The Midnight Cool

Also by LYDIA PEELLE

Reasons for and Advantages of Breathing

The
Midnight Cool

A NOVEL

Lydia Peelle

HARPER

An Imprint of HarperCollins*Publishers*

HarperCollins
PUBLISHERS
Since 1817

HarperCollins books may be purchased for educational, business, or sales promotional use. For information, please email the Special Markets Department at SPsales@harpercollins.com.

FIRST EDITION

Designed by Leah Carlson-Stanisic

Library of Congress Cataloging-in-Publication Data
Names: Peelle, Lydia, author.
Title: The midnight cool : a novel / Lydia Peelle.
Description: First edition. | New York : Harper, [2017]
Identifiers: LCCN 2016032307| ISBN 9780062475466 (hardback) | ISBN 9780062475497 (ebook)
Subjects: | BISAC: FICTION / Literary. | FICTION / Historical.
Classification: LCC PS3616.E327 M53 2017 | DDC 813/.6—dc23 LC record available at https://lccn.loc.gov/2016032307

17 18 19 20 21 RRD 10 9 8 7 6 5 4 3 2 1

For the mules

Four things greater than all things are,—
Women and Horses and Power and War.

RUDYARD KIPLING, "THE BALLAD OF THE KING'S JEST"

Part One

IN THE ARGONNE FOREST

France
OCTOBER 1918

Another shell explodes in the distance. Charles and the mule are stuck, mired in the mud. It is dawn, and the sky is the color of mud, the earth is mud, the whole world is mud. The only thing that is not mud is a stand of wasted trees ahead. Beyond those trees the rest of Charles's unit moves towards the Argonne Forest along a road that is a river of mud, studded with nails and barbed wire the Germans scattered to slow them. A unit was supposed to come through in front of them and clean it up. Nobody seems to know what happened to them.

Charles tugs on his mule's lead. They have fallen far behind the rest. The mule's load is heavy: a Vickers machine gun and its tripod, ammo boxes with twenty pounds of ammunition. Sometimes he just plain quits.

Get along, you old mule, Charles pleads. Get along. Come on, Champ.

The mud sucks the animal's feet. Charles tugs at the animal's head again. He is thinking of Jones, dead now. Jones used to call Champ Sonofabitch Number Two.

Get along, Sonofabitch Number Two, he pleads. Get.

Jones is dead. Jones was a sonofabitch himself, but he misses him, his bad jokes, the constant drone of his voice. He was a city boy who knew nothing about mules. Now Jones is dead and so is Sonofabitch Number One, a bighearted mule whose real name was Rose. Both her front legs were blown off by a shell and she fell into a pit of mud and she would not quit trying to get up, scrambling with her back legs until they put a pistol to the hollow spot behind her eye and shot her, both of them crying, together, him and Jones. She was a real good mule, Rose.

Champ lurches, slips, goes down to his knees. He struggles, only working himself farther into the mud, which covers him to his withers, covers the machine gun, sucks at his sides. Charles hears another shell in the distance. Whizbangs, they call them. The *whiz* sets his teeth, whistles inside his skull. The *bang* makes his guts jump and turns his stomach inside out. He throws himself against the mule. The men beyond the trees shout. A great wall of mud rains upwards. Guns toss into the air like matchsticks. Then, for a rare, odd moment: nothing.

The mule is still, resting for a moment in his struggle. His ears are slung forward towards the place of the explosion, but his big intelligent eyes are calm. Mud on his cheeks and in his shaved mane. Charles rolls over and tries to work loose the hitch that holds the heavy gun to the animal. His hands fumble, useless in the muck, cold and trembling. He is crying now, cursing his hands. The tears run down his face and into his mouth. He isn't going to leave him here. Another shell bursts. Charles lays his head against the mule's wet warm shoulder. That one was close. Jesus. Damn close. He can feel the animal's big heart pounding. He closes his eyes. He takes a breath.

THE PRETTIEST HORSE EVER DREW BREATH

Their boxes were packed and the wagon nearly loaded. The morning had broken bright and almost cool, at least for a Tennessee August. It was a perfect day, Billy and Charles agreed, heading out to the pasture gate, the perfect day for traveling.

Charles McLaughlin and Billy Monday were on their way out of town. The last thing left to do now was catch the black mare out in the pasture, and then leave this place as they left all places, headed nowhere in particular, just on, trading horses as they went, a night here, two weeks there, always on, on to what might lie around the next bend in the road. The spring trading season had been miserable. In Celina they had been robbed blind by a ten-year-old boy. Along the Red River, they got lost in the woods and wandered for three days before coming out exactly where they started. The only good to come of the summer, as far as Charles could see, had been that sweet farm girl in Tuckertown, Kentucky, only they'd been run out of town just when he was getting somewhere with her. When last week they landed here, just hardly south of the border, in Richfield, Tennessee, it seemed like it would be more of the same. Then last night Charles hit the jackpot with the deal he got on this beautiful high-dollar horse.

She was a jewel, out there in the green pasture. Her black hide shone in the morning sun. Delicate pipestem legs. Tail set high and proud on her hindquarters. If you drew a line around her she would fit into a square. The kind of horse that people stopped to watch on the street. She made him want to shout for joy.

He had bought her from the richest man in town. Never mind that he had spent nearly everything they had on her, even after Billy had given him that speech about putting all his eggs in one basket. Look at her! She was a hell of a basket.

Billy paused at the gate, tugging one big ear. Blue sun-shot eyes full of mirth.

I bet you think that little Tuckertown girl would swoon to see you come riding in on a horse like this.

Charles gave him the same long-suffering look he had given him after the egg speech. Billy was getting soft, in his opinion, taking fewer risks in his old age. Charles was eighteen and certain of one truth: that he would, as his mother promised years ago, someday rise up and win the bread of life.

He opened the gate, whistling. The mare flung her head around at the sound of it and he should have noticed the change in her, but he strode right up and swung the lead rope to catch around her neck, and when it touched her she went after him, up on her hind legs, front hooves pummeling the air. He dodged and she came down hard, then reared again. Against the green of the grass she rose, a blur of black velvet hide and iron shoes and the yellow-white ivory of blunt horse-teeth. He shouted and went to grab her mane, and for the third time she screamed and reared, thrashed the air just inches from his temple. When she landed she went after him with her teeth. That was when he dove for the fence, and she spun and thundered across the pasture.

Billy was laughing so hard it took him a minute to give him a hand up. Charles stood and shook out his long lanky frame.

Quit laughing.

Haven't ever seen you move that fast without a girl in the near vicinity, Charlie boy.

Charles dug dust out of his eye with his thumb. The horse was far away, watching them.

Sonofabitch, he said. Something was slowly coming to him. She must have been doped up.

He looked at Billy, who regarded him with one eyebrow tented, the corner of his mouth upturned. His hair stuck out wild beneath the brim of his hat. Billy's laugh was like a force of nature and always left him looking like a stiff wind had knocked him around.

You knew it, didn't you? Knew it soon as I brought her in here last night.

Billy only grinned.

Monday, you sonofabitch.

Billy jogged out to retrieve Charles's hat where it had landed in the grass. Before returning it he flipped it in the air, where it somersaulted three times.

Charles took it and jammed it back on his head.

Ah, don't look so glum, Billy said. She's only a touch hot.

Charles spat and yanked his shirt.

Touch hot? Liked to have killed me.

They must have had her doped to the gills. Wonder what they used. Did a beautiful job of it. Just enough of a dose.

But I don't understand. Charles shook his head. This wasn't no usual place. It was high-class. Fellow's got a pedigree long as the horse does. He drives a damn Pierce-Arrow.

Up on the road, a passing Model T sounded its horn at the landlord's flock of chickens. The noise set the horse off again. She sprang into the air and cartwheeled to the other end of the pasture. Clods of grass flew up behind her. When she tore past the oak tree, four crows startled out of it, cackling.

Sonofabitch, Charles said, watching her. She's bughouse crazy. He grabbed his forelock and groaned. All that money.

Billy put his hand on Charles's shoulder. A strong big-spanned hand that Charles had felt on his shoulder a thousand times, with a weight which, after all the years, could speak to him nearly as plain as words.

Think of it as an investment in your education, Charlie boy. Like I always say, you get burned you got to learn to sit on the blister. If it makes you feel better, you got burned on what's got to be one of the prettiest horses ever drew breath.

Let that damn horse catch herself, Charles said, shrugging off Billy's hand and turning back to the shack. I need a drink.

Ain't got nothing to drink, Billy called after him.

In Tuckertown, where they had spent the end of June and most of July, camped in the back of a cornfield, eating beans and tinned sardines, Billy had tried to teach two spotted ponies how to bow. They had been hauling the ponies around in their string for weeks, unable to unload them, and when they saw the poster for a coming circus on the side of the Tuckertown general store, Billy got the bright idea: teach the ponies a couple tricks, sell them to the circus for good cash money, make back everything the kid in Celina stole from them, get back on their feet in time for the fall season.

It hadn't taken long for Charles to find the girl: Fern, sweet and cool as her name.

I got to be honest with you, he said to her after a week, the fireworks set off by young boys popping in the street behind them. They were standing across from the general store, in a little crowd waiting to see the town parade. We're just here till the circus comes.

The circus?

He pointed to the poster on the side of the building.

Fern strained to see around the woman in front of her, then shook her head.

There ain't no circus coming. That there poster is two years old.

When Charles reported this back to Billy, Billy only laughed, and in a couple of weeks got the two ponies traded off to a hayseed farmer for a crate of peaches and a bicycle, just by the skin of his teeth. When he demonstrated their trick, the farmer watched the animals bend their knees with his brow furrowed over dull suspicious eyes.

What on God's green earth do I need with two ponies that can bow?

They ain't bowing, Billy said, as always hiding his Irish brogue behind a dead-on imitation of the man's accent. Nossir, they ain't bowing. They praying.

The next day Billy rode the bicycle out the Franklin Road and came back on an old pelter with a pint of homemade whiskey he'd taken as boot in the trade. They filed the horse's teeth, blackened his gray hairs, fed him some corn mash, tied him up outside the store, and sat down nearby, minding their own business. Soon enough a man had come along to look the horse over.

Billy got up to meet him. It was the town sheriff.

You in the market for a horse?

Maybe.

Well I wasn't planning on selling him, Billy said. But I like the looks of you.

The sheriff hemmed and hawed and muttered over the horse while Billy stood silently, letting the man talk himself into it. Finally he did and Billy piped up to name a price. They went back and forth for a while before settling on one with a handshake. Then Billy stepped close.

One last thing, Mister Sheriff. Do you believe that horses go to heaven?

The sheriff was already pulling out his wallet. He looked up and shrugged. I don't see why not.

This little horse here is going to go to heaven.

Well a good honest horse is just what I need.

Two mornings later, the sheriff was standing above their bedrolls in the cornfield, his pistol in his hand.

That horse you sold me. Well I walked into that horse's stall this morning. And he was dead.

Dead? Billy said, rubbing his face.

Dead.

Charles looked at Billy and shrugged. He's never done that before.

The sheriff raised the pistol. Well you got some explaining to do.

Billy looked back at him, cool as anything.

Now, Mister Sheriff, sir. I told you that horse was going to go to heaven, didn't I? He grinned and tapped the side of his nose. I just didn't say how soon.

They got out of Tuckertown sort of quick. Coming down off the Highland Rim Charles had seen a boulder painted with one word: REPENT.

Hell, he thought, with a feeling it had been put there just for him. Poor Fern. He was always doing it to them, girls. Picking them up and leaving them like that. It made him feel awful, but he couldn't help it. She was probably still waiting for him to meet her in their spot by the tobacco warehouse. The thought was terrible: her waiting, hopeful. Billy tried to cheer him up. There will be plenty more girls, Charlie boy. But what did Billy know about girls.

Over by the shack, in the measly shade of a sick poplar, Gin was standing in the wagon traces. She perked up when Charles passed. Gin was Billy's horse and devoted to him, but she was always polite to Charles, as she was to all creatures. She lifted a front hoof and scraped the ground once, lightly, with decorum. Blinked her deer eyes.

Don't look at me like that, he told her. I'm ready to get out of here too.

Gin snorted and shook her head. The yard around her was worn down to dirt, littered with the trash of previous tenants. Cans, broken chairs, a water trough gone to rust, hemmed with lacy holes. Billy had managed to convince the farmer who owned it to rent it to them for just a few nights. Dillehay was his name. There had been a sign up in the yard of his place across the road. When they knocked he had told them he would not rent to Negroes, gamblers, drinkers, Dagos, Chinks, Yankees, or Irishmen. As he spoke he refused to open the front door more than halfway. His wife, watching, was a hand at the curtain in the window.

We're good respectable men, Billy assured him.

Dillehay shifted first the tobacco in his lip and then his beady turkey eyes.

A man can't trust anyone these days, he said. Just look at what happened up there in New York City.

On the thirtieth of July there had been an explosion in New York Harbor. Two million pounds of explosives and ammunition, bound for the war and packed in freight cars and barges at a place called Black Tom Island in New Jersey, had caught fire and blown up. The blast picked up boats out of the water, busted the windows of buildings all the way from the Battery to Saint Patrick's Cathedral, rang church bells in Philadelphia. Killed seven people asleep in their beds, including an infant thrown from his cradle. And the word was that it had blown the arm off the Statue of Liberty, and set her skirts on fire.

Dillehay had a wattle at his neck to match his turkey eyes, and it wobbled furiously while he recounted these details. In the past days they had heard the story told by many men. New York City was a long way away, but the gross injury to the Statue of Liberty made the news everyone's business, even an old farmer like Dillehay.

Well it's the Irish dockworkers they can blame, he said. Lazy careless cheats cut every corner they can and look what happens.

His small eyes moved between them. From Charles to Billy back to Charles.

You ain't Irish, are you?

At the window, the wife disappeared like a fish in a creek. Billy sucked a tooth. Charles was staring at the wash line, thinking about Fern. The way the wind had whipped her thin dress against her legs while she stretched to pin up the laundry, the first day he saw her out in her father's yard.

We come from Kentucky, Billy said. Which was not a lie.

Passing Gin, Charles kicked a rusted sardine tin against the side of the house. He flung open the loose-hinged door and went inside, where the smell of salt pork and woodsmoke and the stink of laboring men leached from deep in the lath. The walls for years had been insulated with layers of newspaper and magazine print and now the whole place was a crazy patchwork of words and pictures, floor to ceiling. Headlines, Sunday comics, baseball scores. Advertisements for safety razors, health tonics, toothpaste, chewing gum.

**DO NOT TINKER WITH YOUR DORT. TRUST ONLY
A LICENSED SERVICEMAN FOR ALL REPAIRS.**

**GERMAN U-BOAT SINKS PASSENGER LINER
LUSITANIA. 1,154 DEAD, 114 AMERICANS.
MANY WOMEN AND CHILDREN.**

**STRAW HAT SEASON IS HERE. GET YOURS
AT CASTNER-KNOTT, NASHVILLE.**

Charles didn't bother to shut the door behind him. Let the flies in, hell. They were leaving.

He searched for the Tuckertown whiskey in the boxes lined up to be loaded. It was the jar they had gotten in boot for the trade of the horse they sold to the sheriff who ran them out of town.

Bad luck. Would it never end. The girl in the garden last night had warned him, hadn't she? She had, in plain words. But he had been too awestruck by her, slack-jawed as a hayseed farmer, to even hear it.

He lifted a pasteboard box, which fell to pieces in his hands. He threw it down and a tangle of harness spilled out of it, along with the green smell of moldy leather. When the kid in Celina cleaned them out he had stolen their crates too. Ever since they had been making do with these damn pasteboard boxes.

Against the far wall sat the toilet they had been hauling around all summer, boot in another trade. When they brought all of this junk in, this house had seemed like high living. Two beds and a stove and a water pump in the lean-to kitchen. But it was nothing more than a shabby old rattrap. The floor was covered in a gaudy purple-and-green Congoleum rug, worn clear through at the door by the feet of countless tenants. Where was that whiskey? Charles ran his hands through his hair and looked around wildly. A worthless crazy horse, doped to the gills. He couldn't believe he had been so blind.

FEED YOUR CHILDREN CREAM OF WHEAT.

BATTLE OF VERDUN RAGES ON. CASUALTIES
APPROACH ONE HUNDRED THOUSAND.

TRUST FIRESTONE TIRES.

His eyes moved to the picture just beside the door, the face of a pretty girl selling Pears' soap. Her cheeks were painted pink and her lips were parted as if she was about to laugh. Her hair sat on her forehead in a soft swoop. For four days Billy had not entered or exited the place without giving the picture a little sweet talk and a kiss. Last night, back from town and tight as a drum, Charles had been so happy he had kissed her too, rolled up the last of his cheap Corn Cake tobacco and smoked it, and declared that after they sold the black mare, only the high-dollar stuff would do.

He studied the smiling face. He should have listened to the girl in the garden. Hell, he should have listened to his gut, which told him to bolt even before he had seen the house, from the moment he turned Gin off the Nashville Pike and passed through the great stone pillars of the gate. The word Everbright was etched in each one, only you couldn't see the place at all from the road, just a long winding drive, newly graveled, which crunched neatly under Gin's hooves. At the moment he passed through, an owl hooted in the neighboring wood, and he felt a chill at his neck. It was bad luck, Billy always said, hearing an owl at dusk. Charles halted Gin and reached into his pocket to touch the rabbit's foot he carried. Then he reached into the other pocket and pulled out a nickel. Heads, he'd go in. Tails, turn around. He tossed it and slapped it down on the pommel of the saddle and lifted his hand.

Heads. In he went.

The house appeared on the hill above him like a great white face, its windows watchful eyes, the roof bristling with chimneys. In front of it spread two big black magnolias, old as time. A man was up on a ladder in one of them. Charles hardly had the nerve to dismount and leave Gin, but he did, and got himself up onto the porch, so big you could have held a dance on it. Through the windows, a colored woman was setting the dining room table. As she put out each glass, she first folded a cloth around the lip and gave it a brisk quarter turn. He watched, entranced, his sweaty hands shoved in his pockets, one clenched around the classified ad he had torn from the paper, the other around the rabbit's foot, his thumb working the worn place at its tip. The walls behind the maid were hung with old portraits of women in frothy dresses and eagle-faced men with purebred dogs at their feet. The oil paint gleamed and shone. The maid disappeared before it occurred to him to knock. When he did, no one came.

He stood there at the door. There was no way in hell he was going to be able to afford this horse, no matter if the ad in the paper said, Must go. No serious offer turned down. When he left the shack he had emptied out their cigar box of cash and folded it all into his breast pocket. He patted it now, to be sure of it. Finally he looked up at the porch's pale blue ceiling. A dove perched on a blade of the ceiling fan peered down at him, eyes two black beads pressed in clay.

Alright, he thought. If the bird flies, I go. If she stays, I stay. He counted to ten. The bird did not ruffle a feather.

He went over to the magnolia with the ladder in its branches to speak to the man hidden in the patent leather leaves. He asked for the name on the ad. Leland Hatcher.

The man climbed down slowly, wiping his brow, and told him to try up at the stable. But when Charles asked if he would take him there, he refused.

Soon as I get done with this, the man said shortly, snapping a rag against his leg, I got to do the front windows. And I don't go near the stable if I can help it, he added mysteriously. He looked Charles up and down. He expecting you?

Charles toed an old dry magnolia cone that lay on the ground beneath the tree.

Nossir.

Well you come at just about the worst time there is. Now let me get back to washing these leaves.

Washing the . . . leaves?

The man nodded, one foot on the ladder. Mister Hatcher's got company coming. Likes to have everything just so.

The wind gusted and the big trees shook themselves like dogs. The man went up the ladder and disappeared back into the branches. Charles picked up the cone and squeezed it, feeling the prick of its scales in his palm, then headed in the direction the man had pointed for the stable.

In the side yard a Model T up on blocks had a belt run under the hood to power a band saw, a half-built gazebo beside it. It looked as affronted as a man with his mouth cranked open in a dentist chair. Charles was beginning to feel like he was trespassing, that he might look up to see a shotgun in a window. He stopped at a walled garden, where a white cat crouched on a sundial and rosebushes bloomed in riots of red, and palmed the magnolia cone, his eye on a concrete birdbath at the far side.

It goes in, I go on to the stable. If it misses, I get the hell out of here.

It went in with a splash. The cat streaked away.

Someone applauded.

He started. He would have sworn that the garden, save the cat, was uninhabited. But when he looked there she was, not eight feet from him, standing on a wrought iron bench and half hidden in a tree, just as the man in the front yard had been, only this tree was small and delicate, bearing flowers like silk tassels. He could see only a blue skirt and a white blouse with a wide sailor collar, the brim of a straw hat. Above her swung the paper lantern she had just hung, a pale moon.

She climbed down and came over to him. Watching her come his mouth was already going dry, his head emptying of words, and when she was before him he found he could not look directly at her face, this high-class girl, the kind of girl who crossed to the other side of the street when she saw him coming, and he caught only a glimpse of her hair dark and clean-looking beneath her hat and her collarbone at the place where the tie of her blouse was undone, and then he dropped his eyes.

Are you the iceman? she said. Where on earth have you been? Don't you know we can't have a party without ice? I was thinking I might have to send my brother to the North Pole and he doesn't like to travel.

He dared look up at her. She was smiling at him. She had a gap between her front teeth, just like his mother. It hit him like a hammer in his chest and his eyes went straight back to the ground.

Here to see about a horse, he managed to say.

Don't buy that horse.

Miss?

I'd get out of here, if I were you.

A car was coming around the house, a Pierce-Arrow, big and

slick and high. An incredible car—Charles had only ever seen them in pictures. He watched it coming, still rocked by the strange shock of seeing his mother's smile on this high-class girl, in this high-class garden. And now, this car, the headlights staring him down. If it could talk it would have said, To hell with you.

The Pierce-Arrow stopped at the opposite wall. A pale boy leaned over to the passenger window and pulled a cigarette from his mouth. He wore a brand-new Panama hat with a pencil-curl brim.

Catherine, he said over the engine growl. We've got to go pick up the cake.

You go on without me, she said.

Someone's got to hold it or it'll get smashed up.

The boy in the Pierce-Arrow looked over, noticing Charles for the first time. He hooked his elbow over the door frame and looked back and forth between the two of them. His eyebrows lifted under the brim of his hat.

If you keep looking for trouble, dear Cat, one of these days you're gonna find it.

Charles's hand closed into a fist. Blood will tell, his mother always said. Blood will tell. He had repeated it to many men, but never one in a Pierce-Arrow.

I'll be waiting for you by the front door, Cat. All you need to do is hold the damn thing in your lap. Or hell. You drive. I'll hold the damn cake.

The boy had driven away fast, gravel scattering under the Pierce-Arrow's wheels.

The girl took a step closer. Charles held his breath. He could still only half look at her.

Don't mind my brother, she said. He's in a hurry to get up there and get his whiskey before the bootlegger takes off. Otherwise it's going to be one dull party. Thanks to Edmund, our father's now a teetotaler. The hardest thing he's serving tonight is lemonade.

He didn't like you talking to me.

She sighed roughly. Ed's had a difficult spring. In fact it's been an awful year. And I can't say this in front of him. But look—trust me. You don't want that horse.

Well, Miss. I seen all kinds of horses in my time. I been all around the world.

Well then you must feel as I do. That the world's been absolutely turned upside down. Knocked off kilter. The war in Europe. The terrible bloodshed, never ending. And now that business last week on Black Tom Island. A poor little baby was killed, did you hear?

Terrible, was all he could think to say.

Yes, she said. Terrible.

He stole another look at her and realized she was waiting for him to say something more. He groped around, came up with nothing.

Well it was a terrible accident, he finally said.

See! That's the trouble.

Miss?

She waved at the house. In 1862, she said, the Yankees took Nashville. Two months later Union soldiers marched up this hill and through that front door and moved in. They were here for two years. Just walked right in, while the family stood there clutching their silver, still saying, 'It will never happen here.' Well just because you say something's impossible doesn't mean it is.

Miss?

Why is everyone saying it was an accident? They blew up those ships on purpose. It's plain to see.

Charles thought of old wattle-necked Dillehay.

Who did? he said. The Irish?

The Irish! Her hand went up, as if to wave away a fly. The Irish! Of course not. The *Germans*. All that ammunition was bound for the Allies. It was clearly an act of sabotage.

He looked around the garden for a clue as to how to proceed. The branches of the rosebushes looked as if they might break under the weight of all the blooms, red and pink and white, impossibly fat. The tassels of the tree above the girl were like no flowers he had ever seen, so elaborate they made the lanterns she had hung seem unnecessary. He didn't think too often about the war in Europe. In towns sometimes he heard people argue about whether or not the United States should get into it, but out in the country it had nothing to do with anything and men just left it alone. He rubbed the back of his neck, stalling. Then he opened his mouth, with the hope that something smart might escape it.

I heard the Statue of Liberty caught on fire. Now that's a shame.

Oh! she said. She was agreeing, he thought, and he looked at her, relieved. Now, if only he could make her smile again. But she was shaking her head so violently her hat had slipped, and now her nostrils flared. A lock of hair had come loose. She pushed it out of her eyes and reached up and repinned her hat.

A shame! That's the one good thing that came of it, if you ask me. I wish they had blown that thing into the ocean. It's a howling farce, is what that statue is. She lowered her voice then. But you can't say that to anyone around here.

Well you can say it to me because I'm just passing through. I reckon we'll be gone tomorrow or the next.

At this, she brightened. Where to?

Oh. He waved his hand. Everywhere. We're always going.

Life on the road. How exciting.

You could call it that, sure.

She stepped closer. He could feel her trying to meet his eye.

Is it—is it dangerous?

No, he said. Then, sensing her disappointment, he pulled in a long breath, rubbed the back of his neck, studied the ground, and said, Well. I reckon maybe. There's bear and there's wildcat and some of these farmers, they don't want you around none. We used to carry a gun but Billy done traded it.

That was the end of it. The man from the magnolia came around, calling to him, having had a change of heart about taking him to the stable. Charles had turned to follow without even the wits to say goodbye to the girl, stumbling along through the manicured grass.

And when Leland Hatcher came out to the stable to meet him, wearing a pristine pair of coveralls and a big smile on a pleasant, handsome face, he had treated him so kindly. Pumped his hand, explaining that it was a good, sound, well-bred horse, that he was only selling because he was getting out of horses, should have done it years ago, it was the way everything was headed. Charles nodded along. He was used to standing a head above men, but this fellow was almost small, and he would have thought the man of a place like this would have towered. Hatcher kept rubbing his fingers with a square of washleather, so generous with that big white smile that did not quite go up to his eyes, apologizing for the trouble it was to find him.

Party tonight, he said. Terribly busy.

Then a stablehand brought the mare out, and she was so damn perfect Charles forgot about everything else. Hatcher took his offer without a kick, folding the cash into the pocket of his coveralls. Disappeared quick.

She's a touch hot, buddy, the stablehand said, handing over the lead.

I can handle hot, Charles said, too happy to notice how sluggish she seemed as he tugged her along to the front yard. When he passed the garden and saw the girl was gone, he was more glad than disappointed. He could hardly believe that he had even had the nerve to attempt to talk to her.

Finally he found the whiskey, in a box of broken pocket watches. He unscrewed the top and took it down in one pull.

Last night he and Billy had gone up to Richfield's blind tiger, a dank basement room near the depot where a sign hung behind the bar:

THE SALE OF INTOXICATING BEVERAGES IS ILLEGAL

Billy had gotten right to work, trying to drum up a trade. Take a look at this penknife. Nice one, ain't it? What would you give me for it?

Charles had stood there, spinning his glass on the bar and studying himself in the mirror, his head high above the rest of the crowd. Sometimes girls said he was too tall for his own good, but the girl in the garden had seemed nearly as tall as he was. Catherine Hatcher. Her brother had called her Cat: You keep looking for trouble, Cat, you're going to find it. What had she called the Statue of Liberty? A howling farce. What on earth could she have meant?

The man next to him had a red nose ruined by drink and cheap charms on his watch chain. When they came in he had been complaining to the barkeep about the money his wife had just spent on a dress in Nashville.

I never go to Nashville, the barkeep said. You'll lose more than your money down there.

Now Charles turned to the man and asked him what he thought about Black Tom Island. If it had crossed his mind that someone had done it on purpose.

Such as who? the man said, rubbing his swollen nose.

Such as—Charles coughed—the Germans.

He felt foolish even saying it. The man just laughed.

Son, America is neutral. Neutral as the color white. Neutral we are and neutral we will remain, in spite of what the preparedness folks try to stir up. We haven't a single enemy in the entire world.

Charles nodded. The man was right. It was crazy, the notion that Germans had blown up an island in New York Harbor, crazy as thinking he had any right even lifting his hat to a high-class girl like Catherine Hatcher, no matter who his father might have been. And his thoughts turned to the black mare, now asleep in the pasture, and there came over him a flicker of doubt about her. A prickle at the back of his neck. When Billy saw the horse he had folded his arms and sucked his tooth. Just folded his arms and sucked his tooth and said, Huh.

Charles took another slug of whiskey.

What do you know about Leland Hatcher?

What do I know about him? I work for him, son. Up at the shoe factory. Half the town does, and the half that don't, they got a brother or an uncle who does.

Real high-class, then, Charles said, feeling better. Upright.

The man shrugged. He pays us good. Tonight's his big party. All the big bugs in town are up there at Everbright right now. Wouldn't I like to be a fly on the wall.

At the other end of the bar, Billy had his arm around somebody, talking low and quick. Trying to trade watches, just for the hell of it.

The red-nosed man, growing philosophical, started talking about Black Tom Island again. It just goes to show, he said. When your number's up, it's up. Those people went to bed that night without the slightest inkling they might wake up dead. And the Statue of Liberty without the slightest inkling she was about to catch fire.

Charles called for another drink. A warm calm spread through him with the whiskey. Everything was going to be fine. They were going to make a killing on that horse. The man was saying that the statue would stand for ten thousand years. Of course it would. His mother had a picture postcard of the statue. When she first arrived in New York Harbor as a girl alone in the world, she had elbowed up onto the deck trying to get a glimpse of it, managed to fight through the bodies all the way up to the rail and had had just enough time to see the big arm and hear someone say, And there's the beautiful lady! before a child had been seasick on her.

She always laughed when she told that story. She had a free and reckless laugh, the laugh of someone who had learned through terrible loss that it was the one thing that could not be taken from her. Charles loved it and loved her and had always imagined that the statue should have looked like her, a beauty with a heart-shaped face and a sly, foxy smile with a gap between the two front teeth.

Seeing that smile on the girl today—well sometimes it was too much to bear, all the girls he had to leave behind. All he could do was pin the memory of Catherine Hatcher's face to his chest, just as he had pinned Fern's, just as he did with every girl everywhere. He would pull it out some cold lonesome night trying to sleep by a fire of smoldering coals while Billy snored and somewhere far away beautiful girls danced and laughed and ate cake and drank lemonade on ice out of cut-crystal glasses.

Gold and silver in the ditches, his mother always said. That's what they told me when I was a girl. In America there's gold and silver in the ditches, and nothing to do but gather it. She used to take him to a neighborhood full of houses nearly as grand as Everbright, and they would wait for dusk, the space of time after the lamps had been lit and before the curtains had been drawn, the best time to see in all the windows.

He turned back to the red-nosed man.

My ma loved that statue, he said.

Who doesn't?

Well she drew a real tough lot, my ma.

And Charles had tried to tell the man the story he would have liked to have explained to the joker in the Pierce-Arrow who had called him trouble. The story of how his mother had come from Ireland with nothing, met and married his father, a man rich as Leland Hatcher, richer even, then lost it all when he was struck by a streetcar and killed just before Charles was born.

The man held up his hand.

Kid. The world's got a million sad stories, and I got to work in the morning.

Charles paced across the room to the window, the empty jar in his hand, shoving the broken pasteboard box with one foot. He could see the mare out there, bunched up in the corner of the pasture, and Billy, sitting on the fence, looked like he was having a conversation with the crows in the oak tree.

He turned back to the girl in the Pears' soap advertisement.

Last night while he smoked his last cigarette Billy had sung to her, packing.

> *Daisy, Daisy, give me your answer, do*
> *I'm half crazy all for the love of you*
> *It won't be a stylish marriage*
> *I can't afford a carriage*
> *But you'll look sweet upon the seat*
> *Of a bicycle built for two*

Now he stood there, clutching the empty jar, studying her. His mother used to sing the same song. Or rather, she always sang the answer.

> *William, William, I'll give you my answer true*
> *I'd be crazy to marry the likes of you*
> *If you can't afford a carriage*
> *How can you afford a marriage?*
> *Yes I'll be damned if I'll be crammed*
> *On a bicycle built for two*

She would sing it and then laugh her free and reckless laugh. She came to America all the way from Ireland expecting gold and silver in the ditches and nothing to do but gather it, and she had died in a whorehouse with nothing. And if, like the man in the blind tiger said, if tomorrow Charles should wake up dead, he would die with nothing too.

He threw the empty jar across the room. It hit the wall but did not break. Rolled down the sloping floor and came to rest under one of the beds. That kind of thinking was no use. Crazy or not, that horse still looked good as gold. All they had to do was catch her and dope her up themselves. By tomorrow she could be someone else's problem. And they would be in a new town. New horses. New girls. A thousand possibilities.

He snatched a long rope out of one of the boxes and flung open the door. Burst back out into the glare. Racing past Gin, he blew her a kiss.

Wish me luck!

Billy was grinning at him when he got to the fence.

I got it now, Billy said. I know exactly what we gotta do.

Well good. Because I'm about to go out there and I don't intend to come back until I got her by the pretty little nose.

Billy scratched at his cheek. OK. Here's what we do. We go on up to Dillehay's place. Ask to use his telephone.

And?

And then call up the four riders of the apocalypse. Tell em to get down here. Surely one of them fellows is in the market for another horse.

Bill Monday. You. Son. Of. A. Bitch.

Billy looked back at the horse and kept on scratching his cheek.

He must have used morphine, that Hatcher fellow. For it to last as long as it did.

Hatcher! Charles shook his head. Hatcher wouldn't have done it. It was the stablehand, surely. I knew I didn't like the looks of him.

Charles tested the weight of the loop, watching the horse. A man with a place like that didn't go around doping up horses, he knew that much. For Christ's sake, he'd had someone washing the leaves of his magnolia.

He looked at Billy. What do you think we could get for her? Considering her mental state.

Find the right kind of high-dollar fellow, dope her up on something stronger than that old Hatcher boy up there used? Two, three thousand. Maybe thirty-five hundred. What's important is that we got to find a bigger sucker than you.

Charles knocked the loop of rope against his thigh. Thirty-five hundred dollars! He looked at Billy from under his hat. Smiled.

Billy looked at the rope. You ain't gonna cowboy her.

Yes I am.

I don't think she's gonna like it.

If I don't come back, Monday, see that they put it on my head-stone. 'He went down fighting.'

This time Charles stayed downwind. If she was going to act like a wild animal, he would treat her like one. He stalked up behind her glossy black hindquarters, close enough that he could hear the rip of the grass in her teeth. Easy. Easy. The rope in his hand was shaking. He threw a loop, but it missed the mark, smacked the mare's rump, and then slid to the ground. She spun around and screamed as if the sun itself had dropped from the sky. Took off running and Charles took off after her. He could hear Billy shouting from the fence line but not what he was saying. It was just him and the horse now and he was going to catch her no matter what it took. He ran her into the fence corner, where she slid to a stop and spun to face him, nowhere to run. He moved in, his arms stretched like wings.

The mare pinned her ears, making her face into a hideous arrow. Then she reared up. Ten stories tall. Jesus, she was huge. When she came down, her front hooves hit him like fireworks, like two million pounds of ammunition exploding, and lifted him into the air. He saw a tumble of ground and sky and leaves. He heard Billy shout, or maybe it was just the horse's snort, or his own blood in his ears, and then he heard nothing at all.

CAVEAT EMPTOR

It was four days later, and the summer heat had returned in full force, when Billy tied the two old mules to the sick poplar tree to paint them.

In one pocket he had a tin of black shoe polish. In the other, a boiled egg.

The mules groaned. Their old bones creaked and popped. They had been gray in their prime, but were now faded white as snow. With their long mule ears they looked like a couple of overgrown Easter rabbits. At this age they were next to worthless. He had traded the moldy harness for them.

Three crows watched him through the worm-eaten yellow leaves above, shifting and rattling their wings. He looked up at them and winked. He had sent Charles up to town in search of black fabric dye, but still no sign of him, and he would have to make do without it if they were going to get to the auction on time. Fabric dye or no, he was going to work magic on these mules.

Billy's kit sat at the base of the tree. An old lunch pail, once painted red, with a lid on rusted hinges. In it, in order to cover up nearly any shortcoming or ailment a horse might suffer, were various colors of thread, wads of cotton, green coffee beans, a carved-up piece of gingerroot, castor oil, a metal file. Vials of carbolic acid, quinine, a box of Epsom salts. Wool to stuff the ears of an excitable horse, cocaine to inspire a lazy one. Linseed oil for a heaver. Arsenic, of which a knife's edge could sometimes work wonders, but you had to be careful. A few grains too many and you had a dead horse on your hands.

He lifted the lid and fished out a hypodermic needle and the metal file. Then he took the egg and the shoe polish out of his pockets and set them on the ground. He stepped back and studied the mules. One of them was already dozing, head bobbing. Billy nudged his shoulder.

Need a cup of coffee, old boy?

He checked his watch, a cheap watch with another man's initials on it, taken as boot in a trade. What was keeping Charles? Four days since the black mare punted him into the fence, and he was still in a fog. He had been lucky, that was for sure. It should have been a hell of a lot worse. The mare had been vicious as a rattle-snake that day, and ever since. She was out there now, in the corner of the pasture, watching him, every muscle tensed, ready to run or fight. On the afternoon of the first day, she had even gone after Gin, who now gave her a wide berth. Smart Gin.

Charles had been burned bad. But he was taking it too hard. Sometimes Billy would find him sitting on the fence, just staring at her. Or he'd come in muttering about what he was going to do to the Everbright stablehand. He still refused to believe that such a high-class fellow as Leland Hatcher could have deceived him, and held on to the crazy notion that it was the stablehand who had doped her, and that the stablehand surely had been deceiving this Hatcher all along too. Billy kept his mouth shut. If Charles was still green enough to think that rich men achieved their station in life because they deserved it, because of some purity of character or righteousness of heart, he hated to be the one to tell him otherwise.

Charles had decided to try to cure her. It would take time and patience, but if they could win her trust and start over with her training from square one, he argued, they could make even more than they would if they just doped her up and passed her off again.

Billy suspected that they ought to just cut their losses and run.

As the saying went, trade her for a dog and drown the dog. But again he kept his mouth shut.

Caveat emptor. Buyer beware. That was the cardinal rule in trading. But one you only ever learned the hard way.

As for their current situation, they were dead broke. When Dillehay demanded another week's rent up front, Billy had managed to talk him into taking the toilet in trade, in spite of the fact that the old man did not have indoor plumbing. When he came down to the shack to pick it up, he had stopped at the pasture gate.

That ain't Leland Hatcher's horse out there, is it?

Was, Billy said. Ours now.

Dillehay's small eyes had narrowed.

Said I didn't want no funny business down here.

No funny business. We bought that horse fair and square. Let me help you get that there toilet up in your wagon.

Then Billy had cleaned up the moldy harness and gone into the hills and traded it for these two half-dead mules. Convinced the farmer he was doing him a favor, taking two old hayburners off his hands. Today they would take them to the auction house and make a little cash and soon enough they would be back on their feet.

He picked up the shoe polish tin and turned the key, wishing once again he had the fabric dye. He pulled the egg from his coat pocket and pressed it into the cake of polish, twisting it until it was good and black. With the contents of his kit, and a little smooth talking, Billy could make anything possible. *Caveat emptor.*

Before he began, he paused one last time to look over the mule. Any fool could file down an animal's teeth or shove gingerroot up his bunghole. But to paint a white horse or mule dapple-gray— and do a convincing job of it—required the touch of an artist.

He had learned the trick years ago, when he was young and green himself, from a Levantine in Damascus, Virginia, who wore a gold hoop in one earlobe and hustled Billy out of a fine team of plow horses. It worked on the fact that a dapple-gray horse or mule was born black and then changed color over his lifetime, growing lighter every year, dark dapples fading, until he ended up almost pure white. For this reason just one glance at a dapple-gray could give you the animal's age.

Way back then in Damascus, the painted horse that the Levantine passed off on Billy turned out to be so old he could not even stand up in the morning. When Billy went back to the man's campsite and demanded he give back his team of plow horses, he had refused, but finally agreed to teach him the trick. Sooner you learn, the better, boy, he had said, pulling on his earring. You get burned, you got to learn how to sit on the blister.

Billy stepped forward, egg poised. Here goes nothing, he said, and both mules' ears swiveled. He made his first mark, stamping a fat black dapple on the near animal's shoulder. Beautiful. He inked the egg and made another. The mule closed his eyes again and sighed.

Those days when he was a greenhorn traveling by himself seemed so distant as to have been lived by another man. Weeks of not seeing another person, talking only to the horses. He could hardly now remember what it was like to be alone. For nearly ten years, all he had to do was open his mouth and say his piece and Charles was right there beside him to hear it. And he did have a habit of saying everything and anything on his mind. Everything, except the one thing that could never be spoken.

As he worked the sun drew higher over Dillehay's tobacco fields, and the pasture's green intensified. At one point the black mare suddenly screamed and wheeled, spooked by something, but he hardly looked up, he had grown so used to this.

Demon, he had taken to calling her. Also: the Maniac, the Black Devil, Sweetheart, Angelface, Sugarpie. Out there slashing that tail that she held high and proud as a bride's bouquet, flaunting her fraudulent beauty. How she swindled! Yesterday she had allowed him to come right up and put his hand on her shoulder. Then spun around and bit him in the meat of his arm.

He had already fallen in love with her. He only fell for horses anymore, but he did fall hard. He would have thought by now, after everything, his heart would be just a hunk of petrified wood. Instead with the years it seemed to grow more tender and more reckless. And now here he was in love with a maniac horse out for his blood. He knew she had suffered something terrible.

This place she came from, Leland Hatcher's Everbright, had made such an impression on Charles that he was telling the story about his father again. Billy had heard him tell it in the blind tiger, the night he came back with the mare, and the red-nosed drunk listening had looked at the boy like he had two heads.

The blackened egg lengthwise in his hand, he began to print the mule's belly, moving back towards his tail. The oblong shape of the egg, as well as its size, made perfect dapples, as if it had been invented for the job. He worked slowly, from time to time pausing to reink the egg and give the drowsy mule a scratch behind the ears.

Leland Hatcher, in addition to employing most of Richfield, seemed to spend a lot of time telling its people what to think and what to do. He wrote a column for the local paper. Money Matters, it was called. Billy had overheard half a dozen discussions on the week's installment, which addressed the temperance issue. In fact, the man Billy got these mules off of had been reading it when he showed up at his place. After the usual exchange about weather, crops, and horses, Billy had asked what he thought about it. He had taken off his glasses and rubbed the bridge of his nose.

It is a bit perplexing, the man said. Six months ago Mister Hatcher was railing against temperance. Said it was a threat to a man's liberty and that Tennessee should never have passed the law. Now he says drink's the path to ruin and the whole nation ought to go dry. Says right here—he pointed to the paper—'I've learned that the inalienable truth of America is that its people sometimes must be saved from themselves.'

Billy clucked his tongue. Hard to trust a man who changes his mind as often as he changes his collar.

The man had shrugged and put his glasses back on. They were held together with baling wire.

I suppose when you're as important a man as Mister Hatcher is, you always got to be thinking about what's best for the people.

The place was up on the Highland Rim, so deep in a holler that it was dark even in the middle of the day. Dirt on everything. Dirt in the meal the wife had served. It had crunched in Billy's back teeth. An enormous, gut-busting meal. Always the poorest ones who fed you the most.

The mule sighed. Billy swiped sweat from his brow. If it was a hot sale at the auction today, they might make four hundred bucks off of these mules. Four hundred blessed bucks out of nearly nothing. That was the inalienable truth that Billy had learned about America. Here in the land of plenty you could live mighty well off the trash. Coming from an Irish island of two hundred souls where no one had anything save what was pulled from the sea had helped him to see that. He had come over at the age of fourteen with the same fierce drive Charles now had, though in his case the desire was not to get rich. Simply to never die hungry.

There was something to being a greenhorn that you never did get back. The notion that all you hoped for was within reach. Charles had an idea that life was like the old song 'Climbing up the Golden Stairs.' That it was bound to be up and up and up. He had come back from town yesterday grinning out from underneath a brand-new pencil-brim Panama hat. Lord knew where he got it or how he paid for it, but he thought it made him look high-class. He was already talking about all the fine clothes he would buy when they sold the black mare.

There had been a time, when he was still a scrap of a boy, that Billy thought he'd lost him. He remembered it after seeing him get punted by the black mare, in those awful moments of stillness after he hit the ground and before he scrambled up. That time, long ago now, they had both been on horseback, riding through back-woods in Kentucky. Charles on the hot horse, an excitable stallion, so that Billy could say to potential customers, If this scrawny kid can handle him, surely you can too! The stallion had spooked and thrown Charles hard. Billy had been a ways behind, and galloping up to the little body, he was certain of the worst. He had jumped down and knelt over Charles's crumpled body, not daring to touch him. It did not look like he was breathing. A sinister-looking rock was inches from his skull. Dead, Billy thought, and it's my fault, and the world around him at once went black and treacherous. Trying to fight this mean-hearted darkness he sat back on his heels and swallowed around the lump in his throat and said, There's easier ways to dismount, you know.

Charles had cracked one eye and without missing a beat said, Ah, but I get bored of em.

Finished with the mule's belly on both sides, Billy turned the egg and inked the fat end to make the smaller, rounder leg and shoulder dapples. He began to whistle. When he made his way to the rear leg the mule stomped his foot, thinking the tickle of the egg was a fly.

Easy now. That's a handsome fellow.

When all four legs were done to his liking, he pressed the small tip of the egg in the polish. This he used to press in the delicate little dapples of the curve in the mule's stifle. Nearly finished. From white to dark in the space of half an hour. In the bad light of an auction ring he would fool the sharpest eye. But really the truth was that men saw what they wanted to see. He had learned that too along the way.

Caveat emptor, that was the first rule. The second was to never lie. Twist the truth, yes, hide it, decorate it, do what you would with it, of course, but you never looked a man in the face and opened your mouth and spoke an outright lie. You never knew when you might come through a town again, and you wanted to maintain a reputation. Besides, it took the fun out of it. Trading was a game, after all, nothing but a match of wits, and what fun was a game without rules.

If someone asked the dissembled mules' ages today, he might say, They've seen it all, or Check for yourself, or avoid the question entirely. Leland Hatcher, on the other hand, had looked Charles straight in the eye and lied, told him the mare was a good honest horse, not even giving Charles the chance to speculate otherwise.

There was surely a story behind why he had needed to unload that horse so quickly, and surely not a happy one. Billy suspected the man had more secrets than simply why he had jumped the fence on the temperance issue.

But Leland Hatcher could keep his secrets, for all Billy cared. Soon enough they would have his mare cured, healed of the pain of whatever injustices had made her so skittish. And they would be long gone from here.

He stepped back from the mule, stuck his tongue in his cheek, then put in one last dapple. Not bad at all. There now stood before him not an ancient white plug but a darkly dappled gray mule who looked for all the world as if he was in the prime of his life. Once he trimmed his whiskers and filed his teeth and puffed up the sunken spots behind his eyes, even the mule's own mother wouldn't recognize him.

Yes, Billy thought, giving him a last pat, Leland Hatcher could keep his secrets. A man was entitled to a secret or two. Billy knew that as well as anyone. He had his share of them.

KUNTZ AND SON

When Charles finally got back from town, it was with no fabric dye and no explanation, the telltale white line of a new haircut at the back of his neck. They got Gin hitched and the mules tied up fast and got on the road. But once out, Billy refused to hurry. If the mules broke a sweat it would ruin their paint job.

The auction house was on the north side of town, on the Westmoreland Road, and on their way they passed acres of tobacco, a sprawling stud farm, a poorhouse with women working a vegetable garden in the side yard. Gin's and the mules' hooves clop-clop-clopped on the road and Billy boasted about his paint job and Charles nodded silently. At the bridge over Defeated Creek a hare streaked out of the bushes and across the road.

How do you do! Billy called after him. It was bad luck if a hare crossed your path and you did not address him.

They caught wind of a slaughterhouse, then passed it. Finally they heard the commotion of a sale, and saw the sign painted in big letters on the side of the massive barn.

KUNTZ AND SON AUCTION HOUSE.
HORSES AND MULES BOUGHT AND SOLD.
SALE EVERY WEDNESDAY AND SATURDAY.

When they pulled in a curtain of flies descended. In front of the barn, two pens were packed with horses of every size, color, breed, and condition you could think of. At the edges of the lot sat clusters of wagons and automobiles and more horses and mules tied to hitching posts and trees, tails working against the relentless flies. An assembly of men myriad as the horses, town men and farmers, local dealers, colored men and boys. Skinny dogs trotted through it all like they had someplace to be, crescents of hoof trimmings from the blacksmith held like cigarettes between their teeth.

A boxcar on the siding behind the barn was being unloaded, mule after mule, a chorus of brays that shaded off into shrieks and groans. A man selling heeler pups from a crate on his wagon fished one out by the scruff of the neck to show it to someone, then slung it back in.

Sonofabitch, Shorty! someone was yelling.

Charles jumped down to ask a fellow raking the yard where the office was. He was a great big fellow with a back like a planed board, but when Charles spoke he startled like a doe and dropped the rake. When he swung his head to regard them Billy saw the blank face of an imbecile under the shadow of the jutting brow.

Sorry, pal, Charles said, stepping back. Didn't mean to scare you.

Every little scrap of shade was taken. They went down to the back of the lot and tied Gin to a post rail. Charles was chewing his knuckle, a nervous habit. The smell of offal from the slaughterhouse strengthened with each gust of hot wind.

You really think we'll do alright?

Billy regarded the mules. The shoe polish had held up well. He untied the animals from the wagon and brought them around and tied them to the rail next to Gin. Then he gave each one of them a good-luck kiss.

They found the office and went in and got their paperwork. They came back out and gave it to a kid who handed them their tail numbers and pointed them back to the barn. He wore a pair of stained overalls, rolled at the ankles, and a man's tweed cap. One eye was pink and swollen, crusted at the edges. He couldn't have been more than eight or nine. Billy reached behind his ear and pulled out a penny and handed it to him and asked his name.

Shorty, the kid said, stuffing the penny in his pocket.

Shorty. It's a fine day, ain't it, Shorty? Awful bright though. I got a quarter here with your name on it if you'll go in there and bust one of the lightbulbs above the ring.

Shorty's good eye lit up and he ran off. Billy turned to Charles and winked.

I'd say we'll do just fine.

Over at their wagon, someone was looking at their mules. A high-class fellow, impeccably dressed, in a stiff old-fashioned derby hat. Surely a dealer. He walked around behind the animals and pulled out a small notebook and made a note of their number and walked away.

Billy clapped Charles on the back.

Now hold on a minute there. See that? We might do more than fine.

They untied the mules and took them inside. Once they had them settled they walked down the dim aisles together, looking over the animals. Around them men were doing the same, or standing in knots talking about their crops, their roofs, what tobacco prices would do in the fall.

A farmer, sweating heavy, was looking at a team of tobacco mules, and Billy told him that if he was in the market for mules he ought to go have a look at the dapple-gray mules in stall fifty-two.

Pretty as a painting, he said with a wink.

In the next stall was a plow horse with a nasty-looking poll evil. Then a big mealy-nosed sugar mule. A red mare with a foal sucking her teat.

They stopped in front of a fine saddle horse, a bright bay, almost the caliber of Hatcher's mare. He was too pretty. Too sharp.

After a while Charles pointed to the horse's thick and showy tail.

Falsie, he said.

Billy grinned. Well hell, boy. If it ain't so.

The false tail that someone had fixed to the horse had come loose just enough that you could see where it had been woven in with a piece of black ribbon. Underneath it his own tail was surely ratty and thin, rubbed to nothing against a barn wall or fence.

At the next stall, someone sneezed so loud the horse startled. Billy looked over. A boy stood there with a load of hay in a wheelbarrow, a pitchfork in his hand. He knocked his hair out of his eyes and sneezed again.

Damn horses!

He tossed the fork over the door at the horse, who leapt into the far corner with a squeal.

Billy went into the stall and picked up the fork and brought it out. The animal was still trembling in the corner.

They'll treat you nice if you treat them nice, he said to the boy, handing the pitchfork back. You ought to try it.

Ah, to hell with em. They're big and dumb and they make me sneeze.

He put down the pitchfork and wiped away snot with the palm of his hand. The features of his face were crowded together around a flat nose, as if he had been pinched like a change purse. Charles was eyeing him.

The kid stuck out his hand. He said that everyone called him Twitch.

Billy shook the offered hand, but Charles just nodded, and did not uncross his arms. Twitch let his hand drop. His close-set eyes went back to Billy.

He your boy?

Took him in when he was just a pup.

Billy looked up the aisle. Shorty was hustling through with a handful of rope halters. He wondered if he had even bothered to look at the lights in the ring.

You're in the wrong line of business, ain't you, Twitch?

Soon as my pa kicks off I'm going down to Nashville. I don't care what it is, but I'll do it. Anything to get out of here. I'd shovel any shit other than horse shit. Sheep shit. Hog shit. Hell. Even cow shit.

Twitch looked at Charles. A shadow of mistrust crossed his face.

Where you two from, anyway?

Boy, we been all around the world, Billy said. He took a step closer. Tell me something. Who's the high-dollar fellow in the derby hat?

Lloyd Bonnyman. He comes up here from Nashville every week. Got a mule barn down there half mile long. He works for Roan and Huntington.

Charles snorted. Roan and Huntington? Never heard of em.

Twitch raised his eyebrows. You been living under a rock somewhere?

Charles scowled. Like he said. We just pulled into town.

Well wherever you're from you ought to know Roan and Huntington.

Twitch went on to explain that they were the biggest mule outfit this side of the Mississippi and that they moved thousands of mules every month. They had an exclusive contract with the British Army and shipped animals to India, to South Africa, all over the world. These days, most of them went to the Western Front. Dozens every week. Billy had heard of them. Years ago, during the Boer War, you couldn't go anywhere without a Roan and Huntington man having been there first.

Shorty came by, and Twitch reached out and stopped him. Took the halters and handed him the pitchfork.

Hey, Shorty. Take this hay down to stall fifteen, will ya? Twitch looked at Billy again. Soon as my old man kicks the bucket, I'm going. I've had just about enough of this place, I'll tell you that. Had just about enough of these damn horses. He gave the little boy's cap an affectionate yank. And had just about enough of squirts like Shorty here, who ought to quit standing around and take this hay before I switch him.

Shorty took the wheelbarrow. He turned to Billy.

Busted two of them lights for you. Chunked a rock.

Well I only got one quarter.

Sullenly Shorty accepted the quarter and pivoted the wheelbarrow and went up the aisle.

Charles was studying the horse across from them.

He must make good money, he said to nobody.

Who? Twitch wiped his nose with his shirttail. Bonnyman? Oh, sure. Lloyd Bonnyman's got nothing to complain about. I reckon he could buy this place if he wanted to. Could buy it right out from under Kuntz tomorrow if the fancy struck him. Down there in Nashville he's got a great big house and a French wife. He's got dozens of agents who work for him, but he likes to come up here for this sale personally himself. Friend of Kuntz's, and he says we get the best mules for miles around. Buys a boxcar full every Saturday.

He looked up at the ceiling, pulled an imaginary cord.

I hear his house has got one of them dumbwaiters in it.

How about this Hatcher fellow? Charles said. You reckon he's got a dumbwaiter?

Twitch sniffed. Probably.

He's—he's got a daughter, don't he?

Miss Catherine Hatcher? Oh, buddy. Twitch held up his palms. Don't you and me both want to know. Course, ever since Missus Hatcher died, it's been different with them Hatchers.

A commotion rose at the other end of the barn, two stallions fighting over the wall of a stall, squealing like girls. Twitch sighed and went to see to it.

Billy looked at Charles. Well? That would be a story, huh. Them two painted-up mules going over to fight in the big European war.

Charles frowned. We've had nothing to eat the past three days but potatoes.

It's a damn fine paint job, if I don't say so myself.

Potatoes, potatoes, potatoes. Charles pulled a sandwich out of his pocket. He lifted the top piece of bread and peered inside and then closed it again.

What'd you pay for that? Billy said.

Charles frowned. A dime. In the office back there.

That slice of ham's so thin you could read a newspaper through it.

It's plain crazy, Charles said.

I'd say you were robbed.

Shit, Billy. Ain't talking about the sandwich. To think that Nashville fellow's going to buy them sorry old mules. Ain't even worth the breath to speculate.

They pressed against the stall door to let through a man leading a Percheron team with feathered hooves big as tree stumps. It took days for them to pass.

Charles looked down at the sandwich. You can have this. I need a smoke.

He walked away, towards the bright light streaming in through the door at the far end of the barn. Billy walked up the aisle eating the sandwich and looking over the rest of the horses. When he finished he wiped his mouth on his sleeve and packed his pipe and lit it. He was standing under a big NO SMOKING sign, but it was just a sign, just like the one about the sale of alcohol in the blind tiger. The world was full of signs, but it didn't mean you ever had to read them. He watched the men coming in and hoped they had full wallets, and that Shorty had done what he said he'd done, and even more that there was someone who looked after the kid wherever he went when he left here at night. And he hoped that they really did make four hundred dollars today. He'd find a way to make a million dollars, if that was what Charles wanted.

They found each other again just before the opening bell rang and followed the crowd taking the back way through the in-gate to the sales ring. From the ceiling hung four bare bulbs, two dark, smashed.

Good boy, Shorty, Billy said under his breath.

In front of them, men sat shoulder to shoulder on bleachers that went up to the back ceiling. The ring in which they stood was not big, ten horse lengths long by five deep, but thirty or forty men lined the perimeter. Big-time dealers stood down here, close to the action. They had their hickory sticks propped on their shoulders and their lips loaded up with tobacco. The spotters were taking their positions at the base of the bleachers and two bookkeepers were opening books up on the podium. No one was talking now. It was all business from here on out.

Lloyd Bonnyman occupied the prime spot between the auctioneer's podium and the exit gate. He had his stick against his shoulder and he was leafing through his little notebook, his derby pulled down low.

The auctioneer appeared above them, grunting as he climbed to the podium. This was Kuntz. He had jowls and a walrus mustache waxed and curled and a big diamond horseshoe on one pinky. He shoved this hand into a bag of peanuts and with the other he picked up a length of plaited leather and rapped it impatiently against the podium. Cracked and ate a dozen peanuts one-handed in rapid succession and finally peered into the ring.

What the hell is taking so long? Anybody seen Twitch back there?

I seen his dog a minute ago, someone called out.

Kuntz craned his head. His jowls rocked. Twitch!

Twitch struggled out of the in-gate, tugging a reluctant yearling draft horse.

Ain't sure I trust that fellow—Charles started to say, but like a freight train the sale was off. Kuntz rattling along a mile a minute and the spotters yelping and yipping and jumping around, up on the rail and back down again, pointing to dealers and men in the bleachers and once in a while up to the colored seats in the back.

IgotaonedollarbillfromthemanonthehillwhosgotonefiftyIgot-onefiftythankyouverymuchonefiftyonefiftythataintshiftywho'sgottwo? So! Two? Two? Two? Fine little mare! She'll grow into money!

Yip! Yip!

The mare sold at two twenty-five. Kuntz slapped his plait hard and threw a fistful of peanut shells after her as she was led out. On the other side of the podium, another horse was already coming in, no halter, naked as a jaybird, driven by two colored boys with hickory sticks. She raced to the center of the ring and tossed her head, wild-eyed. Every time she made a dash for the out-gate, the dealers there would step forward and lash their sticks at her.

Alright, boys, away we go. This one here's never been to town!

Kuntz's diamond horseshoe ring flashed. The horses came and went. Ten seconds, twelve seconds tops. Peanut shells flying. Men darting out to pick up a hoof or measure a horse with their sticks or wrench open his mouth to see his teeth. The spotters jumping around like monkeys. Men bidding with a wink, a raised thumb, a nod. One old fellow across the ring made his bids with nothing but a twitch of his ear. Up in the back, men sat with their arms tightly clamped on their chests, and nothing moved but eyes.

A team of good cat-hammed tobacco mules was led into the ring. The bidding kept up, lively as anything. Charles was chewing his knuckle again.

Fellow back there, he said, jabbing his thumb over his shoulder towards the stalls, we got to talking. Said President Wilson rides around Washington in one of them cars.

Billy didn't take his eyes off the mules, who looked like they could go and go and go. Nothing like a pair of nice mules. He could look at them all day. Bonnyman was bidding on them.

In one of what cars?

In one of them Pierce-Arrows. Said Hatcher once paid to have a whole orchestra come up from Nashville for a party. Said that the black mare beat up another horse at the hitching post one Sunday morning a few months ago while he was at church and no one's seen her in town since. This fellow thought he had sold her back then.

Now Billy was watching Bonnyman. He had noticed that Kuntz always looked at him before slapping the plait for a final sale. Bonnyman would give the slightest shake of his head. Pass, or yes. Then the plait would come down. Smack. Sold.

Well all I know is, a horse don't get that mean without some real meanness done to her.

You don't know nothing about him, Charles said shortly.

That's true. I don't. Billy looked over. Don't care to either.

Smack! The mules were sold. Lloyd Bonnyman got them. Five bills.

By noon, when the sale paused just long enough for Kuntz to eat four hard-boiled eggs and brush the shells onto the hats of the men below, maybe a hundred animals had been run through. Billy had kept his eye on Lloyd Bonnyman. By the time their team came up, he had bought twenty-six mules, for two twenty-five to two fifty a piece.

When their two painted mules appeared out of the darkness of the in-gate, Shorty was between them, just two skinny legs and two little hands hanging on to the leads.

Billy worked his way over to Bonnyman, squeezing between men and hickory sticks.

Good-looking, these two.

Bonnyman said nothing.

Billy nodded. Oh yes. Them two will go high.

The bids came in slow. Shorty was leading the mules back and forth. A couple fellows in the middle rows were bidding. Nothing was catching fire. Billy saw he needed to do something. He ducked behind Bonnyman to rap the podium. Kuntz paused and looked down at him, jowls wagging.

Billy grinned. Tell em these two been all around the world.

Kuntz looked up and repeated it to the crowd. Man here says they been all around this world. Still the bidding went sluggishly along. Two fifty. Two fifty-five. Finally he dropped the plait, at two seventy-five for the pair.

The mules disappeared out the gate. Kuntz's peanut shells hit them on the rump and slid down into the sawdust. Billy realized he had been holding his breath. He hadn't noticed that Charles had also made his way over behind him. They stood there next to Lloyd Bonnyman.

Somebody stole them mules, Billy said to Lloyd Bonnyman. He smelled like an apothecary. He was looking through his book, and he did not lift his head.

Those yours?

They were until a few seconds ago.

Bonnyman looked straight at him from under the shadow of the derby. Long deep lines stretched from the wings of his nose to the corners of his mouth.

Next time use fabric dye, he said. It's a hell of a lot more convincing than shoe polish.

Billy was still trying to think of the perfect retort to this when the next lot came in, another mule team, and Bonnyman turned to bid.

The sale lasted until ten o'clock that night. When it was over a couple of bootleggers came down in a big Reo and set up behind the barn. The Johnson twins, regular fixtures of the Saturday sale. They stood beside the car, identical, with eyes like cross sections of hard-boiled eggs while men lined up to buy pints of whiskey smuggled down over the Kentucky border. From the moonlit yard came the sound of starting motors and clopping hooves and occasionally a plaintive whinny, the sound of hundreds of uneasy horses and mules being moved on to new fates.

Charles bought a pint of whiskey and they took it to the side of the barn, where men squatted and smoked, going over the sale.

We did good, Billy said to Charles, but Charles only grunted.

Looking up at the sign on the side of the building, he asked the man next to them who the son was, of Kuntz and Son.

You seen that big idiot around with the rake? the man said,

pushing his tobacco with his tongue. The one who looks like a big dumb ape?

Charles nodded. Nearly scared him to death when we pulled in today.

That's the son. That's Gus Kuntz.

He told them the story. When Missus Kuntz had had her first and only child, and it came out a boy, Kuntz had been so excited by his vision of a family business that he had hired a sign painter to change the sign the very next day. Six months later, their nurse dropped the little baby on his head. Broke something in his brain, and he had never amounted to anything but an overgrown child, good for nothing but raking and baiting mousetraps. Yet all the years gone by, Kuntz had never had the heart to repaint the sign.

Well, Billy said, packing his pipe with his thumb. You never do know what life's going to give you. A man can't be certain of nothing but that everything's gonna change. Wouldn't you say so, Charles?

Charles was counting the money they had made. He looked up, squinting, smiling at some private vision of his own.

Gospel truth, he said.

Money Matters

by Leland Hatcher
The Richfield Gazette

What is the value of a man's life?

It has occurred to me that Richfield's young men would comport themselves differently on a Saturday night if they knew the answer to the question posed above.

The figure? $54,000.

I have arrived at this amount by ballpark estimation, of course. The men who work on my factory floor are paid four dollars a day. That is twenty-four dollars a week, $1200 a year. Over a forty-five-year period, not accounting for inflation, this adds up to $54,000 earned. Yet time and again, I see these men dangerously carousing on a Saturday night as if their lives are worth precisely nothing. In the worst cases, I see lives that otherwise might have been industrious and prosperous utterly ruined by the use of alcohol. If every bottle of illegal whiskey came with a $54,000 price tag, wouldn't these young men think twice before shelling out to the bootlegger?

This town stands on the precipice of greatness; indeed so stands our country. When the current war is over, a new war—an economic war—will decide the fates of nations. Richfield stands the chance to be on the leading edge, when the time comes, if and only if our young men begin to act as if they knew what their own lives are worth.

SCHRECKLICHKEIT

PROFESSOR JAMES C. LITTON OF
VANDERBILT UNIVERSITY
WILL LECTURE ON
THE GROWING GERMAN THREAT TO CIVILIZATION
READING ROOM OF THE SUMNER HOTEL
FRIDAY 3:00
ALL WELCOME AND ENCOURAGED TO ATTEND
HOSTED BY THE RICHFIELD SOCIETY FOR THE AID
OF THE FATHERLESS CHILDREN OF FRANCE

When Charles saw the notice on the board at the courthouse he tore it down and shoved it in his pocket. It sounded like just the place he would find her. Catherine Hatcher. For two weeks he had been searching, with only one success. She was sitting in the window of the soda fountain on Front Street, alone, eating an ice cream sundae. He stood there on the street, unnoticed by her, watching the way the spoon slipped in between her lips and the way she so earnestly studied it and licked the back of it after every bite. He had never seen anything more beautiful in his whole life and he knew that he would not again as long as he lived.

In the shack that night with a new pouch of Corn Cake, he had lain on his bed smoking, studying the girl in the Pears' soap ad.

She looks a little like that, he said after a while. Leland Hatcher's daughter.

Across the room, Billy looked up. He was whittling, a little bird taking shape out of a hunk of wood in his lap. He blew the picture a kiss off the tip of his knife.

Surely not. She can't be as pretty as my Daisy Bell.

You ought to see her, Billy. She's something else. I can't get her out of my head.

He asked about her whenever and wherever he could. Most times, men just shook their heads. Or puffed out their cheeks and said something like what Twitch had said: Don't you and me both want to know. She went to the women's college on the north side of town. She sat at the suffrage booth at political rallies, handing out pamphlets on Votes for Women. Last summer she had walked down East Main Street, smoking a cigar. Her brother, Edmund, had just graduated from Vanderbilt and was a good-timing boy. People said that ever since their mother died, killed when her car went off the bridge on Defeated Creek, they had both been a little wild.

Charles took a drag and tapped his lip.

She's got this gap, he said. It's something, I tell you, Billy.

A gap between her teeth? Billy picked up the bird and held it to eye level. He studied it for some time. Well send me a wedding invitation, he finally said.

Don't tease me. Someday I'm gonna make a million dollars. Hire an orchestra from Nashville just because I feel like it.

Maybe you ought to make your million before you go chasing your million-dollar girl.

Charles folded his arms across his eyes. Ah, forget it. They ought to paint it on a sign and hang it around my neck. World's biggest fool. He looked over at Billy. What's the use? I ain't ever gonna have no orchestra. No dumbwaiter.

Billy pointed the tip of his knife at him.

Now hang on. Talk like that will get you nowhere.

Charles touched his lip again. This smile—ah, you wouldn't understand. I see it at night when I'm lying in bed. See it all day long. Makes it so I can't eat. Can't sleep. He sat up and put his feet on the floor, grabbed his forelock and tugged. She had studied that ice cream so seriously, as seriously as she had spoken about Black Tom Island. Billy was right, of course. What would a girl like that ever want to do with a man like him?

My poor ma, he said to the ground. It ain't fair. The tricks life played on her.

Billy looked down at his knife, snapped it shut, pressed it against his knee. He closed his hand around the half-formed little bird. Looked up at the girl on the wall and sighed a heavy sigh that made the candle next to him go out. He pointed his knife at a newspaper that Charles had tossed on the floor. The headline read, GOVERNOR RYE SAYS SUFFRAGE IS COMING.

Don't know what they want the vote for, he said somberly. They already rule the world.

The afternoon of the lecture, Charles wet his hair and combed it until it clung to his skull and took the interurban to town. When he got to the hotel, the program was already well along. Standing in the doorway, looking in at the sea of people, he had the same feeling he had at the gates of Everbright, an intimidation that made his head feel light as a balloon. Then a gray-haired lady in the back row turned and slid along her bench and beckoned to him. Next thing he knew he had sat down, quick and quiet as an obedient dog.

There was a map of Europe tacked up on the wall, a jagged red line drawn down the center of it to indicate the Front. A stocky stone-faced man traced it with a pointer.

The Battle of the Somme has raged like wildfire all summer, he was saying. Six weeks of fighting. Thousands upon thousands dead already. And no sign of a break in the German line. Not a budge.

Charles scanned the room. Leland Hatcher was in the front row. His son was beside him. There were a dozen pretty girls to the left and right of them. But not her. He knew just by the shape of their ears and the curve of their necks that none of them were her. After watching her eat that sundae, he could pick the line of her neck out of ten thousand girls, easy.

Schrecklichkeit, the professor said, whapping the map with his pointer. A bit of saliva flew from his mouth. It means frightfulness. The term the Germans have coined for the kind of war they are waging. Kaiser Wilhelm has raised up an army of godless men, trained them to understand that the rules of battle are null and void. They are merciless. They are bloodthirsty. The kaiser himself has become a soulless maniac.

Charles turned his head to the big windows along the wall. A hard breeze shepherded big clouds across the sky. He began to jounce his knee as the situation settled on him. He was here, and she was not, and he didn't understand half the words the fellow up there was saying. Like being locked up in a schoolhouse, only worse. He ought to have stayed to help Billy with the mare. He looked around, wondering if he could sneak back out. But he was hemmed in on all sides. No escape.

The professor was cataloging a list of Germany's war crimes. They cut off the hands of little Belgian children. Enslave their parents to work in their coal mines. Burn orchards, bomb churches, tear Jesus down off of the cross. Leave a wake of destruction wherever they pass. What we need to consider is that Kaiser Wilhelm's plan is to terrify the civilian population so thoroughly that the Allied forces, regardless of what happens on the battlefield—he whacked the map again with the pointer—have no choice but to surrender. And then? He swept his eyes over the room. To take over the world.

In the front row, Leland Hatcher's head was bobbing up and down.

The professor raised his pointer to the window.

Look out there. Imagine the sudden appearance of a zeppe-lin. Hoving into view, a massive gray cloud. One moment, clear blue sky. Families having breakfast. Women bathing babies in the kitchen sink. Then you look out the window and there it is, from nowhere, and you have no chance to think. Next moment the bombs fall. And—*ʒumph!*—nothing.

The gray-haired lady next to Charles jumped, and her hip brushed against him.

Pardon me, ma'am, he muttered, and slid far to the edge of the bench.

When it was over he applauded long and loud. He helped the lady up and handed her her purse. She smiled at him.

Gracious, son, you're a tall drink of water.

A few of the girls from the front row had fanned out with col-lection boxes. Up at the front of the room, a cluster of people had formed around the professor, and another around Leland Hatcher, who was shaking everybody's hand, a head shorter than everyone else but clearly the commanding center. Charles stood there watch-ing the smooth way he piloted the discussion, wondering what it felt like, to have men listen to you with rapt attention. After a while he felt himself being watched. He turned. A girl with a collection box was looking him up and down. Her lips were painted and her cheeks too. His ears began to burn.

She was in front of him now. She put her collection box under her arm.

Are you new in town? she asked with a little ruffle of her hip. Because I know everybody.

She told him her name was Cherry Orchard Tisdale, and she held out her hand and he took it and squeezed her fingers. He knew the name Tisdale. There was the Tisdale building and the Tisdale School and the Tisdale addition. Close up her lips were the red of blackberries just before they ripened to black.

He told her his name, and when she asked what line of work he was in he hesitated, and coughed into his fist. Only passing through, he said, and when he did he saw a change in her face. A widening of her eyes, a realization. Her tongue darted out.

Oh, she said slowly. *You*. You're the fellow who bought the horse.

She took him in again, her eyes dragging along from his waist to the top of his head.

But Cat said you were long gone. She said you were the kind who's been everywhere and that you were probably in Chicago or New York by now.

At the sound of Catherine's name his heart floated an inch higher in his chest. He rocked forward on his toes.

Well we decided to stick around.

The girl's face changed, a flash of fear in her eyes.

You don't still have that horse?

When he said he did she stepped closer and dropped her voice. Her perfume smelled like the inside of a lily on the hottest summer day.

Listen, she whispered. I got to tell you something. That horse. That horse is a bad horse.

He laughed a little. Oh, believe me, Miss Tisdale, we know.

No. That's the thing. No one knows. Cat swore me to secrecy but—well—what if it got you too? I'd have that on my soul for the rest of my life.

She leaned in and raised her penciled brows. Her voice so low he could barely hear her.

That horse killed a man. A colored man, in Nashville.

It took a moment to understand. Charles looked over at Leland Hatcher. His group had joined the professor's, but he was still at the center. Hatcher was slapping one hand into the other, making a point to his audience. Charles remembered counting out his bills into that hand, nearly everything they had, the big white smile Hatcher had flashed when he snapped shut his fingers and tucked the wad into his coverall's hip pocket. If she had killed a man— no, no one did that. Even the lowest trader wouldn't just pass on a mankiller like that. And if he did, he'd at least give you fair warning.

He looked back at Cherry. He felt suddenly confused.

She's got top-shelf bloodlines, that horse, he said. Top-shelf. She's quality, that mare. She's— He faltered.

Cherry frowned. I'll tell you what Mister Hatcher said to Catherine, but you got to swear not to repeat it. She was so upset, you see. He told her that the money he paid the dead man's family was more than the poor man would make in a year. He said, the world doesn't mourn a man like that. Not much more than it does a dead dog . . .

She kept going, but now Charles was just watching her redblack lips. All he could hear was a voice in his head: I ain't no dog!

His hand clenched at his side. He could not shake the voice nor the confusion. He began to babble.

You're mistaken, Miss Tisdale! That horse has got bloodlines better than anybody in this here room! I been all around this world, Miss Tisdale, and I seen all kind of horses and I know horses better than most men know their own selves. And that horse is— Let me tell you something about horses, Miss Tisdale. When you breed a horse—when you bring a stallion to a mare with the intention of breeding them—well you don't know what's gonna happen.

Cherry's cheeks and neck flared with streaks of red and her eyes had gotten big. Her dark mouth hung a little ways open. He realized with horror that the subject of horse breeding was not one you brought up with a girl like this. But he could not stop. His mouth just kept going.

That horse, she might kick him in the teeth and walk off and be done with it and that's that or she might turn around and lift her tail—

Cherry put her hand to her mouth.

Lift her tail and take him, Charles finished, miserable. He turned. Edmund Hatcher was standing beside him. How long had he been there? Christ!

You don't say, Edmund Hatcher said coolly. And if that's the case, he said, what do you think about a human girl? Seems to me she'd kick a fellow like you in the teeth before you even opened your mouth.

Well I don't know nothing about human girls, Charles muttered, dropping his chin. I do know about horses.

Misery. Complete and utter humiliation. Edmund Hatcher reached across him to take Cherry's arm. His eyes bore the rawness of a bad hangover.

If you're finished here, Cherry, Edmund said harshly, Missus Dimwiddle wants to make a donation.

By some miracle Charles managed to scrape himself together.

Now hold on a minute, he said, and reached into his pocket. I was fixing to make a donation too.

Just as the words left his mouth he realized he had no money on him. He groped around. He looked at Cherry. She had the box out, waiting. Her cheeks were still crimson.

Every bit counts, she said weakly.

He hasn't got any money, Cherry, Edmund said sharply, and then they were mercifully gone.

Charles paced in the bright sunlight on East Main, the world's biggest fool. He could hardly get his thoughts in order. Flower boxes along the sidewalk burst with red and white geraniums. COMPLIMENTS OF THE RICHFIELD LADIES' BEAUTIFICATION CLUB. Old men dozed on the benches. He kicked a rock that skidded to the middle of the street, then stopped to roll a cigarette. When he had it lit he looked up at the sky, tried to imagine a zeppelin like a gray ghost, silently hoving into view. And then—*ʒumph!*—all of it crumbling. Awful. Unthinkable. But at least it would erase the terrible humiliation of his encounter with the girl.

He tried to remember the German word the professor had used but he could not. It had sounded so strange, like a sneeze. His thoughts were still tangled in confusion.

A mankiller! She couldn't be. She was so beautiful, that horse!

He turned on Second Street, towards the depot. Halfway down the block he heard a jangle of bells and the creak and clatter of wooden wheels. He stopped. Coming towards him, helter-skelter down the middle of the street, a ramshackle low-slung conveyance rumbled, pulled by two goats and driven by a gigantic colored man with such arms and legs and hands and feet that Charles could only imagine that if he stood up he would be eight feet tall. He looked like something from a bad dream, a prophet or a madman. The cart jumped and lurched forward and sideways all at once. Turned the corner of Water Street, then was gone.

Charles realized he had been holding his breath. Time to get the hell out of this place, he said aloud.

He walked all the way to the edge of town, where the Hatcher Boot and Shoe factory dominated the bank of Defeated Creek. At the corner of the humming building, next to a set of side stairs, a few willow trees leaned out over the water. He went and stood beneath them, then picked up a rock and threw it into the sluggish water below. Then another. Above, a kingfisher rattled at him and flew from one branch to another.

Someone called his name.

He turned. It was Twitch. He had just come down the side stairs. A scowl made his pinched-up face even smaller.

If you're here to see about the janitor position, it done been filled.

Charles bristled. I ain't interested in no janitor position.

Well then you got a smoke? Because I just made a damn fool of myself in there, Twitch said.

Charles heard the echo of his own voice at the lecture: Well I don't know nothing about human girls. He softened, and went over to Twitch.

I'm sure it couldn't have been too bad, he said.

They sat down on the step and Charles rolled two cigarettes. Twitch smoked fast, holding the cigarette between thumb and forefinger, from time to time pausing to groan in embarrassment. When the secretary told him the job wasn't available, he had stood there and begged her to check and see if any other positions were open until she told him he had to leave. He was desperate, he said. His mother had run off years ago, and his father was sick and couldn't work, and it was left to him to earn the bread and take care of his three young siblings. Everything getting more expensive. Listening to his story, Charles wondered if he had been wrong about him. He was a good man, Twitch. Plenty in his shoes would have bolted.

Well I made a fool of myself this afternoon too, Charles said, flicking his cigarette into the dirt. Put my foot in my mouth trying to impress a girl.

Girls, Twitch said. Shoot.

You're telling me.

Look at us sitting here all hangdog, Twitch said after a while. It's Friday afternoon. We ought to be tearing it up. Sometimes I wonder if I ought to run bootleg whiskey. Like those Johnson twins. Worth getting killed for that kind of money. He screwed up his face, thinking. But then I suppose you got to consider an eternity in hell.

I might trade an eternity in hell for a million dollars.

What are you talking about? Twitch turned to face Charles. You got it made. You can leave whenever you want. Go wherever you want. No one to take care of. No one to answer to. What's a traveling man need other than the clothes on his back and some grub once in a while?

Yeah. That's the thing, Twitch. Charles stood up and considered the throbbing building. He could see the sweep of machinery in the upper windows. I ain't just a vagrant. See, my father was a man like Leland Hatcher here. Bigger than Leland Hatcher. Why, it wouldn't just be his name on the sign, it'd be his name on the cornerstone too. By rights I ought to be sitting pretty somewhere. Philadelphia, maybe—that's where he was from. Where his people had been since the beginning of time. That's where my mother met him and where they got married.

Philadelphia, Twitch said, as if it was on the other side of the world.

Yeah. Things ought to have been real different. Only one day when she was pregnant with me he went out to buy her a new fur coat in a snowstorm. A streetcar killed him. Knocked him dead. His family disowned her. You ever hear of such a thing? Cast her out without a penny. She got out of there, but she only made it as far as Bristol before she had me. And ever since I've been under the heel of the world. The world's full of liars, ain't it, Twitch? Full of cheats and liars and prevaricating individuals.

Twitch nodded solemnly.

Charles crossed his arms and dug at the dirt with his toe.

She kept me alive, my ma, when I probably should have ended up dead. She worked damn hard. She was too proud to beg. She pulled some fast hustles, but she never begged. She had to stoop pretty low.

He paused. He never spoke of the lowest place, because somewhere in the deepest pit of his heart he did not forgive her for whoring herself at the Crimson Shawl. By that time, already so weak from the consumption that killed her, it was that or starve, and he knew it then. Even with this knowledge, the bitterness lingered, and he hated it. But there it was.

One time, Twitch, we had nothing to eat and had nothing left to our names but an old hen that wouldn't lay no more eggs. So she hoisted that hen up under one arm and me under the other and went door-to-door, asking people if they wanted to buy it. Well each woman took one look at her and one look at me and said, 'You can't sell your last hen, you poor woman, with that tiny child,' and each one would load her up with bread and milk and things to eat. And she'd stash it in the alley and go on to the next house. Every damn house, all the way down the block. Why, we ate for days off of that one damn worthless bird. And then we ate the bird.

With his heel he smoothed the hole he had dug in the dirt.

She got the bum deal, my ma.

Well that's shit luck, Twitch said, frowning.

Don't I know it.

You know, I could tell when I met you, Twitch said. You're different than the average joker who comes around. It's the way you hold your chin. You hold your chin like a rich fella.

All I got of my father is this rabbit's foot, Charles said, pulling it out of his pocket. It's the real thing, this one, the hind foot of a hare killed on a full moon by a cross-eyed man. They aren't any luck otherwise, bet you didn't know that.

Twitch held his knees. He looked mightily impressed.

Blood will tell, Charles said. That's what my ma always said. Sometimes she'd take me to the ball game and point out the rich boys and say, 'Charles, see those boys out there. You got it coming same as they do, them Kings and Dukes.'

Kings and Dukes?

Those were the big names in Bristol. King and Duke.

Well shit. Twitch shook his head. And they told me it was a democracy.

No, Twitch, that's the thing. It is! Charles sat down next to him. His heart was pounding like the machines above them. This is America. You, me, anybody can do it. You don't even need to have a name. Look at Andrew Carnegie! Look at Russell Sage!

Ah, that's bullshit.

Don't talk like that, Twitch. You can do anything you want. You could own a factory like this someday. A man's just got to write his own story. You can win the bread of life same as anybody.

Twitch stuck out his jaw. He was studying Charles with his pinched-together eyes.

It's the way you hold your chin. Maybe you can teach me how to do it. Bet the girls go crazy for it.

At this Charles remembered the way Cherry Orchard Tisdale's little tongue had darted out when he told her who he was, run a course between her teeth before she said, Oh. *You.*

He jumped up again. He leapt and batted the curtain of a willow tree's branches. Then he spun around, grinning.

Twitch! he cried. Let's go get a drink. I'm buying!

For the moment he had forgotten he didn't have a cent on him. It didn't matter. His heart was going like a dynamo.

She had told her friend about him. Sonofabitch! She had told her friend about him.

EDISON MACHINE

A mankiller.

Yes, Billy thought, it made all the sense in the world. He had known plenty of hot horses, dangerous horses too. But this mare was different. Every day this became more evident. She did not even act like a horse, but stalked and plotted like a wolf. No doubt she had been beaten viciously and repeatedly, until something in her mind had broken.

She's good for nothing but the rendering plant, he said after listening to Charles tell the story. It's what Hatcher ought to have done. What the lowest trader would do. No one passes on a mankiller.

But Charles had looked so crestfallen that Billy began to back-pedal. Then again, maybe that girl made the story up, he said. Who is this girl, anyhow? And Charles had brightened so much at this that Billy went on. Sometimes you got to listen to your gut, he said. And what does your gut tell you?

It tells me I spent a hell of a lot of money on that horse.

In the end Billy ended up convincing him that maybe he ought not give up yet. They had made some progress, he pointed out. While Charles was up at the lecture, he had managed to catch her and tie her to the fence. She was mad as hell, swinging herself like a ship's boom, until Billy began to whistle, and she had immediately calmed down. He had started to sing, anything that came to mind, and while he did she was so calm she actually allowed him to run a brush over her, which was more than she had stood for in nearly three weeks.

You're right, Charles said, smiling for the first time that day. A man's got to trust his gut.

Music, Billy said, ignoring his own. Who knows? Maybe that's all she needs.

They had among their possessions an Edison cylinder machine, and Billy dug it out that afternoon, but he could only find two cylinders. A William Jennings Bryan speech against the railroad trusts and the Virginia Reel. He pulled out a stack of agricultural yearbooks to trade, saddled up Gin and headed for the used bookstore on a street near the depot.

The man behind the register, fanning himself with a paper fan from a funeral home, peered at Billy from behind smudged glasses. Around him books were stacked in precarious columns, tobacco stains on the floor. It looked as if he had not had a customer in years.

It's mostly that ragtime trash, he said when Billy asked to see his music, grunting towards a box of cylinders in the corner. You new here?

Billy nodded. Nice town.

It's going to hell in a handbag.

Oh?

Man who owns this building just raised my rent again. Gonna have to close. Well it's just as well. Soon enough no one's going to read books. Just the magazines and the papers. Won't write letters either. Just those awful postcards. Postcard will be the death of the letter. 'Weather is beautiful, wish you were here.' Soon enough no one's going to know how to express a true sentiment. Nor spell correctly.

Well I don't fool with letters, Billy said. Got nobody to write to.

He picked up a scrapbook no bigger than a wallet. It was tied at the side with black ribbon, and when he opened it up it unfolded like an accordion, a single strip of paper folded a dozen times. The snapshots were dark and poorly framed, people's heads hidden in the shadows of buggy awnings, blurry dogs, men cut off at the legs.

You like that? You can take that. I've probably got two months left before I'll have to close up. Maybe I'll move out of town. Lived here all my life. First time I've ever thought about moving. Better go now. Those railroad men strike and it's going to shut down this whole country.

Billy closed the little accordion book and put it in his pocket. He looked out the window. Two little girls crossed the street, holding hands.

Seems like a fine enough town.

It's named for a murderer. I'll tell you the story, because it's just like everything else. Back in the palmy days long before the war. Nothing but raw land and nothing to do but steal it from the Indians. The Rich plantation went on for miles. Young Master Rich, the most eligible bachelor in the county, his father works out a deal with another family up near Portland to marry their daughter. Together they're going to own an empire, only young Rich in the end seems to have been a man governed by his heart, not his account books. You see, the night before the wedding, the bride's family throws a party. At some point she and her groom go off into a parlor together. Everybody hears a shot, comes running. My gun, Rich says, got tangled in her dress. In his attempts to untangle his bride-to-be, the trigger got pulled.

The man took off his glasses and rubbed them on his shirt and returned them to his face, no less greasy than they had been before.

The gun got tangled in her dress. Imagine. The chances of such a thing happening. A tragedy for the poor young man. So heart-broken, in fact, that three months later, he goes down to Nashville and soothes his sorrow by marrying a pretty debutante. He had known her for some time, it seemed. Folks had seen them walking. Well he married her and brought her back up here. Town grew up around the plantation. Here we stand.

He motioned to the window.

Now we got men like Leland Hatcher, coming in here from away, no sense of the place's history.

Billy's ears perked. He put his hand on a stack of books and leaned over the desk.

Let me ask you something, sir. Does he strike you as a shifty fellow, Leland Hatcher?

They all are. The man snorted. All of them with a lick of power.

Dangerous?

He's from away, the man said, as if this was not an excuse for not knowing the answer but itself an answer.

I see, Billy said, giving up. He wasn't going to get a straight word out of this fellow.

Ain't it just the way people do things. Tell a story enough times, it don't matter that it's a bald-faced lie. Tell a story enough times and it becomes good as true.

The man coughed.

Hell in a handbag, yessir.

ROUND ROBIN

The day Charles finally found her again, he wasn't even looking. He and Billy had been at the auction that morning and bought a couple of pelters to doctor up. Billy wanted to keep them a week and bring them to the opening night of the county fair, where they were bound to make more money. Until then they would have to keep living off potatoes and snared rabbits.

Charles was coming up towards Court Square from the depot, where he had spent the afternoon watching the trains come in. The giant colored man on the goat cart had been there. Bud Morgan, he now knew. He sold picture postcards of himself and his goats and met the trains like clockwork. Charles had tried to buy a postcard for a nickel, but Bud Morgan hustled him into three for a dime.

The matinee show at the Paradise Theater had just let out. Cherry Orchard Tisdale stood outside the door with her collection box, soliciting donations for the Richfield Society for the Aid of the Fatherless Children of France. She waved him over. She was wearing an elaborate little hat, trimmed with a trembling ostrich feather, dyed black, and a little whip that kept shaking at him like a scolding finger.

Afraid I still got no money, he said, looking at his feet. She was standing awfully close to him, so close the whip on her hat almost tickled his chin. Sweat sprang out under his arms.

Oh, that's alright! Her voice was bright and tinny. I just want to talk to you.

We nearly got that horse cured, he said shortly.

She said she didn't want to talk about the horse, that she only wanted to apologize for Edmund. They were engaged, she explained, and he tended to get jealous. It was a secret engagement, she added with a wink. They had to figure out how to convince her father to let them get married.

He doesn't like Mister Hatcher, she whispered, pressing a finger to her painted lips.

A woman came over and dropped some change in the box and said a few words to Cherry and then went away. Charles felt a wave of unease. Billy said that, mankiller or not, he was sure that Hatcher was responsible for the mare's madness, and that a man capable of doing that to a horse was capable of the vilest acts. Charles could not reconcile this with the man in the impeccable coveralls and the big white smile, the man behind the big thrumming factory on the bank of the creek. If she really was a mankiller, and he had sold her off to him without a blink—he didn't want to think what that said about his character.

Doesn't like Leland Hatcher? he repeated.

Because, Cherry whispered, rolling her eyes, he's a parvenu.

A what?

Because he's new money.

There was no time to work this out, because Catherine Hatcher was coming out of the theater. Seeing her Charles's blood ran hot and fast through his heart. She wore an apple-green tailored silk suit and also held a collection box. The way her hips swayed made his teeth ache.

He saw a look pass between her and Cherry, and then Cherry introduced him, giggling. Though I think you've met before, she said.

Catherine's eyes dropped shyly to her box. Would you like to make a donation? For the Fatherless Children of France?

The fatherless children of France? he repeated. Then said the first thing that came to mind. What about the fatherless children of America?

The girls looked at each other.

Well there's plenty, ain't there? Dozens of em right here in Richfield. Scrapping around with nothing to eat. Ain't no war done it to em, but what's the difference?

Catherine reconsidered him. She was wearing a hat similar to Cherry's, with an ostrich feather big as a foxtail, although on her it was not silly but becoming. Her eyes were brown and gray, all at once. He held his breath. Once again, just as he had done at the lecture, his nerves had gotten the best of him and he had begun to babble. But he believed what he had said, and he could tell by the look on Catherine's face that his point was well taken.

Well hold on, Cherry said. I didn't call Mister McLaughlin over to *solicit*, Catherine. I told him I had a question but no one's given me the blessed space to ask. She turned to him. Can you do the Turkey Trot?

What?

Or the Grizzly Bear? The Bunny Hug?

A man came over to make a donation. Cherry flashed a big bright smile.

Come back tomorrow, she called after him. We're giving out kisses tomorrow.

She lowered her voice when he was gone. That was Mister Stackpole. Isn't he handsome? He drinks.

Poor Mister Stackpole, Catherine said. It's not his fault, Cherry. Ever since his wife got sick.

The girls discussed the man's troubles for a moment. Charles rubbed the side of his face. His blood had fast gone cool. What in the hell was the Bunny Hug? Was she trying to make a fool out of him? He stole a look at Catherine. She gave him a gentle smile.

We've been trying to find someone to teach us, Catherine said. For the dance tonight.

Cherry cut in. And you just know so much about horses I said to Catherine—

Well I don't know nothing about dancing, Charles said unhappily.

You don't? Cherry said. That's a shame. Well I sure wouldn't expect a fellow like you to waltz, but surely the new steps—why, you'd fill up all the dance cards sure as you're born. She raised her eyebrows and dropped her voice. Cat says you keep a knife in your boot.

Cherry! Catherine shrieked.

Can I see it?

Cherry!

He tried to turn his back on Cherry, to speak to Catherine as if they were alone. The sun reflected off her green shoulders was nearly blinding.

Maybe we could take a walk, you and me. Or I could buy us an ice cream. Or just buy you an ice cream. And maybe I could sit with you.

Oh, she said, and he swore some understanding passed between them, but then her eyes darted past him to Cherry. They exploded in laughter.

He looked around. This was impossible.

What? he said.

We've got to make tracks to the club. We'll be late for the Round Robin.

Round Robin? This time he came out and said it. What in creation is a Round Robin?

More laughter. It burst like rain out of their lips. Charles looked hopelessly between them. There was a difference in their laughter, he noticed. Catherine's was heavier than Cherry's, with a dark abandon to it and hard edges. He thought about what people said, that ever since her mother died her father could not control her. He wondered what that meant, exactly.

Parvenu. Turkey Trot. Bunny Hug. Round Robin. It was like some kind of code they were speaking. Or another language. He felt as confused as he had in the garden when she told him she thought that the Statue of Liberty ought to be pushed into the sea.

Two men walked by quickly, and when Cherry thrust her box at them they dropped in a few pennies and kept going. Charles, with a bolt of courage, started after them.

Pardon me! he said. Sir! Look at these two pretty girls out here. Spending their Saturday afternoon working for a cause. You can give them more than that, surely.

One of the men hesitated, turned back, dug into his pockets, pulled out a dollar's worth of change, and poured it into the box. The girls giggled, and Catherine beamed at Charles, but the victory was short-lived, because Edmund Hatcher was coming down the street.

Charles took a step into the shadow of the building. Edmund Hatcher, dressed in tennis clothes, was less intimidating than he had been at the lecture, but Charles had no desire to explain himself or make himself further into a fool. Another young man was with him, a cripple who was dragging himself along with a cane, but like a good horse who had fallen out of condition it was clear at one glance that he had once been an athlete.

Edmund Hatcher spun his racket on the tip of his finger, tossed it in the air, and caught it behind his back. Cherry kissed him on the cheek, and he introduced her to the fellow he was with. Wad Taylor.

My old partner in crime. We roomed together in Kissam, Edmund said, laughing. Wad. Ought I tell her what they called you?

Wad Taylor blushed and studied the knob of his cane.

Edmund grinned. Kissam Quick Taylor. He drew out the first syllable. *Kissssss-am.*

Not anymore, Wad Taylor said quietly. Hello, Catherine.

Hello, Wad.

Come on, Cat, Edmund said, we'll be late.

You three go on, Catherine said. Just give me half a minute. I've got something I've got to do inside.

They left her there, finally, after more discussion about getting to the tennis courts on time and a few weighted looks between Catherine and Cherry. Catherine stepped into the shadow of the building beside Charles. In an apartment above them someone was playing the same note on a piano, over and over.

I got to ask you something, he said. Is it true? About the horse killing a man?

She looked at him for a moment. All the light went out of her face. She was a different girl than the one she had been, laughing, just moments before. An understanding came into her eyes.

Cherry.

He nodded.

I am so tired of secrets, she said heavily.

Don't look like that. We've nearly got that horse fixed up, you know. Hey. Cheer up. Listen. If I come back tomorrow, do I get a kiss?

This got a smile out of her, but a small one. A woman passed and she held out her box. Above them a different note, higher, rang out over and over. She looked back at him, one eyebrow up.

You're awfully confident.

I'm not who you think I am, he said, lifting his chin.

Well. Neither am I. Listen. I better go.

So I'll see you here tomorrow then. Same time and place.

I won't be here tomorrow. We're rehearsing the living tableau. It's the First Thanksgiving. The Pilgrim costumes are simply the worst. Nuns' habits. But the squaw costumes are pretty swell. She raised an eyebrow, brightening. Not much to them though.

Twitch had told him about the living tableau, put on every year on opening night of the fair by the women's college. It was the most popular attraction at the county fair and every year the costumes grew more scandalous.

Charles swallowed around a lump in his throat.

Well what are you? A Pilgrim or a squaw?

She looked up at him from under her lashes.

I guess you'll just have to come see for yourself.

BRAVE

Sonofabitch, Charles said aloud.

She was a squaw.

When the curtain opened it had taken a minute to find her. He was at the back of the packed exhibition hall, trying to see over all the heads. There were so many girls on the stage itself—girls hugging shocks of wheat, girls with cornucopias, girls holding swaddled baby dolls, all clothed either in heavy black dresses, or what seemed to be nothing at all. All of a sudden, he picked her out, the squaw over on the edge, with a feather in her hair and a basketful of papier-mâché trout on her hip. Her skirt was the color of flesh and her bare knees were looking straight at him and he had to drop his eyes. His face was on fire. He didn't like it one bit.

The man next to him had his arms crossed and was working his hand up and down his biceps. Up and down, up and down, shifting his weight from one foot to the other.

Wouldn't I like to have me a poke of them fish, he grunted.

Charles walked out. The sun had set. Lights glowed in the trees. He went up to the sideshow and paid a nickel to see the Genuine Snake Lady, entering a small hot tent that stank of human urine, where a coiled length of stuffed cotton painted with rattlesnake diamonds ended in the head of a woman, a colored girl with her head stuck through a hole in the false floor. Her eyes slowly moved around to meet Charles's and she gave him such a look of contempt that his blood ran cold and he fled.

It is hopeless, he thought, skirting the edge of the midway. He had spent most of the afternoon trolling it with Twitch, back and forth, up and down. Twitch was talking again about moving to Nashville. If my pa wasn't around, he said, I'd take all them urchins down there with me and start us a new life.

Nashville! Charles said. The place sounded overwhelming to him. Too many people, too many streets, too many automobiles. What would you do in Nashville?

I don't know. Maybe Lloyd Bonnyman would hire me down there at his mule barn. Everybody says it's where the money is these days, mules for the war.

That's high cotton, Charles said, thinking of Bonnyman's undertaker face in the shadow of his derby. That's a whole class of work I can't even imagine.

Now by a candy apple stand Charles saw Kuntz and his son, Gus, stopped right in the middle of the midway, where Kuntz was squatting to tie Gus's shoe. Gus looked huge and a little bit spooked by all the activity, but he recognized Charles and waved happily. Charles waved back.

Now let's try it again, Gus, Kuntz was saying patiently, one lace in each hand. The rabbit goes around the tree, through the hole . . .

Charles walked on. He winced, remembering the sight of her bare knees. He was always watching her from afar. And she did seem to speak another language. He had turned their last conversation over and over in his mind. She hadn't said the horse was a mankiller, had she? She had only said she was tired of secrets. And when she told him to come see her tonight, it had sounded so much like an invitation.

Around him boys were holding girls close. Up by the produce building he saw Dillehay's son, who had just graduated from the Agricultural and Normal Institute, down in Madison, and was home to help his father with the harvest. He was walking with a gorgeous girl. Where did a fellow like him find a girl like that? Even Twitch had gone off to meet a date. It seemed that everywhere all around him life was happening for other people. But not for him.

Feeling too low to stick around, he went out through the turnstile to get the horse he and Billy had traded one of their pelters for, earlier in the day.

Got to stamp your hand if you're coming back in, the man called out.

Ain't coming back in.

The horse was next to Gin, who was dozing in the traces. Charles untied him and mounted up to go. But before he got too far up the road he remembered the poor creature had been standing there all day without a drop of water. He doubled back and cut through the neighboring field to the place where the creek ran behind the fairgrounds, skirting the fence and the back side of the livestock buildings. He rode the horse down a draw in the bank and into the water. The creek was loud with crickets, and while the horse sucked greedily Charles took a deep breath, glad to be away from the flash and noise of the midway.

Then the horse quit drinking and jerked up his head, pricked his ears towards the bank.

Someone was coming.

Catherine.

She was still in her costume. Pale rawhide and paler flesh, her dark hair hanging like ropes in two braids. When she saw him she did not seem surprised.

She stood there above him, on the bank. They were nearly eye to eye.

Howdy, he said.

Hello.

Fine night for the fair.

Her feet in the little moccasins slipped on the slope, and she reached over to the trunk of the tree next to her, steadying herself. Her braids swung. In the darkness her flesh glowed.

He lit a cigarette and crossed his wrists on the pommel of the saddle. The horse, impatient, pawed at the water.

She sat down on the bank, folding her bare legs to the side. He looked away. A bawdy song came into his head. 'Mary Took Her Calves to the Fair.' *All the farmers joked, said they'd never, never stroked, such beautiful calves as Mary's.*

Well I'm glad to see you one more time before I go, he said.

Go?

The horse dropped his head to drink again. Big loud gulps.

Sure. Soon as we get that mare cured we'll be back on the road.

You've really almost got her fixed? I've been—well I've been worried about you.

He clucked to the horse and rode up the steep embankment. A scramble of dirt and falling leaves and then he was above her. He sat a moment before he jumped down, tied the horse to the tree, and got down beside her.

What are you doing back here all by yourself?

She shrugged. Thinking about jumping in and going for a swim.

He looked at the water, churned up, the color of coffee in the dark.

A little cold for swimming, don't you think?

She looked at him.

What?

That was a joke. She flashed her knockout smile. Then her face drew down. They say drowning's one of the most peaceful ways to go, once you quit struggling, that is. But it can't be peaceful while you're struggling. It must be quite the opposite. Terrifying.

There was a silence. A frog chirped. Charles tossed his cigarette into the water. She sighed and touched the fringe of her costume.

Did you like the show?

I did but I didn't.

Why not?

Because the whole time I was thinking about how much all them other fellows liked it too.

She laughed a little. When my father heard about the costumes he told me if I played the part of a squaw he was going to lock me up in the house for the rest of the month.

Well? Will he?

Guess I've got to wait till I get home to find out. If you don't see me around town, then you'll know.

I would come get you out, he said, looking to the water.

You would? And carry me away from here?

Sure. I can pick a lock.

Where would we go?

Anywhere in the world, he said. Kentucky. Arkansas. West Tennessee.

God, not West Tennessee.

Alright. Wherever you want.

She looked at him. You *are* a mystery. You are so awfully sure of yourself.

What do you mean?

That I would go with you. I don't know you. I don't know anything about you.

She laughed again, this time a nervous laugh. He could not read her. He moved a little farther away, trying not to look at her bare calf.

All the farmers joked, said they'd never, never stroked—

She played again with the fringe of her skirt, considering it.

It's real deer hide, she said. Mary Clausen's brother got it for us.

It looks real nice. You looked real nice up there.

It's the softest thing. She looked at him. There were shadows on her face. Do you want to feel it?

Now it was Charles who laughed. A quick nervous burst. His ears burned.

What? she said.

I don't think it's a good idea. Me feeling that skirt of yours.

Why not? she asked.

It just ain't.

She didn't say anything to that. She turned back to the creek. Bats were looping and darting over the water. After a while she said she was cold. He gave her his coat. The horse sighed heavily. He rolled a cigarette. She watched him and asked if she could have one. This surprised him, but he took it from his lips and wordlessly gave it to her, then rolled a new one for himself. He took great care in the job, needing something to do with his hands. She drew up her knees and hooked one arm around them and watched him. Finally he was finished with it and they sat there smoking in silence, watching the bats work the water. Scattered sounds of the midway. The brass band at the dance pavilion, the bells of a game, a barker's drawl.

If he does lock me up—

He wouldn't do that.

I can't be so sure. Want to know where my brother is right now? Home, packing his bags. He's leaving for the war, going over to drive an ambulance. In France! It's too much to bear. My father signed him up. He got in trouble down at school this spring and Father had to go bail him out. This was the deal. Him going over to volunteer will save face, Father said, if it should ever get out what happened.

What happened?

I'm not supposed to know. Her eyes darkened. There's a lot that I know that I'm not supposed to know. Well it was a girl, a woman—the wrong sort of woman, and Father saved him by the skin of his teeth. Went down there, talked to his cronies. They agreed to let him graduate after Father promised to switch sides on the temperance question. Now Ed's at his mercy. But he's always been at his mercy. When he comes back he'll move right into the office across from Father's up at the factory. Where Wad Taylor's working now. That office has been Ed's destiny all his life. On his twentieth birthday my father had the desk in there made to his exact specifications. It fits him perfectly.

She shivered. My father has done so many terrible things. Things that I can't forgive him for. This is just another. But I suppose I'm lucky to be his daughter and not his son. He doesn't care a whit for me.

She paused. Her voice was trembling with fury.

Once I'm finished up at the college, I'll be able to go wherever I please. New York. Chicago. Go down to the depot, get on the first train to wherever, and jump feetfirst into life. I think that's what my mother would have done when she was my age, if she could. Set off on her own. But back then a girl couldn't. Running off with my father was the closest she could come to it. I always think she was robbed of something she didn't even know she had.

Now hold on a minute there, Miss Hatcher. Go wherever you please? I thought you were gonna run away with me.

She ground out her cigarette. Looked at the side of his face. He could feel her smiling coyly.

Well maybe I'll bring you along with me when I go.

He turned and studied her face, trying to read her.

My mother, he said, she got robbed too. If she hadn't I'd be in a real different position than I am now. She's dead.

I'm sorry.

He paused, gathered courage.

She had a smile just like you.

Catherine groaned. Her hand flew up to cover her mouth.

Don't talk about my smile. Cherry says it's my downfall. Cherry says it's why I'll never be a true beauty.

Don't listen to Cherry. She don't know nothing.

After that, more silence. Catherine was staring at the water.

What was her name? she said. Your mother?

Maura, he said.

Her head jerked up. She spun to look at him. Did you say Morning?

No. Maura.

That gave me a chill. She rubbed her bare legs. My mother's name was Morning.

Mourning? Pardon me for saying, but that's an awful sorrowful name for a woman.

No, she said. *Morning*. The dawn of the day.

Oh. That's real pretty.

Maura's a pretty name too.

He put one hand in the cool grass, just beside her hip. He leaned over. He kissed her. She kissed him back, long and hard. Then he pulled away, worried by the thought of whoever it was who had taught her to do all those things with her tongue.

Well, she said.

I gotta tell you up front, he said in a rush. As of my present situation, I got no money. Not yet, anyway. I bet—I bet at your house you have steak for supper every day.

Sure. We eat it off of solid gold plates.

Charles whistled.

She looked at him. Laughed.

I get the feeling you believe everything I say, she said.

Why shouldn't I?

That seemed to surprise her. She considered him.

Can I ask you something straight? Charles said quickly. That Wad Taylor, he used to be your boyfriend? Kissam Quick Taylor?

She laughed, but then her face fell.

Wad? Oh—poor Wad. It's all ruined for him and he never even got started. No girl's ever going to marry him now. Two years ago he had everything going for him and now it's ruined. One bad collision on the football field.

She was quiet for a while. She picked a blade of grass, let it drop.

Ruined. He was so big and strong. A poet, too. You should have seen him in those days.

Charles cleared his throat, wondering why the hell he had thought it was a good idea to bring up Wad Taylor.

You sure looked pretty up there tonight.

She plucked another blade of grass. Well if you want to know the whole truth, they wouldn't let me be what I wanted to be. I didn't want to be a Pilgrim and I didn't want to be a squaw. I wanted to be a brave. I had it all planned. Use my brother's old bow and quiver of arrows. Have Mary Clausen sew me up a pair of leggings. I would be cutting up a deer haunch at my feet, just back from the hunt. Blood on the knife.

She got up on her knees, to demonstrate. Looked at him over her shoulder, braids swinging. Her hips were maddeningly close.

Wouldn't that have been something? But old Missus Dimwiddle wouldn't even hear my argument. She said it was not appropriate. Instead I had to stand there with that dumb basket of fish.

The horse got impatient and began to paw rhythmically at the dry bank, bringing up dust. Catherine said she ought to get back. He helped her up. Her hand was surprisingly strong, and when she gripped his, tight, it sent little waves up his arm and into his spine. When she took off his coat and handed it to him, the flash of her bare shoulders nearly knocked him over.

He went over and untied the horse. She came close and looked up at him from under her lashes. He kissed her again, blood throbbing, but she pulled away quicker this time. Then she gave him another sly smile.

So when are we getting married? she said.

The throb cooled instantly. Married?

Well sure. Isn't that your intention, kissing me?

He fumbled for a long moment before she threw back her head and laughed.

I'm teasing you, she said. I could say anything, couldn't I? I could say anything and you would believe it.

They walked up towards the midway together, him leading the horse. She showed him the gap in the fence where she had snuck out, and they slipped back through it together, the horse hesitating before he too stepped through. They parted at the edge of the midway's brightness. Charles tried to close his lips around his grin, but he couldn't. He smashed his hat down over his eyes. Then he led the horse over to the Test Your Strength booth. The barker was looking at him over his crossed arms. Charles handed him a coin and the horse's reins. Swung the mallet so hard the ball shot up and broke the clapper.

Hey, buddy, the barker said. Easy. It's just a game.

Money Matters

by Leland Hatcher
The Richfield Gazette

I have long held to the belief that a young man's soul can only be forged in the divine crucible of war. My generation, born too late to fight in the conflict between the states, never had its great chance. This missed opportunity of my own makes me even prouder to announce that my son, Edmund, has bravely volunteered to serve with the Norton-Harjes Ambulance Corps. He has chosen to go forth to fight the great fight raging across the ocean, the fight for what is right, for what is good, the fight for freedom. The fight for nothing less than civilization itself.

AT THE DEPOT

Charles and Billy stood at the depot, where so many people had suddenly gathered you would have thought the president was pulling in. Bud Morgan was in the center of everything selling postcards, his goats jumpy from the excitement. Even the birds were worked up, reeling around, and beneath them boys laid out crossed nails on the rails for the train to flatten into crucifixes, and old ladies chattered, and the crowd heaved.

Edmund Hatcher was departing, on his way to Nashville, then New York, then to drive an ambulance for the war. When he showed up with his father, a cheer rose up, but he hung back with his suitcase while Hatcher shook everybody's hand.

Where is she? Charles said, craning his neck. How could she not be here?

Billy patted his shoulder. Well that's alright. Enough pretty girls here to float that fellow's ship all the way over to France. And I imagine plenty of em would let you kiss them behind the fairgrounds too. More than kiss em, probably, if you picked one that wasn't on such a high shelf.

Billy was in a buoyant mood. He'd had a good morning with Hatcher's mare, who had let him saddle and bridle her and work her on a long line. And he always did love a crowd. He had traded his penknife with the fellow to his left and then turned around and traded the new one with the fellow to his right.

So there he is, Billy said. So that's the famous Leland Hatcher. Littler than I expected. But I can see it in his face.

See what? Charles kept looking. She had to be there somewhere.

Ah, Charles. That horse. That poor beautiful confused creature. Ragtime, Charles! That just might be the secret to her. I played her 'The Darktown Strutters' Ball' and the next minute she's nearly eating out of my hand. Remarkable. Incredible. How about that? My maniac sweetheart is a ragtime fan. I should have known she was at heart a good-timing sort of gal . . .

Billy kept rattling on and then Catherine came pushing through to join her father and brother. At the sight of her Charles grabbed Billy's arm.

There she is, he said. Billy. Jesus. Shut up a minute. There she is. Do you see her? That smile, Billy. It's just like my mother's—

Just then she turned and saw him and flashed a sly secret smile. Made all the more sly by that wide dark gap.

Do you see that, Billy? Sonofabitch. She just smiled at me.

He looked at Billy, who was still looking at the Hatchers. But he had gone silent, his face slack.

Hey, Billy. Billy.

Huh?

You OK? Billy?

Sure. I'm OK, Charlie boy.

BOOM BOOM

That afternoon, Billy left Charles up in town and went straight back to Dillehay's.

Straight to the pasture.

Enough of this nonsense already, he said to Hatcher's mare. I'm tired of looking at you.

He caught her and tied her to the fence next to the Edison machine and grabbed a cylinder out of the box and put it on. It was 'Daisy Bell' and he pulled it off immediately. Not that. He was too shaken for that now. He dug until he found a ragtime number, 'Alexander's Ragtime Band.' He cranked the machine and lowered the needle. The horse stood obediently while he ran his hands over her. Her black coat was hot with the day's sun. They were something else, horses. Even one like her, who had suffered a terrible existence, was always here, now. Only *here*. Always *now*.

Watching Leland Hatcher at the depot, he had seen in his face what he expected all along. Behind the mask of his smile, something warped and cold-blooded. He had recognized it instantly. Leland Hatcher was a dangerous man.

When the song ended he went over and pulled off the cylinder. He knew there was another ragtime number in the box somewhere. Rummaging for it, his hand closed on the little accordion book that the bookseller has given him. The ribbon was untied, and when he pulled it out it fell open like a Jacob's ladder toy, all the blurred and shadowed faces hanging there in the air. He tossed it back into the box and kept digging and found what he was looking for. Another ragtime tune. 'Everybody's Doin' It Now.' He put it on. The mare lowered her head and sighed.

He saddled her up. No problem. When he went to put on the bridle she even dropped her head for it. He crossed himself and mounted up. She stood like a dream. Before he did anything he made the exchange he had with any horse, gently playing one rein, asking for submission or permission or comradeship or patience, he never really knew. Maybe just asking. She dropped her head and chewed the bit, swung her nose to touch his toe. Yes, this said. Yes.

Look at you, he told her happily. Should have done this weeks ago.

He asked her for a trot. Beautiful. Hooves snapping smart and high, like she was fixing to knock out her own front teeth. Moving out so calm and sure that he laughed at himself for having grown so afraid of her.

Well it serves you right, Monday, he thought. Wasting all this time hanging around, when you were just being a yellow-bellied fool.

His thoughts swung back to the depot and his heart heaved. It was not Leland Hatcher who had shaken him so badly, who made him want to get out of town quick as he could.

It was the girl. That smile.

He brought the mare down to a walk and spun her around and tried her in the other direction, bringing her up through her paces, the green of the world framed between her perfect ears. But he could not shake the girl out of his head.

Now that he had seen her, he understood. It was no wonder Charles had been such a fool about her.

It was high time they got out of here. Start moving again.

Time had crashed in on him, up at the depot, and he did not like the feeling at all. It was just like that old snapshot book. Time was no arrow, no straight line. If you kept moving it stayed stretched out neatly behind you. But time could just as easily fold and collapse like an accordion, just like that album when you closed it. In his mind as in the photographs, faces pressed on faces, distance crumpled, crushed.

Maybe because he was distracted, or maybe simply because she hit a stone or a hole, the horse stumbled. It made her mad. She tossed her head and wrung her tail.

Steady now, he said. He had lost his stirrup. He groped for it with his foot. The loose stirrup iron knocked against her side. She didn't like that. She threw a buck. He gathered her back in and she settled down.

The girl's smile had done it, collapsed time, just like that. Charles was right. It was a smile just exactly like his mother's.

The mare bucked again. Pitched herself good.

Easy, Billy said. His heart was pounding.

Another buck. This time she spun herself so that her belly and her back swapped places. Wrung herself like a rag until she unseated him. He sailed over her head and landed hard in the grass. It knocked the wind out of him and when he got it back he sat up and grabbed his hat and as the shock waves passed through him and he became dimly aware that his ribs and perhaps his left shoulder had not made out alright the mare came at him in a fury. Screaming. Front legs striking. He clutched his head and tried to roll away, but a hoof caught him in the back, another in the side. He felt the blow of an iron shoe against his skull. The last thing he saw before the world went black was her face. Not the girl's. But Maura's.

Foxy little Maura McLaughlin. Oh, how he had loved her.

IN THE DEAD LEAVES

Bristol, Tennessee-Virginia
JULY 1897

Someday I will buy you a bed, Billy tells her.

Solid brass, Maura says. The best one they make.

Anything you want, he says. I promise. Anything at all.

They fuck like animals, in the woods. They don't have anywhere else to go. Afterwards, there are tiny twigs caught in her hair. Bits of moss, decaying bark, a black slippery-looking beetle. She reaches up and plucks this out, crushes it between her fingernails, laughing.

She is afraid of nothing. Cunning, quick, and ravenous. There is an insatiable gleam in her green eyes.

Anything you want at all, he tells her again. The woods are quiet. There is a faint, musky smell of deer shit on the air, and rotting blackberries, and rain.

Afterwards, they walk up to Solar Hill, as they sometimes do, to look at the big houses. Maura lingers, despite the suspicious looks from people in passing carriages. She makes him wait until dusk, the moment just after the lights are lit and just before the curtains are drawn, so that she can see in the windows to the riches inside.

He watches her eyes take it all in. Seeing that insatiable green gleam fills him with desire too. He feels himself rising, wanting her again.

He'll buy her that bed. He'll buy her one of these houses. He'll do something as crazy as marry her, little Maura McLaughlin. He'll do anything she asks him to do, so long as she'll always stick with him.

THE NEW SUIT

Bristol

This is how it all begins, with a suit of clothes. If not for the suit, he never would have found her. He would have left Bristol when the roads dried out, never knowing a girl like her could even exist.

It is a very good suit, dark blue serge, a coat with padded shoulders, shirt, studs, collar, toothpick shoes. He took it for boot in a trade for a horse, and though he's got no use for finery, it is all folded up in paper and stowed away in his saddlebag until he runs into someone who does.

He is twenty-five years old, and traveling alone with his string of horses in the hazy blue mountains of southwest Virginia. He has been in America for eleven years, out of the honeycombed hell of the Neversink mine for one, though sometimes he still can't believe he made it out at all. Working in the mine had been to live under a tyranny worse than the sea's. At least a broken fisherman could just lie down and die. The joke in the mines was that if you lay down and died the company would make you get up and work until you had paid off your coffin.

But Billy had escaped. He had started trading with the other miners, penknives, cans of beans, bread, not for any gain, just to amuse himself, just to break up the darkness of the underground days. But pretty soon he was doing almost as good business as the company store, and the company caught wind of it and fired him, and when he left without paying his bill they sent two men after him. To shake them off his tail he spent three days hiding out in the green hills of Pennsylvania, snaring rabbits, drinking from creeks, sleeping under his coat. The woods were bountiful as Eden. The second night out there he realized he did not care if the Neversink men caught up with him and shot him dead. What he had found in those woods was worth dying for.

And for a year he has been free. Or nearly. He goes wherever he pleases, trading with whoever he happens to meet, camping at night in hay fields. He is tethered to only one thing in the world and that is the island. Home. All the money he makes, mostly five or ten dollars here and there for boot, he dutifully sends back to his mother, widowed now six years.

With love from your son, who has struck it rich in America, his accompanying letter invariably reads. Where there is gold and silver in the ditches, and nothing to do but gather it.

But things changed two weeks ago, in Abingdon, Virginia, where he stopped for a spell to wait out some bad weather. While there he wrote a letter to a man back up at the Neversink, asking him to send the rest of his belongings. Included in the small package he received in return was a ten-month-old letter from the island with the news that his mother was dead.

It brought the place back to him, in a rush, so real he could feel the sting of salt air. Fourteen years old he was when he left it. The summer after the Winter of Darkness. That winter for ten ghastly weeks storms had kept the men off the sea and cut them off entirely from the mainland, until food dwindled to nothing, until food ran out. His baby sister was one of the first to die. A little bright-eyed girl, not yet two. There was no consecrated ground on the island and so they buried her by the dolmen on top of East Hill, and by the time the weather had settled a dozen more were laid out beside her, shallow in the rocky soil. There was talk of abandoning the place, of the entire island picking up and going to the mainland, where the young people had begun to go, anyway, in recent years. His four older sisters were all married to men in Skibbereen. Without them and without the baby his father's house was sorrowfully quiet, all winter rocked by the howling wolflike wind.

If I live, Billy would say to the wind at night, half-mad with hunger. If I live through this I am going to America.

And he did live, and he did go, six months later, after making his passage money bit by bit, selling rabbit skins at the market in Skib.

When he told his parents of his plan his father had only sucked in a breath and pulled his chin to his chest. His mother's chair creaked when she rose from it and went to the window, and it pained him to know she was looking towards the makeshift grave on East Hill and at a vision of herself alone and old beside an empty hearth. At that moment he nearly told her he would abandon the whole idea. Then, from above, came a squawk. One of the hens which roosted in the thatch of the roof laid an egg, and it fell through, clean through the hole that needed fixing, fell straight down between them and burst on the floor. They all stared at the oozing golden yolk for a minute before they all three began to laugh and his mother embraced him and still laughing told him it was a sign, that he was bound to meet with great fortune in America. In no time at all he was gone, never to return.

Readying his string of horses in Abingdon that morning, the suit packed away in his saddlebag, he can hear for the first time in a decade her laughter when that chicken egg dropped, and he has to stop and lean against the horse's neck for a long time, weak with grief, both for the loss and for all the days he has spent in ignorance of the fact that the world no longer contains her.

But he feels something else, behind all this. A weight lifting.

He heads south, aiming for Tennessee. The roads are still a mess and it is slow going. A few nights later he is camped in the hills above Bristol when a ring shows up around the moon. More rain coming.

He breaks camp at dawn, but the rain has already started. The road gets bad fast as the swollen creeks overflow and water rushes downhill by any path it can find. The horses slog along, their ears at half-mast. Mud sucking their hooves. He is thinking again of his mother. She had not cried when they buried her baby girl. Only crossed herself and said, The good Lord wills it so. But she had wept when he left for America, down at the harbor, waving with the rest of the island.

She is free now, he thinks, God rest her soul.

The rain falls in white sheets. And in it he understands what he is feeling, the weight lifting. He too is free. Responsible for nothing and no one but himself. Coming down off the mountain he overtakes a fellow in a buckboard who is whipping a balky mule.

This keeps up the road won't be passable, he calls after Billy.

Passable? Billy shouts, his heart buoyant with joy. Mister, it won't even be jackassable!

The sky begins to clear by the time the smokestacks of Bristol come into view. Billy finds a dry place to tie up on the edge of town, an overhang of rock hidden in rhododendrons, takes care of the wet horses as best he can, and ponders his next move. Trying to get any farther on these kinds of roads is foolish, but he's got no money for a boardinghouse and is in no shape for town, wet as a drowned rat with mud halfway up his pants legs.

Then he remembers the suit. When he pulls it out of the saddlebag, he finds that by some miracle it has stayed dry. He washes and shaves in a swollen creek, combs back his hair. Strips off his wet clothes and puts it on. Settles the horses one more time. Heads down into town.

And so this is how Billy Monday, with no money in his pockets but looking like a millionaire, comes into Bristol on that wet afternoon. Bristol. He has heard plenty about it, the town that straddles Tennessee and Virginia so tidily that the state line runs right down the center of Main Street. The town with two of everything: two police stations, two post offices, two libraries, two schools, and sixty-four saloons. The town where a man can break the law on one side of the street and evade the sheriff simply by crossing to the other.

He keeps the good shoes tucked under his arm until he gets to Main Street and then, stashing his muddy shoes behind an ash bin, puts them on. Bristol jangles and bustles, Main Street opening back up after a rain. On either side of the street, shopkeepers are jabbing their awnings with broom handles to knock off the rainwater. A grocer is drying off a great green pyramid of watermelons. The windows are stacked with boxes, cans, factory bread, factory clothes, buttons, spools of thread, gloves from Knoxville, leather goods from Chicago, bananas from God knows where. Billy falls in with a group of men who have gathered to read a job board. King Coke and Fuel is hiring, as well as the N&W Railway. There are dozens of men jostling for the same sorry positions that would all break their back and spirit. A dollar a day. Two dollars a day. Five dollars a week. To spend in the shops on leather goods from Chicago, gloves from Knoxville, furniture from North Carolina, furniture polish in a jar to keep all that furniture nice and new-looking.

I am free, Billy is thinking happily. I am free free free free.

He laughs out loud. He knows now what a dead man knows. The distance between the pit and the snare can be measured with time clocks and paychecks. There is only one way out. And that is down. Down below even the bottom rail, to slip out free on the other side.

Somebody turns and looks him over, and then steps aside to let him up to the front of the crowd. He thinks nothing of it until he walks away and a couple of urchins ask him for change. Then an important-looking fellow strolling past gives him a knowing nod.

Suddenly it hits him. The suit!

He stops and looks at his reflection in a shop window.

Well look at that. He squares his shoulders. If he didn't know better, he would think he was somebody. Why, in this suit he could go anywhere. And when the man inside the shop comes out and, smiling broadly, wants to know if he can help him, Billy asks him where the best place in town is. The fellow points him up the street. To the Nichols House Hotel.

THE MONKEY TRICK

Bristol

It is too easy. All he's got to do is keep his mouth shut. Nobody in the Nichols House parlor gives him a second glance. In fact, the fellow sitting next to him, a speculator from Cincinnati, Ohio, chewing a fat cigar, thinks he is a local. He even asks if Billy is a King. Billy bites his lip to keep from laughing, and the man mistakes this for a nod. He nearly tears out his pocket digging for his card and hands it across the brass spittoon between them.

The colored man at the piano is playing a number Billy recognizes. 'The Sunshine of Paradise Alley.' He is blind, his unseeing eyes fixed on a spot between the wall and the ceiling, and his big hands move sleepily up and down the keyboard. His cap lies on top of the piano, turned up for tips. At the foot of his stool sits a threadbare carpetbag.

The Cincinnati man goes on about taxes and the price of raw land, the fine quality of Bristol's water, the agreeable climate, the railroads, but Billy keeps his eye on the piano player's bag. When he sat down, he could have sworn he saw it move. But now it looks like just a run-of-the-mill carpetbag. The truth is, he is restless and bored. The men in the parlor remind him of seals crowded on a rock: fat and torpid, snapping at one another, blowing hot air. There's a sad desperation to the fellow from Cincinnati. Better fed and better heeled, but isn't he clawing out of the same pit and into the same snare as the workingmen huddled at the job board?

Where I'm from every pie's already got too many fingers in it, he is saying. That's what brings me here. I happen to know, on good reliable sources, that Bristol is about to boom. In fifteen years this town will be big as Knoxville. In forty, Chicago.

He settles back into his chair and stabs the air with his cigar.

And I'll be able to say I was on the leading edge.

His eyes wander over Billy's shoulder.

Well if that isn't the ugliest little colored boy I ever seen.

Billy turns. Out of the carpetbag has climbed a monkey. A moonfaced creature dressed in a brocade vest and top hat. It scampers onto the piano to retrieve the player's cap and begins to work the room for tips, holding its tail over its back to display its ass like an insult. When it approaches, the Cincinnati man pushes it away with his foot in disgust. Billy, pitying it, digs in his pocket and finds a nickel. When he reaches down to drop it in the hat, the monkey snatches it out of his hand with thin leathery fingers.

Outside, a train slowing for the station blows its whistle. It passes so close to the back wall of the hotel that the floor shakes and the rose-colored glass globes of the parlor lamps rattle. The Cincinnati man is talking about a tract of land along Beaver Creek, hundreds of acres, limitless possibility for development. Billy watches another man across the room push the monkey away with his foot, without breaking his conversation. So far his nickel is the only one in the creature's cap.

He looks at the man at the piano, his blind eyes raised to the ceiling, now on to 'The Picture That Is Turned Toward the Wall.' Poor old fellow, he thinks. Probably spent his last dollar on that monkey. Creature probably doesn't even earn its keep.

A chambermaid has come in, darting along the wall, quick as a mouse. When she begins to draw the drapes of the big windows, Billy gives her the once-over, dismisses her. Just a sour-looking girl, with downcast eyes and hunched shoulders, dark hair pulled back severely from her scowling face.

The piano player begins to play 'Beautiful Dreamer,' flourishing every note. Without breaking the melody he reaches up to pat the monkey, which has scampered to the top of the piano to sit on its haunches and eat a crust of bread, glaring at the crowd.

The Cincinnati man sings along, his lips working around his cigar.

Beautiful dreamer, wake unto me
Starlight and dewdrops are waiting for thee

Billy hardly hears him. He is watching the monkey. Some sort of spell has come over the animal. It has dropped its bread and is watching the chambermaid with rapt concentration. Finished with the drapes, she is now turning up the gas lamps along the back wall. As if in a trance, the monkey climbs down off the piano and begins moving towards her. Billy looks around the room. A handful of men have noticed the creature's odd behavior and have turned to watch.

Sounds of the rude world, heard in the day . . .

The Cincinnati man is one of the last to notice. He abruptly quits singing, looks at Billy and raises his eyebrows.

Would you look at that little sonofabitch, he says. If I didn't know better I would say it was lovestruck.

The whole room is watching. All eyes are on the creature. In fact, the girl and the piano player seem to be the only two unaware of the fact that the monkey is stalking her, drawing closer and closer.

It is six feet from her now. Five. Four. Three.

The girl is up on her toes, straining to reach one of the light fixtures. The black skirt of her dress sways. The monkey is now only a step behind her. The last notes of the song fade. In the silence, the monkey sits back on its haunches, turns, and gives the room a conspiring look. Then it snatches up the hem of her dress and sticks its head inside.

The girl screams. And what a scream. They could probably hear it back in Abingdon. She snatches up her skirts, beats out the monkey as if beating out a flame, and flees. The beads of the portiere clack wildly behind her.

The room rocks with laughter nearly as hard as it shook with the passing train. Feet pound the floor. Somebody calls after her.

Hey, honey, come back, he only wants a little kiss!

The player looks up, pretends to grope around for the monkey, shrugs, turns to the room, and pulls a grin. Brings his hands back down to the keyboard.

Shave and a haircut, two bits!

The Cincinnati man is laughing so hard it sends him into a coughing fit. The monkey scampers onto the piano for the hat and goes back around for tips. This time, no one kicks him away. The coins rain in. And the fellow at the piano is grinning like his face is going to split in two.

Billy shakes his head. What a brilliant trick. Jesus, Joseph, and Mary. It's the best hustle he's seen in all his travels.

In the morning, after sleeping under the overhang with the horses, he realizes he left his hat at the hotel. He puts the suit back on and heads back into town along the railroad tracks. Better traveling than the roads, which are a churned mess. Ruts so deep, the Cincinnati man said yesterday, that you can hear voices coming up from below.

Where to? Billy thinks, hearing the whistle of a distant train. His evening at the Nichols House has only made him more grateful that he has nothing to his name. He's freer even than the birds wheeling above the tracks, which after all have to hustle back to the nest at the end of the day. But for him—no limits. Where to? What next?

When he gets to the Nichols House, he sees that someone has left a back door propped open. When he slips in, it brings him to the foot of a dark, narrow stairwell. The clatter of pans and smells of the kitchen rise up from below. From above, the sound of creaking stairs.

He looks up. A small girl with a basketful of linens on her hip is coming down backwards. She goes carefully, one hand sliding along the banister, placing each foot square in the center of each tread.

Irish, he thinks, admiring the slow swing of her backside. All Irish girls in America go down staircases backwards, accustomed as they are to ladders back at home.

She looks over her shoulder and catches his eye, then lets out a yelp. He jumps. The basket falls from her hip, spilling its contents. She unleashes a string of curses as satisfying as any Billy has ever heard in any barroom. He laughs, amazed that such filth can come from such a wisp of a girl.

She spins around, clutching her hand to her mouth. Even with half her face covered he can see that she is beautiful. Her eyes are green and sharp. They move over him slowly, taking in more, it somehow feels, than just the suit and the shoes.

Lowering her hand, she grins. It's a big, disarming smile, revealing a gap between the two front teeth.

Barked my knuckles, she says. Then she runs her tongue over her lip, looking him over again. You were in the parlor last night, weren't you?

I was. An important business meeting. This town's going to be big as Chicago someday, you know— He hesitates, suddenly confused. But how do you know? You weren't there. I would have noticed a girl so pretty as you.

Ah! she says. But I was there, sure enough.

He shakes his head. She is standing three steps above him, looking down. Remembering the basket, he bends down to right it and begins to pick up the linens.

There was only one girl I saw, he says, straightening. And she was nothing to look at. Just a homely little mouse.

She smiles bigger at this and winks. Then she drops her gaze, rounds her shoulders, bites the insides of her cheeks. She is transformed into the sour little chambermaid who was chased by the monkey.

Billy sucks in his breath.

Jesus, Joseph, and Mary. How did you do that?

She throws back her head and laughs a big glittering laugh. When she does, the ugly girl disappears, as if the sun has suddenly burst forth from behind dark clouds.

He stands there dumbfounded, clutching his armload of dirty rags. She is still three stairs above him, looking down.

You— he says.

That's right, she says proudly. Me. I play that old monkey trick three nights a week and twice on Saturdays. Me and old Joe, we split the take.

He's a smart one, that old fellow, Billy says admiringly.

Joe? She shakes her head. Joe's about as smart as that monkey of his.

Well, my girl, a man's got to have some brains in his head, dreaming up a trick as brilliant as that.

Wasn't his idea, she says shortly.

No?

She squares her shoulders. Oh no. 'Twas mine.

In a few days, he won't be able to believe that he doubted her. But other than witnessing her transformation from ugly to beautiful, he doesn't yet know her powers. He doesn't even know her name.

Well if that's so, what's with the disguise? Why does a pretty little thing like you go and turn into an ugly mouse?

She shrugs. Didn't take me long to figure out that men would rather see a monkey goose an ugly girl than a pretty one. See, I've learned a thing or two about men. I know what they want.

And what's that?

She doesn't answer. Just smiles. The gap is a hole you could fall into. Or a door you could climb through. She looks back at her injured hand and shakes it.

Look at that, she says. Took the skin right off.

She takes the rest of the stairs to stand before him, lifts her hand to her mouth, then draws in a sharp breath. Looks up at him from under her lashes.

Blow on it, will you? she says, holding out her hand. It'll feel better than if I do.

He looks at it. The knuckles are red and chapped, and there are black lines of dirt under her fingernails. He hesitates. His mouth has gone dry. His thoughts are all twisted around. Somewhere in the tangle, he wonders if he is being hustled.

If he is, for the moment, he does not care.

He takes her hand in his and brings it to his mouth. He purses his lips. He blows.

CHICKEN OF THE WOODS

Bristol

Her parents are dead, her brothers and sisters are all dead, all of them long gone and buried back in County Galway. She came to New York at the age of thirteen with a cousin who did terrible things to her and then died drunk facedown in a basement in Hell's Kitchen, where rats ate him.

Truly, she says to Billy, when she tells him this story, the first day they spend together. Ate him up, bones and all. She draws an X across her heart. Swear on my mother's grave.

All alone in the city, she registered with an intelligence office and found a job as a domestic servant. After a month, the old widow she worked for choked on a chicken bone one night at supper and died and Maura only just escaped being tried for murder and that was the end of her career as a domestic. After that she did anything to get by, sold week-old bread on a street corner and did piecework for a glove factory at night. She lived in a room on Mulberry Street with ten other people and two pigs and then cholera struck and they all began to die. She managed to escape, but landed in a filthy shed full of lecherous drunks so crowded she was forced to sleep sitting up when she dared sleep at all. By some miracle she found a flyer about jobs in Virginia. Scraped together money for the train fare. She has been at the Nichols House for a year. She is seventeen years old.

Oh, I ought to be dead ten times over, she laughs. It is a wonder I am still on this earth. Every morning I wake up and thank my lucky stars. The world is full of liars, isn't it? Liars and sneaks and shams. It's all a girl can do to keep two steps ahead of them.

It is her afternoon off, and they are walking down Main Street. Billy told her he would take her to lunch. But he is panicking now, realizing that in the finely tailored pocket of his high-class suit, he's only got a nickel and a couple of pennies.

Where shall we eat? she says, taking his arm. The hotel? Or have you got a private railroad car?

He tells her he's got to confess something. The suit is nothing but a suit. I ain't rich, he says.

She laughs so hard tears come to her eyes. Bill Monday, I saw through that suit the moment I saw you across the parlor. I says to myself, Maura, there's two people in disguise here tonight. Yourself and that handsome boy over there with the grim look on his face like he's stuck in the schoolhouse on a sunny day.

You've known all along? Then why did you agree to lunch?

I liked the show you were putting on, she says, wiping her eyes. Wanted to see how far you'd carry it.

They walk along muddy Main Street with the rest of the Sunday afternoon crowd. She darts in and out of alleys, checking ash barrels, stooping to pick up dropped pennies that he never would have noticed. With her, in fact, treasure reveals itself everywhere. Later she shows him some of her prized scavenged possessions. A Masonic watch charm with a broken clip, a moldy copy of *Robinson Crusoe* with pink covers. That afternoon, when she triumphantly holds up her fourth found penny for him to see, he can't believe her luck. In time, he will come to understand that it is more than luck, but a certain combination of qualities that bring her all this good fortune: her animal alertness, the green-eyed charm, that fearlessness. She can flutter her eyelashes at a butcher and talk him into giving her a soup bone as easy as she can catch a wayward chicken and break its neck with a snap of her wrist, do both as if she has absolutely nothing to lose in the world.

That day he gives her a rabbit's foot he's been carrying. Tells her the man he got it off of said it was the real deal: the left hind leg of a male jackrabbit killed on a full moon by a cross-eyed man. Which was not a lie, because it was what the man told him. And when she asks if it has brought him luck he says, It brought me to you, didn't it?

Later it is Maura who finally finds them something to eat, mushrooms that she gathers out in the woods and fries over a little fire he builds on the bank of Beaver Creek. He will learn that many of her meals are scavenged, if not from the rubbish bins of town then from the hills above it, the old fields, the vacant lots. Mushrooms, greens, nuts, windfall fruit, even flowers.

There's a feast to be had out here, and it's all free for the taking, she tells him. Anyone who goes hungry in America isn't paying attention.

Gold and silver in the ditches, he says, certain she heard that one back home too, and nothing to do but gather it. He points to the mushrooms, smiles and winks. Suppose there's our gold and silver.

She straightens up suddenly. Her nostrils flare.

Oh, I'll have my share of gold and silver, alright. I'll be eating off of fine china and wearing ropes of pearls.

The flame-colored mushroom is called chicken of the woods. Later, when they scramble up the hill looking for a hidden place to be together, he sees it everywhere, growing on the sides of trees, fleshy, sulfur-bright, and it makes him ache for her even more urgently.

But that is still ahead of them. He has not yet dared touch her. While they eat, the sun drops slowly in the west. Birds are rustling around on the bank and kingfishers dart over the water, chattering. A cow lows in a field.

Maura, he starts. He has been trying to think of a way to tell her that he is leaving as soon as the roads dry up. He is already sure he never wants to hurt her, or disappoint her, or even cause her to frown.

He fishes another piece of mushroom out of the pan. Warm and soft as flesh, slippery from the butter. The cool evening, the hot food, the smell of her, makes him feel strong and happy. It's no time to talk of leaving. He'll tell her tomorrow. Or the next day.

Smiling, she watches him.

Now don't go gathering mushrooms without me, she says. Some of them out there is poison and they look just exactly like the good ones. Kill you dead faster than a bullet. Girl who taught me about em once got so sick herself they were measuring her for her coffin before she sat up and asked for a glass of water.

He freezes, the bite of mushroom halfway to his mouth.

She laughs. Look at you. Don't worry. I won't kill you. You've got my word on that.

She brushes the hair back from her face and squats to stir the mushrooms still frying in the pan.

I won't kill you. But I got to tell you something, Bill Monday. I'll be leaving you someday. I just want to say so now. I'll be taking to the road, and I don't want you to get your poor heart broken.

BUSTED

Charles had stayed up at the depot until Edmund Hatcher's train pulled out and the crowd filtered away, still vibrating from the rush of the locomotive in his feet, the rush of seeing her smile at him through the crowd.

Then she had come running back around the corner.

You're still here, she said, her face so close to his he could feel her breath. Where do you live? How can I find you?

He thought about the shack, the peeling newsprint on the walls, the mice in the kitchen, cobwebs hung with flies.

I'll find you, he said.

He pulled her behind the freight shed and kissed her, once, quick, before she ran off again. Afterwards he had paced around town, walking big loops, feeling as if he might lift up over the tops of the buildings and into the clouds. Finally he climbed onto the interurban car and headed back out to the shack. When the car passed the Everbright gates, just south of town on the Pike, he laid his head against the back of his seat and laughed.

He got off at the stop whistling. It was a fine day, the air cool and bright, the tobacco being brought in, the trees beginning to change. He laughed again, remembering the taste of her mouth, the sweetness, the faint thrill of cigarettes.

When he turned down the drive towards their place, it took a moment to make sense of the scene. Dillehay's son's bicycle lay in the yard, the front wheel sticking straight up. A Ford was parked behind it. Hatcher's mare, standing in the corner of the pasture, was still saddled, the broken reins hanging from the bit. The Edison machine was out in the pasture with the lid propped open, a gaping mouth. He started to run. He knew whose Ford it was. A doctor's. And he knew how bad it had to be. Because if Billy was in any shape at all, he would have never let anybody call a doctor for him.

Inside, there were too many bodies. Dillehay and his son, and the doctor leaning over a lump in the bed. The sharp scent of chloroform.

Dillehay's bird eyes ratcheted around to him. He shifted his tobacco. Told you that horse was no good.

Charles went over to the bed. Billy looked as if he had been worked over by a gang of roughnecks. But it wasn't the blood or the terrible bruises that made the bottom drop out of his stomach in fear. It was Billy's silence. His stillness.

The doctor was sewing a flap of his scalp.

Jesus. He ain't gonna die, is he?

The doctor finished the stitches, tying them off carefully, before he answered. His eyes, behind thick glasses, were the eyes of a man who had delivered a lifetime's worth of bad news.

I don't think so.

There was a chair pulled up next to the bed. Charles sat down.

The doctor opened his bag and put the chloroform into it.

For the shape he's in I don't know how he even had it in him. Couldn't even quite understand what he was saying. But when I got here I do believe he was trying to sell me a horse.

A laugh burst out of Charles. Desperate and startled. Yeah?

I told him he isn't the best advertising for that particular means of conveyance at the current moment.

Dillehay and his son went back out to the fields. Be careful, now, the old man muttered as the door closed behind them, the closest he could come to condolences.

When the doctor was through Charles went outside with him. Walker was his name. He said he had never seen a joint as out of place as Billy's shoulder. His collarbone was probably broken. He had four busted ribs, as many teeth missing, and the blow to the head—well, he said, they would just have to wait and see. It was a wonder it hadn't killed him instantly.

Are you sure you ought to go, Doc? Given all that?

I've done what I can do. He's got to rest now.

But don't you think you ought to stick around? Just in case something happens?

You call me if something happens.

We ain't got a telephone.

The doctor laid his hand on his shoulder and looked at him with his kind eyes. You go on up to your landlord's, son, and call me if you need me.

When he cranked the Ford, Charles stood there watching him. It was settling on him that he was going to have to walk back into the shack and take care of everything on his own.

The doctor smiled and patted the hood of the Ford, shook his head, and said, A horse, never again. He went around to the door and stood there with his hand on the handle. Never again will I have to take the time to brush and feed and blanket a horse in a freezing stable after a call that takes me out in the middle of the night.

Charles stood close. He wanted to reach out and take the man's arm. He did not want him to go. He did not know what he was going to do.

Why is it, Doc, that people always get sick in the middle of the night?

Oh, they get sick at all hours, son. He opened the door and got into the car and sighed. But they don't get scared until the middle of the night.

NICKERSON'S

Two days later Charles went out to the pasture and caught Hatcher's mare. He put a muzzle on her, and a chain over her nose, and gave her a dose of Billy's morphine. While he waited for it to set in, he hitched Gin to the wagon. Then he tied the mare to the back and headed up to town. She went quietly all the way, gentle as a lamb. Her black coat gleamed in the cool autumn sun.

When he arrived at Nickerson's slaughterhouse, the low characters who worked there came out of the woodwork at the sight of her. Somebody catcalled. When he untied her from the wagon she lowered her head and sighed. Her breath smelled of grass and grain. Clumsily, she tried to itch her forehead against Charles's back. Sleepy and sweet from the morphine.

Hot damn, someone said.

Hell of a horse.

Who do I see to fill out the paperwork? Charles said. His throat filled up when he said it.

You got the wrong place, boy, said a man with a measles-pocked face. This here's the killing floor.

That ain't Leland Hatcher's horse, is it? someone else asked.

Somebody get me the damn paperwork. Charles could feel tears coming on. He blinked them back and swallowed around the lump in his throat. Come on, he growled. Haven't got all day.

The man with the pitted face sucked his teeth. In his eyes flashed a shady idea so plain he might as well have spoken it.

Let me take her, he said, stepping forward. Hand her over here.

If I see this horse for sale anywhere I'm gonna come up here and twist your balls off, Charles told him. You hear that? If you try anything funny I'll come up here and I'll twist em right off with my bare hand.

When he got back to the shack Billy was trying to sit up. He went over and helped him. Stuffed the pillow and a folded horse blanket behind him. He smelled of chloroform. The bruises. The crooked railroad track of stitches. You'd never think a horse could do that to a man.

She gone? Billy's voice was slurred, heavy, heartbroken.

Charles nodded. Sat down heavily. Jesus. You look like hell.

Billy brightened a little at that. I do, don't I. Bring me a mirror. I want to see.

Charles went and got the mirror off the wall, and when Billy saw his face he smiled, or tried to smile.

Hoo-whee, Billy said to his reflection. What happened to that poor fellow?

He laid the mirror down. If you happen to find my teeth, the Doc says put em in a glass of milk.

We don't got no milk, Charles said. We got nothing. Mouse shit in all the cupboards and in the food.

Well that's alright. I ain't got the teeth to eat it anyway. Billy tried to smile again. Maybe Dillehay's got my teeth.

If he does maybe he'll keep em in trade for the rent.

Billy started to laugh, then grimaced and put his hand on his side. Don't make me laugh, Charlie boy.

Charles laughed too. It was all so awful and it was all his fault. He ran his hand through his hair.

It ain't your fault, Billy said.

Yes it is.

No it ain't.

Then it's Leland Hatcher's fault. I believe you now, Billy.

Billy tried to raise his hand, then laid it on his chest.

Any man does that to a horse, Charlie boy, he's suffered something awful himself. And probably at the hand of another man, who suffered something awful. At the hand of another man before him. And on and on. You want to blame somebody, you got to trace it all the way back to the days of Noah's ark.

Ah, Billy. I'm gonna make up for it. I'm gonna turn it around. I'm gonna make us some money. Get us back on our feet.

Billy was breathing hard. It had taken a lot out of him, all those words.

I think it's gonna take more than money to get me back on my feet.

Charles could hear a mouse now, gnawing through something in the kitchen. How could such a small creature make such a big sound?

I'm gonna get me a real job, he said. An alarm clock and a paycheck. Make some real money. Get us out of this dump.

Billy's swollen eyes moved in his black-and-yellow face. Slowly closed.

Charlie my boy. I think you ought to have whatever the hell you want. You oughta be president of the United States, if that's what you want to do.

What the hell are you talking about? I don't want to be president.

Good. Whoever would want that job would have to be bughouse crazy.

Charles laughed, tears in his eyes. If Billy died he did not know what he would do. Where he would go. He did not know.

Billy started to laugh too.

Now, Charles. He drew in a shallow breath. Cut that out. I told you.

Billy tried to shift his weight. His broad shoulders fell back on the folded blanket behind him.

Who said anything about being president, Charles said, wiping his face. I think your brain's still addled.

Billy closed his eyes. From the kitchen came the snap of one of the mousetraps Charles had set. Then the small silence that was the mouse, dead.

I think you oughta quit talking and get some rest.

Whatever you say, Charlie boy. You're the boss.

CALIFORNIA

Bristol

Maura has a plan. She is going to be rich.

I didn't come all this way to empty chamber pots, she tells Billy. Nor to be chained to a stove with a dozen little brats tugging my apron. I'm going to rise up.

To Solar Hill? he asks. Why do you want to go there? No fun up there.

Solar Hill! I'll live in a place that makes those houses look like tenant shacks. I'm going to California. To San Francisco. Get my name up on a marquee.

She keeps a scrapbook, pictures of famous actresses. Newspaper stories of their wealth and talents. She can't read, but someone has read it all to her enough times that she can recite them, word for word, from memory.

Lillian Russell, who pedaled lazily around Central Park on a bicycle monogrammed with diamonds.

Sarah Bernhardt. The Divine Miss Sarah, who, when she traveled, had to take out an extra suite in her hotels for the flowers sent by admirers.

Lola Montez. Who, by showing a little leg while she sang and danced, shook more money out of the California gold rushers than the gold rushers ever shook out of the California hills. Who kept so many coins in her stockings that they jangled when she walked. Who kept a bear cub as a pet. Just for fun.

She rattles off all of this for Billy. Then she points to a photograph of Sarah Bernhardt. Ropes of pearls and smoky eyes.

If you look closely, she says, you see it. They all have something in common.

Billy looks. They sure are pretty.

Come now, Bill Monday! Look closer. Use your eyes.

He looks, but all he sees is finery, feathers, jewels, silk, and lace.

She puts the scrapbook away after that, carefully wrapping it in paper. He makes a joke about it, but she has grown serious, a furrow between her dark brows. Then she shows him the cigar box where she saves her money. She has a stack of bills, more money than he would have imagined, nearly enough for a train ticket. When he sees it he feels himself sober up. An emptiness in his heart, as if he has already lost her.

They named a gold mine after Lola Montez, she says solemnly. They named a mountain after her too.

A PLAN

The plan came to Charles in a flash, up at the auction house that Saturday. Hit him on the head with a handful of Kuntz's peanut shells. Lloyd Bonnyman had been out in the lot that morning, showing off some of the mules he had bought for the British Army.

Don't just do your bit for the war, he had said to the gathered young men. Don't just do your bit, but do your all.

In the ring the peanut shells rained down on Charles and he looked over at Lloyd Bonnyman in his derby on the other side of the podium and it hit him. If all the money was in war mules, like Twitch kept saying, then he would get into the war mule business. He could do it. All he needed to do was show up with some knockout mules, parade them around in front of Bonnyman, and then tell him he knew where to get plenty more. And he knew right where to go for the mules. There was a breeder just over the line in Kentucky. He was famous up there. Pen Pendergrass was his name. Bred the best mules in the state. Charles wagered he was too far out of Bonnyman's territory for Bonnyman to have discovered him. He could go up there and buy mules on credit, bring them down here and sell them to Bonnyman. Pay for the mules. Start collecting his paycheck. Take care of Billy. Go see Catherine Hatcher outside the Paradise Theater and stuff ten bucks in her collection box.

After the auction he went straight to town and sent Pendergrass a wire. Then went to the depot to buy a train ticket, without even thinking he ought to wait for a telegram in reply. He went back to the shack and told Billy what he had done, and Billy winced and smiled around his missing teeth.

Somebody taught you good, he said.

PLENTY OF NAME

Billy could never tell him. Never. He would sooner die than tell him.

He had once known an old colored man, born a slave. A welded knot of scars crisscrossed his back from whippings. His name was James Washington Pliny Abraham Page.

When I was born we had nothing, the old man told Billy. My mother, she said, when a child's born with nothing, you give him plenty of name.

Billy understood that Charles's story was the same. He had been born with nothing and his mother had given him that story because she had nothing else to give him. And who was Billy to take it away?

In the end, it was simple. Maura's gift to Charles had been that story. Billy's was allowing him to keep it.

Breed More Mules!

By Chancellor "Pen" Pendergrass
The Southern Kentucky Agriculturalist
October 1914

What is the future, the young folk sometimes ask me. And I always reply with the same:
What? Mules! When? Now!

Consider the mule, my friends: a special animal indeed. God did not make him. Man made him. He is a hybrid. The perfect result of an imperfect union. His father is a donkey and his mother is a horse, and he combines the best traits of both species and inherits the bad traits of neither, is more intelligent than the two put together, and is truly greater than the sum of his parts. He can do double the work of a horse on half the feed and worse care. He plows straighter, lives longer, and hardly ever needs to see the doctor.

Yet the humble long-ear has been the victim of much mud-slinging. Stubborn, stupid, and dull are only some of the epithets bestowed by the misinformed. But a mule is not stubborn. No, he is smart. He understands his own limitations; unlike a horse, he will never work himself to death.

The mighty mule has but one fault. This is his inability to make more mules. His hybridism means sterility, and his sterility means that every mule is the end of his line. The last branch of a stunted family tree. The period at the end of a short sentence. No hope of progeny, no pride of posterity for these humble beasts.

Young men, take heed: we need you to make more of 'em.

Let us eschew the eagle as the symbol of this country. Let us adopt instead as the symbol of our great nation the unsung hero of these shores, the muscle behind all great American endeavors. Yes, let's see a golden statue of a long-ear atop every capitol dome from sea to shining sea. A mule on the lawn of the White House. On the face of the dollar bill.

This is the greatest nation in the history of the world. Our future is dazzlingly bright. But to get there we'll need even more power, more muscle, more brute effort. And who built this country? Mules, my friends, and don't you forget it.

The framed article hung by the door of Pendergrass's office, surrounded by photographs of his champion donkey jack studs, the sires of his beloved hybrids. Big black jackasses with white noses and balls big as grapefruits. Each frame bore a silver plate engraved with the animal's name. JUPITER. QUEEQUEG. ARCHIMEDES. BLACKJACK. PONDEROSA.

Charles straightened his collar in the reflection of one of the frames. He had been waiting long enough now to read the article three times. No hope of progeny, no pride of posterity—he had committed that one to memory. He had studied every donkey in turn. Top-shelf asses. Even finer quality than he had expected. He knew it as soon as they made the turn off the main road and he saw the sign.

PENDERGRASS'S ASSES
JACKS AT STUD
JACKSTOCK AND MULES FOR SALE
HOME OF PONDEROSA
GRAND CHAMPION DONKEY JACK, KENTUCKY STATE FAIR
1913-1914-1915-

Now he was getting nervous. He crossed to the window on the other side of the office, chewing his knuckle. Pendergrass had wired him back telling him he was welcome to come, but that he had nothing for sale at the time. He had to figure out a way to convince him to sell mules he did not want to sell for money Charles did not have.

Well, he thought, stranger things are happening.

Two days ago, Catherine had shown up at the shack. Came right down and knocked on the door. He began to sweat, just remembering it. Doc Walker had told her what had happened, and she wanted to see Billy. When she sat down by his bed he had taken her hands and patted them for a long time. Just patted them and patted them, his hand on hers making a little cupping sound. A wistful doped-up look on his face. Charles had stood by the door, frozen, madly jealous of the attention she was giving Billy, ashamed of the smell of the place, the strip of flypaper behind the woodstove, the dirty horse blankets piled on Billy's bed.

I tried to warn you, she said, looking from Billy to Charles with tears in her eyes.

It's my fault, Charles said weakly. I didn't listen.

It's nobody's damn fault, Billy said.

She said that after the horse had killed the man in Nashville she had begged her father not to sell her.

He told me that it was a freak accident, she said, shaking her head. He convinced me that it could have happened anywhere, with any horse. But I should have known better than to trust my father. The only reason that poor man was killed was because of his secrecy and double-talk. You see, it all happened when he went to bail Edmund out at school. He took the mare and surrey instead of the Pierce-Arrow because he didn't want to draw attention to his trip, and then he left her at a low-class stable for the same reason. He didn't want word getting back to Richfield, what he was doing down there. When the man was found dead in her stall that morning, he even managed to keep it out of the newspaper. Same as Edmund's trouble.

She pulled her hands away from Billy's, and clasped them in her lap. All this secrecy. All this equivocating. My father's reputation means more to him than . . . oh, that poor man! His poor family. I tried to go see them. My father found out, and forbade me. Practically locked me up in my room.

And how on earth did you talk him into letting you come down here? Billy had leaned back against the folded blankets. He looked completely drained. Charles was still glued to the doorway.

He's got no idea I'm here.

Well then you ought to get on out of here, Billy said gently. Don't know how we'd explain you if anyone came along.

She shot a colluding look at Charles that made his knees weak. Don't worry about that. I've thought about that. And the thing is, Mister Monday, I'm a fast talker myself.

Even here in the office at the front of Pendergrass's house Charles could hear the racket of the braying mules. He looked out the window. The barns were up on a hill, in great long shed rows. All around them, cross-fenced pastures shone. A man on horseback was riding through a pasture of little jennet donkeys. Out in the yard a magnolia nearly as big as the ones at Everbright spread its black arms. Near it stood a small rose garden.

Pen Pendergrass burst into the office, swearing at someone behind him in the hall.

If they want to murder that animal, he was saying, they can do it on their own goddamn land.

Hardly looking at Charles, he crossed to the desk and began to search through the stacks of paper. He was older than Charles had expected. White hair, white mustache, stooped shoulders. It took a few moments to notice he only had one arm. The empty sleeve hung by his side. He had either forgotten or not bothered to pin it up.

Welcome, welcome, welcome, he said, still shuffling papers. The white mustache jumped. How the hell are you, how was your trip. Always happy to show a man around the place but you're wasting your time. Got nothing for sale this time of year.

Well— Charles stammered.

Speak up, boy! Speak up! A man's got to assert himself. This country was not built by the meek.

Pendergrass pointed to the portrait of Washington above the desk.

That man right there. General Washington. You think he stammered when he met a man? Hell no. He stuck out his hand and said, 'Hello, I'm George Goddamn Washington, and who the hell are you?'

Well I'm Charles Goddamn McLaughlin. And I need some mules.

Ha! Good boy! Pendergrass smiled. You want to know why I keep him up there, son? Not because he's the father of this country. But because he's the father of the American mule.

Charles grinned.

It's not a joke, boy! They ought to teach it in school. Trust you've heard of a little war called the American Revolution. Well when that was finally over, General Washington was a happy man, because now he could get down to what he really wanted to do, which was study the problem of animal power for this brand-new country. The ox was too slow and the horse too delicate for the virgin fields. He had a hunch about mules, but American donkeys were too puny to breed good ones. American donkeys' equipment just snapped off in the big American horse mares.

Pendergrass snapped his fingers. He was still smiling up at the portrait. Charles could see his chest rising and falling.

Well the general knew for a fact that Spain had the best mules in the world, and the best donkeys to make them with. Lucky he's got connections. Calls up his old friend Lafayette, who calls the king of Spain. Says, 'Send your best donkey to Mount Vernon.' And he did. Name was Royal Gift.

Pendergrass put his hand over his heart.

Wouldn't I love to go back in time and see that donkey. He must have been impressive. Washington set him up at Mount Vernon, put out the call for the best horse mares. And they came from all directions, only Royal Gift—he didn't deliver! They couldn't get him in the mood. Wouldn't even look at a mare. It's a complicated business, you know, trying to breed a horse to a donkey. Like trying to bring together two magnets at the same pole. Poor George. But give up? Never! Not on the Delaware, not with a jackass! He got right down to finding another donkey. This one all the way from Malta. This was his life's work, remember! Put his best men on the job of getting him delivered. Finally got that breeding program going. Started breeding good jackasses, and men from all over came to him to breed their horses to them. The American mule was born. The general's greatest contribution to this country.

Pendergrass saluted the portrait. Charles, caught up in the moment, did the same.

You see, my boy, George Washington was a man of vision. He might have been a great military man, but his quest to make the perfect mule shows that at heart he was a man of the *imagination*. Like Edison, or Ford. And the power of the imagination is stronger than the power of the sword, at the end of the day.

Pen Pendergrass leapt towards the door. Charles's heart was pounding with excitement.

But what are we doing sitting here talking, son? You want to meet my mules!

They headed up the hill to the barns. Pendergrass charged ahead, his one arm pumping, toes pointing out to the sides, his empty sleeve flapping like a banner. Charles struggled to keep up with him. The old man was like a locomotive.

His heart had pounded like this in the shack when Catherine gave him that conspiring look. And just as she had promised, when Dillehay's son showed up a few minutes later to collect the rent, she smooth-talked him so fast. Charmed him out of any suspicion. She flashed him a big smile and said she was canvassing for the Fatherless Children of France. Natural as anything. You would have never known that a moment ago she had been sitting there crying. When he told her she was wasting her time trying to get anything from Billy and Charles, she took his arm and batted her eyes and said, Well then, Jack, let's go up and see your mother. And out she had swept with him, the poor fellow looking equally helpless and thrilled. It was like some kind of magic trick. As soon as she was gone Charles could not believe she had even been there.

The brays grew louder as they approached the barns, and Pendergrass raised his voice to compete until he was nearly shouting. A wolf had been killing his neighbors' chickens for weeks, he said. Several had gone after him with dogs and guns but had no luck. Now they were all setting out poisoned meat. Pendergrass refused to cooperate.

He paused and swept his good arm towards the distant woods.

I don't care if he's killing your goddamn chickens, he growled. That wolf's life is worth ten thousand goddamn chickens. A wolf, he's the wilderness. And we need wilderness. Because a man cannot be a man without the wilderness at his back.

They arrived at the first barn. Someone was driving a manure spreader out to the fields. Charles whistled at the team. They were fine mules, perfectly matched. Pendergrass beamed and said they were Kate and Duplicate, full sisters. Another team, Pete and Repeat, were standing in a paddock nearby.

Sometimes I think, if only I could churn em out on an assembly line. The way old Mister Ford does up there in his factory in Detroit. Then I'd really be making some money.

Yessir, Charles said.

Slaves and mules, boy. Slaves and mules built the South. Everything.

It's awful ugly, what they did to those people.

You can't build a country this great this fast without a whole lot of ugliness and that's just a fact. Washington knew that and it pained his heart all his life. Jefferson knew it too. Neither of them could figure out how to get around it.

They went on to the line of small paddocks where the jacks were kept. The donkeys watched them approach.

Pendergrass lifted his empty sleeve and shook it. The nearest jack perked up his head and swung his big ears towards them.

Ain't he something, Pendergrass said. That there's my Ponderosa.

The donkey was huge, not only in size but in presence. A great dark gravity to him, ears that went on and on. He regarded them with his mysterious donkey eyes.

Pendergrass rubbed the donkey's nose.

Tough life, ain't it? Eat, sleep, screw. Drew the short straw, didn't you, you old fool?

He stood back and admired the animal for a moment.

Just a big nuisance, is what he is.

Then he beckoned to Charles to come along. He had just installed mechanical water troughs in every paddock. An alarm sounded in the main barn when the water level dropped too low. He explained the engineering of it in great detail. He was nearly as proud of it as his animals.

Finally they came to the pasture Charles had had his eye on. Four big coffee-colored mules grazed peacefully. They looked to be about four years old, eleven hundred pounds apiece. Prime. Just the kind of mules Bonnyman was always snatching up at the auction.

When Charles asked about them Pendergrass grinned and tapped his nose.

You got good taste, son. Them boys are my reputation mules. Gonna take em to the state fair in two weeks and win every damn blue ribbon with em. Get everybody talking. Best advertising I got, them mules in there.

Interested in selling them?

Selling them! Pendergrass wiped his mustache and laughed.

A hawk lifted from the hay field. Charles's confidence went with it.

Oh, son. I'm not laughing at you. Sell them! They're my best advertising. Selling them would be throwing out the baby with the bathwater!

They went back down to the office. Pendergrass's wife waved from the rose garden. Her silver hair was done in perfect waves. Light of my life, Pen said, blowing her a kiss.

Catherine. After she was gone Billy had closed his eyes for a long time, though Charles knew he wasn't sleeping. Charles had sat down on his bed with the stunned feeling that a bright bird had just flown through the window and then back out again.

Some girl, ain't she?

Billy smiled behind his closed eyes. She sure fast-talked that poor Jack Dillehay.

She makes me want to be a good man.

That girl's got a weight on her shoulders, Billy said. She's carrying around something awful heavy.

Charles got up and tore down the fly-studded flypaper. He picked up a dirty plate he had left in the middle of the floor. Then he went to the little mirror on the wall and looked into it for a long time. He thought about Leland Hatcher shaking hands with all the people who came to the depot to see Edmund off. And about what it must have taken to keep news of the stablehand's death out of the papers. Shifty, yes. But he could understand why a man in Hatcher's position had to take his reputation seriously. After all, he had the eyes of the entire town on him.

I got to shape up if I think I'll get anywhere with a girl like that, he said.

You be careful, Charlie boy, Billy said, and then he went quiet. After a while he said, Give me a little more of that dope, would you? Pain won't let me be.

Inside Pendergrass poured two drinks and sat down behind his desk.

Charles sat across from him and threw back the drink. He had to do something. It couldn't be that he came all the way to Scottsville, Kentucky, for one lousy drink.

Quite a place, isn't it? Pendergrass smiled.

Charles nodded. He thought of the sign at the bottom of the drive, the dash already painted in for another championship year to be added to Ponderosa's list. He could picture Pendergrass down there, waving his one arm and hollering at the sign painter to go ahead and paint it in, with the optimism—no, the certainty—that the animal would win again.

Glad to show you around, son. I've got the best animals in the state, and I consider it a personal crusade, encouraging the next generation of mule breeders. There's men out there will try to tell you there's no future in it. No future in mules!

He pointed to a photograph on the wall behind him. Charles had studied it while he was waiting. It was a remarkable photo, a broad view of a wheat field, three enormous combine machines each being pulled by a twenty-mule team. Sixty mules in one field. Five of them were Pendergrass mules, Pendergrass explained happily, and it just went to show that mules would never go out, that even if trucks began to move all the freight and deliver all the milk and ice and coal and mail and build all the roads, men would never be able to make the machine both nimble and strong enough to work a crop row. In fact, he went on to say, the way the population was growing, the demand for food was increasing by bounds, and more food meant bigger farms, and bigger farms only meant more mules.

He leaned across the desk. His eyes were blazing. I'd give anything to be in your shoes, boy! Everything lies ahead of you. Your potential is limitless!

He paused. Where are you from, anyway?

When Charles said Richfield, Pendergrass nodded.

We were doing business with a fellow down there, Charles said tentatively. Leland Hatcher.

Pendergrass's eyes changed. Leland Hatcher, he repeated.

You know Hatcher?

Pendergrass's eyes went to the ceiling. He put his hand over his heart. Knew his wife. Morning Roberson. The Robersons, from up near Franklin. Big money, those Robersons. And Morning Roberson, my my my. I remember when she came out. The boys around here were all scrambling for her. Then that fellow came up here and stole her while the rest of the boys were asleep. A nobody. A farm boy from West Tennessee. Of course, her father did not approve. Her father cut her off without a cent.

She's dead, Charles said bluntly.

Pendergrass sighed. Yes, I know. She died in an accident last year. Her car went off a bridge. They ought not to drive. They ought not drive, nor vote, nor hold office, nor run around in gymnasiums with medicine balls. Missus Pendergrass calls me old-fashioned, but I'm a man of my times.

Pendergrass looked to the window. This is when you know you're old, son. When the little girls aren't just gone off and married, but gone on to their heavenly rest. And your old bones are still creaking around. That's what happens, boy. You get old, and then you die, before you've had the chance to make the perfect jackass. That's the sad fact.

He sat back in his chair. His eyes were still on the window. Charles could see he was far away. Lost in the past. He thought about Catherine, wondering if her mother had looked like her. And he remembered her by the creek behind the fairgrounds, talking about what it was like to drown. Serious and melancholy. My father has done so many terrible things, she said. Things I can't forgive him for. Sitting by Billy's bed in the shack, she had seemed so overcome by guilt about the Nashville man. But it was an accident, after all. Even if her father had acted irresponsibly. Even if he had mistreated the horse so badly as to make her into a vicious beast. The man's death had still been an accident.

You be careful, Billy had said, after she left. Charles had taken this to mean that he needed to watch out for himself. But maybe Billy had meant that he needed to watch out for *her*. That she was the one who needed looking after. He didn't know. She seemed awfully capable of looking after herself. Something about Catherine was like Pendergrass's wolf. Her wildness was thrilling. Essential.

Sir. Charles swallowed. I want your four best mules. Them ones in the front pasture. You say they ain't for sale, but this is different. He paused. They're for the war. For the British Army. For the Allies.

Pendergrass's eyes got wide.

Don't get me started about that war. We cannot get into it. Me, I'm a textbook isolationist. If we start acting as the world's schoolmaster, it's going to be trouble. No. Leave it to England and France. We've got to keep the blinders on. Stay the course here. America's got too much potential. We ought to take this war as opportunity to improve upon our own self-reliance. Why, there's no reason why we should need to import any raw material except rubber. But soon enough we should be able to replace rubber. I've been studying the rubber problem . . .

Pendergrass trailed off, looking to the window again. Charles rubbed his face. That was a bust. Not at all what he expected. He wondered what Billy would do. Then, suddenly, he knew exactly what Billy would do. How many times had he watched Billy talk a man into trading simply by first talking him out of it?

Well, he said slowly, I shouldn't try anyway. Fellow I'm buying for says he only wants Tennessee mules.

What? Pendergrass spun around. Why? Kentucky mules are the best mules in the country. There's no argument.

This fellow says that of Tennessee mules. Heard him say it just the other day. Suppose that's where I ought to look. Tennessee bluegrass is better. Girls down there are prettier too. Suppose that can't be because of the grass. He shrugged. Maybe it's the water.

He stood up as if making to leave.

You know of anybody down there who can sell me some good mules on credit? I need the best, now. Cream of the crop.

Pendergrass jumped out of his chair. Only place you're going to get cream of the crop is right here. Tennessee mules finest in the country—what kind of rubbish is that? He got up and paced to the window. Those Brits wouldn't even know what to do with mules like mine. Their heads would spin just to see em.

Charles's eyes moved to the portrait of Washington on the wall. He had an idea.

Mister Pendergrass, sir. What do you think old George Washington up there would say?

He'd tell you Kentucky mules are the finest in the country, Pendergrass growled, and American mules are the finest mules in the world.

And what would General Washington do if his old friend Lafayette over there called him up, saying he needed some good mules?

On the train home Charles pressed his grin against the window. He couldn't believe he had done it, convinced Pen Pendergrass to sell him those four top-shelf mules on credit. He could still hear him muttering as he went up to the barn to arrange to ship them.

Tennessee mules! Finest in the country! What kind of rubbish is that!

WORKING STIFF

Charles brought Pendergrass's four reputation mules to Kuntz's on Saturday. When they came up in the ring Bonnyman bought every single one of them, bing bing bing bing. After the sale he sought Charles out, tugging on his undertaker face and wanting to know where he had found them.

I know where to get more just like em, Mister Bonnyman. Just tell me how many you need.

How many do I need? Bonnyman raised his eyes to the sky. How many do I need? A multitude. Mules don't keep. They're not hams, or ammunition, or bandages. The Allies need a steady supply. My agents work night and day. They work like dogs.

Charles squared his shoulders and took a breath. I'm your man, he said.

The job was his, on one condition. No funny business, Bonnyman said. He looked at him long and hard. No shoe polish.

Yessir. No shoe polish.

Bonnyman gave him a checkbook. It was big and leather, with gilt edges. ROAN AND HUNTINGTON MULE COMPANY was embossed on the front. Charles stared at it in awe.

There's one thing, Mister Bonnyman. I got a partner and he's got to be in on it too.

I don't care if it's you, your ma, your pa, and three uncles, Bonnyman replied. You bring me the mules, I write you the paycheck.

————————

Back at the shack, Billy had run out of dope. He had pulled himself out of bed and was digging through the kit, looking for something to take. When Charles showed him the checkbook, he seemed to forget all about the pain. Sat down and held his ribs and laughed.

I should have known you would do it, Charlie boy. Look at you. Paycheck and a real job. Reckon the first thing you're gonna want to do is run tell Leland Hatcher your blood's as blue as his.

Leland Hatcher's a farm boy. Pen Pendergrass told me so. It was Catherine's mother who came from good people. Hatcher, he came up from nothing. Charles studied the checkbook. Gives a fellow hope, actually. That a man can make a fortune like that, coming up from nothing.

Well what's his daughter going to say when she hears you're working for the British Army?

Charles grinned.

I do believe she'll like it just fine.

It was a week of cool weather, perfect for traveling. In the trees industrious squirrels labored and the smell of skunk was on the air. Charles went out to the feedlots, places out beyond the edge of town where young mules were fattened and sold. Many run by shady characters. At some of those places he would look over sixty head of mules and not take any. Bonnyman had schooled him on the specifications for size and weight and condition. Once they went down to Nashville they had to pass a strict inspection by the British officers.

When he came back through town with mules tied to the back of the wagon, he tipped his hat to everyone who passed.

Where you taking them mules?

To the war!

On Friday afternoon he finally saw Catherine on one of these trips through town. He halted Gin at the corner and looked down at her from the wagon bench, grinning.

She looked up at him and smiled big. My, she said, her eyes going to the mules and back to him. You've got your hands full.

Nothing I can't handle. His heart felt as if it might burst out of his shirt.

Well I don't doubt that, she said, looking at him through her lashes.

He stuttered a moment, remembering how she had charmed Jack Dillehay with the exact same look. Then he composed himself, shifting the reins in his hand and sitting up straighter.

I've got a big job to do. I'm working for the British Army now.

Her smile changed at this. Fell a little.

But I thought you were going to take me away from here. She was joking, he knew. Yet there was real disappointment in her voice.

Well, he said, these days it's not just do your bit for the war. It's do your all.

He could feel the mules shifting around behind him, all that muscle and power and strength. He thought of Pen Pendergrass and grinned again.

And Tennessee mules are the finest mules in the whole wide world.

The next day he delivered the mules to Bonnyman at Kuntz's. Bonnyman had brought with him a mule gas mask, and out in the lot he took one of Charles's mules from the line at the fence and showed him how it worked, slipping it over the mule's nose and buckling it behind his ears. It looked like a giant paper bag and the mule stood there with a long-suffering look in his eyes until Bonnyman unbuckled it.

That's all we do, he said, hanging it on the fence and retying the mule. That's the sole training we give them, before we send them over, is get them used to one of these. There's a big difference between a war horse and a war mule. War horse, you've got to prepare him, train him to ignore the gunfire and the shells and the confusion of the battlefield. But you can't train a mule for that. Mule's too smart. When it comes down to the action, a horse reacts. But a mule thinks, then *acts*. You can't simply just inure him to the bullets and shells.

Shorty was standing there, listening. His crusty eye had cleared up. He was wearing a new cap, many sizes too big but new all the same.

I'd rather have me a war horse than a war mule, Shorty said. Any day.

Bonnyman looked down at him. Well I'm sorry to say the days of the glorious cavalry charge are over. The days of brisk, decisive battles are over. In this war, ground is gained by mere feet, mere inches, carved out in the mud by men wriggling on their balls and bellies. Not by galloping charges on swift stallions. No. This is a mule's war.

The mule reached out and lipped the gas mask, curious. Bonnyman pushed his big ironing board head away.

The gas, he said, they say it smells like lilacs. Or new-mown hay. He tapped the mask. You smell that and you got about twenty seconds to get this on before your lungs turn to a bloody pulp. The animals are the worst gas cases. Because you can't explain to them what's happened. They go mad with the pain.

He tugged the brim of his derby. Shorty. Take these mules on back to the boxcar.

How much longer they gonna keep fighting, anyway?

Twitch, passing with a wheelbarrow, heard this and stopped.

The longer they keep at it, the more money you make off of it, right, Mister Bonnyman?

Bonnyman rubbed his jaw. His long face seemed to grow longer. I was there when it began, he said. We had been over to visit my wife's family and we were in Paris that August, on our way home. I remember we were sitting at a little café. Suddenly there was a huge mass of men in the street. They were piling into taxicabs, shouting, singing. What's going on? I said. War! It was going to be over in a month, maybe two. They would win back from Germany what was rightfully theirs. Yet no one could quite get their minds wrapped around it. It was too huge. Forces too great to comprehend. I remember one girl, from the red-light district, to every passing young man she called gaily, 'Promise you'll bring me a pretzel from Berlin!' When she turned I saw that her face was wrecked with tears.

During this story, Charles fussed happily with the mule to his left, hardly listening. Yesterday he had climbed down out of the wagon and slipped with Catherine into an alley. They had shared a cigarette and kissed. He had made her laugh, doing tricks with his hat. He had assured her Billy was going to be fine. And it was true, he would be fine. Soon enough he'd be back on his feet. Everything was happening. Everything was looking up. Ever since the trip to Kentucky Charles's blood had been humming. Pendergrass's energy had been contagious. And the success with Bonnyman made him feel not only lucky but invincible.

War is what Sherman said it is, ain't it, Twitch said, sniffling and pivoting the wheelbarrow.

Bonnyman untied the mule closest to him and grabbed him by the nose and opened his mouth to check his teeth one more time before handing the lead to Shorty.

I've seen it firsthand and I'll tell you. The greatest tragedy of war is the realization that what lies at its center is the human heart.

HEAT

Hunt mules, look after Billy, see Catherine. This was all Charles now did.

There was a loose stone in the Everbright wall where they would leave notes. Just a few words. A time and a place to meet.

Four days a week she went to classes up at the women's college, and on those days they met there, late in the afternoon, in a little unused boathouse on a pond. Sometimes they met in the vacant lot behind the icehouse, around the corner from a laundry called the Citizens' Club. It was owned by a young colored man with a sense of humor who put a different sign up in the window every week. WE CLEAN EVERYTHING BUT YOUR REPUTATION. WE WILL DYE FOR YOU.

Charles would wait for her in the decided spot, his heart pounding, jumping at every creaking branch or squirrel rustle. When she came they would kiss until their faces were raw in the cool autumn air. It would get cold when the sun dropped, but they never noticed. Heat. That was all he felt. Heat rising up off of her skin. Heat in his blood. Heat in his bones. Heat between their knocking front teeth. Once, an old groundskeeper walked into the boathouse, and Charles had pulled Catherine so close to him against the shadows, and they had stood so long, hardly breathing, until the old man went back out, that it took hours that night for his hot blood to cool down.

That day he told her the story about his father. The streetcar accident in Philadelphia, the heartless family, his mother left with nothing. As she listened her eyes got sad. She reached out and touched his face, eyes full of understanding. Yet she rarely talked about her own family, except to say how much she missed Edmund, who had written to say that he had arrived in Paris. Let's change the subject, she would say, if he asked her about it, or she would find something to tease him about. She did love to tease, which made it so hard to read her. One time she said she had a dress for every day of the week, and as he laughed he realized it wasn't a joke. Another time she told him she wasn't a virgin and when he nodded gravely she gave him a shove and said, Shame on you, Charles! It was odd but she reminded him of Billy sometimes. The way Billy could tell any story in the world as if it was gospel truth and you'd never know until later that half of it was made up.

She still gave him a hard time for believing her when she said they ate off of gold plates. After a while it became a little game they played.

What's for supper at Everbright tonight? he would ask, wrapping his arms around her, and she would wave her hand and say, Oh, quail with dollar bills and crushed diamond sauce. Oysters— and pearls. And for dessert nothing but a dish of ice cream with bananas and walnuts and rubies on top.

How long ago it seemed now, the day he had watched her eat that sundae in the window of the soda fountain. And yet sometimes she still felt so out of reach, even after he had kissed her hot mouth all evening. When his first paycheck arrived he had gone up to Court Square and bought a new hat at Suddarth's department store. When he came out she was sitting on a bench, eating a bag of popcorn, and he ducked into an alley and watched her, awestruck, just stood there and watched her hand lift each golden kernel to her perfect lips.

NAMES

Bristol

Maura likes to try out her stage names on him.

Dusty Rose, she says. Lillian Loveworthy. Maybelle Mayhem. Princess M.

Billy laughs. How about the Mysterious Monkey Mistress?

His own name is invented, he admits to her. He was William O'Maonlai when he left the island, but when he stepped off the boat onto American soil, he was William Monday.

No reason, he says to her. I changed it just because I could.

She sighs happily, nodding.

This is a hell of a country, isn't it? she says. You choose your story. Then you go out and make it happen.

BONESHAKERS

Bristol

There are bicycles everywhere in Bristol. It is the height of the craze. The horses hate them. There are countless accidents. Buggies overturned, riders thrown. The streets are nothing short of chaos.

Maura is a crack rider. She has sewn lead into the hem of her skirts, to keep them out of the way of the wheels. She tries to teach Billy. He is hopeless.

I see why they call these things boneshakers, Billy grumbles. He has fallen again. He rights himself, kicks the tire. Give me a horse any day.

He looks at her. Anyway where the hell did you learn to ride a bicycle?

Fella taught me, she says, and his face burns and he gives the thing another kick.

It takes all afternoon, but she teaches him. They ride all the way out to see a baseball game, Bristol against the Johnson City Miners. He sits beside her proudly. She spends the whole game watching the Dukes and the Kings. Their children sit in a row, eating popcorn and peanuts.

Those little boys will never want for anything, she says. They are practically aristocrats.

Well, he points out. After all, they're Dukes. And Kings.

When they ride back to town, they pass a house that burned to the ground in the spring. There is still rubble everywhere and they stop to see if there is anything of value. A cheap tin frame around a blackened photo, the newel of a bedstead. Something catches on the leaded hem of Maura's dress, and Billy bends to carefully extract it. Someone's spectacles, lenses gone, wire frames twisted.

Later that day they are up on the knob, collecting persimmons. He calls them permissions, a weak joke, maybe, but it makes her laugh.

With your permission, Miss Maura, he says, slowly unbuttoning her shirtwaist. In the air is the first snap of autumn. Here and there, a few leaves, red and yellow, as if paint has dripped on the trees. A perfect stillness. The mountains around them are a bluish bowl. Nothing beyond even exists. Certainly not California. His fingers taste of her, and the sweet sloppy orange fruit. He lays his head in her lap and she puts her fingers in his hair. Above the trees is a cloud shaped like a hand. He looks up at it and whistles.

> *Daisy, Daisy, give me your answer, do*
> *I'm half crazy all for the love of you*
> *It won't be a stylish marriage*
> *I can't afford a carriage*
> *But you'll look sweet upon the seat*
> *Of a bicycle built for two*

She sings back to him, as she always does:

> *William, William, I'll give you my answer true*
> *I'd be crazy to marry the likes of you*
> *If you can't afford a carriage*
> *How can you afford a marriage?*
> *Yes I'll be damned if I'll be crammed*
> *On a bicycle built for two*

They laugh. Then her brow wrinkles.

What's the matter?

I'm just thinking of that house down there. That poor family. God rest their souls.

You ain't afraid to die, are you?

No I ain't. Not at all. But I'll miss you when I do.

Well then I've got it.

What?

Let's not die.

CLIMBING UP THE GOLDEN STAIRS

You're a good secret, Catherine said to Charles one night.

I don't want to be no secret, he said. They were sitting on the rickety staircase on the back side of the Paradise. He was watching a rat nose around in the alley. He felt about as good as that rat. She had been at a party, and had been late meeting him. Earlier he had been tying up two mules on Court Square when he saw her heading there with Cherry and a pack of boys. She was walking next to Wad Taylor, and had taken his free arm and laughed at something he said, causing him to take an awkward misstep with his cane. Charles's hand had curled into a fist around the mule's lead.

That's not what I mean, she said. She sighed. I've never known anyone like you. I like being with you. Even if we have to sneak around.

Moths were weaving in and out of the streetlight's glow. Late in the year for moths. One fluttered past them and Charles reached up and closed his hand around it and then let it go. He had followed the group all the way to the house where the party was going on. Then he had stood in the boxwood hedge and watched them through the window. Cherry Tisdale played the piano and they all sang along. 'Come On and Kiss Your Baby.' 'Climbing Up the Golden Stairs.' 'The Ragtime Mockingbird.'

Well then, he said, let's quit sneaking around.

Below them a man walked around the corner into the alley, whistling. Catherine started.

She had been saying lately that she was afraid her father suspected that she was up to something. She said that he had been acting strangely, distracted, that he had been shorter with her than usual and even more distant. But when Charles pressed her for more, she would close up, as she always did when she talked about her family.

I'm not afraid of your father, Charles said. He looked up at the streetlight, thinking of Billy's busted face. No matter what he did to that horse.

She looked at him, confused. What he did to the horse? What do you mean?

Ah, I don't want to tell you, Cat. It's too ugly.

I can handle anything, she said. Believe me. Nothing shocks me anymore. Tell me.

He explained to her that the black mare, to end up so vicious, had most likely been beaten, terribly and repeatedly. Just talking about it made him angry, that men could be so cruel. She listened silently, nodding, biting her lip.

Well then that poor animal's just another thing he ruined, she said finally, and shivered. She rubbed her arms. She was wearing a heavy blue coat, though the evening was warm for October. She was all done up for the party, her hair swept back.

She looked up at the moths.

Sometime I just feel like I'm on an island, all alone, looking out at everyone else on shore.

One of the moths circled down and flew between them. She turned to him. There was a furrow between her eyebrows. Her mouth was pinched, serious.

Can I trust you?

I told you, Catherine. I told you I'd always be a gentleman. I told you.

She shook her head. Oh, Charles. That's not what I mean. There's no one in this town I can talk to—

She leaned forward and pulled an envelope from the pocket of her coat and handed it to him.

This is Ed's latest letter. She tapped it. Go on. Read it.

Charles unfolded it.

Dearest Cat,

Well I moved again, and now they've got us stationed at a big old chateau. Photo enclosed. You'll agree it makes old Everbright look small. They're keeping us too busy for much fun, though. French lessons and driving lessons from dawn to dusk. Does Cherry miss me something terrible? Tell her to be good. Tell her if I'm home by Christmas I'll bring her a little something from Paris that will make her knees knock.

And you. I do worry about you, Cat. Now that I'm here I can see how bad it is there. It's a hell of a weight for you to bear, Cat. It might be for the best, in the end, how it happened. If she were still alive I hate to think how life would be. You need to forgive him, Cat. I think you're in worse straits than I am, Cat, and I am headed to the Front.

With it was a photograph of the chateau. Edmund had drawn an X over one of the windows and written on the back, My room. Charles looked at it for a long time. He was right about it making Everbright look small. What was she trying to tell him? He had no idea.

She was looking at him expectantly.

I don't understand.

She shook her head. I don't even know where to begin.

He put his arms around her. After a while she reached out and took the letter. She touched her fingertips to her forehead.

Have you got a cigarette?

He rolled and lit two cigarettes and handed one to her. She took one pull and then ground it out on the landing. She folded the letter carefully. Before she tucked it back into the envelope, she kissed it. Her hands were shaking. She said she sometimes dreamed that she could go over to Europe too. She had read a story in a magazine written by an American girl who had gone to the war as a nurse. The girl had said it was the only worthwhile thing she could think to do with her life.

Charles hurled his cigarette on the ground. He did not like all this talk of leaving. The war's no place for a girl like you, he said.

At this she reared back, nostrils flaring.

Look at Mata Hari! Or Edith Cavell. Florence Nightingale. There's plenty a woman can do. Why, in Paris girls are driving taxicabs!

Is that what you're trying to tell me? You're going to Paris to drive a taxicab? But Cat. We're only getting started.

She shook her head, pulling farther away.

That's the thing, Charles. You're only passing through here yourself. Someday you'll be gone and I'll still be here—

She wrapped her arms around her knees and looked over the edge of the staircase to the alley below.

I'm so tired of being on the outside, looking in. At that party tonight, that's exactly how I felt. Wad Taylor recited one of his poems and I nearly cried. How did it go? It was called 'Brothers of the Gridiron.' 'Valorous men—*something*—*something*—' Wait. I have it now. 'Valorous men, they spar and clash, free of doubt and—*something*—and fear. While here I sit, just half a man, no power but to cheer.'

She looked at him, her eyebrows knit together.

That's how I feel, she said. Powerless.

His face burned, remembering the way she had taken Wad Taylor's arm and made him laugh and stumble.

Maybe you'd be better off with another fellow, he said sharply.

Charles. Please. I don't think you're understanding me. She stood up suddenly. Let's not sit up here any longer. Let's walk.

Walk? he said. They never dared walk together.

It's dark. No one will see us. She was already standing, groping for his hand. Come on.

_____

They walked down the alley, along the back sides of the buildings, past the ash bins and rubbish pails. He was mad at himself for getting so sore about Wad Taylor. Sometimes he felt his jealousy was a wall he put up between himself and the power of his feelings for her. Like some sort of fire curtain. Otherwise the heat was too much to bear.

What had she been trying to tell him? You need to forgive him, Cat, her brother had written. He thought of what Billy had said: That girl's got a weight on her shoulders. He wanted to lift it for her, if she would let him. But the more time he spent with her, the more her mystery deepened, and the more he feared that whatever the weight was, he might not be strong enough to shoulder it. Sometimes it made his heart quail. Lately just looking at Billy's battered face could make him sink into panic that he was in over his head, had been since the moment he paid Leland Hatcher for that maniac horse. Poor Billy. The bruises on his face had faded to a sickly yellow-and-green patchwork, and his gone teeth made his cheeks drawn as an old man's. He could still hardly drag himself across the room.

Just another thing he ruined, she had said about the horse. What did she mean?

Now that they were walking she had cheered up. She was teasing him and had slipped her hand into his coat pocket, and it was so exciting, to be out in the open with her, walking, even if it was in an alley. They walked all the way out to a quiet neighborhood behind Court Square, where there were no streetlights and no one was around. He found himself trying to steal a glimpse through windows, just as when his mother used to take him up to Solar Hill in Bristol, and he would try to filch for his own self a bit of the happiness he perceived in the people inside. In one house a man and a woman, alone, were in their living room, waltzing to a record on a gramophone.

I'm tired of it too, he said to Catherine, watching them. Being on the outside looking in.

He pulled her to him and kissed her. Right there in the middle of the street.

She stepped back from him.

I'm sorry I've been so blue, she said. I haven't scared you off, have I? Cherry always tells me there's nothing a fellow likes less than a girl who's blue.

He shook his head and pulled her back to him, his blood throbbing with desire. I can't think of a single thing that would keep me away from you, he said.

They went back towards Court Square, keeping to the alleys. She said she wanted to see his mules. She said she didn't care who saw them. Her sadness had disappeared completely, replaced by a boldness that seemed on the edge of reckless. It excited him.

Alright, he said. Let's go see the mules.

They stood right there together in Court Square. At first he jumped at the few figures who appeared out of the shadows, but they were all low types, coming or going from the blind tiger, paying them no mind. She was making a big fuss over the mules, petting them and talking to them. He lit a cigarette and watched her, so pretty next to those pretty mules in the dark. Strange to see her with them but it had been a strange night. He felt as if he knew her somehow better and somehow less. She had started to open up and then had closed up tighter than before. Thinking of how she had let him kiss her in the middle of the street, he smiled. She was a hell of a girl. Someday when he was better set up with a place and a position they wouldn't have to sneak around and it would all be different.

Over on East Main, two drunks shouted at each other. Catherine didn't even seem to notice. She reached over and took his cigarette from between his fingers and took a pull.

King Midas, she said, letting out a thin line of smoke.

Who?

She handed the cigarette back. They make me think of King Midas.

Charles had never heard of anybody named King Midas. But he made a noise that he hoped made out like he had. The drunks moved on up the street, still arguing, in the direction of the depot. Now they were alone.

Catherine touched the mule's neck.

Well everyone knows the story of how he wished that everything he touched would turn to gold. Bad thing to wish for, it turns out. Wife turned to gold. Children turned gold. Got pretty lonely to be King Midas. But there's another story, how afterwards he was cursed. The gods gave him donkey ears. He was so ashamed he kept them hidden under his hat all the time, even in bed, except to have his hair cut. Only one day his barber couldn't keep the secret to himself. So he ran down to the river and whispered it on the bank. After that, whenever the wind blew, all the reeds and rushes would whisper his secret. 'King Midas has ass's ears! Ass's ears!'

She sighed. The mule next to her stuck his head between them. She reached up and touched his nose.

My brother told me that story, a long time ago. It reminds me of my father.

The mule swung his big head towards Charles. Charles stuck the cigarette between his lips and reached up and gave the animal a pat behind the ear, roughed him up a little and talked sweet to him. Then pulled away suddenly, embarrassed by his tenderness.

This mule right here might be joining your brother in the fight, he said, businesslike as he could.

Might be seeing him before I do. She laughed a little. I ought to give him a message to deliver.

Go right ahead, Charles said, motioning with the cigarette.

She looked at him and smiled. Then she got up on her toes and grabbed the mule's ear and whispered into it.

Well. Charles handed her the cigarette. What'd you tell him?

She smiled again, her teasing smile. She would share no secrets tonight.

I told him to tell Ed what we were having for breakfast at Everbright tomorrow, of course. Bowls of cold sapphires and orange juice. Ham and eggs and emeralds.

FREEDMAN'S HILL

One morning Billy looked over from his bed and said, Take me mule hunting with you, Charles, or else I just might go crazy in here.

Charles had to help him across the yard to the wagon. He made a big fuss over Gin and then Charles realized it was because he couldn't climb in on his own. So Charles hefted him up, taking hold of his big strong hand. He didn't complain about the pain. That meant it was bad.

But as soon as they got going, Billy cheered up. He delighted in every tree, every bird, every cow and horse they passed. They went to a feedlot on the north side of town and Billy did all the talking. There had been a Money Matters column that week about conserving food titled 'Food Will Win the War.' Charles grinned when he overheard Billy's big pitch to the feedlot manager.

You know what will win the war? he was saying to the man. *Mules* will win the war.

A little colored boy had been watching them from the fence. When Charles was tying the mules to the wagon Billy coaxed him over.

I know where some good mules are, the boy said. I'll take you there if you give me a piece of it.

Billy grinned at him, and he climbed into the back of the wagon. At his direction they headed off for the colored neighborhood out beyond the depot that was known as Freedman's Hill. On the way they passed two men trying to get a Ford out of a gully by the road, and when Gin trotted smartly past them Billy leaned over and shouted to them, Git a hoss! Then he made Charles turn around and unhitch Gin and pull them out. And afterwards wouldn't let them drive off until he told them his favorite joke, the one about the farmer and the banker. Charles had heard it a hundred times.

Well the banker buys himself a brand-new automobile and takes his wife out for a Sunday drive in the country. Soon enough he gets the thing stuck in a ditch in front of somebody's cornfield. His wife is hollering at him but he pushes and shoves until he's covered in mud and there's nothing to be done, he can't budge it. Finally along comes the farmer in his hay wagon. The banker gets out and pleads for help. The farmer, he unhitches old Dobbins from the wagon, hitches him to the car, pulls it out in a jiffy. Just like we did for you here. The banker is beside himself. Pulls out a nice fresh dollar bill and hands it to the farmer. Says, 'You must make money day and night, pulling folks out of these ditches.' The farmer tucks the dollar into his overalls and smiles. 'Not quite,' he says.

Billy looked between the two men, eyes flashing.

'Not quite. At night I got to dig the ditches.'

The men laughed, but Billy laughed the hardest, the laugh that took over him like a strong wind, and he didn't even hold on to his broken ribs. Charles had taken out his stitches a few days before, and the angry red gash at his hairline was covered by his hat. His bruises seemed to be fading by the minute. He looked almost as if nothing had ever happened. It felt good as hell to have him back.

The men drove away and the little boy helped him hitch Gin back up and they set off. Soon they got up to Freedman's Hill. As they were coming up it, a couple of kids in an apple cart rigged with roller skates tore past them, though Gin didn't blink. A dog cried like a woman. A man came out of a house to empty a bucket, an excuse to look at them.

The boy brought them to a place near the top of the hill, where they bought two mules off of an old man who ran a delivery business. When Charles wrote out the check the kid watched with bloodthirsty eyes. He took a dollar out of his pocket and gave it to him.

You keep on your toes, kid, you'll make a million bucks someday.

The kid ran off. Billy had propped himself against the back of the bench, twisted nearly backwards to lean on his good shoulder. He whistled to Charles and then pointed in the direction they had come from, where Leland Hatcher's Pierce-Arrow had glided out from an alley. It turned onto the road and disappeared down the hill.

Charles's heart began to pound in his ears. Shit, he said.

I can't think of a single thing that would keep me away from you, he had told Catherine in the middle of the dark deserted street. But with the Pierce-Arrow staring him down like that, he did not feel quite so brave.

You look a little nervous, Charlie boy.

Charles watched the place the car had come from, chewing his knuckle.

You don't think he followed me?

A man with that kind of money can go just about any damn place he pleases, I suppose, Billy said thoughtfully. He's like a shark in the ocean, Charlie boy. Go anywhere he pleases, do anything he pleases, say anything he pleases.

Billy tugged his ear and looked at the mules. And you and me can too, you know. Look at me. I'm right as rain. Why, we could pack up and be out of here by first light tomorrow. We might not be sharks. But we could be free as a couple of gulls.

SCANDAL

Bristol

There is a scandal in Bristol that summer. The youngest King brother announces that he has discovered a health spring in a secret location up on Holston Mountain and unveils a plan to build a grand resort there. He and his business partner begin recruiting investors, and they have raised thousands of dollars when his partner has a heart attack, nearly dies, and confesses the whole thing is a hoax. There is no spring, he announces. And with this ailment God had punished me for the lie.

The investors pull out quickly. There is talk. The Kings take a long vacation in West Virginia.

When they return, Maura gets a job working for them, at their house up on Solar Hill. She makes twice the money she did at the Nichols House, even taking the monkey trick into consideration.

She whispers to Billy about the beauty of the house, the silver settings, the Oriental carpet. Missus King's fur coat, mink, is kept in a special box in the closet.

I don't like you working for em, Billy tells her. To make the kind of money that man has, you got to be something of a shark.

Oh, Maura says simply. I don't mind a shark.

But he's a liar too.

Ah, Billy, no one will even remember this nonsense soon enough. And what's the harm he's done, anyway? If you ask me the way the world works isn't gonna change. You either figure out how to make it work for you, or you don't. If it wasn't Mister King it'd be somebody else making all that money. No. I admire Mister King. He goes after it, he does. The world's a goose, Bill Monday. Them that do not pluck will get no feathers.

Soon the Kings purchase an automobile, Bristol's first. They take it out only on Sundays, puttering into the country. Mister King hires someone just to look after it, to clean the acetylene lights, to polish the chrome, to buy the gasoline.

Sometimes he drives it downtown and lets young boys take turns sitting in it. It sends the horses on the street into greater paroxysms of panic than the bicycles do and smells terrible. And Maura is right. Soon everyone is talking about the automobile, and no one is talking about the scandal.

THE BATTLE OF THE SOMME

Four months, nearly one million dead. Six miles won. Six miles.

CORNHUSKING

The bright half-moon hung above Kuntz's like something you might want to lick. Charles and Billy had been at the sale to buy mules, and he and Twitch and a few others were waiting for the Johnson twins, but it was clear now they weren't going to show. Billy had taken the wagon back to Dillehay's with the mules they had bought. He was still unsteady on his feet, but as he said, if anything happened to him, Gin knew the way.

Charles was stalling. Catherine had left a note in the wall for him, breaking their date to meet that evening. It was the second date she had broken in a week. And the last time they were together, she hadn't let him kiss her. She was convinced her father was on to her. Charles had not told her about seeing the Pierce-Arrow on Freedman's Hill, afraid that if he did she might refuse to see him at all.

He had explained all of this to Billy. Charlie boy, Billy had said. Be sensible. Remember who we're talking about. The richest fellow in town. If he knew that something was going on that he didn't like, don't you think he would put an end to it without a moment's pause?

Billy was right. But Charles could not convince Catherine. You don't understand, she said. It is so strange. He'll drift off in the middle of a sentence. I'll find him staring out the window. Just staring. I'm just waiting for him to turn to me and tell me he knows about us. Then—well I don't know what then. But that would be the end of it, I do know that.

Charles studied the brilliant moon. He was full of energy, all jumped up from the auction, and he did not want to go back to the shack and stare at the newsprint on the walls all night. He had been doing such a fine job finding mules that today Bonnyman had not come up to Kuntz's, and instead entrusted him with the buying at the sale. He and Billy had stood in his prime spot beneath the podium and bought one thousand dollars' worth of mules. One thousand dollars, just like that. Kuntz looked down at Charles always just before he dropped the plait, as he did with Bonnyman, his waxed mustache trembling, giving him the final chance. Pass or yes. It made Charles's chest swell every time. It made him feel about ten feet tall.

Twitch was headed to a party. A cornhusking, up in the Barrens. There would be good strong liquor, he said. Homemade. Strong enough to eat the intestines out of a coyote.

Come on, he said. The girls up there, they're prettier than you'd think.

They walked up along the moonlit road. No horses, no wagons, no cars. As they went up the hill, the houses got smaller, the fields scrappier. The tobacco gave way to shabby little acres of corn, now all harvested, just the bent pale stalks left. An owl boomed from the dark woods when they turned in at Twitch's place so that he could look in on his father. An unpainted frame foursquare with a skinny dog asleep on the porch, its spine sharp as a knife. Inside, Twitch lit a coal oil lamp and said, Make yourself comfortable.

Charles looked around. In the room was a stove, two ladder-back chairs, a table covered with oilcloth. A 1915 calendar tacked to the wall, torn to February, was the sole decoration. The picture, printed cheaply, was of Jesus on the cross. Along the bottom someone had written, It is easier for a camel to pass through the eye of a needle than a rich man to enter heaven. The meek shall inherit the earth. He could hear the old man cursing Twitch as Twitch coaxed him to eat. Twitch's voice was patient and gentle, the opposite of the way he talked to the horses.

With the money he was making, Charles had bought all kinds of things. A new wool suit, and a chain for his watch, and a two-volume set called *Poems to Make You a Better Man*, and a silverware chest a traveling peddler brought to the door of the shack, even though Billy tried to stop him, even though he didn't have any silverware to put in it, and two framed water-spotted Currier and Ives prints. He had spent five whole dollars on a gift for Catherine, a brooch. And for a dollar he had bought a subscription to a magazine called *Ambition*.

He stood there regarding Jesus. He had never understood that, about the camel and the needle. He hadn't had the best of luck with his purchases, he did know that. The book of poems, he had abandoned after a few pages. He couldn't make heads or tails of it. The brooch had turned out to be a fake, glass and paste, which he thankfully discovered before he tried to give it to Catherine. That was a good thing, because these days he could not figure out what she wanted from him anyway. She had been so distant. So guarded.

And *Ambition*, he had discovered, was a sham. Every article was a thinly veiled advertisement for a business correspondence school. He wrote a letter demanding his dollar back, but the letter came back marked Undeliverable.

Sleep well, Pa, he heard Twitch say.

Be careful, Vernon.

When Twitch came out Charles still hadn't sat down.

Your name's Vernon?

Come on. Let's get the hell out of here.

At the party the barn floor was piled knee-high, wall to wall, with unshucked corn that hid half a dozen jars of moonshine. Charles drank hard and flew through the corn, tearing off the husks and throwing the cobs into the huge growing pile. Whenever a red ear was discovered, a girl was kissed. It took Charles a long time and a lot of liquor to find one. When he did he looked around. There was one girl no one had yet kissed, with a patch over her eye. The smile she gave him when he lifted her up and spun her around and kissed her was a thousand watts. For the rest of the night, he could feel her watching him. The liquor was running hot in his blood.

Catherine had pushed him away again and again, looking over her shoulder, saying that they had to be more careful. That was the thing. He didn't want to have to be careful at all. Didn't want to sneak around. And there was some relief, not being with her. With her he was always weighing his words, wondering how he came across. Here he could just drink whiskey and tell a joke and snatch up a girl and spin her around.

When the husks were swept away a couple of the older men brought out a fiddle and a banjo. Twitch, he saw, was a good dancer, light on his feet. He handled the girls delicately. For one dance they ended up across the square from each other. Twitch winked.

You're a saint, McLaughlin. You ain't got to kiss Sally. They're all swooning over you.

The fiddle rang out. The caller hooted. Charles reached between the two girls on either side of their square. They danced. Across the barn, the girl with the patch over her eye was watching him. Every time he spun he could see her. The floor was shaking. The girls smelled of hay and sweat.

After the last dance Twitch disappeared. Charles took the girl with the patch outside. Sally. He was woozy with the liquor. When he put his hand on her back, her homemade dress felt so coarse compared to Catherine's fine clothes.

He kissed her, sloppy, at the edge of the woods.

She took off the patch and where her eye should have been was a shiny mass of flesh.

Lost it harvesting tobacco, she said. Leaned too fast over one of them there spikes.

He wished she would put it back on but she didn't, so he closed his eyes so he wouldn't have to see it. It made him awfully sad. She would have been pretty but now no man was ever going to want to marry her. He could see the life that stretched out before her, poor and lonesome and toiling, all because of one stroke of bad luck, leaning over too fast at the wrong moment in the tobacco field. And then he realized she was going to let him do whatever he wanted and he knew he would and then he quit thinking at all. Her dress was hitched up around her breasts. She was shivering. He turned her around and yanked at his belt and pulled himself out of his pants and had her quick. When he pulled out of her it was with the thought of Catherine Hatcher's bare legs in the deerskin skirt that he came on the leaves at her feet.

He walked the girl home. In the moonlight everything was clear. There were even shadows. She had put the eye patch back on. Below the road the tobacco clung to the steep hills.

Kind of place where the cows got legs shorter on one side than the other, he said.

This made her laugh.

You're a swell girl, he said, when they got to her house. He strung the words together carefully as he could but still wasn't sure they had come out in the right order. It was powerful liquor. You got some warm blankets in there?

I'm plenty warm now, she said before stepping up onto the porch.

He went back to Twitch's. The place was dark. Twitch wasn't home, or had already gone to bed.

He slept on the floor in the front room with his coat as a pillow. He felt fleas gnawing at his ankles, picked up in the corn, and thick corncrib dust in his throat. All night the mice ran across his legs. He would open his eyes and see Jesus up on the cross and then roll over and try to sleep again.

He woke to the sound of two boys beating a dog. It was past midmorning but the holler was so dark you wouldn't know it. There was the smell of burn coming from the kitchen. The boys came in, trailed by a little girl working her thumb into the cleft of her bottom through her dress. Where had these children been last night? He rubbed his eyes. They felt full of sand. His mouth was thick with a dark brown film. The soul-forsaking hangover of homemade liquor.

Twitch followed the children in, batting the little girl's thumb away from her backside.

They all got damn worms, Twitch said. I just burned the damn biscuits. You get a piece of tail last night?

Charles rubbed the side of his face.

Shoot. The girls they won't hardly blink at me and you come up here for one dance and walk off with a piece of tail.

Charles's head was pounding. The dog howled shrilly. He put on his hat and asked Twitch if he wanted to go to town and get something to eat. Twitch looked back at the smoky kitchen.

Shoot, he said, I ain't going nowhere. Sometimes I think it's lost on you, McLaughlin. You don't know how good you got it.

COLD

Cold days, colder nights. Every morning, a carpet of frost covered the pasture. Hog-killing weather. Dillehay dragged his scalding tub into his front yard and the neighbors brought their hogs. One by one their bodies went up on the oak trees in the front yard until there were three, legs strung taught, bellies slit.

Dillehay's son, Jack, had moved in. He was going to help his father modernize his operation and was building a house, right next door to his parents'. It was nearly all framed out. Down at the shack, Charles could hear the steady *thwock thwock thwock* of his hammer. It was like the ticking of a clock, and it had begun to drive him mad. All day every day, *thwock thwock thwock*, keeping track of his lost time.

These days kids everywhere were playing with the slaughtered hogs' bladders, which they inflated like balloons and tossed around the barnyards. After a few days the bladders ended up deflated and forgotten, beside a barn or behind a stove, shriveled up, fair game for varmints and ants. Charles's heart felt like one of these forgotten balloons.

Two weeks had passed since the night Charles spent up in the Barrens. In that time Catherine had broken all their dates but one, saying it was too cold, or she was too busy, or a party had come up. He did not understand what was happening. He had begun to wonder if she somehow knew what he had done with the girl. He would take out a nickel ten times a day and flip it. Heads, she knew. Tails, she didn't. No matter which way it came out it left him miserable.

Billy, he said.

Charlie boy.

I'm gonna quit drinking whiskey.

Fine.

I'm gonna walk the righteous path.

Who said you were crooked?

He went back up to see the girl. One blustery afternoon when the wind was making short work of the few leaves left on the trees he was nearby, hunting mules, and he found the house and knocked on the door and she came to it with a dish and a flour sack in her hand. A chicken with a filthy bottom came out around her legs. Then a kitten, all bone, stumbling as if drunk.

Just so you know, I got a steady girl.

She looked at him with her one eye. Someone was calling to her from inside the house.

I gotta get, she said.

He felt even worse, after that.

He now ran an advertisement in the paper. WANTED. GOOD MULES. Men sometimes showed up at the shack with all kinds of animals, from good stout quality mules to the sorriest worn-out creatures. A colored man sold them a mule to pay for a lawyer. He had been arrested after two white women accused him of not stepping down off the sidewalk to let them pass. He had a wife and three children and two jobs and stood to lose everything if he was found guilty.

They wrote him a check for the mule and he set off determinedly up the road. Charles sat down on the step and tossed the checkbook aside and put his head in his hands.

It's an awful mean world, Billy. It's a messed-up world.

The next day they went out to the sawmill to look at some mules. It was on the eastern edge of town, out beyond the Rich addition.

The stone plantation wall still stood along the roadside, nearly a mile long.

They looked at two mules, log skidders.

Oh, them mules can pull, the man said. They could pull the devil offa the cross.

When they departed Charles turned back and regarded the mules, now tied to the back of the wagon. It was a raw day. Little needles of rain had begun to sting his face.

We could just up and go, couldn't we, Billy?

Billy had his collar clenched up around his neck. Charles knew his pain was worse in this weather.

In a heartbeat, Charlie boy.

Oh, Catherine. Charles knocked his head. What am I gonna do about that girl?

Well, Billy said from deep in his collar. Women like a man they can depend on, don't they? Maybe you ought to buy yourself a little patch of dirt.

Charles bit his lip, studying this. Billy was right. That was exactly what he needed to do. Buy some land and build a house like Jack Dillehay was doing. Invest in the future. To stay in one spot was the only way to get ahead in life. The only way to be a man in full. But what an odd thing to come out of Billy, who always said he had long ago given up on the pursuit of what other men called success.

He looked over at him. Maybe the mare's attack had changed something in him. Maybe it had helped him realize a man could not wander forever.

Really, Monday?

Billy smiled, pointing across the road. Why, there's a place for sale right there.

Charles looked. A foursquare farmhouse, a couple of cows. A few acres of tobacco. There was a sign in the front field. He had to squint, trying to read it through the rain. When they got a bit closer he finally saw it. HAY FOR SALE.

That place? How do you know it's even for sale?

Well look at that sign. A grin cracked Billy's face. Hey, for sale.

Sonofabitch, Monday. Sometimes I could sock you.

On Thanksgiving Day Charles and Billy ate two cans of beans and a rabbit Billy snared. Darkness fell fast and Charles lay on his bed smoking and listening to the mules braying in the pasture and thinking about Catherine in her squaw's costume. It seemed a lifetime ago.

He pulled out a nickel. Heads, he would tell her he had not been true. Tails, he would tell her nothing. He flipped it.

Heads. He couldn't remember what heads was.

He left her a note in the Everbright wall to meet him behind the icehouse. He went up there early. A train was coming in. In the distance he could hear the bells of Bud Morgan's goats as he went to meet it. There was a sign in the window of the Citizens' Club laundry. WE SMOOTH EVERYTHING BUT YOUR FAMILY TROUBLES.

She was already there, waiting. Just seeing her, his blood ran fast and hot. He lifted her by the elbows and set her on the fence, and she kissed him, a little recklessly. But kissing her his thoughts wandered to the girl in the Barrens, Sally, her sharp animal teeth and cold nose. Her hunger.

What's the matter? Catherine said.

He knocked the side of his head with his knuckles.

It's you, he said. You're the only girl for me.

She pulled back to look at him. There was a freckle near her ear he had never noticed before.

If I went away, she said, would you be true to me?

His blood ran cold. He wondered if she had read his thoughts.

What kind of a question is that?

She was leaving, she explained. She had not known how to tell him. Every year they went to see her father's family in West Tennessee. They would be gone for eight weeks. Longer than usual.

My father, she said bitterly, claims he needs to clear his head.

Charles's heart fell, smashed down by the idea of eight weeks without her. He had no idea how to express what he felt.

You gonna be alright? was all he said.

She shivered.

Oh, it's awful, she said. It's an awful place. The farm. Nothing around for miles. And every year he tells everyone we're going west. Just—she waved her hand—west. He likes for them to think we're going to *the* West—someplace far, exotic. The mountains. Maybe even the coast.

There was desperation in her voice but as she spoke Charles's mind was elsewhere. His heart was lifting again. He saw that this could be an opportunity. He had a second chance. Eight weeks was a long time. When she returned, everything would be different. He thought of something Billy sometimes said: When opportunity knocks, you got to know enough to open the door. He had almost missed his chance but he wouldn't again. He was going to become the kind of man he had always wanted to be. A good man. The kind who won the bread of life. Whose name wasn't just on the sign above the building but the cornerstone at its base.

Kiss me again, she said. It's so cold.

But it was too cold to be out and they gave up after a while. She told him she would write to him. He walked away with that now too-familiar icy tangle in his guts, the ache in his balls, the pent-up desire. But on top of it, the thrumming power of his resolve.

A few days later, there it was, in the society column of the paper.

LELAND HATCHER AND MISS CATHERINE HATCHER HAVE GONE WEST FOR THE HOLIDAYS. THEY WILL RETURN IN THE NEW YEAR.

MONUMENTS

Charles sometimes stood in front of the Court Square monument for the men of Richfield who fought in the Spanish-American War. He would mouth the names as he read them. Rich, Markham, Sawyer, Shipp. There was something beautiful about the way the lichen filled in the letters, making them darker, austere, and noble. He would think about what Pendergrass said, about how George Washington's greatest deed for the country had been not an act of military force but an act of the imagination. That a man could do more for his country with a vision than with a sword. And he would feel in his chest the dynamo of energy, the beautiful potential of America, the might of sixty mules pulling combine machines across oceans of golden wheat.

His mother had loved America. Charles reckoned she had loved it as much as General Washington had, the way she talked about it. Or at least loved the vision of it, the promise of it, the picture of it that she held in her imagination. And she had fought for it too, fought to keep him alive and fed so that he might one day embody this vision. But no monument bore her name. She was buried with all the other whores in the paupers' graveyard in Bristol, no headstone, no nothing. If he ever went back there he wouldn't even know where to look for her. There was nothing to mark her now but grass. Those hundreds of mornings she made sure he got up to the schoolhouse. The thousand jokes she told to distract him from hunger. Or how she wiped the tears from her eyes and put on rosewater to mask the smell of the men at the Crimson Shawl. The times she rocked him to sleep at night. The countless songs she sang him. All that was left of it, all of it, was grass.

YOUR CROWDED HOUR

The tobacco markets opened, and Kuntz's closed for six weeks. Charles and Billy were out all the time buying mules now, flashing the gilt-edged checkbook, giving a little speech about how George Washington was the father of the American mule and how mules would win the war. Every week Charles would ship them down to Bonnyman on a boxcar. His paycheck was more money than he knew what to do with. And with Catherine gone he didn't know what to do with the long winter evening hours either. He had sworn off liquor and the blind tiger. Most nights, to the tune of Billy's snores across the room, he counted his money into a cigar box he kept under the bed. Counted and recounted it. Still he had loads more than he knew what to do with. He bought himself a new hat, beaver, and when Twitch admired it he bought him one too. He would go up to see a picture and buy tickets for the boys who hung around outside the theater. They all called him the mule man.

One day the week before Christmas he got an invitation from Kuntz. He had just moved into his new house and was having Lloyd Bonnyman up to lunch, and Bonnyman had suggested that Charles join them.

When he told Twitch, he knocked his shoulder.

You're in with the big bugs now, you lucky dog.

He went to Suddarth's and bought a new collar and, when he saw how dingy it made his shirt look, a new shirt too. He bought a pair of mercerized socks with gold stitching at the toe. The morning of the lunch he got a shave and a haircut and a shoeshine. He put on his new beaver hat.

Kuntz's house was on the edge of the Rich addition. It looked solid and respectable in a field of fresh thin snow, young saplings staked in front, an evergreen wreath on the front door, a finger of smoke reaching up from the chimney. There was a small barn with a few nice horses out in the paddock. On the white ground, steaming dark heaps of manure.

A maid greeted him at the door. Stood there with a funny look on her face for a long time before Charles realized she was waiting to take his coat and hat. He held the hat a moment, feeling its plush quality. He did hate to hand it away.

Bonnyman was already there. Kuntz was giving him a tour. When Charles joined them in the sunroom off the kitchen Kuntz hardly paused in his narration. It was a kit house, ordered through the mail, delivered from Michigan in pieces in three boxcars, everything except the windows and the nails. The pride with which Kuntz pointed out the details, you would have thought he built it himself from lumber he cut and hewed with his own hands. He took them from room to room, speaking with the same jumping drive he had on the auction podium. Charles was surprised he wasn't cracking peanuts and tossing the shells on the floor. He reminded him of Pendergrass, showing off his donkeys and automatic waterers, and filled him with the same contagious energy.

They went upstairs. Gus Kuntz was mopping an empty room that still smelled of sawdust.

Get on top of that mop, Gus! Kuntz said. What do I always tell you? Get on top of a mop, and behind a broom.

He looked at them and shook his head in mock exasperation.

Apple of my eye, that boy.

He took them into his own bedroom. There was a photograph of Theodore Roosevelt next to his bed.

The greatest president of them all, Kuntz said, studying the picture. And the finest American who has ever drawn breath. His charge on San Juan Hill is the crystallizing moment of this country's history. The fire, the tenacity, the overcoming of the odds. The rush and the push and the planting of the flag. As Roosevelt called it, his crowded hour.

By his wife's bed hung a needlepoint and a cross she'd brought from Germany. Charles stood in the doorway and looked at it and thought of the picture of Jesus on the cross at Twitch's house. *The meek shall inherit the earth*. And he thought of Pen Pendergrass pumping his hand with his one good arm. *This country was not built by the meek*. For some time now he had been turning a new question over and over in his mind. How could a man set his course by both of those stars?

He could just read the needlepoint from this distance.

When I was a child, I spake as a child, I understood as a child, I thought as a child: but when I became a man, I put away childish things.

I CORINTHIANS 13:11

Kuntz was humming happily. He squeezed the tip of his mustache. His diamond ring caught the December light coming through the window.

Well it's nothing like your place in Nashville, Bonnyman, but it's not bad, is it?

They ate lunch in the dining room at a table laid with a cloth and a mess of forks, knives, and spoons, waited on by Kuntz's wife and the colored maid. Charles hunched and ate while Kuntz and Bonnyman talked. He had never seen Bonnyman without the derby hat on before, and his head was enormous, big as a bandbox, glaringly bald on the top. The maid and Missus Kuntz brought out dish after dish. Charles ate ravenously. Last week Billy had come back from town having traded the Edison cylinder player for three cases of Corn Flakes cereal. Nearly one hundred boxes of cereal. They had been eating Corn Flakes morning, noon, and night. Feeding them to the horses. Stacking up the boxes to make a card table. Billy was delighted. He said he'd got the deal of the century.

Kuntz was talking about the time he spent buying cotton mules in Mississippi. Hundreds of mules were employed on every plantation.

Those that say the horse and mule is going out, he said, I'd like to take them on a trip to see those cotton plantations.

Oh, they'll never go out, Bonnyman said, lifting his glass.

Outside a blue jay landed on the windowsill, looked in, took off. The women were laughing in the kitchen.

Kuntz turned to Charles. What do you think?

Charles shrugged. I don't know, sir.

You don't say much, do you, kid?

Nossir. I guess not unless I got something to say.

Charles shrank, realizing that Kuntz had taken offense at this. He was scowling, his fork in his fist on the table.

Well. Good for you. My wife tells me to shut my trap all the time. She says I ought to go into politics.

If they get the vote that'll be it, Bonnyman said. He took his thumb and forefinger and ran them slowly down the lines on either side of his nose, stopping at the corners of his mouth. None of them will be able to make up their minds, queues will form at the polling places two miles long, and the wheels of democracy will screech to a halt.

Kuntz quit scowling, pushed back from the table, and smiled to himself.

Sometimes I think I ought to get into politics. I've got the thing a man needs, to have any effect at all in public office. He pointed between his eyes and looked directly at Charles. Optimism. Blind, ferocious optimism.

After the meal they went to sit in the parlor to smoke. The maid brought in a pitcher of iced tea.

Drink it all year long, Kuntz boasted, pouring their glasses. Never touched a drop of liquor in my entire life.

The armchairs were the color of butter. Charles sat on the very edge of his chair, terrified he would get it dirty. There was a doily on each arm and one behind his head. When he sat down Kuntz's wife had adjusted it behind him and he had jumped.

Outside, the snow had begun to fall again. Missus Kuntz came in to speak to Kuntz. Then she went out and got the car to drive the colored girl home.

Can only afford to keep her half days, Kuntz said, watching them go. We've been through three in as many months. But Missus Kuntz won't take white help. Colored only. It was a white girl dropped Gus and she'll never forget it. Every day she drives this one back and forth to the foot of Freedman's Hill. He grimaced. I know the fellow who owns most of those places up there. Says you wouldn't believe the way they live. On a summer day, the smell of the outhouses.

Charles put his hands on his knees. Well if he don't like it then maybe he ought to plumb the houses.

Kuntz gave him a pitying look. Plumbing on Freedman's Hill? What next?

Bonnyman gave a little bark of a laugh. Charles's ears burned. He excused himself and headed to the bathroom down the hall. He was really fouling this up. He wondered if Bonnyman had brought him here to fire him. Wouldn't that be a fitting end to it.

Catherine had sent a letter. Not much to it, just a few lines. It had made him miss her so much he rode out to their old meeting places. The women's college boathouse, with the college out of session, was lonesome and haunted-looking. Ducks swimming forlorn circles on the pond. The lot behind the icehouse had all the color wrung out of it. He knew these places the way he knew her lips and tongue and teeth, secretly and intimately and as if they were a part of his own body. Every scrappy weed and resident crow and thornbush. Where the burrs would get you if you tried to lie down. Someday he wanted to kiss her someplace where he did not afterwards have to pick burrs off the hem of her skirt. Yet the idea felt so far out of reach.

In the hall he passed a half-open door. He heard a moan, and when he looked in he saw Gus Kuntz, pants open, a half dozen stereoscope cards spread out on the bed. Gus looked up and scrambled around, trying to hide the cards and tugging at his pants.

Charles went in and picked up one of the cards.

Where'd you get this?

Gus looked up at him guiltily from under his jutting brow.

Fellow at the auction house sold em to me.

The card was greasy and well handled. Fat girl with her legs spread and her head tossed back. Black triangle of fur. Double image. Ugly as sin in both of them.

He handed it back. What you pay for em?

Three dollars.

Three dollars? Ah, Gus. You were fleeced. I can get you a better set than these. I can get you some will blow your mind. You get yourself a viewer for those cards and they'll really be something.

My pa took all the others and put them in the fireplace. He says I'm gonna go blind.

You ain't gonna go blind.

They burned! Gus's eyes got wide. They burned all up.

Listen. You ain't gonna go blind. Don't worry about nothing, Gus. You don't got to worry about nothing.

When he came back to the parlor Bonnyman was talking about the Belgian workhorses he imported before working for Roan and Huntington. He had a faraway look in his eye. Saying how the horses, perfected after years of careful breeding, made strong and stout on the fine Belgian grasslands, were the color of wheat beer, the color of honey, the color of a kind of apple he used to eat by the handful.

He went quiet, and stared into his iced tea. Charles looked at him. Such tenderness coming out of Bonnyman's undertaker mouth was a surprise.

How is your wife? Kuntz asked.

Fair, Bonnyman said, making it clear that he wished to say no more.

The conversation moved on to the latest war news. In November a British ocean liner had been torpedoed without warning in the Mediterranean, and Kuntz pointed out that, all other things aside, this further proved the undeniable engineering genius of the German submarine.

Now it was Bonnyman who excused himself. When he left Kuntz picked up his pipe and raised his eyebrows at Charles.

His wife is in a sanatorium. Did you know? She lost her whole family at the start of the war. Though they were French they had lived in Belgium since she was born. Lost both parents when their village was sacked, and her brother died at the Battle of Mons that first August. It has hit her badly. She is not doing well at all.

Out the window, something had stirred up the horses. They were whinnying in unison.

Wonder if the coyote's coming around again, Kuntz said to himself. He looked into the fire. It will be a glad day when this war is over, McLaughlin. It will be the dawning of a new age. A great age of peace and progress and brotherhood between all men. You'll have the opportunity for greatness. If only Gus— He stopped himself and gazed back out at the horses for a moment. Then he clapped his hands. This town is poised for anything! Why, look at what Leland Hatcher has managed to come in and do. A fellow could learn a lot by studying him. When my father brought us here from Germany back in 1867 he very carefully picked this place. Tennessee, America! His neighbors had never heard of it. But he knew the War between the States had left a vacuum. He knew it was here for the taking. He brought my mother big with child—he jabbed his chest—and that was me.

Bonnyman had come back in and had been standing in the archway, listening. Taking his seat, he pinched the thighs of his pants and tugged on them.

I always forget that you're a Kraut.

I am not. Kuntz brought down his hand as if he was smacking his leather plait. I am an American. He looked at Charles. You ought to buy yourself a piece of land, son. Best investment a man can make. Only thing they're not making more of. I hear the Tisdale addition's being divided into lots. How much do you have in your bank account?

Don't have one.

Ach! Kuntz looked back at Bonnyman. Did you hear that? Shameful! He shook his head. And you, calling me a Kraut. What does Roosevelt say? He says, 'No hyphenated Americans. Only Americans.'

Charles wondered if Kuntz included the folks on Freedman's Hill in this definition. But he knew enough just to put the cigarette in his mouth and not say anything. His face was burning. It had never occurred to him to open a bank account.

Now Kuntz was talking about Henry Ford, how he taught all his workers English, how he sent women into their homes to teach their wives how to cook American food.

Organizes baseball leagues for them, he said proudly. Keeps them from doing all the voodoo they might do back in the old country on a Sunday afternoon.

He lifted his glass.

Here's to Henry Ford!

Well I think it's terrible, Bonnyman said. They got to remember where they came from. My wife. Her home meant everything to her.

Kuntz took a mouthful of iced tea, set his glass down with a bang. This is exactly my point! You've got a French wife. I was conceived in Germany. Our two nations are engaged in the bitterest of wars. Yet here we sit, smoking together, talking peaceably. It is a beautiful place, America. The melting pot! The alchemy of it!

If, after this war, the whole world could be like this, then it would not matter where a man came from, or who his parents were. All men could meet on the level, bringing together their knowledge and experience and backgrounds—think of the possibility.

Bonnyman turned to Charles and gave him an exasperated look. The light was bouncing off the top of his head.

How about you, McLaughlin? From where did your people scramble over?

Well, Mister Bonnyman, sir, he began, choosing his words carefully, my father—

Son! Kuntz boomed. You don't even answer him. This is my point entirely. It does not matter where a man comes from. Everything great in America has been achieved through hard work and common sense. Except for the raw land, and we stole that from the Indians. But listen. No bank account? What are you doing?

Bonnyman was looking at Charles over crossed arms.

You've got an uncanny eye for animals, McLaughlin. Was just telling Mister Kuntz. And you hustle. You could go far in this business. That fellow you're with. Monday. You ever think about cutting him loose and going out on your own?

Charles shifted uncomfortably, knocking a doily off the arm of the chair. He leaned to pick it up, then decided to leave it. It had no more occurred to him that he ought to cut loose from Billy than it had that he ought to open a bank account.

He took care of me when I was a kid, he said quietly. I didn't have nobody and he took care of me.

Well so did my mother, Bonnyman said, but you don't see me hanging on her apron strings.

Charles finally reached down and picked up the doily and put it back in place. He coughed and fidgeted.

Bonnyman rubbed the top of his head. You'll only ever get so far until you realize it's every man for himself. Most important thing Virgil Huntington ever taught me. In business it's every man for himself.

I agree with you there, Lloyd, Kuntz said.

Charles was thinking about Billy eating a big bowl of Corn Flakes with the new dentures he had bought him. All those damn boxes of cereal. They made him think of the time he'd been laid up weeks in that Kentucky boardinghouse when he was a kid, after a hot horse had thrown him in the woods and broken his arm and collarbone. He had asked Billy for oranges, and Billy had gone out with an old plug to trade and come back with three crates of oranges. Charles had gorged himself on the sweet juicy fruit, forgetting his pain. He had felt like a prince, like the luckiest kid on earth. In the years since he had often asked Billy where he managed to find all those oranges, at that time of year. But Billy would only ever wink.

Well, sir, he said simply. We're a team.

There was a crash from the back of the house. Gus's room. Bonnyman flinched. What in the hell was that?

Kuntz frowned and waved his hand dismissively, diamonds flashing. Charles thought about how he had stopped himself a moment ago from speculating on what Gus might have accomplished if he had not been crippled. And he saw a glimmer of deep pain in Kuntz's eyes. Charles silently vowed to find Gus that stereoscope. Help teach him how to tie his shoes. Maybe there was hope for Gus. It might take a miracle, but miracles happened, didn't they?

But it did not last long. In a moment Kuntz was galloping ahead, praising the house and its craftsmanship again. He got up to demonstrate the smooth slide of the room's pocket doors.

Why, God willing, we'll live here the rest of our lives, he said happily, sitting back down. I can still hardly believe I had the wallet for it. This war has been good for the mule business, hasn't it, Lloyd?

Been good for all business, Bonnyman said matter-of-factly.

Well thanks to you, Lloyd, you old profiteer, it's paid for this house, Kuntz said. He smiled. What is it they say? A rising tide lifts all ships.

Except a sub, Charles volunteered.

Kuntz looked at him a moment. His mustache tips began to quiver. Then he began to laugh. He slapped his thick thigh and laughed until his jowls shivered. He showed as many teeth as old Teddy Roosevelt in the photo upstairs. Charles's heart swelled.

Yes! Yes! Kuntz cried. Except a sub.

Bonnyman smiled wanly and reached out to the table, where the iced tea pitcher sat between their three glasses. He touched his own glass.

My friend Mister Kuntz here, he's a half-full man if I've ever seen one. Always and forevermore. As a half-empty man, I can appreciate that.

He pushed Charles's glass towards him.

What are you, McLaughlin?

Charles looked at the glass. He looked at Bonnyman and then at Kuntz, still buoyed by the success of his joke.

Neither, he said.

Neither?

He smiled and seized the heavy pitcher and pulled it off the table and filled the glass to the brim.

Top it off! he said triumphantly. That's what I say. Top it off!

Money Matters

by Leland Hatcher
The Richfield Gazette

I send my holiday greetings to you from afar, dear Richfield, and all the best for a prosperous 1917. And I keep this week's column short, for as we welcome in the New Year, I know as well as any man that there are only two questions on people's minds:

War or no war? And how high can prices go?

MONEY

Bristol

Billy makes a little money working at Harkleroad's Livery Stable, enough to pay for his room and all the trifles for Maura: the chocolate and peppermints, the bottles of cheap perfume, hair combs of imitation tortoiseshell, sprays of artificial violets and lilacs for her hat, cards printed with cherubs and hearts that he buys from the drugstore on the corner of Main and Fifth. These things do add up.

Harkleroad is convinced the bicycles are going to run him out of business. Billy helps him paint a sign, which he puts out in front of the stable door.

> COME ON FELLAS—TAKE HER FOR A SUNDAY
> CARRIAGE RIDE—HER SKIRTS WON'T GET
> MUDDY—HER LEGS WON'T GET TIRED—
> YOU'LL BE COZY SIDE BY SIDE

He is a bighearted man, Harkleroad, a veteran of Chickamauga and twenty years a widow, who keeps his account book with a quill pen, pays Billy too well, and feeds the boys who hang around the stable and jump in the rain barrels on hot days. The horses are better looked after than any livery stable horses Billy has ever come across. One august gray gelding is a veteran of the war, just like Harkleroad himself, retired but allowed to stick around because he seems to enjoy the activity, his ears perked at all the comings and goings of the day. Three bullets are lodged in his chest. Harkleroad keeps him in a big box stall and lets the boys spoil him with apples. Every time he passes, he greets him in his rich, growling old corporal's voice, still strong in spite of his years.

Onward, Christian Soldier!

Billy sometimes employs a boy or two to run an errand for him, sending them up to the drugstore with instructions on which hat pin or scented soap to buy. For my secret Valentine, Billy says with a wink. When they come back with the little packages Harkleroad watches and laughs, his white mustache quivering beneath his high stiff derby.

Let me give you some advice, Monday. Marry her now. It's cheaper in the long run.

Marry her!

Don't look so frightened, son. Someday you'll be an old man like me and you'll realize none of it was so serious, after all. And that you don't have the chance to go back and do it all over again.

A few days later he and Harkleroad bring the old gray gelding out into the yard to trim his feet.

A man on a bicycle flies around the corner, collides with a telephone pole. The horse's head shoots up and he pulls back from Billy's grasp. Before the man collects himself and his contraption and rides away, Harkleroad booms at him.

Keep riding that thing like a madman and they'll be using it to dig your grave!

Harkleroad smooths and pats the gelding's mane, telling him it's alright. One of the boys, with a face freckled like a turkey egg, is squatting in the corner, sorting his marbles. He looks up.

Why you always talking to that horse, Mister Harkleroad? He can't understand you. He's nothing but a dumb animal.

The boy points to a group of sparrows that, after scattering at the racket of the crash, has come back down to perch on the telephone pole.

Horses are no different than them birds up there, and them birds don't know nothing but to eat, sleep, and fly like hell when the cat pounces. Spend their whole life either asleep or afraid.

Harkleroad stands back from the horse. Then he takes off his hat and lifts it. The horse's ears move towards it. He moves it one way and the ears follow, then the other and the ears follow still. The old horse has his head up, watching Harkleroad intently, and Billy can see the shadow of his former glory on the battlefield. When Harkleroad brings the hat down fast to his knee the old horse tenses, a small change that registers in every muscle of his body. The slightest shift. He is still standing there at the end of Billy's lead, but he is ready to run.

See what I mean, the boy says. Always afraid.

Harkleroad puts his hat back on. He rubs the horse's mane again. I could have done that twenty yards from here and he would have known it. He's like a spider at the center of a web who knows the second a fly hits it way off in another corner. He ain't afraid. He's aware.

Squinting up at the sparrows, Harkleroad goes on.

Same as those birds up there. Aware. They can hear the wind blowing through the hay. They can hear a worm roll over under the dirt. And I do believe that's close to God. Because this must be how God sees the world. All at once, everything, all around Him. Every footfall, every breath, every broken twig. To know is to love, the Bible says. To know a thing, to understand a thing, with not just your thoughts but your heart and your blood, is to love it. I once watched a wolf take down one of my neighbor's sheep. It wasn't a battle, it was a dance. The wolf loves the sheep and the sheep, in a way, loves the wolf. Because he is completely and utterly attuned to him.

This sends the boy into a convulsion of laughter. Harkleroad turns to Billy.

Well what do you think, Mister Monday? Does it make you laugh, the thought that an animal could love the world and everything in it? Including you?

Billy looks at the boy and winks.

If the rabbits love me, why don't they jump into the snares I set for em two days ago in the field behind the post office?

Harkleroad smiles patiently, showing his yellow teeth beneath his mustache.

Maybe you've got to woo them, the boy said with a big grin. Whisper sweet nothings in their ears!

Why, I will try that directly, Billy says, and winks at him again, giving him a smile that says, Let's humor the old man.

They finish with the horse and put him away and Billy heads up towards Main Street. He is meeting Maura in an hour, and Harkleroad has paid him. If he hurries he can get to the drugstore before they close and pick up the new little music box she is always admiring.

A horse! Loving the world!

Harkleroad may be going a little soft in the head.

BILLY'S PAIN

The hand-painted sign on Freedman's Hill said:

SKULLS READ

FORTUNES TOLD

LAUNDRY WASHED AND FOLDED

I SPEAK WITH THE DEAD

The house was halfway up the hill, with a dirt yard swept clean and lined carefully all the way around with white stones. In it stood a big coffee-colored mule, head like an anvil, well-fed and brushed to a shine. He nickered to Gin when Billy tied her at the fence, maybe feeling somewhere in his mysterious mule brain a memory of the horse mare who had borne him into the world. Gin ignored him, poor fellow.

Billy stood for a moment, getting his legs under him. It was the first time he had ridden since the mare's attack. It had taken ten minutes just to heft himself into the saddle, but Gin stood stock-still for him. Riding up the Pike, he was not much better than a sack of meal, but she made infinite small adjustments to his shifting weight to keep him in the saddle. Bless her, Gin. It could break a man's heart, a horse like her. Everything she did reminded you that you weren't worthy of it.

He went up unto the porch and knocked on the door. At Kuntz's he had heard about this woman, Aunt Ernestine, who told fortunes and knew herbs. Someone swore she had cured his gallstones, another that she knew the scripture that stopped blood. Billy was ready to try anything. In the months since the mare's attack the pain had only grown worse. A pain in his head that came and went, a pain in his side that made it so he couldn't sleep. All kinds of other pains, big and small and in between.

He knocked again, harder, and rubbed his hands to warm them. The air was brittle and he could see his breath.

It made him ornerier than a hurt dog, this pain. Charles had come back from his lunch at Kuntz's with a catalog for kit houses. Aladdin Homes, with a picture of a genie coming out of a bottle, and according to Charles it took little more than a wish to get one of these houses built. They had names: the Senator, the Charleston, the Belle. Kuntz's was on page twenty-four: the Magnolia. They send everything but the windows and the nails, Charles said happily, to anyone who would listen. Send it on a boxcar!

The cheapest was called the Raymond: $325, COD. This was the one Charles had his eye on. When he showed him the picture and the blueprints, four rooms, a pantry, a little front porch, Billy had snapped his teeth.

Couldn't they have given it a better name? What fool's gonna shell out three hundred twenty-five dollars for something called the damn Raymond?

He knocked again. Finally someone came to the door. A tiny colored woman in a pair of men's shoes stuffed with newspaper and a coat that almost swallowed her. Her face was etched with a thousand lines of age, yet she was delicate as a child. Aunt Ernestine.

When she asked what he needed he put his hand on his gut.

Horse threw me. Got me pretty good right here, he said. Pain won't leave me be.

She brought him inside. A shock of warmth. A small table at the center of the room, covered in oilcloth, flanked by two stools. Stack of playing cards. Big fire in an open fireplace, with a phrenologist's skull on the rough-hewn mantel. Next to it, a turtle shell.

That's a mighty fine mule you got out there, he said, looking out the window.

She went to the wall, where a shelf of jars and bottles caught the light. Her gnarled hand hovered, went back and forth between two bottles.

What color was the horse that did it to you?

Black, he said, and she nodded and picked up the bottle on the left.

You mean the damn thing's color makes a difference what you give me?

Course not, she said, her face unchanging. Just wondering.

Billy laughed. Well I'll tell you what, she belonged to a real high-class fellow down there. Name of Hatcher. We saw his automobile up here a while back. Maybe you know him.

He my best customer, she said, without missing a beat.

Billy laughed again. He liked this woman. She had a sense of humor. It was good to be out of the empty shack. Charles had been gone two days on a mule-buying trip. All this talk of houses and land hit Billy with a lonesome, desperate feeling, especially when Charles was out on the road. He couldn't imagine the kid would really do it. He certainly wasn't being too smart with his money. Last week Bonnyman had given him a raise and what had he done but spend two dollars on a stack of stereoscope cards and a stereoscope and given it all to Gus Kuntz. Then bought a cheap portrait of George Washington, and one of Teddy Roosevelt, and hung them up side by side on the wall.

She filled a small bottle halfway with the contents of the one from the shelf. Instructed him on how and when to take it.

That'll be fifty cents, she said, uncurling her small hand.

Fifty cents?

Don't try to bargain with me, she said. I don't bargain. Prices are high on everything, these days. And besides. My son's about to put me out of the laundry business. You know that Citizens' Club down there? she said proudly. That's him. He does real good, my boy. Smart boy.

Billy thought of the punning signs in the window. WE WILL DYE FOR YOU.

Well I see where he gets it from, he said.

When he left she followed him out. She went to the mule and rubbed him along his back and picked a bit of grass out of his mane.

Old Rattler here, he getting soft. Used to be it was his job, going down to town to collect the laundry. Your own son running you out of business. She clucked her tongue. Best a woman can hope for, I reckon.

You want me to take him off your hands? Billy was looking him over and couldn't find a fault. Mules are high. Highest they've ever been.

She kept rubbing. The mule sighed.

He'll be a hero, Billy added.

I had me a mule before him. Name was Robespierre. Worst mule ever walked this earth.

What kind of a name is that?

He come to me with that name. We was working a share back then. My husband was still alive. That mule, he was a smart mule! A bad mule too. If you was plowing and didn't give him a rest every hour, why he'd just start stepping on the plants. Just start throwing his hooves trampling them until you gave him a rest.

Rattler stuck his nose out to Billy, nostrils working, checking him over. Ernestine put her hand on his big dark shoulder.

Rattler here, he's a good mule. But Robespierre, he was a smart mule. He got what he wanted, whatever he had to do to get it.

She gave the mule a hard scratch behind the ears.

Well no more laundry anymore, right, Rattler? Maybe it's better he's retiring. White folk never liked seeing him in town. They thought he was too good a mule for an old colored woman. My son, he just built a new house. I told him, you better leave it unpainted, boy, or the white folk gonna think you're getting above yourself. I had eight children and he's the only one alive today. My littlest boy got killed by lightning hiding under a tree from a storm.

I've worked all my life. I done everything from take in laundry to work shares to read fortunes and I reckon I will always get by.

Someone was coming up through the side gate, a young colored girl with a crying baby on her hip and two children behind. Aunt Ernestine left him to meet them.

Now you come back for more of that medicine when you run out, she called to him. You come right on back. Now you know where I am.

FALSE SPRING

On the thirty-first of January, a glanders scare hit Kuntz's. Panic. Pandemonium in the lot. Men were cussing at one another, jostling horses and mules out of the barn and pens fast as they could move them.

Glanders. The dread disease. Billy had seen it before and never wanted to again. It meant certain and agonizing death, eating a horse from the inside out until he was nothing but a pile of sores, an ulcerated skeleton racked with pain. And it started like nothing, only a peculiar, clammy, bird-limy drip of snot from the animal's left nostril. Not only was it deadly but it spread like wildfire. Just the word itself was ugly. The name of a wanton woman who'd steal all your money and give you the clap for boot.

It turned out to be a false alarm. The sick horse was put in quarantine, and after two days the veterinarian declared it was nothing but a cold. Kuntz had the whole premises cleaned and disinfected anyway. He personally supervised the removal of every scrap of sawdust, every cobweb. All the hay was hauled away, new hay trucked in. The floors were stripped and limed and every wood surface painted with turpentine. Shorty was made to crawl along the rafters and scrub each joist.

Kuntz ran an ad in the newspaper, announcing the precautions he had taken. But when the sale opened up on Saturday it was sparsely attended. Those there were still telling glanders stories. Someone had heard of a lion in a zoo that had been fed the meat of a glandered horse and was dead by morning. Someone else had a friend who had a dog that had licked blood from the carcass of a glandered horse before it could be incinerated. Dead within the hour. Stories of empty barns where the disease had lingered for a year until a new string of horses was brought in and infected nearly immediately.

Men were jumpy for another reason too. The Germans had declared their intention to sink American ships, anywhere and everywhere they found them. Any day now, people were saying, we would get into it. Washington had no choice now.

In the aisle at Kuntz's one farmer boasted that he had buried all his money in a safe behind his barn.

My grandpa did the same thing when the Yankees came through, he said, standing in the middle of a knot of men. Only after the war he never could remember where he put it.

Laughter. Nervous, loud.

Maybe I ought to go up to Freedman's Hill, the man said. Go to that old woman who speaks to the dead. Ask her to call up heaven, ask him if he knows where it is.

Ah, that woman's nothing but a hoax! someone said.

Oh no she ain't, said someone else. She's bona fide.

The weather was warm that day, a false spring. Flies had hatched, along with little clouds of midges. The smell of mud and thawing earth and the unfamiliar feel of warm sun on your shoulders. Yet the pall of the glanders scare gave the warm weather an air of pestilence. The bidding was slow. It was all over by dusk. The place cleared out quickly. The Johnson twins hadn't even come down.

Billy and Charles bought only one mule, dark with a half-moon of white on his face. Billy walked outside while Charles went into the office. The change in the weather had brought on the ache in his ribs and all down his left side. He sat down on a stack of boards. Whatever it was Aunt Ernestine had given him, it was the only thing that worked on the pain. But he had run out of the medicine the day Charles went up to town and opened himself a bank account. The kid was talking about renting an apartment now. Getting out of the shack until he could build his own place.

Twitch, coming by with a load of hay, stopped in front of him.

You alright, Monday?

Sure.

Looked for a minute like you might be coming down with it yourself. Glanders.

Twitch spat and blew out a glob of snot. Shit. Kuntz had me in here picking up bits of straw with a tweezer. Don't know how much longer I'm gonna last here. McLaughlin's been showing me that catalog he's got. Them kit houses. Says there ain't no reason why any man can't do it. I reminded him that his paycheck's three times as big as mine. He said, it's a free country! A man works hard, he can have anything he wants.

As Twitch spoke Billy could hear Charles saying it, truly believing it, and he knew that he had no right to try to talk him out of any of it.

Twitch, he said, shaking his head. Sometimes I feel like the last free man in the entire U. S. of A.

He stood up. In the lot a stranger was circling Gin.

Billy hadn't moved so quick in a long time.

What the hell are you doing, buddy?

What'll you take for her?

She ain't for sale.

I'll give you two hundred dollars.

Mister, her left hind foot's worth more'n two hundred dollars.

Two seventy-five.

Billy let out a breath. Well shoo. You don't mess around.

Two eighty-five. She looks just like one my wife lost last year.

Nossir. This horse ain't for sale.

The man recircled her.

She's got a thick ankle back there.

Like hell she's got a thick ankle. That's no thick ankle.

Three hundred.

The man kept going up and Billy kept shaking his head. Finally he got to three twenty-five. Precisely the number Charles was walking around chanting. Billy told him to take his money and go to hell, and he gave up, spat once, and walked off.

Billy put his arm on Gin's mane.

He put his forehead on his arm.

He put his face against her warm neck and closed his eyes for a minute.

Because, Jesus, Joseph, and Mary, three hundred twenty-five dollars was a hell of a lot of money.

FREE

On Sunday, February 4, there were two items of note in the news-paper. The German ambassador had packed up and left Washington for good. And the Hatchers had returned to Richfield.

In Charles's mind, these were both pieces of good news. War, so many men were now saying, was necessary if the stalemate was ever to be broken. Bonnyman said that this business of sinking American ships would surely be the thing that tipped President Wilson's hand. The ambassador's departure seemed to prove him right.

Get ready, he had told Charles. If we get in it, you're going to need to work twice as hard as you do now.

Charles was ready. For anything. He had pinned up above his bed a line he clipped from an old Money Matters column.

IN THE WORDS OF ANDREW CARNEGIE, FRIENDS: NOTHING
CAN KEEP SUCCESS FROM THE MAN PREPARED FOR IT.

He had opened a bank account, and already had almost enough money in it to afford the Raymond. Lately he had been going out to the Tisdale addition and just sitting, watching the work being done to divide the field into lots. To him it was a beautiful place, peace-ful even when it was full of shouting men and trucks and mules pulling graders. He loved the possibility it held, and he loved the vision of all the houses, the streets, children playing, men coming and going to work. Happy, safe, industrious lives. He could see it all so clearly, even though now it was nothing but an old torn-up cow field full of tire ruts.

All through the cold bitter days of January, out in the wagon hunting mules, he had thought about Kuntz and Pendergrass. Both men were driven by a great optimistic energy. But while Pendergrass's vision of the future was of an America that was an island unto itself, Kuntz's utopia stretched all the way around the globe.

Charles now believed Kuntz was right. That America not only should get into the war but needed to. Same as he had to get that bank account, and now a piece of land and a house built. The only road to the bright future was through responsibility and hard work and, yes, sacrifice. As it said in the needlepoint by Kuntz's wife's bed, it was time to put aside childish things.

As soon as he put down the paper he went up to Everbright and left a note in the wall. The next evening they found each other behind the icehouse, together after two months. She wore a heavy fur coat, and it gave him a new thrill, as if he was kissing some sort of wild animal.

You look different, she said, finally pulling back to study him.

I should, he said happily. I'm a new man.

He helped her up onto the fence and she took off her coat and draped it over both of them, and they sat close, sharing a cigarette. She told him the same things as what her few letters had all said, that the winter had been terrible.

Cows and mud, she said, shaking her head. Nothing but cows and mud. I thought I was going to go out of my mind. I have never been happier to pull in at the Richfield train depot.

Charles searched the side of her face, looking for the freckle he had discovered the last time they were together. Couldn't find it.

And your father?

She took a drag, let out smoke. You want to know something, Charles? I realized something. He never suspected me. He hardly even knows I'm alive. Why, these days he's so lost up here—she tapped her temple. Something's going on. I heard him talking one night to my uncle about heaven and hell. Other realms. He's never been a churchman, my father. Oh, he goes, every Sunday, but he just shows up and sits there. But I think I've figured it out. I think—she lowered her voice to a whisper—I think he might be seeing a spirit medium.

What?

I think he's trying to communicate with my mother.

Charles thought of the woman on Freedman's Hill who sold Billy the medicine. Billy said that she had joked that Leland Hatcher was her best customer.

That don't make sense, he said. A man like your father.

You never know with my father. Catherine took a long drag. Her body was tense. He presents one face to the world. But what's going on behind it—it's a complete mystery.

You think—you think people really can speak to the dead?

Not if my father's gone in for it. It has to be a hoax. She let out a stream of smoke and studied the tip of the cigarette. You know how I know? Because if there really was a line to heaven, my mother would refuse to speak to him. If I was dead, I'd refuse to speak to him too.

She shivered and pulled closer to him, grinding out the cigarette. He could not resist her magnetic heat and kissed her. It was better to kiss than to sit there talking about her father, anyway. For a while they were quiet, close beneath the heavy fur, breathing the cold air together. They watched a fox sneak across the grassy lot. She asked about the mules and he told her about his travels, the men who so willingly gave up their animals for the cause. She nodded soberly. Her brother was at the Front now, she said, and the war, which had felt so far away, suddenly felt so close.

Can I ask you something? he said. That day we met. In your garden. You told me the Statue of Liberty was a farce. You said it should have been blown into the ocean. Don't you love America?

I do, she said, matter-of-factly.

Good. My mother always said it is the greatest country in the history of the world.

Catherine pulled the fur coat closer around her shoulder. This knocked her hip against his. He felt another shiver of desire.

But I still think that statue's a farce, she said. Liberty. My mother didn't have it. I don't. No woman does. Not the colored folks. They don't have it either. I love this country for what it might be. Not what it is. And there's nothing wrong with that, is there? Loving something's potential? I see it through a clouded glass, I suppose. But you can't say that to anyone in this town. They'd call it treason.

He kissed her again, in spite of the cold knot already bound up in his gut. The kisses could be torture. He wanted her so badly. It occurred to him that he could simply say that to her. Just say that unspeakable thing. This thought made him burn with shame. No. He had already nearly ruined it once. And she wasn't that kind of girl, and he wasn't that kind of man anymore. He pulled away, ducking out from under the coat.

If it was true, about her father. That he did not and had never suspected them. Charles thought this ought to mean that they were free. That he might even come up and knock on the Everbright door, sit with her in the parlor like a proper courting. He was that kind of man, now. Wasn't he? No more sneaking around.

When they parted he held her a minute, bursting to tell her about the Raymond and about the land in the Tisdale addition. But no. Not yet. There would be time for that. A time for war and a time for peace, men were saying these days. A time to reap and a time to sow. Or, as it said it the window of the Citizens' Club around the corner, A TIME TO RIP AND A TIME TO SEW.

BONE DRY

On March 1 the Woman's Christian Temperance Union threw a party. They were celebrating the new stricter prohibition law that, after eight years of temperance had left Tennessee wet as ever, now promised to make it not just dry, but bone dry.

I'll be at the party, Charles had written on the note he stuffed in the hole in the Everbright wall. I got good news.

He had been gone, out buying mules, and had not seen her in weeks. Lately things were happening at such a speed his heart was always going like a flywheel. He had the plat for the Tisdale addition land auction. Just as with the Aladdin catalog, he had opened it and studied it so many times its creases were white and soft. He had circled the best lots. The sale was on Friday, only three days away.

At the auction that Saturday, Bonnyman had come up to meet him, and given him another raise. Any day now, he said. We'll be in the fight. Get ready.

That evening he had filled out the order form at the back of the Aladdin Homes catalog. Sent off for the Raymond. It was easy as that. Just sat down on the shack steps after feeding the mules and checked a box marked COD.

Afterwards he had walked up to Jack Dillehay's house. He was on the roof, hammering shingles. Charles walked around the house and admired it. Said, with a lift in his voice, that he would soon be building one of his own.

Jack Dillehay nodded. I love this place, he said, sweeping his hammer to encompass the tobacco fields behind him. I love every tree. I love every bird in these trees. There's been a mockingbird singing in that tree since I was knee high. I swear it's the same bird now. I swear he'll live to be a hundred. When I die I want them to bury me right there so I can keep listening to that damn mockingbird.

He went back to pounding shingles. Charles shaded his eyes and looked into the setting sun. The world was getting greener by the day. All around him he felt the energy of spring, the birds getting busy making their nests, the first buds popping on the trees. Buying a house was the easiest thing he had ever done. Just checked that box marked COD. Put it in an envelope. Put a stamp in the corner. He looked up at Jack Dillehay against the blue sky. What a feeling it must be, to love a place like that. Someday he would feel the same way.

Well remember what a man needs, above all, Jack.

What's that? He looked over the edge, nails between his lips.

Charles grinned up at him. Above all he needs a roof.

The party was in the auditorium on the second floor of town hall, which was hung with crepe paper streamers and the femur bones of cows with BONE DRY written on them. A banner over the stage read NEXT THE NATION. Above it, a carved wooden eagle glared. At a long table ladies stood behind crystal bowls of cherry smash punch. Charles got in line for a glass. A man he had bought a mule from a few weeks before came over to talk. He wanted to know if his mule was in the fight yet.

Charles grinned. He's on the path to glory, sir, sure enough. Mules are gonna win the war.

In front of another table boys and girls were lined up to sign a pledge against liquor, tobacco, and caffeine. Two girls chanted together, The lips that touch liquor shall never touch mine. One boy reached into his mouth and hooked out a wad of tobacco and threw it on the floor just before he picked up the pen to sign.

Where you planning on putting this Raymond? Billy had said when Charles told him what he had done.

I'm gonna buy a little lot.

He should have known he had set himself up.

Well which is it, Charlie boy? A little, or a lot?

With his glass of punch he went looking for her in the crowd. His heart was whirring. Around him all the talk was of the intercepted secret telegram that had just been published. The Zimmermann telegram. It was outrageous, this telegram, everyone agreed. An invitation from Germany to Mexico to wage war together on the United States. Fight together, make peace together. Win back for Mexico the lost lands of Texas, New Mexico, and Arizona.

Preposterous! an old woman said.

Surely this will shake Wilson to action, a man said. First they attack our ships. Now they tell Mexico they'll take back Texas and Arizona? Insanity!

You know who wants us to fight? said another. J. P. Morgan wants us to fight, and all his fat-cat friends on Wall Street. They got millions sunk into it already and they can't stand to lose on their investment. Well I ain't fighting for them.

I heard there are U-boats off of Long Island.

That don't worry me. Long Island's a damn sight far from here.

They told Mexico they'd help em win back Texas and Arizona!

Mexico can have em, if you ask me.

I hear old Kaiser Bill is shut up in a concrete bunker. They lower down his food and drink through a two-foot-wide hole.

You'd have to lower down more than food and drink if it was me in there.

Ah, German women are too fat. They'd stop you up in there like a cork in a bunghole.

Well as long as they got the right end in, I wouldn't mind.

Which end is that?

Ah, I ain't gotta tell you. Take what you want from her whenever you want and not have to listen to her yammer all day.

Where was Catherine? A flash of doubt struck Charles. The last time he saw her she had told him the second anniversary of her mother's death was approaching. Then disappeared behind a curtain of melancholy that he could not shift, hard as he tried. She was still such a mystery to him. Sometimes he felt he hardly even knew her.

He went back and got more punch and drank it in one toss. Red and sweet and not much else. He walked over to the stage and looked up, studying the eagle. He wondered if anything would be different, with the new liquor law. One thing was sure. The Johnson twins would hike their prices.

A man was saying his name. The manager from a delivery company they had bought a bunch of mules from back in November. The kind of man who stood too close. Awful breath.

Well who let the mule man in? he crowed disdainfully.

Charles stammered a moment, caught off guard, until the man put a hand on his shoulder.

A joke! he said, in a burst of bad air. Come with me. There's someone I want you to meet.

He steered Charles to a group of men standing around a table in the corner. High class. George Tisdale and John Rich. On the far side of them was Leland Hatcher. He had one of the femur bones resting on his shoulder, like a club. In his other hand was a glass of cherry smash. Charles felt his knees go a little soft.

This is the fellow I was telling you about, the manager said, presenting Charles to Hatcher like a prize. The one who works for the British Army.

Leland Hatcher smiled at Charles, the smile that looked as if it was pulled on a string. Charles had forgotten how short he was. He looked down at him, struck dumb a moment. Coming face-to-face with him after all these months was disorienting.

Have we met? Hatcher said pleasantly.

Charles said the one thing that came into his head.

I bought your horse, sir.

Oh yes. Hatcher cleared his throat. A tiny sound. He shot a glance at the manager, who was standing there smiling. Whatever happened to that horse?

Did the only responsible thing, Charles said. Took her up to the killing floor.

Hatcher looked again at the other man. Well. As I recall. She was a bit hard to handle. He cleared his throat, knocked the femur bone twice against his shoulder. Now tell me. What is it you do for the British Army, exactly?

Charles began to tell him, and Hatcher listened intently for a minute, nodding, growing obviously impressed, then stopped him midsentence so that he could introduce him to Tisdale and Rich. Charles was in his hands now, he could see that. Nothing to do but submit to it.

Finally, Hatcher was saying, here we have a young man of decisive action in Richfield.

Charles swallowed and shook their hands. He thought of Twitch saying, You're in with the big bugs now, when he had his lunch with Kuntz and Bonnyman. If Twitch could see him now.

Tisdale was big and barrel-chested, with a jaw like a gate. He asked him about the mules, about what happened to them when they got to France.

Charles did his best to imitate Bonnyman's somber all-business tone.

Everything from pack machine guns to haul kitchen wagons.

We got to send em over constantly, he said. See mules don't keep. They ain't—they're not hams.

The men laughed. Hatcher was knocking the femur bone gently against his shoulder, smiling at Charles.

What was I just saying, George? We need more young men like this one, don't we?

Well, Tisdale said, I agree with you there, Leland. We should have gotten into it two years ago, after the *Lusitania*. They come along and torpedo a passenger ship full of Americans and we give them a slap on the wrist.

We can't get into it, Rich said. His voice was weak, and he had the whitest, finest hair Charles had ever seen on a man. We've got five hundred thousand German nationals living in this country. Imagine the power they would have if they united.

Well if they do, Hatcher said, we got five hundred thousand lampposts we can hang them from.

Silence, after this.

If old schoolmaster Wilson doesn't quit this nonsense, Hatcher finally said, I'm going to go up there and pick up his telephone and make the damn call myself.

Tisdale told a story about how the day before he had encountered a young mother he knew on Court Square. Her two young boys were licking ice cream cones by the fountain and she was sitting on a bench, crying.

Tisdale put his hand on his cheek and tossed his head, imitating the young woman.

'I can't stand to see them eating ice cream,' she told me. 'Can't stand it, knowing that at this very moment in Armenia little children are starving to death, worse than starving, being herded together and shot, children just like my own boys.' And mark my words, with tears streaming down her face she stood up and snatched those ice cream cones right out of their little hands.

Rich shook his head. Women, he said.

Hatcher had put his glass on the table and was beckoning to

someone. Charles looked and felt his heart jump. It was Catherine. She was wearing a blue-black dress that shimmered. Pearls at her neck and in her ears. She looked beautiful.

He drew his shoulder blades together.

Someone here I'd like you to meet, Hatcher said to her. This fellow works for the British Army.

She smiled at him. Her eyes were red.

This is my daughter, Catherine, Hatcher said.

Charles held out his hand. Hello, Miss Hatcher. Pleased to meet you.

Hatcher asked him where he was from, and he stammered and said Bristol.

Oh, have I got a story about Bristol, Tisdale said, eyes big. He stole a look at Catherine. But it's not for mixed company. You kin to the Kings?

Nossir.

Tisdale raised one bushy eyebrow. Where'd you go to school up there?

Charles mumbled something. He suddenly wanted to run, or sock the man in his big gate jaw. Then Hatcher stepped forward.

For God's sake, George. Don't grill the boy.

Charles stole a look at Catherine. She was standing next to her father, her dress shining like beetle wings. She seemed miles away. He slipped his hand into his pocket and felt for the auction plat. He needed to be alone with her. If only all these men would disappear.

Tisdale emptied his glass of cherry smash. Now what is it they say about mules, Mister McLaughlin?

Well they say a lot of things, Charles said, to laughter from the men. He thought of the framed article on Pendergrass's wall. But some like to say, 'No hope of progeny, no pride of posterity.'

Tisdale nodded, pleased. 'He hath neither child nor brother: yet there is no end of all his labor.' Ecclesiastes, chapter four, verse eight.

Lonesome life, Rich said, for the humble beast.

Well what I wanted to point out, Tisdale said, thrusting his empty glass at Hatcher, is that the lowly mule can always do what the Hatchet here did. Just buy himself a family tree.

His tone was harsh, nearly cruel. Charles looked back at Catherine. She was looking at the ground.

Hatcher ignored Tisdale. He lifted the femur bone and with it made an arc that encompassed the room.

Bone dry! he boomed. Look around, Mister McLaughlin. Remember this day. A fine day for Tennessee. Next, the nation. Think of it! The Negro will be saved from himself. Your children will grow up in a country free of the evils of vice. Crime. Adultery. They will grow to be the finest instruments of God the world has ever seen.

That is, said Rich, swallowing the last of his punch and smiling wryly, if they're not speaking German.

Hatcher spun to face him. His eyes were suddenly wild.

It is talk like that that keeps us down! Talk like that that works against us! Talk like that will destroy us!

He lifted the cow bone above his head and swung it down on the table. Half a dozen cups of cherry smash went flying. Red arcing everywhere. Charles saw a spray of it hit Catherine's face at the same moment he felt it hit his neck, then the cold sticky drip into his collar. The glasses hit the floor and shattered.

Around them people looked over. The manager scurried off, muttering something about finding a girl to clean it all up. Tisdale had his handkerchief out, mopping his brow. Rich took out his and dabbed at his shirtfront. As if it had been a small spill, a little accident.

Hatcher took a step back, broken glass crunching beneath his shoes. He was still holding the bone, glaring at Tisdale and Rich. His mouth opened as if he was about to say something. Then he dropped the bone and strode to the door at the back of the room.

Tisdale frowned at his handkerchief and looked at Catherine.

I forgot, he said briskly. This must be a difficult night for your father.

He stepped over and handed her a clean handkerchief. She took it, not looking at him. Her eyes brimmed with tears. Lifting her gaze to Charles for the briefest moment, she said, Excuse me. I'm going outside to get some air.

He followed as quickly as he could. Going down the stairs two at a time, his boots echoing in the stairwell.

He found her in the shelter of the building, buckling the belt of a green coat. Beneath it her skirt blew in the gusty wind.

Well now you've seen for yourself, she said, pressing her fingertips to the corners of her eyes. This is what I've been talking about. It's impossible to know what's going on behind that smile of his. When I go home tonight, we'll pretend that never happened. We'll never speak of it again. Oh! Her lip trembled. I don't want to go home at all.

He rolled a cigarette and lit it and handed it to her. Rolled one for himself. He took a long drag.

She held hers, studying the tip. There was a slight red stain on her cheek from the spilled punch.

These are mad times, she said, shaking her head. Sometimes it feels like a bad dream. Germany and Mexico want to attack us and take back Texas. Doesn't that sound just like a bad dream?

What was that Tisdale meant, about your father buying a family tree?

Catherine took a drag and sighed, letting out a stream of smoke. The pearls on her ears quivered. The portraits, she said, in the Everbright dining room. He bought them with the house. The family he bought that place from, the aftermath of the war ruined them. When my father bought the house he bought almost everything in it. I think he's got himself half convinced they really are our ancestors. Oh, he's a liar! I cannot stand to even be in the same room as him tonight—

She pressed her fingers to her eyes again.

Oh. I'm a wreck. I feel I might go to pieces any minute.

She looked at him, drawing her hands away.

What's your good news? I could use some. Did you miss me when you were gone away?

A shiver of remorse caught him by surprise, remembering the girl up in the Barrens, all these months ago. He shook it off and tried to tease her.

When you were away this winter sometimes I got to thinking you'd run off and married a West Tennessee boy.

I'm not marrying anybody, she said sharply. Ever.

Not marrying anybody? That's crazy. He looked at her. She was biting her lip. Oh. I get it. You're pulling my leg.

I'm serious.

All girls ought to get married, he said simply. Especially one as pretty as you.

She glared at him. He put his cigarette in his mouth.

Well I guess that was the wrong thing to say, he said, miserable.

I'm sorry, she said. Tonight's the night— Her voice broke up.

It dawned on Charles then.

Your mother.

She nodded, her mouth tight. It was tonight. Two years ago to-night.

He felt that he should do something, but he did not move any closer. He licked his lips. His mouth was coated with the sickly sweet remains of the cherry smash. He looked at the glowing tip of his cigarette. He had his whole speech lined up, about the house and the land. He had the whole thing lined up, but nothing was going like he had expected.

I'm real sorry, Cat, he said.

How did your mother die, Charles?

He ran his hand through his hair. Just the question filled him with shame. The truth was something he could never tell Catherine, not ever, that his mother died in a whorehouse.

She got sick, he said. He fumbled with the cigarette and dropped it and picked it up. My father, if he hadn't been killed, things would have been a lot different.

There's something I don't understand, Catherine said, turning to him. If your father was such a big man, why have you never tried to find his family? Why, you don't even know his name. You know nothing about him. It's all such a big mystery.

She said this gently enough, but the words stung like a whip. Just as when Tisdale had grilled him at the party. His blood surged. His hand curled into a fist.

My mother was dealt a real bad hand, he said roughly. Someone like you can't ever understand it.

Catherine flinched, and he immediately wanted to take it back. She let out a heavy breath. Well I'll tell you how my mother died, she said. My father killed her.

He looked up at the storefronts across from them, the clothes on mannequins in the window of the department store, eerie headless human shapes. Then up at the hooked claw of the moon over the buildings. He thought about Hatcher's eyes when he brought the bone down on the table. And about what Billy always said about the black mare, that she had suffered at the hands of a man capable of the vilest acts. A murderer? No. That was crazy. Crazy as Mexico taking back Texas.

No, he said.

A gust of wind at once warm and cold swept the litter of East Main Street. The indecision of March. Catherine pulled her collar tighter. She had red knuckles. Her eyes were fixed on a puddle a few feet in front of them.

He did. She would still be alive if it wasn't for him. She drove her car off the bridge that night on purpose. It was no accident. He gave her no choice. No other way out.

She shook her head slowly, still staring at the ground. I know what happened. I heard them argue. He got a girl in trouble and my mother found out and wanted a divorce and he said no. 'What would that look like to people around here,' he said. 'What would that do to me?' They argued. Night after night. And then one night she got in her car and drove out to the Pike and drove it off that bridge. She knew there was no other way out.

Catherine flung her cigarette into the puddle. It sizzled, then went out.

She came into my room before she left that night. I pretended to be asleep. I could hear her breathing. She wasn't crying anymore. She had made her decision by then, I see now. When I heard her car pull out I knew what she was going to do. I just knew.

Catherine, Charles said, gentle as he could.

Most women, they would just live with it, what my father did. As a matter of course. Just smile and keep up appearances. Missus Tisdale would. Missus Rich would. But not my mother. My mother was different.

Charles looked back to the mannequins in the store window. He shook his head. The night felt suddenly so dark and hard.

Your brother—does he know?

Catherine pressed her hands to her eyes, then drew them away. Nodded.

He was down at school. But he had been home for Christmas—we did not go to West Tennessee that year. He had been home and he had seen my father with her—Catherine broke a little—with the girl, with the colored girl.

A colored girl, she said again, almost a whisper. She worked for us.

Charles stood very stiff and very still. He thought about the day they had seen the Pierce-Arrow on Freedman's Hill, and he wondered if that was the explanation, not that Hatcher was going to see some old fortune-teller, but that he still had a girl up there. And he thought of his mother, the straits she faced raising him alone, and could not help feeling sorry for the girl, whoever she was.

The girl, he said slowly. What happened to her?

Oh, who cares? Catherine said sharply. She's gone. Edmund said she left town. I wish she had never been born. At Mother's funeral we all stood there. I must have heard him say it a hundred times. 'What a shocking accident.' He said it to every single person who came down the receiving line and there wasn't a soul in town who didn't come. I think by the end of it he had convinced himself. So terrified of what people would say about a divorce. Well what would they say about a suicide?

She pressed her hands to her face again. When she took them away he expected her to be crying. But she wasn't. Her eyes were fierce.

Those men up there, I've heard them say it: 'Put your wife on a pedestal, and a colored girl in your bed.' She laughed a harsh laugh. Those men he's trying so hard to impress. Those men don't listen to anyone, don't hear anything but the sounds of their own voices. Well he killed her, I'd like to tell them, if they'd listen. To hell with them! To hell with all of them.

The world is full of cheats and shams, Catherine. It's too bad but it's the truth.

She began to sob. The pearls in her ears shook back and forth.

I'll tell you something. I'm never getting married, she said. The whole institution is bogus. There isn't a man in this world I would marry.

Charles did not know what to do. She looked awful, standing there crying, such terrible things coming out of her mouth. He wanted to take it all away from her, the sadness, lift it off of her like a shawl. He knew he had to act. He had to do something, or say something.

Suddenly he had a vision of the black mare. Beautiful, ruined. Catherine had told him not to buy her and he had not listened. Billy had told him to give up on her but he hadn't wanted to hear it, and so Billy had kept working her, against his judgment, just for him, and nearly been killed. So wasn't he just as guilty as those men who did not listen, who did not hear anything but the sounds of their own voices? The thought made him want to run. Just run.

He turned to her and gathered his breath in his chest.

There's good men in the world too, you know, he said.

But those were just words and they felt empty as soon as they left his mouth. He wanted to prove it to her. All he had wanted to do since he met her was prove it to her. She was still crying, standing so far away, out of arm's reach. He realized he had his hand on the plat in his pocket. He pulled it out. His speech was still in the front of his mind, the one he had been rehearsing all day.

I'm buying some land, he said quickly, unfolding the plat. Gonna build a house. Best investment on earth.

He wrestled with it in the wind. See there—these lots are the prime lots—

She wiped her eyes and looked at it, wrinkling her brow in confusion. Oh. Charles. Why are you showing me this?

I'd marry you tonight, you know, he said. He took her hand. She pulled it away.

Don't be foolish!

Her face was so ugly. Red and swollen and shiny with the tears, like scar tissue. He felt his mouth twist with shame.

Ain't I good enough for you?

Charles!

He got down on one knee. So hard he felt a little burst in his kneecap when it hit the ground.

If I had the money I would do it, you know. I would get down like this and I would ask you to marry me.

He couldn't look at her face anymore. He stared at her feet, hanging on to her hand. She wasn't saying anything. A group leaving the party catcalled from across the street, shouting something lewd. He squeezed her hand tighter.

Charles! she hissed. Stop it.

So I ain't good enough. That's it. You don't think I'm good enough for you.

Get up, she pleaded. Please.

She wrenched her hand out of his. Broke free of him and ran around the corner of the building and left him there on one knee, with the wet of the March ground soaking through his pants to his skin.

WOMEN GET THE RAW DEAL

Bristol

Women get the raw deal, Maura tells Billy. There's only one way for them to make it rich. And that is to find a man with a lot of money, or a lot of men with a little money, and shake it out of em. The only power a girl can hope for in this country.

She takes out her scrapbook of actresses, opens it up for him. Points to one of the photographs.

Do you see it now? What they all have?

Tell me, he says.

Look at their eyes. Not just beautiful. Smart. They have figured out what a man wants. Just like I did, when I used to do that monkey trick at the Nichols House.

He thinks of the men's eyes in the parlor, trained on her. The nasty thoughts behind them.

On his knee his hand becomes a fist, then a claw.

Well what is it? What does every man want?

She closes the book with a snap.

It's simple, she says. Every man wants what he wants. The thing to do is figure out how to give it to him.

Billy knocks his knee with his clenched hand, as if he can knock away the memory of the men's eyes in the parlor.

Well it don't strike me as a way to make an honest living, he says. You might as well be a whore.

Her eyes flash. Don't you ever say that. I will never be a whore. I would die before I would be a whore.

SOLD

Two days later Charles went to the land auction.

It was a frigid gray day. No shadows, no hint of warmth. After a hard rain winter had returned. The blossoms on the trees hung on for dear life.

Out in the field, folding chairs were lined up neatly in the dead grass and a table of barbeque sat under a tent. The sweet cooked-flesh smell made Charles's stomach turn. He could hear the faint prickling sound of the rain settling into the earth. The chairs were nearly full, mostly women, balancing plates on their knees.

He picked up a cardboard paddle and found a seat at the back. The auctioneer started the sale. One plot sold, then another, then another. He took out his pencil and the plat and began to makes X's over them as they sold. He could hardly keep up. Soon the plat was a mess of X's. He bid on those that he had circled, but he was outbid every time. After a while it began to feel as if all the other bidders were fighting him. Bidding solely just to keep him down.

He had done it all wrong with her outside the party. He understood that now. The world was full of cheats and shams and he was just as bad as any of them. He glared at the people to his left and right. All these busy women gossiping in their big heavy coats, all these self-satisfied men murmuring to one another. Well to hell with them all, he thought, dropping his paddle, outbid again.

The auctioneer whooped and hollered. A judge's gavel, this fellow used, that he smashed down with every sale, a report like a pistol.

It was an act of violence, what he had done to her, the way he had dropped down on one knee. As violent as the blow Hatcher had dealt the table with that bone. Now it was all he could do to try to beat away the memory with his paddle.

Sold!

Sold!

He won the last lot that came up, the least desirable one, narrow, low, and full of standing water, bidding against a man fast and ferocious, striking the air with his paddle. The gavel fell. Sold.

The woman behind him leaned over to her friend and whispered.

Well that young man overpaid, now, didn't he?

Afterwards he rode the interurban out to the shack. Dropped his head when it passed Everbright. He wanted Billy to see the lot. He wanted him to say it was alright, and not make a joke about it. He just wanted somebody to say it was alright.

They harnessed up Gin and headed back up towards town. The night of the party he had told Billy the story, what Catherine had told him, what he had done. The way Hatcher had smashed the table with the femur.

Poor man, Billy had said.

Poor man! What the hell are you talking about? I could kill that bastard. I swear I would.

I'm just glad I ain't standing in his shoes, is all. Just glad I ain't in the old Hatchet's shiny pair of shoes.

Now, passing the Everbright gates for the second time that day, Charles again looked away.

That day Catherine came down to see you in the shack, he said, looking over at Billy. She said that her father's secrets and lies were to blame for everything. That his reputation was worth more to him than even that dead man's life. She was talking about her mother, wasn't she? Why, it's so ugly and awful. And Hatcher up there strutting around with no remorse. Scot-free.

Billy listening, sucking his tooth. Finally he said, You heard the story about the fellow this town is named for?

What's that got to do with anything?

You mean you haven't heard? Why, the original Mister Rich, he's a murderer. All those years ago, he killed the girl he was supposed to marry, just because he wanted to marry someone else. Told everyone his gun got tangled in her dress. And that was that. But whatever he managed to convince the history books, he had the truth lodged in his heart the rest of his life. Might have grown over thick and hard like a burl grows over a wound in a tree, but it was always there. A man like Hatcher, it's true, he can tell any damn story he wants to. He does something people don't like, well all he's got to do is tell them what they want to hear and they'll believe him. Or hell, just get em talking about something else. Distract em. Buy himself a new automobile and drive it down the road. A man like that can tell any story and people will believe it. But that doesn't mean that in the end he won't have to pay his price.

Billy clucked to Gin. He spoke with his eyes on the road.

A man's got a secret like that, after a while he's got no friend in the world. Only the secret. He's all alone, Charlie boy, and that's the worst place a man can find himself in this world.

Out in the field the chairs were still there, some of them knocked over. Broken tape hung from the stakes. The road cuts looked like raw wounds. Billy stood there. He looked and looked. Charles knew what he was thinking. He was wondering whoever got the crazy notion in his head to go and tear up such a prime piece of pasture.

After a while he took out his pipe and packed it and lit it. Charles stared at the giant puddle in the depression in the center of the lot. Shifted his boots in the soggy ground. A great sinking feeling, as if it might swallow him up.

There was one tree, a hackberry, a trash tree, in the corner by the stake. So young one hard push could have bent the trunk to the ground.

Billy put his hand on it.

Down there's a magnolia, Charles said miserably. I didn't get the one with the magnolia.

Billy gave the hackberry a little shake. This tree will grow.

But Charles hardly heard him. He could not grasp what he had done. They had taken a deposit from him after the sale. Biggest pile of money he had ever shelled out for anything. Then he had signed his name to a hundred sheets of paper.

I ruined it, Billy, he said.

APRIL 6

On March 18 the papers reported that the Germans had sunk two more American ships, the *City of Memphis* and the *Illinois*. A week later Bonnyman sent an urgent telegram. He had lost a load of mules on yet another torpedoed ship. The seas are a battleground, he wrote. We need more mules, and fast.

They went on a buying trip up on the Highland Rim, camping out at night. Charles could hardly sleep. Now that war was inevitable, it seemed impossible. Charles thought of Catherine in the Everbright garden, saying that German spies had blown up Black Tom Island. Just because you say a thing's impossible doesn't mean it is, she had said. He lay on his bedroll and watched the stars in the sky and tried to imagine the nightmare of a zeppelin, the way it would silently appear over the trees, coming slowly but relentlessly, the gray ghost, the big whale's belly of death.

It could not be ruined. No. He would get her back.

When they came back through Richfield something was happening. All the doors of the businesses were propped open. A group of people in the street were singing 'The Star-Spangled Banner,' like the Fourth of July. Only it was not the fourth of July but the sixth of April.

Charles jumped out of the wagon. A man was standing in the doorway of Suddarth's, waving a tiny flag. When Charles asked him what was going on, he quit waving it.

Ain't you heard?

Heard what?

President Wilson finally did it. Dragged his old bones up in front of Congress up there and told em, 'The hell with it, boys. Unleash the sword.'

What?

The fellow grinned. It's good news, buddy. We're going to war.

Part Two

SPRING 1917

In the aisles at Kuntz's the men stood close to one another and spoke in low serious tones.

Well we will wait for what the future holds.

We must. We are making the world safe for democracy.

This means we'll send more guns, more ammo, certainly more money. Not men.

Oh no! Of course not. We won't need to send men. That's one thing they have plenty of, over there. Men.

In May the draft was announced.

To begin there would be a nationwide registration of all men aged twenty-one to thirty. Regardless of their race, creed, or physical health.

Shortly after this announcement, the first service star in Richfield went up in a window. Doc Walker's son, called up from the Mexican border, would go over with the 30th Infantry Division. He was headed to Camp Sevier in just a few weeks.

The paper announced the engagement of Miss Cherry Orchard Tisdale to Mister John Rich IV. There was a rumor going around that married men were going to be exempt from the draft. There had been such a run on the church that there was a term for girls like Cherry: slacker brides.

Kuntz hung an American flag by the door of the office, another over the door of the barn. He added a 3 percent commission to every animal sold and gave it to the Red Cross. A few of the men who worked for him enlisted right away. So did Jack Dillehay, leaving his house unfinished.

Rather decide my own fate, he said, than sit around and wait for it to be decided for me.

In front of the Paradise Theater, instead of girls collecting money for the Society for the Aid of the Fatherless Children of France, there was a little booth set up by the Red Cross. Girls in white nurses' uniforms with red crosses on their hats sold flowers and rattled collection boxes. They were organizing chapters up on Freedman's Hill, teaching the colored women how to roll bandages and how to knit and how to go around collecting money too.

A sign on the wall of the restaurant at the Sumner Hotel read: USE LESS SUGAR, AND STIR LIKE HELL.

Charles put a note in the Everbright wall asking Catherine to meet him behind the icehouse. He went up there and waited, even knowing she would not show.

He had thought for a long time about the letter from Edmund, the one she showed him all those months ago on the staircase of the Paradise: You've got it worse than I do and I'm headed to the Front. Secrets, he could hear her say. I'm so tired of secrets. He knew, now, what she had meant. He knew the weight on her shoulders. How was it that he could now know so much more about her, yet understand so much less?

Stores were sold out of American flags. Women traded recipes for cooking wheatless, meatless, and sugarless. A dozen new clubs were formed every week. Mothers of Enlisted Boys. The Calvin

Avenue Society of Knitters. Everywhere you went, women knitting socks for soldiers.

A gang of college boys stole a dachshund dog and staged a trial on Court Square. The boys found it guilty, as charged, of treason and were about to hang it from a tiny gallows when somebody took pity on the creature and intervened.

Now, whenever you went to a movie, a man would come out before the show and give a talk for four minutes on some subject concerning the war. These men—lawyers, bankers, businessmen—were called the Four Minute Men, a division of Washington's new Committee on Public Information, and their local chairman was Leland Hatcher.

Wad Taylor began to publish patriotic poems in the newspaper, with titles like 'My Star-Spangled Heart' and 'Ode to a Soldier's Mother.' People memorized them and recited them in the streets. Every week there were several letters to the editor, requesting more.

Bonnyman came up to the auction one Saturday. The lines around his mouth had deepened. He was sober as a judge.

His standards were lower, now that he was buying for Uncle Sam. The Americans are a hell of a lot less picky than the Brits, he told Charles. Just send em down.

Mules, mules, mules. Charles saw them when he closed his eyes at night. They were the first thing on his mind when he woke up in the morning. Where could he find them and how fast could he get them and how fast could he ship them down to Nashville. The farmers were plowing under tobacco and corn to grow potatoes and hemp for the war. Everyone with a patch of slack land was told to plant a victory garden. Charles went up to his lot and planted a big one. With a mule and a walking plow he tilled a plot on the high side, planted corn and beans and greens and tomatoes.

The Raymond sat under a tarp at the back of the lot, right where the deliverymen had unloaded it, four days after war was declared. He tried not to look at it. He worked without ceasing. As long as he was working, he did not have time to regret it. As long as he was working, he felt like a good man.

As he drove through the fields and up into the hills he thought, Catherine.

He tried to write her a letter. Ripped it up.

Catherine.

The days passed. The earth steadily warmed. In the few fields still set aside for tobacco, the farmers set the tiny tobacco slips in the plowed dark earth, and the cherry blossoms on Court Square bloomed and pinked and fell from the branches, and swirled around in the Tennessee spring breeze, and caught in the girls' hair, and in the backs of wagons, and the windshields of the cars, and piled up in corners like petals on the church steps after a wedding.

Money Matters

by Leland Hatcher
The Richfield Gazette

Note: I received the letter below from my son, Edmund, with the request that it be printed here, for all Richfield. It is an honor to comply with his request.—LH

Dear old friends,

If I could I would tell you where I am at present, but alas, on account of the censors, I must say only that I am "somewhere in France." How I wish instead I was back in old Richfield, Tennessee.

As for my current situation, it can be described as 99 percent mud. And the remainder—mud.

I have been through many trials that I know would be of interest, but it is nearly impossible to relate any of it in a letter. The censors take their jobs seriously. I can say that at [blacked out] I had [blacked out] men die in the back of my car before we could even make it to the hospital. I use that word lightly, as "the hospital" was nothing more than some burlap sacks stretched over the ruins of a church. All day, twenty cars went back and forth to the Front, retrieving the dead and dying. When night fell, for fear of attracting the enemy, we could not use our lights. A man walked along in front of my car, holding a white handkerchief behind his back. I followed this all through the terrible night, and can still see that small white beacon in the dark when I shut my eyes.

But enough of all that. The purpose of this letter, when I sat down to write it, was solely to express to you the enthusiasm and excitement here over the coming arrival of "Les Americains." It is something akin to the happiness of children on Christmas Eve. It sure makes a fellow proud to be an American.

When you all get over here, we will kick the Boche in the teeth and be back home before anyone has time to blink.

Get over here just as quick as you can.

May God bless Richfield, and may God bless America.

Your friend,
Edmund Hatcher

GET IN THE GAME WITH UNCLE SAM

June 5. Registration day.

The predicted rain had held and the day had turned out dry and hot, no cloud in the clean sky. The mayor had declared a holiday so that all the men of draft age could get up to the high school for the registration. Things had gone without a hitch. Better than expected, everyone was saying. Registration was over and done by ten o'clock. Now it was time for the parade.

On his way to East Main, Billy stopped to study the poster in the window of the post office. It showed a gawky Uncle Sam on the pitching mound, winding up, pipestem arms and legs accordioned. The batter at the plate was a young man in uniform, smiling.

GET IN THE GAME WITH UNCLE SAM

A boy in short pants was standing there, looking at the poster while he scratched his armpit with his thumb. He had a wide white face like a halved apple.

Wish I was old enough to go over, the boy said.

Billy acted surprised. You mean you ain't of age?

Nossir.

Surely next year.

The boy scowled. Won't even be eleven till next Tuesday.

Billy winked at him. Well here's to ten years from next Tuesday.

If they're still going at it then, you'll surely be the man to take it over the top.

*   *   *

Charles cut through an alley and came out on Maple Street, right into the middle of the staging area. On the wall behind the marching band a poster of the Statue of Liberty read, DO YOUR PART. A woman was trying to help an old man button the coat of his Confederate uniform. One sleeve was pinned up over the stump of his long-gone arm. The other trembled at one of the brass buttons. The woman kept reaching out, and he kept batting her hand away.

I can manage, Susannah, he growled.

I'm Mary, Father, the woman said patiently, reaching again for the button. Mary. Remember. Susannah's gone.

On East Main, the crowd stood six men deep. Chatter and laughter. Parasols and straw hats. All the young men wore red, white, and blue buttons in their lapels to show they had registered. A boy was handing out cheap cardboard fans. Charles took one.

COMPLIMENTS OF HATCHER BOOT AND SHOE.

Catherine. Finally he had spoken to her, the day of Cherry Orchard Tisdale's wedding. She had been sitting on the back steps of the church, all dressed up for the wedding. He was coming up the alley with a mule. Seeing her, his heart leapt. His blood rose with the familiar heat. He thought she might run, but she did not.

I heard the news, he said cautiously. Cherry and John Rich.

Catherine screwed up her mouth.

She's a turncoat, she said bitterly. A traitor. She didn't even tell Ed. He heard about it from Wad Taylor, then he wrote me a letter. You know what it said? 'I hope to God they're happy. Because I am in hell.'

She put her face in her hands. He tied up the mule and sat down next to her and didn't care who saw them. He just sat there next to her, watching her shoulders shake. Wanting to put his arm around her but not daring.

I'll never forgive her, she said.

I'm real sorry I did what I did the night of the party, Cat. The way I got down on my knee. Wish I'd never done that.

She spread her hands and looked at him. Ed always says I ought not be so hard on people. He says I'm pure Roberson, too proud. You know, what I've been so angry about all this time isn't that you got down on your knee like that. I've been angry with you all this time for saying you weren't good enough for me. That was a terrible thing to say.

I shouldn't have said it, Charles said.

It was a lie and an ugly and terrible thing to say and you should have known better than to say it. She looked him in the eye and took a long breath. Don't ever say that again, alright?

Alright.

Above them the church bells started clanging. She looked up, then back at him.

Did you get your land?

He nodded. And a house too. Only I'm too busy to get it built.

Good, she said, standing. He stood with her. So close. They nearly touched.

I'm glad you got what you wanted. She smiled at him, tenderly. I think you ought to have everything you want, Charles.

The bells kept clanging. She turned to go. He watched her disappear through the back door of the church, because he did not know how to say what he was thinking. That what he wanted was not land or a house or anything else. That all he wanted was her.

Charles slipped the fan into his hatband. Just seeing her name on it made blood rush to his face. He would see her today. He felt certain of it. He must. He and Billy had been invited to sit on the podium during the speeches after the parade. The letter had come from the Richfield draft board. Chair, Leland Hatcher.

Behind him, two girls giggled. A father hoisted a little boy up onto his shoulders.

Here they come!

First were three lines of National Guardsmen, bearing flags and bayonets, marching in step, and at the sight of them Charles, along with every other man along the block, stood up taller and squared his shoulders, removing his hat for the flag. Behind the soldiers came two sloppy lines of schoolboys bearing two hand-painted banners:

IT MAY BE HOT, BUT IT'LL BE HOTTER IN BERLIN!
WATCH YOUR BACK, KIZER BILL

Beside him a woman, fat and well powdered, violently flapped her Hatcher fan and huffed to her companion.

With the dust they're raising, mercy, I won't be able to hang washing out till Wednesday.

The first float rattled down the street: a trailer towed by a Model T, draped in banners, carrying schoolboys dressed as soldiers, all with wooden bayonets. One stood poised, ready to toss a magnolia cone grenade. At the back, on a riser, sat a girl dressed as Winged Victory, in a bedsheet and chicken-feather wings. Her arms, thick pink ham hocks, were wrapped around a boy who was lying across her lap, trying very hard to look dead.

The crowd cheered. A gust of wind lifted the cloth beneath her, revealing a stack of hay bales. Lifted her bedsheet, too, enough to reveal her bare legs for an instant. Charles felt the blood-rush of desire, coughed and shifted his pants.

The high school marching band came through playing 'Are You from Dixie?' The woman who had earlier complained about the dust clapped along, her chest heaving.

Charles felt the drums in the walls of his heart. America! He loved it. Lately he loved it more with every passing day. One day last month he had repeated to Kuntz the story George Tisdale had told at the Bone Dry party, about the mother on Court Square who took away her children's ice cream cones because children in Armenia were staving to death. That's a tragedy! Kuntz had barked. Who is this woman? I'd like to buy those children another ice cream myself! Because if the children of America aren't eating ice cream cones, McLaughlin, then where in God's name can the rest of the world set its sights and aspirations?

Now came the float carrying the Confederate veterans. You could hardly see the men on the float for all the flags: the American flag and the Confederate flag, the Tennessee flag, a mess of regimental flags, a billowing jumble of stars, stripes, and bars, blues, reds, and whites. Every so often one would snap aside in the wind to reveal a waving hand or a weathered, fringe-bearded face before it closed back up like a curtain.

The crowd was going wild. Charles thought he saw the man who had been trying to button his coat back in the alley, but he wasn't sure. Then from behind the flags came a rebel yell, half fox yelp, half grizzly roar. Part mad glory, part pants-pissing fear, and it was him, Charles saw as the flags parted, the man from the alley, his eyes far gone to some battlefield of his youth.

Billy had told him about the draft riots in New York during the Civil War, which he himself had heard about from a man who had lived through them, who claimed that since that day his sense of smell had forever been burned out of his nose.

Police cracking the skulls of Irish men cracking the skulls of colored men, Billy said. Well Uncle Sam sure as hell won't let that happen this time, will he? This time they're throwing us a parade.

The veterans rattled past. Charles put his hat back on. The Hatcher fan fell from the band, and he reached down to pick it up, suddenly in a different world, now at the level of trouser legs and shoes and litter. He fumbled for the fan, caught under someone's heel, and then from above he heard a whistle and a man say in a nasty tone, Well looky there.

Lord have mercy, another said. Did her old man let her out of the house in that?

She couldn't—

But she did. Look at her.

Charles felt a burn in his face and straightened up and pushed to the front of the crowd because there was only one girl they could be talking about. At first all he could see was a group of boys in tricorn hats carrying the French flag and a banner that said, LIBERTÉ—ÉGALITÉ—FRATERNITÉ.

Vive la France! the boys shouted, and the crowd, with a roar, shouted it back. But no one was looking at them, and now Charles got around a tall man who had been blocking his view and saw her.

God. She was spectacular. That was what she was. A spectacle.

Even more than all that bare flesh and chain mail, it was the way she sat the horse. Her thin shoulders thrown back, spine straight as an arrow, the pole of her banner not wavering an inch. Around it her fist was steady, her wrist covered by a metal cuff that went half-way to her elbow. From beneath a glittering helmet her fierce eyes were fixed far ahead on East Main Street. As if she saw beyond it, to shores even farther than Europe's. Beyond the war to a distant promised land.

What in the high holy? Charles said. There it was again, ten times stronger than before, the blood-rush to his core. He shifted, feeling it strain his pants. Ashamed of it. Thrilled by it.

The fellow next to him turned. That, buddy, is Miss Catherine Hatcher.

Well I know that, Charles growled. Under her short metallic skirt her bare thigh flashed in the sun. But what's she got up as?

Joan of Arc, the fellow said. Course. When Charles kept looking at him he raised his eyebrows. Buddy. You mean you don't know who Joan of Arc is?

Sure I do.

The man jogged his eyebrows again, rolled his eyes. Around them the crowd was going nearly as wild as they had for the veterans. The slightest smile turned up the corners of Catherine's mouth.

French bird, buddy. God spoke to her. Whispered in her ear that she oughta fight the British, free her people, save her king. Joan of Arc, she saved France. Then they done burned her at the stake.

Oh yeah. Sure. Charles swallowed around the heat in his throat. The dark horse wore a white leather bridle and a white blanket beneath the saddle. Catherine's hips rocked with his enormous stride. He was a magnificent horse. Where on earth did she get that horse?

But man oh man, the fellow was saying. No French bird ever looked as good as that. Wouldn't you like a feel of that? Now I wasn't there, but I heard at last year's fair—

Charles was already pushing through the crowd, trying to follow her. He could hear bits and pieces of what people were saying. He wanted to shout, She's mine! She's mine! But she wasn't, not anymore, maybe never had been, and he knew it. His heart was already falling, she was past now, the horse's tail swaying, and the crowd was packed too tight. A big stocky fellow with a black mustache stopped him. Got up in his face and growled, Where's your button?

Ain't of age, he croaked, and pushed on. She was gone.

*　　*　　*

Billy stood by the bandstand, watching the streaming sea of people, waiting for Charles. He had missed most of the parade. After talking to the boy he had ducked into the grassy lot of an abandoned house to take a leak, where he discovered another boy, the one with the raccoons. He had heard them first, actually, the mewling howls, tiny shrieks of pain, and had followed the sound to the back of the house, where a colored boy squatted under the half-collapsed back stairs, ripping the guts out of a litter of baby raccoons with a razor blade. Two were already dead, tossed in the dust, their guts in whorls like shiny red streamers. Their tiny black hands curled.

Billy had slowly moved closer to the boy, until he stood just beside him. He thought the kid would run, but he only glared up at him and turned back to the creature in his hands. Billy talked him into taking his pipe and tobacco, all he had on him, in trade for the animals. And the boy had taken these things with eyes that had been betrayed by everyone, everywhere, since always.

Billy carried the two that were still alive all the way back to the creek. When he set them down they spun and bumped blindly before disappearing into the brush. He sat down for a long time, just sitting there, staring at the water, and had gone back up towards the parade only because Charles wanted him there. He was wearing the suit Charles had bought for him and he had shined his shoes like he had asked him to, but now, looking down, he saw they were covered in mud from the creek bank.

Charles appeared out of the crowd. He was clutching one of the .Hatcher fans that were everywhere. He looked like he had seen a ghost.

They climbed up onto the bandstand and were shown to their chairs by a smiling young girl. They were in the second row, behind a line of men whose heads sat in their collars like eggs in cups.

In high cotton now, ain't we, Charlie boy?

Charles frowned at Billy's muddy shoes. Thought I told you to get a shoeshine, he said.

The mayor brought out an old woman. She had set the county record in the number of socks she had knitted to send to soldiers. Leland Hatcher put a button on her and the crowd cheered. They helped her back down the stairs and then she was gone.

How about that Joan of Arc? someone at the back of the crowd shouted. There was a tightening at Hatcher's temple, but that was all. He coolly unfolded a piece of paper and began his introduction.

Billy searched for his pipe, forgetting he had traded it away. Sitting like this was no good for the pain. Nowadays, when he went up to Ernestine's for more medicine, she had a line of boys at the door, all waiting to get their fortunes read, wanting to know their fates.

The mayor spoke first, then the president of the draft board, declaring that the day had been 100 percent a success. Then Leland Hatcher got up. Hatcher Boot and Shoe had just hired ten more employees, he announced. And had just taken a government contract to make hobnail shoes for the Army. During the long applause the mayor got back up. He put his hand on Hatcher's back.

It just goes to show, he said. An inalienable truth about war is that it is good for business. He went on to introduce Representative Denning, who had come up all the way from Nashville. He told a long story about a hunting trip they had been on together. He managed to say an awful lot about himself and nothing about the representative. Billy looked at Charles. He was hanging on every word.

Enough hot air up here to float one of them zeppelins, Billy whispered. Charles ignored him.

He sat back in the stiff chair. He wondered about the raccoons. He imagined them in the brush, on an unfamiliar stretch of the creek. Their tiny hearts still beating wild with fear. He hoped they stayed together. Their chances were just about zero.

The representative stood up. He had a forelock of white hair and eyes set deep in his skull. He went to the podium and gripped it and glared out at the crowd.

War! he thundered.

The word echoed off the courthouse. *Wah. Wah. Wah.* Every man in the crowd stood up a little straighter.

Your mayor, ladies and gentleman of Richfield, is wrong. War is not good for business.

There was a long pause. Billy looked over at the mayor, who was frozen, head cocked, a half smile slowly fading.

No, no, no, the representative thundered. War is not good for business. War is *great* for business. War is . . . *tops* for business.

Hoots and cheers. The mayor smiled, and leaned over and whispered to Hatcher, who smiled and nodded.

The representative went on.

Today we are here to talk about duty. To talk about sacrifice. And honor. And service. Loyalty to this great country. Win the war we will—and win it we must.

He paused for the swell of applause.

Because this fight is not just for us. We are fighting for all Western civilization. We are fighting the war that will put an end to fighting. We are fighting for a new world. But I am here today to implore you to cast your gaze on another face of war. I ask each and every one of you—merchants, bankers, farmers, whatever your line of business may be—I ask each one of you to stop and reflect a moment. Ask yourself, have you not felt the effects of this war for years already, in your ledger books? Yes, I am speaking now in dollars and cents, ladies and gentlemen. It is a fact that business is booming in all sectors. Prices are at an all-time high. Commerce moves at a lightning speed. Our farms, our factories, are more prolific than ever. Internationally, the dollar is strong as an ox. Boom times, these are.

He raised his hand. It trembled a little. He shook his forelock out of his eyes.

Consider, if you will, the Oregon cherry farmer. These farmers are sending their pits and stems to the factories for use in the poison gases. Pits and stems—what would normally be a waste product—and their children are wearing new shoes because of it. The great modern advancements with which Europe has waged her fight—the airplane, the machine gun, the torpedo, the submarine—most all of these are *American* inventions. Think of these things and then ask yourself this: When victory comes, to whom will Europe turn when she sets her sights on rebuilding? Whither will she go for her brick, her steel, her glass, to build back up those great cities, to restore peace and unity and harmony to her ravaged lands? It will be American brick, my friends. American steel. American glass. Europe will rise up again on the back of the American eagle. And the final victor that shall emerge? The American dollar!

The crowd went wild. Billy stood up. Charles grabbed his arm.

It ain't through, he whispered.

I know it ain't, but I am.

Billy couldn't quit thinking about the boy's hopeless raging eyes when he reached out and took his tobacco in trade for the raccoons. And about the man in New York all those years ago who had told him about the draft riots and said, What would you have done? The rich men could buy their way out of dying for just two hundred dollars. And he thought about Leland Hatcher's column, way back when they first got to town, putting the price of a man's life at $54,000. When you took everything away, the speeches and the clothes and the houses and the flower boxes on East Main Street, then man was just a naked animal, wasn't he, and his life was worth as much as those baby raccoons'. Which was not nothing, and not something, but everything. Beyond a dollar sign. Real and holy.

Yet here they were, all still applauding. And what they were applauding could be said in one word. Death.

He didn't even create a stir. Just walked away. Not a ripple. Representative Denning had sat down and someone else was speaking now and no one except Charles even noticed that he had gotten up. He walked down the stairs at the edge of the grandstand and out along the edge of the massed crowd and down the center of East Main Street, which was strewn with bits of crepe and silk flowers and paper fans, and he went through an alley to Gin's sweet familiar silhouette. At the sound of his footfall she lifted her head and nickered.

Come on, Gin. Let's go home.

*   *   *

After the speeches the crowd slowly broke apart and people streamed towards the booths set up all around the square, Army and Navy recruiting booths, a Red Cross booth, a dozen other charities and organizations. Four men in a string band carried their instruments up onto the grandstand.

Charles walked out into the throng. The charge in the air held strong. A crackling, sustained surge of unity and purpose. He was consumed by the throb of desire. He wanted to grab every girl he passed and kiss her. They would let him. It was that kind of day.

After the speeches the mayor had gone down the row on the bandstand and one by one introduced the men engaged in war work. He had said Charles's and Billy's names and Charles stood up and the crowd applauded. He knew that it was the finest moment of his life.

He found Catherine over by the Army recruiting booth. She had changed out of her costume into the sailor blouse and skirt she had been wearing the day he first saw her, nearly a year ago, in the Everbright garden. The Army fellow was letting her try on his recruiter's armband.

Charles strode over to them, pushing through the electricity in the air. He knew Catherine felt it, and the Army fellow, damn the skinny sonofabitch, he knew he felt it too. And so did the old lady next to them at the booth of the Richfield Food Preservation Society with her sign that said CAN PRESERVE PICKLE AND DRY. Hell, everyone felt it. It was the beginning of something great, bigger than all of them put together. A day, as Hatcher had said in his introduction of the representative, for the history books.

He went right to her. Didn't say a word, just slipped the armband off of her arm and handed it back to the Army fellow without looking at him and led her away.

You were something out there, he told her.

She gave him a funny smile. As if he was in on some big joke. She asked him if he wanted to walk her home.

Walk you home? His heart leapt. He looked around. Behind

them, the Army man glowered. Don't you think somebody will say something?

Today? She laughed a little. Today I think we can do anything.

Together they walked to the edge of the square. The string band had begun to play. 'Turkey in the Straw.' Where the people had stood to listen to the speeches, they were now sprawled out on picnic blankets, eating, listening to the music, faces turned to the sun as if enjoying nothing more than the happy freedom of a perfect June afternoon.

Charles and Catherine kept walking. They did not speak. Out on the Pike a rabbit stopped to watch them, sun filtering through its ears so that they shone red. Then it crossed their path. Charles cleared his throat, which was dry as the road, and greeted it, as Billy always did, to reverse the luck, and she laughed, the silence broken.

If I didn't know better, Catherine said, I'd say we were the only two people left in the whole world.

That'd be fine by me, he said.

No one could tell us what to do, she said coyly. She looked at him. Or not to do.

His throat filled.

She swept her arm towards the hay field they were passing.

Everything's different, Charles. Do you feel it? Everything's different.

Her sleeve fell back as she gestured, and he stole a look at her bare arm and remembered the wrist cuffs she had worn, half naked and fearless and magnificent astride that magnificent horse.

Oh, I feel it, he said.

She said she had been up at the high school with the Red Cross all morning, handing out free sandwiches to the men after they registered. She said that even Wad Taylor had registered, cheerfully, in spite of being crippled. Just to say, I'm in.

They made me proud to be an American, she said.

He stared at her arm, covered again by her sleeve, its pale skin

forever revealed to him, now and forever burned in his mind—
God—Joan of Arc. He wished he could touch the chain mail of
her skirt, which had looked so cold and unyielding yet had so faith-
fully followed the curve of her, as if it were a curtain of silk. He
wanted to bite down on it, feel its hardness between his teeth, then,
her thigh. He caught the inside of his cheek between his molars.
She was right. Today no one could tell them what to do. Or not to
do. Could she possibly be thinking what he was thinking?

They went up the drive. When they stepped up onto the porch the
house seemed even bigger than he remembered.

She opened the door and he took it and held it for her and then
followed her into the foyer, where he was struck dumb by the cool
smoky air and the grandeur of the place.

Finally she gave him a little smile and asked what was wrong.

Oh, just thinking.

They stood there awkwardly, as if they had never kissed, never
touched, never huddled beneath her fur coat, smoking cigarettes.
He looked into the dining room, at the portraits Leland Hatcher
had bought along with the house, and he felt a miserable flash of
the night of the Bone Dry party. He did not want to foul up again.
He chose his words carefully.

You sure made a real pretty picture on that horse.

Nearly gave my father a heart attack, she said. A smile slowly
spread on her face until it was big enough to show the gap. Nearly
killed him.

Well I believe Miss Joan of Arc probably near killed her father
too, his daughter one day come to tell him God's been whispering
in her ear.

Catherine frowned. That's not the point, she said.

What ain't?

That God spoke to her. It's what she chose to do about it. She
chose to *act*.

Her hand raised to her collarbone, hovered, landed there.

I want to act, she said. Just like all those men did today. I want to meet life head-on. You know what my father said, when he came and found me after the parade? He said, Catherine Roberson Hatcher. Your body is not a weapon. It is not a sword you can simply unsheathe. I was still up on the horse. I just looked down at him until he walked away.

She was moving closer. She was so close he could feel her breath. The ties of her sailor collar were undone. He could hardly stand it.

Tell me something, he said. Where'd you get that horse? I don't think I'm ever going to get that picture of you out of my mind. He put his hand on his forehead. It's burned in there.

She lifted her chin and he put his arms around her and kissed her. When he closed his eyes they were all there, all the people, all the faces of the day, and kissing her, he felt as he had when they were applauding him, the applause coursing like love in his blood. He knew from the way she kissed back that she felt the same as he did, charged, still charged with the energy that had connected every person on the square. And he knew she could feel the hard fact of his desire pressing into her.

She pulled away and looked at him. An invitation, clear as the day.

Let's get out of here, she said.

They walked back outside and around the house, passing the garden, the stable, an old slave cabin. He tripped then, stumbled over a furrow in the ground. She caught him, and they both laughed nervously. She led him to a springhouse at the back side of the property. They went inside. Dark and cool. An old butter churn in the corner, and cobwebs like lace, and shelves of old forgotten preserves. A covered well in the middle of the floor.

They sat on the bare dirt floor. He brushed away a brittle snakeskin quick as he could, hoping she had not seen it.

Nice in here, he said. Cool and dark.

Always is. When I was a girl I used to come in and play with the snakeskins. Once I found one eight feet long.

He shook his head.

What?

You ain't scared of snakes?

Why should I be?

You're some girl.

Something landed on the roof. He started.

Christ!

Just a bird, she said, laughing.

A big one, Christ.

No one's here, she said. I promise. She laughed again, then got serious. Her voice had a certain gravity, in the close dark space.

What would you do, Charles, if you heard the voice of God? If He spoke to you?

Sit up and listen, I suppose.

His eyes had adjusted. He could see her better now. Beautiful, dark, and pale. He took her wrist gently in his hand, circling the place where the cuff had been. She looked down at it. He moved his other hand to the loose tie of her blouse.

She said something he didn't quite hear. He flattened his hand on her chest, feeling the tremor of her heart under it. He moved it lower, slipping his fingers inside her collar. She caught her breath when he did this, but didn't stop him.

He kissed her. She kissed him back.

He pulled her down next to him on the bare dirt floor. He could smell old apples and old milk, so old that the smell was nearly just the smell of dust. Her arms were tight around him. Her flesh was so cool. When he slipped his hand up her skirt he felt her body tense. She reached down and put her hand on his hand, but she did not take it away.

I've never done it before, she whispered.

I won't do it to you.

I want you to. I want to.

Cat, he said. A fly landed in her hair. He reached up and brushed it away. He put his arms around her and rolled over so that he lay on top of her. He pulled at his pants and her skirt and her drawers impatiently, madly, until he found her and fit himself into her and went as deep as he could. He looked down at her face. Her hair was wild. Her lip was caught up in her teeth. Her eyes flashed fierce as they had on East Main Street.

Does it hurt? he breathed into her ear. Knowing that even if she asked him to stop he could not.

She was shaking her head. I'm glad, she was saying. I want to. I'm glad.

THE MONSTER OF LIBERTY

New York City
OCTOBER 28, 1886

Billy and his pack of boys run slipping and sliding through the rainy wet streets of New York. There is going to be a party. A big one, for the unveiling of the new statue in the harbor.

It's a lady in a bedsheet, no joke, says one of the boys.

You can see her bubbies, another says. He puts his pointer fingers on either side of his chest and waggles them. You can see the nipples from Wall Street.

How tall would you say it is? Ten stories?

Jesus. She's a monster.

How'd they get it over here from France?

Put her in a box and shipped her across in steerage. Same as us.

Under all them bedsheets, you think she has or has not?

She's got a cunt so big the whole fleet of the U.S. Navy could pass through it.

They all sell newspapers, these boys. Sleep in the newspaper office. Billy is the oldest and newest. Not yet three months in New York under his belt.

Well it's got to be cold out there in the harbor, ain't it?

As a witch's tit, Billy says, and they all follow him through a hole in a fence.

In the Battery the crowd is massive, an animal with its own moods and movements. The boys, trying to get as close to the water as possible, shove through. It had been one of the first things Billy learned after arriving in New York, how to shove through a crowd. They skirt a dead horse and weave like a train through the people, the umbrellas, the muddy skirts and boots. Billy slips in a pile of manure. Curses long and loud.

They push towards the water's edge. He is hungry to see the statue. In his mind, it is a giant rendition of the goggle-eyed witch, all the way back across the ocean in Ireland, carved in stone deep in the cave on his island's highest hill. You had to wriggle on your belly with your face inches from the rock ceiling to see her, the witch who howled at you with her hands between her spread legs, tearing open the round hole of her cunt.

Back home, Billy was the youngest of the pack. The older boys would dare, Go on in there and see if you can figure out the answer to her riddle. If you can solve the riddle, you'll live forever. But beware. If you get a stiff one while you're in there, you'll go blind.

The riddle itself was maddeningly simple: Was she holding herself open to let in a man? Or to let out a baby?

They would wriggle in and wriggle out, one by one, and then creep behind the fuchsia bushes that bore red swollen flowers that looked like scrotums, slick themselves with spit, and beat out the stiff ones they did not dare reveal to the others. Staring up at the blue island sky and the flowers like red cocks and balls, still terrified by those blank goggle eyes, indifferent and furious, and the clawlike fingers at either side of her cunt. Ripping it open. To take in a cock or push out a baby none could say. Wondering when they would go blind.

That October day in the cold rain on the Battery, Billy is disappointed. There is nothing about this statue that makes you stiff. Nothing that made you want to sneak behind the scarlet-hung fuchsia bushes. Nothing that would make you go blind. No mystery. In fact, the statue doesn't even look like a woman. It looks like a man, a man in a bedsheet.

The dull rain makes everything gray, the color of the dead horse's nostrils. Nothing to see anyway, except all the other souls there trying to see something too. The fireworks have been canceled due to the weather. After a while, the crowd breaks up, and everyone just goes home.

That night Billy goes back out to the edge of the water, alone, because he wants to see the statue's light. In the foggy, heavy air, it is another disappointment, more of a weak glowworm than a torch.

There had been a cluster of dignitaries out on the island for the unveiling, but they had been no more than faceless specks. From the Battery they had hardly seemed human, especially from the midst of that teeming crowd, all those faces, tired faces and fat faces, faces with mouths like gashes, brown-eyed faces and shrewd faces and broken faces and bitter faces and pretty ones too. He is still getting used to it, all the faces, all the lives. He saw more people in his first five minutes in New York City than he had in his whole life before. Saw his first colored man too, curled up asleep in a doorway like a downtrodden dog. There had been no colored men out on the island for the statue's unveiling, of course, and no women either. If he had been in charge he would have let the whole crowd onto the island. Women and babies and newspaper boys and colored folks, anyone who wanted to come. Tired, fat, shrewd, broken, bitter, or pretty, anyone. All of them. He would have packed them in, shoulder to shoulder. He would have had music, and dancing, and beer. No one would have noticed the rain.

When he leaves New York six years later, the statue is still bright copper. By the time Maura arrives, she will tell him later, it has already turned green. She was told at home that it was the color of the moon, and when she sees that it is green it is like a bad joke, this Monster of Liberty, and then someone gets sick on her.

At this moment Billy is working in the Neversink mine, slowly killing himself in Lackawanna, Pennsylvania, still caught between the pit and the snare. Hacking up black phlegm all night. The little mules that pull the coal carts go blind after a year down there, and he figures he will too. One breaks her leg and he has to lead her out to the woods and tie a stick of dynamite to her and run. Cheaper than a bullet, the boss explained.

Billy understands at that moment, running from the sound of the terrible explosion of muleflesh, that he is as expendable as the mule.

Still he goes into the mine, down in the morning, up at night. Down in the morning, up at night. More black phlegm. Half a day off on Sunday morning, and if you don't go to church, they look at you funny. Buy your bread at the company store. The honey-combed underground rooms. A hive of men, like ants, like termites, chipping away at the rock. Irishmen, who had every one been promised the same riches he had. Germans too, and Italians, and Slavs and Russians and Poles. Same promise, different language, all now coughing up the same black phlegm. A man falls through from the seam above one day, just crashes right through the ceiling into the seam Billy is working. Breaks his back, though it doesn't kill him. And when someone rushes over and asks where the hell he came from, he is so confused and stunned, he says, automatically, County Galway. Then, I can't die, I'll lose my job.

By this time Billy has long since quit thinking about the statue, or New York, or even of home. Or faces or fireworks or dancing or beer. Or freedom or love or hope or riches. All he thinks about and dreams about and sees when he closes his eyes at night is the dead black thing worth more than all this and his life and the Galway man's life and that mule's life put together. Coal.

Money Matters

by Leland Hatcher
The Richfield Gazette

Citizens of Richfield, I am ashamed.

I am deeply ashamed of the colored citizens of this town. They call themselves men, and demand certain rights. But they are not men if they cannot assume responsibility.

I am referring to the letter published in this paper last week, suggesting that a Negro need not be included in the draft. That he "will not fight for democracy, until democracy is proven not a sham." The author of that letter ought to be ashamed, and we all must be ashamed. It is a black mark on our town—on our state—on our country—that it was even printed.

We have carried Ham's race for generations. We have shouldered his burdens, fed him, clothed him. This country has given him everything he has. Now she asks something of him in return. Our nation is at war. No man can now sit back and allow others to take care of him. Those days are done. No colored man can now expect to be carried—if he can call himself a man.

BLUING

A week after the parade, Billy and Charles were out hunting mules when Billy announced they were going to Ernestine's so that he could pick up more medicine. It was out of their way but Charles did not protest. All week he had stumbled around like a moonblind horse, consumed by the memory of Catherine in the springhouse. His shock and excitement and terror and elation had fused into one single thought: would she let him do it again?

Ernestine was on her porch sorting through a bag of dried blossoms, shucking the stems into the fold of the newspaper spread in her lap. It was open to Leland Hatcher's column.

Billy pointed to it. Sometimes I think they ought to just give the Hatchet a soapbox on Court Square.

Ernestine said nothing, just sucked her eyetooth. She finished her job and then folded the paper and brushed off her skirt.

My son wrote that letter he's in such a state about, she said. Wrote it the day he closed the laundry and enlisted. I do believe Mister Hatcher missed the point.

After she went inside and got the medicine she asked Billy to take a look at her mule's hoof, which that morning had been punctured by a nail that she could not get out herself. He was in the side yard, wearing a fly suit she had made for him out of burlap sacks. Ridiculous, like a mule in a tea cozy, but Charles knew just by looking at him that underneath it he was as fine as Billy had described him to be.

She bent down to show Billy the nail. Charles leaned against the fence and studied her tiny frame. She was not at all what he had expected. He certainly could not imagine Leland Hatcher sitting down across from this frail bird in men's shoes, trusting her power to reach his wife on the other side. Hatcher did not seem like the kind of man who would believe such hocus-pocus. Let alone from a poor old colored woman.

Say, he said to Ernestine when she stood up. What sort of men do you get up here, wanting their fortunes read?

Oh, she said. All kinds. She looked down at Billy. Be gentle with him please, Mister Monday.

The mule had leaned his weight against Billy. He pushed him off, rebalancing himself.

Fine. If you tell him to be gentle with me.

And when you get people up here, wanting to talk to the dead, Charles pressed, why is it they come?

She reached under a seam of the suit and stroked the mule's neck while Billy went to work at the nail with his knife. Gazed thoughtfully up the road for a while before she answered.

Who knows what goes on in a man's heart. All kinds of people show up at my door. All walks of life. But it's the unhappy ones need to get in touch with their dead. The ones who can't sleep at night.

And what do you tell them?

Tell them? Why, I'm just the medium. It just comes through me.

Sure, Charles said shortly. He wanted to know, one way or another, if Hatcher really did come up here. He wanted to know one true thing about Leland Hatcher that would help him understand the man, one fact he could hang his hat on. If he understood Hatcher, maybe he would understand Catherine. He had not seen her all week. He had no idea what she thought about what happened in the springhouse. Everything moved so quickly these days. Everyone was busy. But busy was better than sitting around waiting. No one knew what was coming.

The mule flinched. Billy grunted. Nearly had it that time.

I appreciate you being gentle with him, Mister Monday, Ernestine said. She put her hand on the animal's shoulder. I never know what the spirits are gonna say, she said quietly. I'll tell you what they all ask for, though. All the living. All them come wanting to ask for forgiveness.

Just then with another grunt Billy got the nail out. He straightened and held it out to her, triumphant. Then he opened his tobacco and took out a pinch and knelt back down to pack the wound with it.

Ernestine, still holding the nail, looked over at Charles.

I do like your friend Mister Monday, she said to him. He's an honest fellow. A lot of men ain't so honest. One fellow in particular, he comes to me, wanting to speak to his departed wife. He ain't such an honest fellow, this one. Him? I charge two dollars a sitting. Twice what I charge other people.

That's awfully crooked, Billy said, standing up.

She looked down the road. He can afford it. Believe me.

That's a fast hustle, Charles said.

Oh, I don't keep it.

What do you mean?

There's a girl in Chicago with a baby who needs it. She made it all the way up there when she got out of here. But now her baby's sick, and the brother she lives with is sick and can't work. I send it to her.

She clucked her tongue and shook her head, studying the tip of the nail.

Two dollars a sitting. It do add up.

Billy reached out and took his bottle of medicine off the fence post. Looked at Charles and winked. Then he cocked his eyebrow at the old woman.

Crooked, he said. Awfully crooked.

She turned her back to them, fussing over the mule.

Oh, I'm so crooked they're gonna have to bury me with a

corkscrew. I'm as crooked as my old mule Robespierre. But it's a crooked world. You been all around it. You ought to know.

She turned and pointed the nail at the bottle in Billy's hand.

And you ought to know that ain't medicine.

Billy looked down. Sure it is.

It ain't nothing but a little bit of bluing in some well water. And here I've been charging you fifty cents a dose.

RAIN

Charles went and found Catherine that evening. She was manning the Red Cross booth outside the theater. But it had begun to rain, a warm soft rain, and no one was on the street.

What he had discovered on Freedman's Hill had burned in him all day. He wanted to tell her. He wanted it to bring them together.

Her cheeks colored when she looked up and saw him. Which made his do the same. They stared at each other a moment, awkward. He wanted to put his arms around her, but she was so out of reach behind the heavy wooden front of the booth. He cursed it silently.

I gotta tell you something, Catherine, he began. It's true. Your father goes to see a woman up on Freedman's Hill. She pretends she's got a direct line to heaven. Like Joan of Arc hearing God. Like that song 'Hello Central Give Me Heaven.' Like she could just pick up a telephone.

Her look of triumph caught him off guard.

I was right! she said, knocking her counter, her white Red Cross hat jouncing a little.

Well there's more, he said. He told her what Ernestine was doing, sending Hatcher's money to the girl. Catherine listened with her teeth hooked on her lip. Her eyes were on two cardinals in a puddle in the middle of the street. Her brow was furrowed, as if she was trying to sort it out.

I see, she said simply.

Charles wondered if he should have kept this part from her. It did seem awfully crooked. Riding back down Freedman's Hill, Billy had laughed about it. He said, Old Ernestine, she's just like the fellow in the joke, making money pulling cars out of the ditches. At night she digs the ditches.

Catherine was still looking at the cardinals, which were fighting now, hopping around the edge of the puddle. She was so far away behind that booth. He could not read her face. The rain slapped the awning above them.

I'm awful sorry to be the one to tell you. There's so many cheats in this world, Cat.

She was quiet for a long time, watching the birds. Finally she looked at him. What does he want to know, my father? What does he ask my mother?

He thought about Ernestine saying that they all came wanting to speak to the dead for the same reason.

Forgiveness, he said.

I see, she said again, but quietly. She looked back at the puddle. Look at those birds. I sometimes envy them, the birds. They have no idea about the war.

He took a step closer. His chest hit the edge of the booth. I gotta know something. Do you wish we hadn't done it—in the spring-house?

Now she looked him straight in the eye. No, she said slowly. I'm glad we did.

His blood surged. We could do it again, you know.

She smiled at him then, broadly, showing the gap, and shook her head.

Well we could.

Her smile went away and her face set with resolve.

I'll tell you why I'm glad, Charles. It helped me to realize what I need to do. I was confused that day. I was so stirred by all those men signing up to fight, I wanted to act too, to do something bold. Something brave. Like—like Joan of Arc.

She told him about a girl she knew who was going to nursing school in Nashville. They taught you everything you needed to know double time. Then you could go over as a war nurse, work in Paris, maybe even at the Front. She wanted to go too. To Nashville, and then to France.

She waved at the booth. Standing here, all day—it's all I can do, but in the end it's so small. Does it even make a whit of difference? I haven't heard from Edmund in a month. I have no idea where he is. I can roll bandages until I'm blue in the face. But if I want to make a real difference, what can I do? I've got to go. My father is right about one thing. My body is not a weapon. I've got to quit thinking like a child. She knocked the counter in front of her. We all do.

The passion in her voice made him think of her that first day in the Everbright garden, all fired up about Black Tom Island. And of her as Joan of Arc with her eyes on a distant horizon. Slowly it settled on him what she was saying, that she wanted to go away. And the thought of this, as desperate as it made him, also stirred him. Stirred him the way the flags on East Main did, or 'The Star-Spangled Banner,' or when enlisted men sang 'Over There.' It made him want do something bold too. To act.

You're some girl, Catherine.

Well it's a long way away. First I've got to do the impossible. Convince my father.

Another girl in a white uniform came flying around the corner through the rain, late to relieve Catherine from her post.

I've got to run, Catherine said. I'm late. I've got to go teach a bandage-making class. She looked at him over her shoulder, going into the theater to change her clothes, and watching her, he felt that this was it, that she was already gone.

It's not just do your bit, these days, she called, as if from a distant shore. Right, Charles? It's do your all.

RED PAINT

On July 20, the draft was published in the Richfield paper, and something shifted in the air. There was more excitement in town that day than the day in April when war was declared.

Charles looked at the newspaper, the columns and columns of names.

What would you do, Billy? If you were of age, and if they called you up?

Ah, they'd never take me. I got flat feet and a case of the heaves.

But what would you do? If they told you you had to fight?

Those boys are better men than me.

But what would you do? If you had to choose?

Billy was quiet for a while.

Those boys.

The next morning, Kuntz woke to find a can of red paint had been splashed across his front porch. GO HOME, KROUT written on the wall. He laughed about it before the sale.

I set up Gus with a scrub brush and a can of paint. If there's anything that boy can do, it is scrub and paint.

He waved his hand. His diamond horseshoe flashed.

I'd like to find whoever did it.

Someone made a fist and shook it. Give him a piece of your mind?

No! A spelling lesson.

FOOD

USE LESS

BUY LOCAL

USE LESS MEAT AND WHEAT

SERVE ONLY WHAT YOU CAN EAT

DON'T WASTE IT

WHEATLESS—MEATLESS—SUGARLESS DAYS

WOMEN OF AMERICA—JOIN THE FIGHT—

VICTORY BEGINS IN THE KITCHEN

WHEATLESS AND MEATLESS

Up in the Barrens, buying mules. Choking heat. Dust whirling above the road, along with black thick clouds of gnats. The corn on the hills chest high. Boys darted out from the fields—*blat! blat! blat!*—and swept their crude wooden machine guns across the road.

In the unpainted house the woman poured them coffee, black, boiled hard, and then poured some onto a rag for the baby to suck on. She had signed her pledge card, she said proudly. She didn't quite understand what it was about. Her two oldest boys had been drafted and they had to report somewhere at a certain time for their physical exam. She showed them the cards they had received in the mail. Maybe you can explain it to me, she said. The baby had begun to wail.

WHERE DO YOU GET YOUR FACTS?

On the hottest, heaviest day of July, Charles got a letter from Catherine. Her brother had been wounded. He was in a hospital in Paris and they did not know the details. She had just heard, she wrote. He was the first person she had thought to tell.

Now I know I have no choice but to go over, she wrote. Now I know I can't live with myself unless I do.

He looked at the envelope. The postmark was three days old. He had been working so hard rounding up mules that he had been sleeping most nights out on the road. Sometimes Billy went with him. But often he stayed behind, saying his side ached, or his head ached, or that he wanted to watch the grass grow.

That evening Charles went up to his lot with cans of water for his garden. He adjusted the tarps over the stack of lumber that was the Raymond, disturbing a mockingbird that flew up into the hackberry, scolding him.

He knew that she meant it, that she had no choice. He had seen it in her eyes at the Red Cross booth, this fierce resolve. He knew that he should not try to talk her out of it. There would be no more dropping to one knee. No more only being able to hear the sound of his own voice. These were extraordinary times and called for extraordinary measures. As the people of Richfield had all learned to say now, *C'est la guerre*. A man had to think not of himself anymore. But of his country.

A time for war and a time for peace, he thought, retying the last tie of the tarp to its stake. A time to reap and a time to sow. A time to put away childish things.

He wrote her a letter in reply, embarrassed by his chicken-scratch handwriting.

You're some girl, Catherine. I know that you'll be alright.

He went to see a picture. He needed to go pick up two mules he had bought from one of the tobacco warehouses, but they could wait. He wanted to sit in the dark, and not think. About Catherine, or about the war. Before the film started a slide came up.

LELAND HATCHER WILL SPEAK FOR FOUR MINUTES ON A SUBJECT OF NATIONAL IMPORTANCE. HE SPEAKS UNDER THE AUTHORITY OF THE COMMITTEE ON PUBLIC INFORMATION.

Ah, hell, Charles thought.

Out strode Hatcher. He smashed one hand into the other and looked up at the balcony.

Where do *you* get your facts? he boomed. Then went on without a pause. Richfield, there is an enemy on our shores. And it is the man who comes to us disguised as the dove of peace, the pacifist who questions this war. His poison spreads in the hearts and minds of men. We must combat this insidious foe. We must overcome his lies with the truth.

Hatcher smacked his hands together again.

Freedom of opinion? Yes. Liberty of speech? We must preserve it at all cost. The government will not stifle honest opinions. Yet it is our job to identify the difference between *honest opinion* and *un-American motives*.

He kept going, smacking his hands and striding back and forth, and then ended with another booming volley at the balcony.

The next time a man speaks to you of peace, you say to him: 'Where do you get your facts?'

Off he walked. No applause, no nothing, just Hatcher's echoing footfall, and then the film began. A train robbery, a girl tied to the tracks. Charles slid down in his seat and lit a cigarette, and in the darkness all he could see was Catherine. His mind wandered for the thousandth time to the hot thrill of thrusting into her.

He tried to follow the story. The villain had the same pinched-up face as Twitch. He had quit Kuntz's last week, leaving him in a lurch, but Kuntz had laughed and said, Well who knows, with all the young men going, next I'll have to hire women! Lord knows Gus would like it.

Twitch was all balled up about the fact he was going to be exempt because, due to the fact of his father's illness, he was the head of his household. For weeks he had been walking around saying, If they let me at him I'd stick it to the kaiser with one damn shot. The reason he gave for quitting Kuntz's was that it just didn't feel right, working for a German. Besides, he said, he still hasn't paid me for the extra time I worked, cleaning up the damn barn when he thought glanders was gonna ruin em. Some thanks. He spat. Well I wish it had been glanders, and I wish it had ruined em.

He had a job down at the sawmill now. Charles missed him. He missed sitting at the depot all afternoon, watching the trains come and go. He missed packing the wagon and heading out of a place at sunrise. He missed going to a picture show and not having somebody holler at you for four minutes before it began.

After the show the brightness of the lobby staggered him a little. There were posters on all the walls. ENLIST. CONSERVE. BUY A LIBERTY BOND. GO OR GIVE. On most of them were stamped the letters C.P.I. The Committee on Public Information. It was almost as bad as the shack, with all the advertisements on the walls. The shack could make you crazy, after a while, words everywhere you looked that told you what to do or buy or think. The war posters did all that and more. Like Hatcher pacing around on the stage, they also told you how you were supposed to *feel*.

There was a comment box in the middle of the room, for questions and comments for the Four Minute Men, though it wasn't clear when or how they would answer you. Charles leaned against it to roll a cigarette. Catherine came out of the theater with a couple of girls. Seeing her, he stood up straight. Desire seized him and he wanted only to taste her and feel her all around him and then he thought of her letter and her brother and felt guilty and base. When she saw him she went right to him. She was smiling big. Beautiful as ever. And with a new lightness to the way she held herself.

He felt a flush of relief.

Then it's good news? About your brother?

She shook her head. We still don't know anything. It's been impossible to get any information about him. But I refuse to let my mind wander to worry. We simply don't know. I've just got to have faith. I can expect the best as well as I can expect the worst, can't I?

I suppose you can.

She smiled again.

Oh, Charles, I've convinced him. I'm going to go over. First to nursing school, and then to the war.

What? Charles's heart lurched. How?

She was still grinning. Well you saw him in there. Pacing around on the stage, whacking his fist in his hand. She lifted her eyebrow. Well I just did what he does. Four minutes. Walked in, walked out. She pounded her fist into her palm. Came back in with the check for him to write out for my enrollment. And he did.

People moved around them, murmuring, laughing, making plans for later. He stood there looking at her beaming with triumph. He loved her. He loved her and she was leaving, going off to the war. He took her in his arms and held her and kissed her, and no one in the theater lobby even gave them a second glance.

HOLSTON MOUNTAIN

Bristol

Billy leaves in November to make some money. He joins a road crew. He has no choice. Winter is breathing down his neck, and Harkleroad is right. A girl is an expensive habit. The night before he leaves, under a thin blanket in his narrow bed, he kisses her again and again, as if he can save up the kisses.

It is bad work. They are cutting in a road up on Holston Mountain. Terrible. Grinding. Men and mules against the mountain. Almost as bad as the Neversink mine. One of the coldest, wettest Novembers in years. They work like the devil, to beat the coming snow. The road seems pointless, connecting nowhere to nothing.

His mule's name is Bertha and she's too smart for her own good. Hour after hour they set their shoulder to the same grueling task. Sometimes he thinks of the old gray veteran horse at Harkleroad's and ponders what Harkleroad meant when he said that he loved the world. If men loved the world, would they cover up mountains like this?

At this distance from Bristol and from Maura she begins to slip from his mind, fainter every day. He talks to the mule about her, trying to keep her close, and swears the animal sometimes gets jealous, pinning her long ears and making a sour face. She is happier when he sings.

Daisy, Daisy, give me your answer, do
I'm half crazy all for the love of you

Many times a day there are blasts, dynamite going off in the cut in front of them. At the sound of the blasts the mules all stop working and look, not scared, just thinking about it. And it makes him think of the poor mule he exploded at the Neversink mine and it gives him a heavy hopeless feeling. On Holston Mountain he is as low as he was then, him and the mule, both so expendable they weren't worth the price of a bullet.

One day he overhears two men talking about their wives. The old ball and chain, one says, and it fills Billy's heart with sadness, to hear a man talk like that. It occurs to him that he traded in his freedom as soon as he discovered it, and this makes him feel even lower. It didn't seem right that he should have to choose. The girl he loves or freedom. Then, looking out to the hills below him, he has an idea. A revelation.

He will take her to California. He will get his hands on a wagon and they will set off together and cross the country, trading along the way, sleeping under the stars, keeping each other warm. They don't need to get married. They will slip along through the big country as two foxes would travel, noses to the ground, needing only each other. Free. Together and free. She will see that it is the same life as the one she thinks she wants, the one with all the diamonds and furs, that to have precisely nothing is the same as having everything.

He quits the next day. Gives Bertha a kiss on her warm white nose, tells her he will never work for another man as long as he lives. His heart swells to bursting. Two months chipping away at big Holston Mountain building a road to nowhere, but it wasn't all for nothing. He sets off for Bristol on foot, whistling, under a white sky and slowly drifting snow.

SACRIFICE

Sacrifice. It was the word on everyone's lips, and it could make you feel good and proud just saying it. There was a woman in Nashville with four sons in the Army, and her picture had been printed in the paper above the words A MOTHER'S SACRIFICE IS THE GREATEST OF THEM ALL. But now that Catherine was leaving, Charles wondered if his own sacrifice wasn't the greatest a person could bear. Some days the fact of losing a girl to the war seemed righteous and noble, while other days it felt like a bad joke, a dirty trick. When he got a wire from Bonnyman asking him to meet at the Sumner Hotel to discuss an important matter, his first thought was that he would do whatever Bonnyman asked. He would take a pay cut. Take on more work, though he wasn't sure if that was possible. Just say the word, he thought. I will give up anything.

They sat at a little table in the restaurant. There was a card on it apologizing for the limited menu and small portions. This was not a mercenary act, it explained, but an act of patriotism.

Bonnyman got right to it. No time for small talk these days, he said, clapping his hands once, as if he had once been a man to make small talk. There was a position opening up at the end of September. Manager of the Roan and Huntington feedlot. In charge of twenty men. It came with lodging, a house right on the premises. Virgil Huntington had called Bonnyman up about it personally, and he would like to be the one who delivered him the man for the job.

Only thing is, he said, it's down in Columbia.

Columbia, Charles said. Of all the things he had expected Bonnyman might ask of him, something like this had not entered his mind. Columbia was seventy-five miles away, nearly in Alabama. It might as well be another country.

I can't go to Columbia, he heard himself say. Just bought a plot of land up here.

Bonnyman was watching the waitress set coffee down in front of three women at another table.

Use less sugar and stir like hell, one of the women said, with a devilish grin. They all laughed.

Right now I got it planted with a victory garden, Charles said.

My wife used to love to garden, Bonnyman said sadly.

I've got some beans and some corn, Charles said. Greens too.

His heart was racing. Columbia! He could not leave Richfield. Not now. When the war was over—and it would be over by Christmas, everyone was saying—Catherine would come back, and they would start new. This was the comfort he always arrived at, on both good days and bad. That somewhere on the other side of all this they would be together. That the sacrifice, in the end, was temporary.

My wife grew flowers, Bonnyman said, his voice quavering. All kinds of flowers. You've never seen flowers like these. Not this year. But next year, God willing, next year—well we've got a new doctor who is giving us some hope. He's from Chicago.

Yessir, Charles said, stalling. Billy, he thought. And then there was Billy. He remembered Kuntz and Bonnyman, back in December, telling him he would never get anywhere until he split from Billy and cast off on his own. There was no place for Billy in the situation Bonnyman described. Manager of a feedlot with twenty men under him. What would Billy do? Lately he had been joking he was going to go someplace no one had ever heard of the war. The moon.

Bonnyman leaned forward and pressed a finger to the table.

Listen. McLaughlin. You'd be a fool not to take this. All I have to do is put in a word with Huntington for you and it's a sealed deal.

I don't know nothing about Columbia, Mister Bonnyman. Or twenty men working under me. Don't know if I'm the man for that. And right now I got this land. Soon enough I'll get the house put up on it. Once the war's over.

Bonnyman leaned back and sighed. Then he clucked his tongue and shook his head.

Someday you will learn, McLaughlin. A man can make plans, but in the end they're worthless, nothing but dust. Things change. That's the one constant a man can count on. That, and death. He clasped his hands. There's a story of a king who wanted to put up an inscription in stone at the gates of his kingdom, and he asked his wisest adviser to think of the words that would last for a thousand years, words that could never be laughed at or spit at or disproved. You know what the wise man came up with? The one immutable phrase he could think of. 'This too shall pass.'

Bonnyman stared at his twined fingers.

There was a time, he said slowly, way back in the long-gone days, we thought we might stay in Belgium, have a little brood of children, breed horses, an orchard, a little farm. But now all of that's gone. Up in smoke. Burned. Gone.

He trailed off, eyes far away. The women's cups clanked against their saucers.

I'd have to think on it, Charles said finally.

Think on it! Bonnyman's eyes came back to Charles. Why? Are you considering enlisting? Racing off to the fight?

Charles cleared his throat. The thought of enlisting, which came to him sometimes now that Catherine was going, left him almost sick with doubt and fear. Though he would never admit that to anyone. Not even Billy.

Listen to me, young man, Bonnyman said. Seize the opportunity. Trust me. You can do more for the war effort with twenty men under you in Columbia than you can blown to bits in a trench on the Western Front.

Sir?

It's how they'll all end up. He thrust his hand at the window. Every boy who goes over there. Human kindling for the great insatiable furnace of war.

Charles's stomach lurched. Mister Bonnyman, sir?

Bonnyman let out a heavy breath and sat back. When he spoke again his voice was almost a whisper.

Do nothing, McLaughlin. Buy yourself a violin and fiddle while it burns. Do nothing. Because nothing any of us do will make a speck of difference. From this sort of madness the world will not recover. Doing nothing in the end is the same as doing something. As doing anything.

Charles looked out the window. Suddenly nothing Bonnyman was saying made sense. A veil of confusion had dropped over him. He felt sweat under his collar. In the street some boys were playing Bear in the Pit. The boy in the middle was throwing his weight around frantically.

Bonnyman took his handkerchief from his pocket, unfolded it all the way, put his elbows on his knees, and pressed his face into it. He did not take it away. Just sat there with his face hidden, one hand over each eye. After a while the table of ladies next to them fell quiet and looked over. Charles cleared his throat and nodded at them, then looked back at Bonnyman. His face was still hidden, and now his shoulders shook.

The ladies began to whisper. One of them was a teacher at the college. Charles used to pass her when he went up to the boathouse to meet Catherine in the hot days of fall. Here it was, nearly fall again, everything changed, everything turned backwards and upside down. Columbia! He could not do it. He could not go. He stole a look at Bonnyman, then gave the women a little smile and a nod. He had no idea what to do and so he just sat there and waited, sweating through his shirt, his hands between his knees. Outside the boy in the middle of the bear pit broke out and ran down the street, hooting.

Finally Bonnyman pulled the handkerchief away. He held it in front of him, matched the corners, folded it, matched the corners, folded again, gave it a tidy shake, slipped it back into his pocket. He straightened the knot of his tie. The lines around his mouth had grown redder and deeper. Otherwise his face was as always. He cleared his throat with one short tidy cough.

Well let me know when you've done your thinking, he said.

DOWN THE STAIRS

Bristol

A few miles out of town, a farmer in a wagon picks up Billy. They are passed by King, in his noisy horseless carriage. He is wearing a skullcap and goggles, his body hidden under a buffalo robe. He looks like a maniac.

Billy wonders if she will be at work at the Kings' when he arrives. He will just knock on the front door and take her away from there.

The automobile smells horrible and makes a racket. When it passes, the farmer's horse jumps sideways.

Wouldn't it be a mess, the farmer says, sawing on the reins, if every man had one of those awful contraptions.

The farmer lets Billy off on the edge of town. He runs up to the Kings' but he doesn't have the nerve to go to the front door. He goes to the back. She is not there.

Late, the cook says, and slams the door in his face. Late. That does not sound like Maura. He runs back to town, to her boardinghouse, dark, cold, and empty. The floorboards creak. An old woman comes to the door and he has to say Maura's name twice before she hears him and disappears up the stairs to get her. He waits, for what seems to be an eternity.

Bill Monday, he hears her say from the top of the stairs. But her voice is different. Weak. Lifeless.

She comes down backwards, as always. The treads creak under her boots. Finally, at the bottom, she turns to face him. Her face is drawn. Dark smudges beneath her eyes.

She reaches out to steady herself on the banister.

My God, he thinks. She is dying.

TWO MINDS

Bristol

Ruined, Maura says, in an empty voice. All of it ruined.

She says she's got to get to work. Her hand on the banister is a gnarled claw. Red and raw from scrubbing the Kings' dirty dishes.

You're in no shape to work, he says. We need to get you to a doctor.

He follows her back up Solar Hill, back up to the Kings'. All the way up Solar Hill, she tries to shoo him off like a dog.

Go on, Bill Monday. You'll get me fired. Go on. You should have never come back. You go on.

A fringe-top buggy passes coming down the hill, pulled by a well-bred horse. The faces inside peer out at them suspiciously. Billy picks up a rock and throws it after them. A panicky blackness is closing in. He cannot lose her.

He takes her arm and turns her towards him.

Remember, he says. We promised. We aren't going to die. A promise is a promise.

Bill Monday, you fool, I ain't gonna die. I'm going to have a damn baby.

That night, the thermometers of Bristol drop below zero. Still Billy walks, in his thin coat, up and down Main Street. He paces from Virginia to Tennessee to Virginia to Tennessee.

The stars in the sky are brittle chips. Not two nights ago, up on Holston Mountain, he had a vision of the two of them, together, free. And now that is gone, blasted to oblivion like the rock of the road cut.

He crosses the street. He could go. Women get the raw deal, he can hear her saying, but pushes the thought away. He could go. She doesn't want him. She has told him herself. He should have never come back. He is no father, no husband. He'd do her no good.

Crossing the street again. No. He can't leave her. Not like this.

His cloud of breath is thick and white and he walks straight through it, as through a fog.

Oh, Maura. I'm so sorry, Maura. No California. No stockings full of gold. No diamond-studded bicycle. No bear cub on a leash.

The cold air bites through his pants legs, rakes across his face. He could leave tonight, easy as a leaf would blow on this bitter mountain air. He could go, and not look back.

Stay. Go. Stay. Go. Back and forth across the street. Tennessee. Virginia. Tennessee.

It's a hell of a good place, Bristol, to be of two minds about something.

AUGUST 7

August 7. The day of the physical examinations.

From the two doors of Richfield High School marked BOYS and GIRLS stretched two lines of men. White and colored. Men from town, farmers, skinny boys from up in the Barrens, all waiting. Cracking jokes, talking tobacco, talking weather. Some just standing quietly. When the line moved, they all shuffled forward. One foot in front of the other.

Charles and Billy stood at the hitching post. The heat squeezed everything like a vice. Birds panted. All the horses and mules were slicked with sweat. It was Billy's idea, to go out there. There'll be a lot of men, he told Charles, and a lot of mules.

The pasture at the shack was already full of mules, always full of mules. Ears and rumps. Big, dark coffee-colored mules. Ready to work. Resting potential. Muscle and sinew and heart. Enough power to move mountains. American mules, the greatest in the world.

When they got to braying it was a racket to raise the roof. Billy would say, There goes the Committee on Public Information again. There goes the C.P.I.

It had been nearly a week since Bonnyman's offer. Charles did not know what to do. He had walked up to Everbright, looking for Catherine. Strange days, these were, that he could just walk up to that big white house on the hill and knock on the big front door. Hatcher himself had answered. She wasn't home, busy working down at the Red Cross canteen by the depot where passing troop trains stopped so the men could get a cup of coffee, stretch their legs, dance with pretty girls. Pretty girls were busy, these days, giving the troops a proper goodbye. Everyone busy all the time.

Come again sometime, Hatcher said, looking him over. An upright fellow like you might be what she needs to talk her out of this nursing nonsense. Lord knows she won't listen to me.

Before he went away Charles asked if he had heard any news about Edmund. Hatcher looked at him for a long time. His face went through a dozen changes. Finally he opened his mouth.

Oh, he's fine, fine! It came out a crazy yelp. Yes, fine! Fine! Fine!

Strange, yes. That had been the same day Kuntz woke to a cross burning in his yard.

At the sale he waved it off, joked about it as he had joked about the red paint.

Richfield's idea of *Schrecklichkeit*, he said. But this time his laugh was strained.

Mercy, he said, did it scare Missus Kuntz. She's afraid they're going to lynch me. And poor Gus. It took all day to calm him down. He don't like fire.

Kuntz shook his head.

Only one thing worse than being a colored man these days. And that is being a German.

A big country fellow came out of the building and took the reins of a good stout mule. Charles went over and gave him the little speech about George Washington and duty and honor and how mules would win the war.

I got no wife, the man said. No family. The man in there says I'm in tip-top shape. So I suppose my fate's decided. Suppose I won't be around much longer to have a need for this old mule. Then, with a smile, he added, Suppose I oughta get used to walking. I hear they make you walk like the devil over there in France.

John Rich IV came out, looking smug. When it was announced that men who had been married after announcement of the draft would not be exempt, his father had gotten busy working on a commission for him. Cherry had told Catherine he was certain he would spend the war behind a desk, far from combat. After a while, Twitch came out, a hangdog look on his face. Anytime Charles saw him in town these days it was with a pack of men from the sawmill, big-shouldered, hard-drinking men, the sort who cussed and brawled outside the blind tiger on Saturday night and on Sunday mornings shouted ugliness at the wagons of families on their way to church from Freedman's Hill.

Just like I figured, Twitch said. He pulled out his lip and stuffed it with tobacco. I'm healthy as an ox. Some good that's gonna do me with those little brats to look after. I could go over there and knock the kaiser down and be back in time for breakfast. Shit. Last week, you know what I done? I prayed. Said, Lord, show me a path.

Well, Billy said, next time ask the Lord what Charles here ought to do too. He's been pacing the floor all week.

Charles explained about the position in Columbia. Twitch's small eyes flared in jealousy.

Shit, he said. Columbia. What they got in Columbia they don't got here?

And he had walked away, muttering, What kind of fool goes to Columbia?

When it was over Doc Walker walked out, wan and spent-looking, followed by Leland Hatcher. They came over to where Billy and Charles were standing with their mules at the fence. Hatcher told Charles he wanted him to speak at the month's Red Cross meeting.

I'd like the people to hear from a man like you. A young man with vision enough to get into the fight long before that pacifist schoolmaster in the White House did.

Charles stammered. Just the thought of speaking in front of

all of Richfield made his blood run cold. They would see right through him, the first word out of his mouth. They would all know he was nothing but a rube.

He overheard Billy ask Doc Walker how it had gone, and he head Doc Walker say something about the men who examined beef cattle up at Nickerson's killing floor.

But instead of sending the culls out to slaughter, the doctor said soberly, I'm sending the good strong healthy ones. The ones in their prime.

Hatcher leaned over, overhearing this too.

Doctor! he hissed. What kind of talk is that? You, with a boy in the Old Hickory division. You of all people.

Well my boy's a bigger man than me, Doc Walker said simply. Then he peered at Hatcher over his glasses. You know, I'm worried about you, Leland. You're run down. Burning the candle at both ends. A man's got to rest. And it's a terrible strain on you, not knowing about Edmund. I can understand. My boy's been in the Army for two years now. I can understand the strain of not knowing.

Not knowing! Hatcher sputtered. Edmund's fine. He paused. I have it on good authority.

Doc Walker raised his eyebrows. And what authority is that?

Don't question me, Walker! Hatcher snapped. I am not worried about the boy. Not one bit. The boy is fine. And what is this nonsense about resting. I have more energy than I've ever had in my life. We cannot rest. We are deciding the fate of civilization! We are making the world safe for democracy! We cannot rest a single moment. The Germans are breathing down our necks!

Come up to my office tomorrow, Doc Walker said gently. I'd like to give you a physical.

Hatcher brought his hand down hard on the fence, causing the mules to start.

Christ almighty! I said I'm fine!

Charles and Billy took the mules back to Dillehay's. They stood at the fence and watched them join the ones in the pasture. One came over and stretched her head to them, and Billy scratched behind her ear.

Charles hung on the fence. He had made his decision and now he could feel the anticipation of it in his fingers and toes. He knew he had to do it. Go to Columbia.

Seeing all those men today, Billy, he said. Up there so cheerful and so willing. A man's got to do his all. That's the plain truth.

Billy raised an eyebrow and slowly shook his head.

Charlie boy. The truth is currently owned by the United States government. They mint it like money and they dole it out and they take it away. For all we know old Kaiser Bill is just a gentle misunderstood soul. I have never met him personally, after all. How do I know? Me, I'd just as well get my facts from these mules here. Or from old Ernestine up there on Freedman's Hill. Leland Hatcher sure seems to listen to her, after all, and he's our authority on the whole damn mess.

That woman, Charles said. I think it might be dangerous, what she's doing to him. Filling his head with crazy notions. You saw him today. Looked like he was about to crack.

Billy shook his head again. If Leland Hatcher cracks, it's no fault of that old woman up there. A man hears what he wants to hear, after all. Hell, she might even be doing him some good. I don't know. All I know is I'm awful tired of working for this war.

Charles turned to face him. The sun beat down on his head like a hammer. All the way home he had felt sheepish about the way he had given his speech to that first man who came out of the high school. Preaching about duty and honor and sacrifice when he himself was shrinking from it.

I'm tired of it too, some days, he said. Can't say that too loud, can you? But what's the alternative? Do nothing? How can a fellow do nothing when everyone else is giving their all?

Billy looked up at the sky and shrugged. I don't know, Charlie boy. That's a question for a better man than me.

Gin came over, and the mule nosed her. It was always a delicate dance, with Gin and the mules. An undeniable fact that they recognized in her their mothers, even if they looked nothing like her. They followed her everywhere. It was sort of touching.

Billy reached out and scratched her mane. She lowered her head, blinking her big deer eyes.

They say we're fighting to end all war, he said, more to Gin than to Charles. But it seems to me you can't end war with war. That seems to me a real backward kind of thinking. Those men up there today, they've been told they are making a choice. That they are choosing the right path by stepping up and putting their name on the dotted line. But they haven't got any choice. There's no choice in what they're doing. Why, a man's hardly free these days to speak his own mind.

Well we're fighting for freedom, Billy. That's what we're fighting for.

Billy kept scratching. Gin groaned and sighed.

You do what you got to do, Charlie boy. I believe I will go to the moon.

That evening Charles went in to Suddarth's to use the telephone to call Bonnyman. The man at the counter boasted that he had passed his physical exam with flying colors. Pointing Charles to the telephone, he sang a line from a new song: *Hello, Central! Give me no-man's-land . . .*

Charles told Bonnyman he wanted the job. Bonnyman said he would set up a meeting with Huntington when he came to Nashville in a few weeks.

Charles hung up. Bonnyman had been curt and businesslike. He had hoped for something more. He just wanted someone to tell him that he had made the right decision.

Outside the air had grown so heavy it had to break. But lately it never broke. It would grow hotter and hotter and heavier and heavier, but the rain would never come. At least to Richfield. You would see the lightning off to the north and know it was raining up in Kentucky, cooling the sweltering earth, and envy the bastards.

Charles sat down on the bench outside the store. He was suddenly bone tired. When he heard the crash, he first thought it was thunder. Then the man from Suddarth's came outside and looked up and down the street. All along East Main, men were coming out of the shops. Two doors down from the Paradise, Leland Hatcher's Pierce-Arrow was halfway through the shattered front window of the furniture store.

They walked over together, Charles and the Suddarth's man. A crowd had already formed. Someone was helping Hatcher out of the driver's seat. Shards of glass on his shoulders and in his hair winked and glittered. His eyes were wild. He looked very small.

Somebody get Edmund for me, Hatcher was saying. Tell him to help me clean up this mess.

Sir?

Go find him! Hatcher snapped. He's around here somewhere. Go check up at the country club. For Christ's sake, hurry!

Mister Hatcher. Sir.

If someone would just go get Edmund we'll get this mess cleaned up!

The Suddarth's man looked at Charles and raised his eyebrows. You reckon that window just jumped out in front of him?

Jesus, Charles said.

Two men came up and got on either side of Hatcher and walked him up the street and helped him into another car and drove off. A boy hurried out of the furniture store with a broom. Probably drunk, someone muttered. A slip of the foot, someone else said. Could happen to any man.

The Suddarth's man was untying his apron, shaking his head. I'm going home, he said. It's been a long day.

SECOND HIGH

Bristol

Billy does not leave. He decides that frigid night on Main Street—he doesn't even know, anymore, which side he is on—that he is going to take care of her.

He rents a house for them down on Second High Street, in a slummy line of identical houses. He takes her to see it that afternoon.

Don't worry, he tells her. I got it all taken care of. I'm gonna marry you.

A weird thaw has come on. The air brings the stench of rotten eggs, something dead. She begins to cry.

He gets a job at the terra-cotta factory, where the kilns are so hot the men strip down and work shirtless, in spite of the snow falling outside. He has worked there three weeks when one day there is an accident and a boy is killed, burned so badly he makes just one sound, like the mewing of a cat, before he dies.

On the way back to Second High that afternoon Billy sits down. He puts his elbows on his knees and his head in his hands. It will be months before the smell of charred flesh will leave his nose and right now it is unbearable. He squeezes at his nostrils. He doesn't want to go home. The nights have been terrible. Maura is sick, tormented by strange pains. He has been sleeping in the front room. They hardly speak.

He looks down the crooked street.

They have to get away from this place.

She is inside, frying potatoes. This is the only thing she can eat, fried potatoes, that does not make her ill. The fat is so expensive, he keeps telling her. But she can not stomach them boiled.

He puts his arms around her. We'll go to California. I'll take you there.

She is stiff in his arms. The potatoes in the pan hiss at him. He looks away from them, seeing again the dead boy's bubbled flesh.

We'll leave tomorrow, he says. Let's go.

Don't say that. You know that would leave us in worse straits than this.

He knows she is right but still he goes back into the other room and takes out a bag and begins to pull things off the shelves. Her meager treasures. Her watch charm, her *Robinson Crusoe*. His gifts. Things he would like to trade back in for the money he spent on them. They need money. Where does she keep that cigar box hidden? He gropes the top shelf. Her scrapbook falls to the floor, lies open like a dead bird with spread wings. He picks it up, hating the photographs of the actresses, hating their false promises.

He looks up. Maura is standing in the doorway, watching him. She snatches the scrapbook away and takes it into the kitchen and opens the stove and throws it in.

Don't ever say the word California again.

He rushes in after her. The potatoes in the pan are black, smoking. For a moment he thinks only of the fat, the thirty cents he spent on it, and he reaches out to save the food before it is ruined and burns his hand on the handle of the frying pan. With the heat flaring in his palm he grabs her, too rough.

Out on the street a woman is yelling. Billy coughs. It all closes in on him, the burned oil, the smoke of the scrapbook issuing out of the poorly drawing stove, the smell of the boy's flesh stuck in his nose. Maura pulls away, flies into the other room, slams the door.

He pounds out the front, down the stairs, to the street. Takes in great gulping breaths of the bad Second High air.

That night he drinks at the saloon by the Crimson Shawl until it closes, pinching at his nostrils. He cannot bring himself to go back to the smoke-filled house. When he finally lurches out a girl tries to talk him into the whorehouse. She is small, walleyed, a bag of bones. He feels so low he considers it, then cusses at her, keeps walking.

THE MIDNIGHT COOL

Charles knew where he could find Catherine. Up at the depot, working at the Red Cross canteen.

She saw him through the window and came outside. She was wearing her Red Cross uniform and the hat that made her look like a nun. A fleeting wish that she was wearing something prettier made him feel unpatriotic. It was dusk, still hot. The brimstone smell of the trains made it feel even hotter. They walked past the freight yard, then past the icehouse. In the lot where they used to meet, construction had begun on a new warehouse.

It had been two days since Hatcher's accident. There had been a small piece in the paper about it. Faulty brakes.

Are you alright? he said.

I've made my decision, she said. I'm sticking to it.

She was leaving for Nashville in two days. Her father was resting and Wad Taylor was taking care of things at the factory. She had convinced him, at least, to rest.

But nothing's going to change, she said, touching her hat, straightening it. Nothing. In a week he'll be back up and going about things as if it never happened.

That woman up on Freedman's Hill, Charles said. It's no good, what she's doing to him. It ain't right.

Catherine shook her head and slowed her stride.

If what you told me is true, she said, that he goes up there and asks my mother for forgiveness. I have thought about that, these days. If that is true, then it helps me understand. The cage he is in. The trap.

She stopped, reached up and touched her temple.

It's a dark place, Charles. He's all alone in there. I can see it now. And I don't think he's ever going to get out of it.

They kept walking. They passed the Citizens' Club laundry, shuttered. Ernestine's son gone off to the army. The sign left in the window: WE WILL DYE FOR YOU.

A firefly flashed in front of them. Charles reached out, grabbed it, let it go.

What about your brother?

Catherine sighed, following the flashing track of the firefly with her eyes. Still not one dependable piece of news. I am trying to keep my hopes up. And now this, with Father. She sighed. But I've got to go. And I won't be far, when he does finally come home. Nashville isn't far.

You're doing what's right, Cat. I'm sure of it.

Right? She looked at him. Oh, Charles, I don't know what's right. How can anyone do one right thing in a world that is so crazy and wrong? Sometimes it seems like the only way to end it would be if we all just threw up our hands and yelled 'Stop.' There'd be no war if every man, woman, and child on earth did that. But we would have to do it all at once. Every single one of us would have to yell 'Stop' at the exact same time. And that will never happen. She bit her lip. So what is left to do? I have to go.

They walked past a line of warehouses, farther than they usually went. Cicadas droned. Fireflies all around. A bead of sweat ran down Charles's forehead.

Catherine looked over her shoulder towards the depot, her face framed in her white wimple.

I ought to get back soon, she said. They call on the phone when the trains are due and tell us in code. It's top secret. Classified information. We never know when they're coming.

Charles rubbed his forehead with his cuff. The tree ahead of them was full of fireflies, blinking almost in unison. The distant hollow sound of a screen door slamming. They turned and walked back the way they came. For a while they walked in silence. Finally he told her that he was going too. He explained the position in Columbia. Twenty men under me, he said. Imagine that.

She bit her lip again, nodding.

Well I suppose I'll miss you, she said.

There was a broken branch in her path. He stopped her and picked it up and hefted it out of her way. Then he looked at her.

Cat. Sometimes I think, if not for the war—sometimes I think we never even really got started.

He tried to kiss her. She kissed him back for only a second and then touched her hair under her hat and looked around. They were right beside the tracks, under a sprawling elm tree at the edge of a vacant lot. In the sky, millions of stars. The kiss had been awkward, a knocking of teeth. They stood there looking at each other, suddenly shy.

My, she said, it is warm.

Another little while and it will cool down, he said. Nights sure have been cool.

Yes. There always is some relief, isn't there. Even in August. It does finally cool, around midnight. Only we're all asleep, not even out to enjoy it.

She paused, looking up into the leaves of the elm.

That was her name, you know.

Whose name?

The black horse, Catherine said. My father's horse. Her name was The Midnight Cool.

Charles followed her gaze up into the leaves of the tree. He thought of all the names they had called Hatcher's mare. He could still hear Billy warbling to her, blowing her a kiss. Just you wait, My Devil, My Maniac, My Own True Love. You and I, Turtledove, we'll be thick as thieves yet. Back when he thought she was nothing but potential. When she was curable, when she was going to turn out to be an incredible horse, the find of a lifetime. Before he knew she was ruined, and that Hatcher had ruined her. He thought about the day he took her to the slaughterhouse. Doped up, she had reached out and nuzzled his arm. Touched it ever so gently with her velvet nose. She was so beautiful.

My mother named her, Catherine said quietly. A few days after she was born.

She could have been a real fine horse, Charles said.

There was a long silence, after that. Both of them with their eyes on the tree. Finally Catherine looked into his face. There had been a new gleam to her eyes since the day in the theater lobby she told him she was leaving. The fierceness had been replaced by something gentler, yet somehow more powerful. An understanding. He saw it now, in the moonlight. Envied it.

All day long my father tells people what to do. Then he goes up there to Freedman's Hill and, instead of telling anyone anything, why, he *asks* for something. He asks for forgiveness. Even if it's all a big hoax, even if it's no way to get it, he wants it. And that's a fair thing to ask for, isn't it, forgiveness? No matter how terrible it is, what you've done. I look at him differently now that I understand that.

He wants me to speak at this month's Red Cross meeting. He invited me the day of the accident.

Well you've been working for the war longer than anybody in this town, Charles. You ought to do it. It's an honor.

Charles shook his head. It was funny. There had been a time not long ago that Leland Hatcher's approval felt like the only thing that stood between him and the rest of his life. And now it meant nothing to him.

You know, I really thought your father had it all figured out.

Well. Plenty of people do, she said. Then she put her hand on his arm.

Do you feel it? Here comes another troop train.

There it was in his feet, the vibration, and in the next moment he heard it. And soon enough he saw it, a flash of light up ahead on the track. They stood and watched the engine thunder towards them, the burn of its headlight splitting the dark, catching them in its blinding glare for a moment before it passed screaming and moaning towards the depot.

GONE

Bristol

When Billy gets back to Second High in the morning, hungover, half dead with cold, Maura is gone. The house is empty like an empty walnut shell, a shed cicada case or snakeskin. Empty in a lifeless, final, used-up way.

He runs all over town, looking for her. On Solar Hill he sees Missus King, stepping into her carriage.

Your maid, he says. Maura. His lungs are seared from the cold and it hurts to speak. His gloveless hands have lost feeling. The burn on his palm is red, blistered. The charred smell of death high in nostrils.

She looks down at him, then through him.

Didn't show up this morning and frankly I'm not surprised.

Finally he thinks to go to the depot.

Two of the boys from Harkleroad's are there.

Sure we seen her. An hour or so ago.

Billy looks up at the board. In the past hour four trains have come through.

Well which damn train did she get on? Even as they speak, another train is coming in.

One boy is certain she was headed west.

East, the other says. I'm sure of it. Cross my heart, Mister Monday. She was going east.

Well Jesus, Joseph, and Mary, boys. Billy looks between them, wanting to shake them. Which goddamn way?

East.

West.

No, one suddenly says. North, Mister Monday. She was heading north.

Billy walks around Bristol for two days, believing she might come back. On the third day something in his heart closes up. He goes to Harkleroad and, with the last of his money, buys a horse and a saddle. And bent into a cold wind that shears down from Holston Mountain, he goes.

SO LONG, RICHFIELD

Two weeks after Catherine's departure, the night of the Red Cross meeting, Charles gave his speech. He had worked on it for days, but when he stood up at the podium in his rented dinner jacket, what he had written, all about George Washington and the American mule and duty and honor and sacrifice, felt empty, a masquerade.

He cleared his throat. Hundreds of faces looked up at him, waiting.

Citizens of Richfield, he began. His voice quavered, sounded strange in his own skull. I know that all of you are doing your bit. Well for a long time now, our mules have been chewing their bit.

Laughter. He looked out at the people. He wondered if he was the only one who felt that with every passing day he understood not more and more but less and less. Not just about the war but about life and himself and what a man was meant to do to be right in the world.

I love this country, he said slowly, and I'm proud of it too. And I'm proud our mules are in the fight. They don't know why we're in it, or what we're fighting for.

He hesitated.

To tell you the truth, sometimes I don't know either. But these mules, they put their whole hearts into it. I do know that. They put their whole hearts in it for us, and then some.

Afterwards in the opera house lobby a crowd of men had come up to shake his hand. Wad Taylor came up on his cane and congratulated him, a genuine smile on his broad face. And Charles saw that he had been a fool, all the times he had been jealous of him. All along he'd had what Wad wanted. Catherine. But he had acted as if it was the other way around.

Leland Hatcher congratulated him too. Catherine's prediction was right. After a week's rest he had been back at it as if nothing had ever happened. Giving speeches, writing columns, crowing at everyone for four minutes before the shows at the Paradise. To-night he was flashing around the smile that did not go up to his eyes. Shaking hands. Clapping shoulders. Working the room.

Kuntz came up and pumped Charles's hand. It was rumored that he had been the Red Cross's single biggest donor that month. Charles told him about the Ford he had just bought, in order to cover more ground when he was out buying mules. Under his mustache Kuntz grinned as big as the picture of Teddy Roosevelt Charles had pinned up in the shack.

That's a boy, McLaughlin. Wise investment. Me, I'm going to tell them to bury me with my Ford. Because there's never been a hole she couldn't get me out of.

Charles was still learning to drive the car, always cursing it and telling it to *whoa*. All alone out on the country roads. Billy didn't come out anymore.

I believe I'm getting out of the war mule business, he had said the day after they went to the high school for the examinations. I can't send another mule over there. They suffer our foolishness enough in peacetime to ask them to get into the middle of that madness.

Charles kept shaking hands and smiling, but without Catherine there, it was all emptiness. He had felt it since she left, and the harder he worked, the more fully he tried to dedicate himself to the cause of the war, the more he thought about her and missed her. The more he missed her, the harder he worked, driving far into the county in the Ford, following every lead.

He shook another hand.

Yessir, he said. Thank you, sir. We've all got to do our all, yessir.

Early that morning he had driven out to the Tisdale addition, thinking, Shit, the garden. The greens lay in withered black lumps. The corn stalks were bent. Even the weeds that had grown up around everything looked dead. He got out of the car and walked over and stood in the middle of it. Touched the brittle arm of a parched tomato plant and it snapped off and floated to the ground.

He had met a young man in his travels, a redheaded boy who quoted scripture and carried a Bible under his arm. He had been drafted and he was torn up about what to do.

On the one hand, he told Charles, I got God saying, 'Thou shalt not kill.' On the other I got Uncle Sam saying, 'I want you to go over there and kill the Hun quick as you can.'

The redheaded boy had held his Bible to his chest.

What's a man to do?

Charles thought of him now, trying to set his course by two stars.

Thou shalt not kill. I need you to fight.

The meek shall inherit the earth. This country was not built by the meek.

Conserve. Spend.

Invest. Divest.

Fight or Go.

It is our job to identify the difference between honest opinion and un-American motives.

Work will win the war. Food will win the war. Mules will win the war.

Sometimes these days Charles wished he could do as Billy had done. Just, quit.

He slipped out of the opera house by the back door. He thought of Kuntz smiling at him, big as Roosevelt, all those men smiling at him, wanting to meet him and shake his hand. My crowded hour, he thought. He could not understand why he felt so low.

Catherine was coming up through the alley, hurrying. Catherine. She was a vision, a dream, a wish. His heart lifted at the sight of her, and he ran to meet her, stumbling, nearly falling, over a broken brick in his path. She was flushed and beautiful and smelled of rosewater. A lock of hair had fallen onto her forehead. When he went to put his arms around her she put up her hand.

I've got to talk to you, she said.

Were you in there, Catherine? His toe was throbbing from the brick but he could hardly feel it.

She shook her head. She would not look him in the eye.

Oh, Cat. I wish you had been in there. I gave a speech. A damn good speech. And they stood when they applauded me, but I got to tell you, it just didn't feel right. I think it's because you weren't there. If you had been there it would have been different. I'm sure of it.

His hands trembled. She was wearing a yellow dress with a high collar. He wanted to put his hands behind her neck and close his eyes and put his face in the space between the collar and her ear and just listen to the beating of her heart.

Charles, she said. The day of the parade. In the springhouse.

Jesus. I miss you. Cat. I could come visit you in Nashville. I'll take you out walking.

He was so happy to see her. He still did not understand what she was saying. He reached out and took her hands. Her mouth was screwed up. Now she looked as if she had been stung by a wasp.

Charles, she said. I'm pregnant.

DUTY

When he went in to Suddarth's the next morning to return his dinner jacket a sign in the window stopped Charles in his tracks.

ATTENTION ALL YOUNG MEN!!
IMPORTANT NOTICE!!!!!
NOW IS THE TIME TO BUY YOUR FALL HAT
IT IS YOUR DUTY TO YOUR COUNTRY
TO LOOK YOUR BEST

It made his heart pound with alarm. They ought not put up a sign like that. It wasn't fair, making men's hearts pound like that. Especially when they hadn't slept all damn night.

He returned the jacket and had his shoes shined, hardly speaking to the men in the store. Then he walked out to Hatcher Boot and Shoe to ask Leland Hatcher for permission to marry his daughter.

He was going to take care of her. He had decided right there in the alley behind the opera house as soon as she told him. Forget everything else. Forget even the war. He loved her and he was a good man and he was going to take care of her. He would go door-to-door with an old hen under his arm the way his mother had, if it came down to that. He knew now how Maura could have stooped so low. How she could have knocked at the Crimson Shawl looking for work when she could find none elsewhere. Offer herself to those despicable men for a few coins. He would do anything, now, for Catherine.

Hatcher's secretary sent him up the stairs to the second floor. His heart was hammering and he was shaky from the sleepless night but now his head was clear. Whatever you do when you ask him, Catherine had said in the alley, her voice hardly a whisper, don't let on about my condition. Promise you'll keep that a secret. I don't know what it would do to him, in the state he's in.

He paused on the landing to catch his breath. He felt like he had nothing to lose. Hatcher could run straight into him same as he had run into that window. He would fight him with his bare hands. He could take anything.

But there was no fight, after all. Leland Hatcher, in his big office above the whirring machines, listened to Charles, then nodded once and said fine.

Charles went on in a rush, explaining the position in Columbia, the house, twenty men under him, that they were in a hurry only because of this opportunity, and because of the war. But Hatcher was nodding as if none of this mattered to him.

I've been hoping someone would talk her out of this nonsense about going to France, he said shortly. A woman has one place. And that's the home.

There was a framed photograph on his desk: Morning Hatcher. Charles would have known her anywhere. Her face was Catherine's face, the fierce dark eyes, the determined mouth. Hatcher turned the frame a quarter inch with his finger and studied it.

These are uncertain days, Mister McLaughlin, he said after a while. The only thing a man can count on is uncertainty.

Yessir.

Hatcher's hand was trembling. His eyes were gone with a terrible sadness. In them Charles caught a glimpse of the cage Catherine had spoken of when she had tapped her temple and said, It's a dark place. Way back in the gone days of March Billy had said, A man's got a secret like that, after a while he's got no friend in the world. Only the secret. But Charles realized that he was the one with the secret now. Not Hatcher. Billy was right. And Catherine was right too. It was a dark lonesome feeling.

Hatcher rubbed his eyes and swung his head to the big clock on the wall. He clapped his hands and reached for the phone. When he spoke again his voice boomed, brisk and efficient. All the sadness swallowed, hidden, gone without a trace.

If I call now we might have time to get the announcement in tomorrow's paper.

A FINE DAY

Bristol
JUNE 1908

More than ten years pass before Billy returns to Bristol. All these years, he has told himself a story. It is a good story. She made it to California, got rid of the baby, and her name is on a marquee. Maura McLaughlin, up in lights. Or her new invented name, whichever one she ended up choosing. In this story she has so much gold and silver her stockings jangle when she walks.

Over time, her face has faded. There are other girls in other towns. Some for a day. Some for a week. And as the years have gone by, even the story has faded too. He will be reminded of her sometimes, at the sight of persimmons growing in the woods, or when he hears a laugh like hers. In 1906, when he hears about the earthquake and fire in San Francisco, his first thought is to wonder if she is alright. He decides quickly that she is. Little Maura Mc-Laughlin could always outfox anything.

In 1908, he is in Johnson City, Tennessee, and hears that over in Bristol, Harkleroad's Livery Stable is closing for good, selling off all its horses. He's got no other leads at the moment and figures he'll go have a look at what old Harkleroad has to sell.

He takes the train, disoriented when it slows through Bristol's new neighborhoods. Beaver Creek is all built up, just as the Cincinnati man predicted in the Nichols House parlor. He arrives in at a new depot, with bright limestone-and-brick walls, where he eats a sandwich and drinks coffee at the lunch counter. A story comes back to him, about the wild strawberry field that was here long ago, before the first depot was built, so bursting with berries that when horses were ridden through they would come out on the other side with their legs stained red as blood.

Things change, he thinks. They're always changing. Only if you keep moving, you don't have to notice it so much.

He walks down Main Street, and even this has changed: State Street, they call it now. The Nichols House is gone, razed. Across the street sits a new hotel, the Tip Top. Up on the knob where he and Maura ate persimmons there is now a dance pavilion, with a streetcar running all the way up to it.

He looks up at the sunlight and shadows on the mountain. The world is in a constant state of becoming. It all flows on and on. They both escaped this place, and it was better so.

He thinks of the last day they spent together, before he went off to join the crew. Those kisses he had tried to store up under the blanket in his narrow bed.

He can see now that he should have known it would only last so long. In the midst of it he was so happy it seemed as if he had arrived at something, that his life was now fixed. But he should have known better. Nothing lasts.

He crosses the street and hops the curb to the sidewalk. Something in a puddle catches his eye. A little India rubber cat, fallen from a baby's pram. He picks it up and puts it in his pocket and goes out to the stable.

Harkleroad is indeed alive, though almost unrecognizable. Stooped and shriveled, brittle as a December leaf.

The stable, dark and unswept, at first feels empty. The few horses left hang back in the corners of their stalls. The sign Billy helped Harkleroad paint all those years ago is covered with cobwebs and velvety dust in the corner of the harness room.

COME ON FELLAS—TAKE HER FOR A SUNDAY
CARRIAGE RIDE—HER SKIRTS WON'T GET
MUDDY—HER LEGS WON'T GET TIRED—
YOU'LL BE COZY SIDE BY SIDE

They stand together a moment, laughing over it.

Well as it turned out, Billy says, the bicycles didn't get you.

No, but if I stick around much longer, Harkleroad says, wheezing, something tells me these damn automobiles surely will.

Billy buys a half dozen horses, although someone has beaten him to the good ones. He arranges to come back for them in the morning.

Before he goes he asks Harkleroad what he is going to do. The stable is being torn down for a new hospital.

Oh, Harkleroad says, I don't know. Sit up at the depot, I reckon, and tell stories.

On Billy's way out, a boy who is washing the wheels of a carriage out in the yard lifts his head. He thinks at first it's one of the pack which used to play in the rain barrel, but all those boys are grown now, of course. Perhaps with boys of their own.

How quickly time passes. It just flows on and on and on. Whether a man sticks around to watch it go or not.

Billy smiles at the boy, then turns his eyes to the swift-moving clouds.

Well, he says. It sure is a fine day for the race.

The kid looks at him. Squints his foxy eyes.

What race? he says.

Billy winks. Why, the human race!

THE LAST MULE IN SUMNER COUNTY

It was all lined up.

Charles had spoken with Bonnyman. Virgil Huntington was due in Nashville a week from Monday, and they arranged that Charles would come down with his next boxcar load to meet him. Bonnyman assured him that the meeting was only a formality. The job is yours, he said. I've told Virgil Huntington all about you. He paused. I just hope you're bringing your best load of mules. Never mind the inspectors. Huntington, he's going to want to go over each and every one of them with a fine-toothed comb.

Charles swallowed around a lump in his throat.

Is it a big house, down there in Columbia? I'm getting married.

Congratulations, came Bonnyman's sober voice, and then the connection broke.

Billy was helping him find the last load. Charles hadn't thought he would. He did not tell him about Catherine until after he spoke to Hatcher. He had expected that Billy might try to talk him out of it. But Billy had not tried to talk him out of it. That was the thing about Billy. Nearly ten years together and he could still surprise him.

You're a good man, Charles, was all he said.

It was the worst time of year for buying mules, with the harvest approaching, and they mined the deepest veins, going out to places in the dark hollers that didn't even have roads leading to them.

Charles even went up to Kentucky to see Pen Pendergrass. HOME OF PONDEROSA, read the sign at the road, GRAND CHAMPION DONKEY JACK, with 1916 added to the line of dates and a new dash in anticipation of this year's fair painted in after it. Just seeing it gave Charles a bolt of Pendergrass's optimism, the feeling that everything was going to work out alright. But when he got up to the place he found Pen Pendergrass a different man, broody and defeated. Only the day before, his neighbor had finally managed to trap and kill the wolf in the woods. Standing at the pasture fence, shoulders slumped, he let his good arm hang as limply as the empty sleeve over his stump.

Without that wolf, he kept saying, what am I?

Pendergrass sold him six mules, but when Charles tried to give him the speech about how they were going to win the war, he cut him off with a chop of his one hand.

Getting into this war, he said, is the most dire mistake ever made in the history of this country. Let the yearbooks attest.

It left Charles a little spooked, seeing Pendergrass so low. And as soon as he returned from the trip a cloud of bad luck moved in over the pasture. One mule was swarmed by bees and swelled up like a balloon. One caught her leg on the fence and got a bad puncture wound. As soon as Charles saw it he knew he could not send her to Bonnyman.

He pulled out his rabbit's foot. Tossed it in the air, caught it. Made like he was going to chuck it into the weeds.

Some good this thing's doing, he said to Billy.

Now hold on a minute, Billy said, catching his wrist. Because you don't know how bad things would be if you didn't have it.

The next day they hunted long and hard and only came back with one mule, ponying her home behind the Ford. The tobacco farmer they bought her from said that whenever his boy had her out plowing and it started to rain, she would let the kid wait it out under her belly. She's like one of the family, he said sadly.

When they got her home, Billy found an abscess on her hoof that Charles had missed. While Charles was standing there swearing he went inside. He came back out with the kit.

What are you doing? Charles said.

Well this one's easy. I can doctor that up quick enough and your Bonnyman down there will never know it.

Charles took the kit out of Billy's hands.

These mules are going to *war*, Billy. To the United States Army.

Uncle Sam ain't too picky, these days. You said so yourself. This mule will be fine enough healed in a couple of weeks.

Charles considered this. Billy was right. But he could hear Lloyd Bonnyman's voice in his head, the day he hired him. No funny business. No shoe polish. He had honored that all along.

Well I'm not even thinking about Uncle Sam, he finally said. Not Bonnyman neither. I'm thinking about Virgil Huntington. Virgil Huntington, of the Roan and Huntington Mule Company. He gonna give me a job if I show up with a doctored-up mule? He handed the kit back to Billy. No. I'll find another mule.

Billy took the kit and turned for the shack. You're the boss. But I don't know where you're gonna find him. Because I think this fellow here was the last mule left in Sumner County.

TWO FIFTY

Billy harnessed Gin and went up Freedman's Hill. Up to Miss Ernestine's.

You here for more bluing water?

No.

She was looking across the yard at Rattler. He was wearing the burlap fly coat and resting one hind foot, dozing in the way only a mule could doze, lower lip like a saucer, trembling.

Billy hesitated. He wondered if he should even bother trying. She didn't want to sell Rattler, and he didn't want to take him from her. But Charles needed him.

Did you hear, he said, stalling. Leland Hatcher went into the furniture store the other day. Only he forgot to get out of his car.

She clucked her tongue. Her dark skin shone with sweat. She had been shelling beans and a pod stuck to her apron, hanging like an empty cicada shell.

These are strange days, she said. She looked at him. He knew she knew what he was there for. He felt too low, joking around.

He pulled out the gilt-edged checkbook.

I'll write you a bigger check than you know what to do with. I'll give you double what we're giving these days.

She walked over to Rattler. It's different now, you know, she said. That war. With my boy going over.

This old mule will be a hero, Billy said. We'll set him on the path to glory.

Ernestine pulled the bean pod from her apron and studied it and then fed it to the mule, who chewed it carefully.

I seen war, Mister Monday, she said. In 1862 the Union men came up here like a swarm of locusts. I was a little girl. Lived on the old Morgan plantation. I hid in the chimney. Those boots on the floorboards. Can still hear them. *Thump thump.* They found me. I held on to the bricks inside that chimney till my fingernails tore off. Still they pulled me out. I seen war. And there ain't no glory in it.

She raised a hand towards Gin, waiting on the other side of the fence.

This little horse of yours. You ever wonder if she got a soul?

If she does she's getting to heaven quicker than me.

Ernestine touched Rattler's shoulder.

I never did believe an animal might have a soul until that bad old mule Robespierre. He convinced me. He had free will, that mule. And if you got free will, you got a soul, don't you? My father, when they sold him away from my mother and us, they put him on the auction block, smeared bacon grease around his mouth so he'd look well fed. That don't mean he didn't have free will, do it? He did, the same as you and me, same as my boy, signing up to go fight that war.

A fly landed on her shoulder. She brushed it away. It landed on Rattler's suit. She brushed it away again.

The Lord gave man dominion over the other animals. From that little fly to the whales in the sea. The Bible tells it so. But that ain't ownership. Same as no man could own another man in anything more than body. No man's ever owned another man's heart or mind or spirit. Ever. Dominion ain't ownership. I take full responsibility for this mule, Mister Monday, same as any of my children. And now the only one I got left is gone off to fight that war.

As she spoke Rattler's ears has been swinging all around, following the rise and fall of her voice. Another fly landed on one and he got it off with a shake of his big head and then went right back to swiveling and listening.

I'll give you two fifty. Billy felt awfully low. If you sell him to me I'll look after him good. At least as long as I can.

Ernestine put out the flat of her hand. The mule dropped his nose into it.

I ain't gonna sell him to you because I don't believe I own him. But I'm gonna give him to you.

YOU'LL SEE THE WORLD

Bristol

When Billy goes back to Harkleroad's the next morning, the boy is there again, sweeping the yard. Wearing a cast-off coat that doesn't hide how skinny he is.

Looks like that boy out there hasn't had a meal for days, Billy says to Harkleroad.

Sometimes I am surprised when he shows up in the morning. He's the kind who turns up dead.

How long he been working here?

Not long. Since his mother—I bet you used to know his mother. She was famous around here for a time. Should have been right around when you came through. The girl who used to do the dirty trick with the monkey down at the Nichols House.

Billy reaches into his pocket. The India rubber cat he picked up out of the gutter is still there, the sort of thing he would send the boys up to the drugstore to buy for Maura. His secret Valentine.

She's—she's here?

She's dead, Harkleroad says simply. Died a year or so ago. Terrible story. But there's a thousand like it in the world.

Harkleroad keeps talking, but now there is an ocean of blood in Billy's ears, and he does not hear. All these years, all the stories he has told himself about her, he has never doubted that she was somewhere. Anywhere. But somewhere.

The old gray war horse finally went to his rest, Billy hears Harkleroad say. You remember him.

Billy takes off his hat and holds it to his chest. The blood in his ears churns. It might pour out and swallow him completely. Drown him.

Well I'm sorry to hear that, he manages to say.

Buried him with full military honors, Harkleroad says wistfully. Last horse left in the county who had served, far as we could tell. That horse had a heart big as this stable.

That boy out there, Billy says, still clutching his hat. What's his—what's his name?

Charles.

Charles, Billy repeats.

Buried him the day McKinley was shot, Harkleroad says. He shakes his head, his sad thin thatch of hair lifting. The world ain't the same.

Nossir, it ain't. That's the truth. It never will be the same again.

When Billy goes out to the front of the stable he asks Charles to help him with the horses. His legs stick out from ragged pants cuffs. He is so thin he looks like he is made of bone. Wordlessly he goes in and fetches them, two at a time, and ties them to the rail. Billy goes to the horses, puts his hands on one of them, but he is watching Charles, the way he moves, hoping to see some small gesture of hers, or the carriage of her shoulders, even a look, a glance. He doesn't see her, not the faintest ghost of her. He sees himself, briefly, in the way Charles knocks the hair out of his eyes with his forearm, as he will see himself many times in the days and months to come. But what good is that? He wants her.

Boy, he says, when the horses are all ready, I know you ain't got prospects here. And I know you don't know me and I can't promise nothing, but come with me, kid, and you'll see the world.

That night they camp in the foothills of the mountains. One of the horses breaks free from where he is staked and ambles slowly up the road, dragging his line, head down to crop grass. Charles takes off running after him. So skinny he seems to just blow along. Comes back breathless.

You don't have to work so hard, Billy says, poking at a poor greenwood fire.

I'm just glad to be out of there. He stakes the horse again, spits and jabs his thumb in the direction of Bristol. Never going back.

Well you don't got to thank me.

The boy puts his hands on his knees to catch his breath. Billy is wondering how he is going to tell him that he is his father. How he will even begin.

Oh, Charles says, I knew I was gonna get out of there. It was just a matter of when.

You sound awfully sure of yourself.

Why shouldn't I be? My father was a real big man.

Then, on the other side of the thick veil of smoke rising from the fire, Charles tells the story. Philadelphia. The husband with the big name going out to buy her a fur coat. The streetcar that took him from her. The family that cast her out, left her with nothing.

Listening, Billy thinks only of her. What a story. Maura. She should have been a horse trader.

It is made of scavenged pieces, the story, like a bird's nest, scraps of string and hair and twigs. But one scrap of it he recognizes. It is a small offering she sends him, from beyond.

Charles pulls out that rabbit's foot. His rabbit's foot. The one he gave her that first night, all those years ago, when they feasted on slippery mushrooms and she told him she was bound to leave him, that she was going off to seek everything she wanted, that she was going to break his heart.

The hind foot of a hare killed on a full moon by a cross-eyed man, Charles says solemnly. She told me it belonged to him, he says, turning it over in his hand, then holds it up proudly for Billy to see.

My pa.

HEAT

By Friday evening, the pasture at Dillehay's was full of mules. Charles went to bed with the sun, exhausted. He needed four more, which he could easily pick up at the Saturday auction. But there was no Saturday auction. On Friday night, someone burned down Kuntz's barn.

When Charles drove in first thing in the morning, the fire was already out. It had burned fast, with a thoroughness. There was hardly any timber left.

A few men working a third shift at the slaughterhouse had seen the flames and run down and gotten all the horses out. Thrown coats over their faces so they would not rush back into the burning barn. When the Kuntzes came down they had to hold Gus Kuntz in the car and cover him, same as the horses. He'd had a fit, screaming and hollering, his eyes rolled back in his head.

They were leaving that afternoon, Shorty said. His wife had a sister somewhere in another state.

Should have left even before that burning cross in the yard. Should have got out of here when they dumped that paint on his porch, someone said. He's been here on borrowed time. Surprised he ain't been killed.

Charles looked over at the office. There was Gus. Calm now. Just sitting limp as a scarecrow on the bench. They must have given him something to calm him.

Charles went to him.

Gus, buddy.

No response. Gus blinked. He reached up and swiped at a fly by his ear.

Charles reached into his pockets, wishing he had something to give him. But he didn't have anything for Gus. All he had was the rabbit's foot. He pulled it out.

Take this, Gus. This ain't doing me no good no more. Maybe it'll help you.

Gus reached out. It disappeared into his big hand.

Charles climbed up on the hood of the Ford and ran his hands through his hair. Next to him a little donkey stood tied up to the iron rail. Men said the dark cross on a donkey's back was a mark of honor for bearing Mary to Bethlehem. Or did they say it was for carrying the cross up Golgotha Hill the day they crucified Jesus. Charles couldn't remember suddenly, but what did it matter to the donkey. It was terrible, the things men did to other men. The donkey, he only bore witness.

Tell me, he said to the silent creature. Where the hell am I going to find me four more mules?

LUCK

Charles drove straight out to Dillehay's. Billy listened to the story quietly, just listening. He shook his head and harnessed Gin.

Come on. I ain't riding in that old rattletrap Ford of yours no more. Come on.

They met the roader not three miles out, passing over the bridge that crossed Calf Kill Creek. Pale eyes, stringy white hair that came to his shoulders. He wore a necklace made of small bones. His spine was twisted up so that it seemed his body had been put together wrong. There was a decrepit goat in a crate in the back of his wagon and four mules tied to the tailgate.

Charles went to look them over. His heart was pounding in his mouth. The goat threw its weight against the side of the cage, rocking it. Its stink rose up.

The man said what Charles expected. That the mules weren't for sale.

We're buying em for the war, he said in a rush. But the man shifted his pale eyes over Charles's face, as if to say, What war? And Charles knew he shouldn't even waste his breath on his speech.

He flashed the checkbook. The man shook his head. The bones of his necklace clacked and clattered. Squirrel bones, maybe. Thin as fingers.

He made a sound with his lips and tilted his head towards their wagon.

I ain't got no use for that piece of paper, he said. But I'll trade em all for that little mare of yourn.

Charles went back over to the wagon and put his foot up on the running board.

Well I should have known, he said. He swung himself up. He won't take money for em.

What does he want?

Charles swallowed. He couldn't look at Billy, because he knew Billy knew what he was going to say.

He wants Gin, he said.

Oh.

Sonofabitch. It's alright. Charles picked up the reins. We'll find something else. It's alright. Let's get up to the feedlot on Greasy Creek before it gets too late.

Billy had not moved. He was studying the ground.

They good mules?

Yeah.

Billy pulled his hat down over his eyes.

Go on, he said. Go on up there and take her out of the traces.

LOVE

Before she was killed with a bolt to the skull and made into dog food, there was a story that Hatcher's black mare knew, not in her brain but in the muscle and blood of her exquisite horse body: the story of a man. A story about love.

Love. That was what it was, even if the man never allowed himself to believe it. But that was what Leland Hatcher felt for the girl, the colored girl, the new maid, felt from the first time he saw her reaching up for something on a shelf in his summer kitchen, a love so powerful, so all-encompassing, so much deeper and hungrier than anything he had ever felt for his wife, that it frightened, shamed, repulsed him. That night he closed the door behind them in the summer kitchen and ran his hands up under the girl's dress and moaned into her hair and had her because he thought this would settle it, this feeling that had taken hold of him, that this would cure it like a tonic. It did not. It never did. There were many nights like this, a year's worth of nights, Hatcher moaning into the girl's hair because there were no words for it, what he felt with her, except to say that he wanted her and he had to have her. The girl said nothing, terrified of this white man, her boss, terrified by the look that would come into his eyes when she entered the room. Said nothing, that is, until the cold winter night she said that she was having his baby, and that she was leaving, and that she wanted the money to get her to Chicago. That night she was in bare feet in the closed-up summer kitchen, had taken off her shoes for the walk home because she had a wound on her toe, a wound with blooms of yellow pus oozing from it, and Hatcher dropped to his knees and held her foot in his hands, and he loved her, he loved the pus, he loved the red gash of the wound, edged in black dirt, and he moaned and made clasps of his hands around her small wrists.

I cannot live without you, he said.

No.

His hands slowly tightened, holding her there.

If you leave me I am not going to give you any money. Do you hear me? Not a cent.

I'm going, she said again. Up north. I got a brother.

I forbid it. I forbid you.

He shook her. Then put his head against her legs. He was weeping. He would not let her leave. He would put that festering toe in his mouth and swallow it. She was his, she belonged to him. But she managed to break away, and she ran down the Everbright drive, ran fast despite her bare feet and her wounded toe and the cold winter ground, ran just as fast she could, ran all the way back to Freedman's Hill. Leland Hatcher knelt in the summer kitchen weeping and then he got up and went out to the stable, where the young black horse stood peacefully in her stall. He took a pitchfork down off the wall and brought it down hard against her side. It made a sound like a heavy bag of flour falling from a shelf and the mare skidded to the other side of the stall and he did it again. *Whump. Whump whump whump.* He did it simply because she was there, and she could not run as the girl had run. And because she was beautiful. The Midnight Cool, named by his wife when she was born two summers before. His wife, who had once forsaken everything just to be with him.

Never in his life had he wanted something that he could not have and he hated the world for it, and now every night after his family had gone to bed, instead of going into the summer kitchen and moaning into the girl's neck, he went out to the stable and beat the black mare. And every night the black mare tensed when she heard his footfall, knowing what was coming, balling herself up in the corner of her stall. *Whump whump whump whump*. This went on for months. One night the horse fought back. He walked into her stall and with a hoof she lashed out against him, this madman with the pitchfork. He beat her harder, after that. And after that she fought back more and more often, not just against the madman with the pitchfork but against the whole world, because now something had broken in her mind, she could trust nothing, not a sheet flapping in the wind, not a strange sound, not even the birds, anything might come after her with an inexplicable fury and she fought against it all. For her, every rule as she understood it had been violated, made null, smashed and burned. For her the world was now always and forever in flame.

Hatcher would hang the pitchfork on the wall. Take out his handkerchief. Wipe his face and then his fingertips, one by one. Straighten his coat, go back into the house, where his wife and his children were asleep in their beds.

Early that spring his wife found out about the girl. Then came the night soon after when she drove her car into the water. Because she refused to stay. Because she could not see, as he saw, what was best. Like the girl, she ran.

That night, he had beat the mare until she dropped to her knees. *Whump whump whump*, the blows came down.

After that night he quit beating the horse. Just quit. Hung up the pitchfork. Walked back into the house. Never did it again. But he had ruined her. Her entire body was a tensed-up ball of nerve and fear, waiting for the next blow to come from the pitchfork handle, always waiting for the pitchfork handle. She might hold together for a day or a week but then she would explode. Then came the day the man took her down to Nashville and the other man came into the strange stall with a shovel in his hands to clean it, and with one terrible scream she reared up and struck him in the skull. Struck him dead.

In the morning they found her trembling in the corner of the stall. Waiting for the next blow. Wondering where it would come from.

After the war there was a word for men who left the battlefields like this. Shell-shocked.

When they carried the man's body away Hatcher had lifted his hand and struck her hard, once, across the nose.

All of this, the mare held in her flesh. This she carried in her ruined beautiful body, impregnated in every muscle, corpuscle of blood, and marrow-fill of bone by the story of Leland Hatcher's love that he could not say for the girl he could not have.

But that story had been ground up and tinned and eaten and shat out in coils by a dozen dogs. And no one was ever going to know it.

A NICE LITTLE STORY

Charles and Catherine stood in the dusk light at the Richfield freight yard, looking out at the pen full of mules. Everything was ready. In the morning he would go to Nashville to deliver them and meet Huntington. Then he would come back up and marry her. The thought of it filled him with a nervous anticipation that tipped over into dread. He had the feeling that it was all some strange dream.

Bud Morgan was over by the express office, giving his goats a drink of water from a pail. Charles remembered how when he had first seen the giant he suspected him to be a soothsayer or a proselytizer or even something violent, dangerous. But Bud Morgan had turned out to be nothing but another hustler trying to get by in the world.

Catherine looked over at the goats, which were bleating and pushing with their horns over the pail.

One for a nickel, three for a dime, she said, her voice a little ragged. When I was a girl I must have had a stack of fifty of his postcards. Coming to the depot to watch the trains was my favorite thing in the world. Just to sit here and wonder where all the people were going, and where they had been.

And now you're up here staring at a bunch of old long-ears, Charles said. He studied the side of her face, trying to read her. He wanted to hear her say that everything would be alright.

She sighed.

Well I ought to get used to it, don't you think? The sight of mules. Where we're headed that'll be the view. Miles and miles of mules.

She had been so stoic. Resigned. One foot in front of the other, in every decision they had made. As much as he wanted to hear her say she was happy, he knew what she must be thinking. Of all the things she had wanted in her life, she was getting Columbia and mules.

He leaned on the rail beside her.

Everything's going to be alright, Cat. Everything's going to be fine.

She looked beautiful, clean, out of place here beside the dusty pen. They had come from a dinner Leland Hatcher had hosted for them at Everbright, and she was still in her evening dress, cream-colored lace and taffeta. A substitute for the wedding dress I'll never wear, she had wryly joked when she met him at the door of Everbright. It would be a simple civil ceremony. Hatcher had decided that. No need to have anyone calling you a slacker, he told Charles.

The guests at the dinner were the Tisdales and the Riches and the Walkers. When the meal was served, Hatcher had grown silent, gazing out the window. The other men talked of the second round of the draft. The Army had not raised the numbers they needed and so had called back all the men they rejected on account of small shortcomings, bad teeth or low weight. Charles, nervous, kept his eyes on the portraits around them: Hatcher's false ancestors. From time to time he would steal a glance at Catherine, her neck so pale and vulnerable above the ruffles of her dress. He thought about the way she had questioned Maura's story about his father, the night of the Bone Dry party, and how it had made him lash out at her. He had hung on to that story for so many years it had become as constant and necessary as a pebble held under the tongue to slack thirst. The day he came to buy the mare he had yearned to shout it into Edmund Hatcher's disdainful face, to holler that he too came from a line as high-blooded as these faces on the dining room walls. He had wanted many times to say it to Hatcher too. But as it turned out Leland Hatcher had muscled into this house the way a cuckoo bird muscled into another bird's nest to lay its egg. He could lay claim to nothing more than what he had made with his own two hands, and Richfield, for better or for worse, had been forced to accept him. His wife's family, on the other hand, never had. Looking across the table at Catherine, Charles could see that because of this their children were of two worlds, of two worlds and at home in neither. And he saw that when she had questioned his story she might have being trying to say that she understood what it felt like to not belong anywhere. She might have been trying to say that where either of them came from did not matter a hill of beans.

And Edmund. Edmund Hatcher was finally coming home, though you would never guess it from the melancholy way Leland Hatcher stared out at the lawn all evening. It was Catherine who answered Tisdale and Rich's questions about him, Catherine who brightly declared what a relief it was to have the waiting over.

After dinner they walked with Cherry and John Rich out to the garden. John had gotten his commission and they were headed to Washington in a week. Cherry was expecting a baby. In the garden she was matronly and serious, going on about how glad she was that Catherine had finally cast aside her childish ideas about never getting married. Catherine only smiled her new stoic smile, the one that was not big enough to show the gap between her teeth. She had told Charles that she forgave Cherry for what she had done to Edmund. I've been rereading his letters from the past year, she said, and I've realized that if he's forgiven her, in the midst of all the awfulness he's been through, then I've simply got to as well.

After the guests' departures, she had looked so tired that Charles was surprised when she asked to go with him to see the mules. When he went up to the house to tell Hatcher what they were doing he found him sitting on the front porch, staring into the dark magnolias. He had a piece of paper in his hands and he was tearing it into smaller and smaller pieces.

I'm going to send a newspaperman with you to Nashville tomorrow, he said flatly. He'll work up a nice little story.

Sir. I don't believe that's necessary.

Nonsense, Hatcher said. His voice was still dead calm, but his fingers clawed and tore frantically at the paper. You have got to let people know what kind of a man you are, McLaughlin. They'll try to drag you down. They'll bury you. They will if you give them an inch.

He let the scraps of paper fall to his feet. His distant eyes narrowed, and his lips drew back in a cold hard smile.

If I've learned one thing in this life, son, it's that you've got to write your own story before the bastards write it for you.

At the depot the moon was coming up enormous. Charles told Catherine how people had shouted and cheered when he and Billy brought the mules through town that afternoon.

She looked out at them.

Imagine it, she said. Every one of these animals. From Tennessee all the way to France. Quite a trip, for a mule. She sighed. You know, it's strange. Now that I'm leaving here I see something. All my life, even when my mother was still alive, I've wanted to get out of Richfield. To leave it for another place. When I met you I thought you might take me there. But now that I am leaving, I see that. I carry it with me, everything I've thought I could leave behind.

She paused, and pressed her hand to her chest.

Why, even if I had gone over to France, I would still carry it in here. I see that now. Tonight, when Cherry told me she knew I'd always come around to getting married, I thought about how I could tell her the truth, the truth about what happened with you and me. But what good would it do? For the hundred times I've wished I could go back to that day and change it, to go back and not open the door of that springhouse—

She faltered, and pressed her fingertips to her eyes.

Well I'm the one with a secret now, aren't I? Only I can't run away. I can't step out of my skin and run. I'm stuck with this. Maybe this is the same as what it's been all along. All along I could never walk away from Richfield and my father, same as now I can't walk away from my own self.

Leaving the garden at Everbright that evening, Charles had once again tripped over a furrow in the grass, same as the day she had led him out to the springhouse. Tonight he had seen it for what it was, a path worn from the slave quarters to the back door of the big house, dug out by generations of feet going back and forth in shackled misery all those years. He thought of it now and understood that Catherine would always carry the burden of her story the same way the land and the place would forever bear the scar of this terrible path, the shameful history.

The two mules in front of them were scratching each other's backs with their teeth. Catherine smiled at them from behind welling tears.

Look at them, she said. Look at those mules. They're something else, aren't they? I do hope they do fine over there. I hope each and every one of them does fine. I can't imagine where they're going. In Edmund's last letter he said, 'Where I am, Catherine, a man doesn't harbor grudges. I forgive everybody. Even the damn Germans shooting at me over there. I forgive everybody except this damn war.'

Charles took a step closer to her.

You can't blame yourself, Catherine. What happened with us. It was a mistake but it ain't nobody's fault. You've got to forgive yourself. Like your brother says. Like you forgive Cherry.

Oh, Cherry. Catherine swallowed hard. I do forgive Cherry. What did Cherry do, really? Ever since April everything's been madness. Cherry's never had much of a head on her shoulders, anyway.

Her eyes, far away, suddenly narrowed, and she made a fist and laid it on top of the fence rail.

But I'll tell you something. That John Rich. I still can't look him in the eye. Running off to Washington to hide out while poor Ed lies alone and hurt in some hospital in France. Well John Rich is a coward. Maybe Ed can forgive everybody but I don't suffer cowards. Not with my brother—not with my poor brother—

She looked at Charles, nostrils flaring. What's he going to tell his children, John Rich? Or his grandchildren? What will he say when they ask him what he did for the Great War?

Charles put his hand next to hers on the fence. Her face was lit with the same fierce intensity that had been in her father's eyes when he shredded that piece of paper and glared into the magnolias. *Write your story before the bastards write it for you.*

Well maybe John Rich will change his mind, he said carefully.

Yes, she said. Maybe he will. She took hold of the fence and drew in a deep breath. And maybe someday I'll forgive everyone.

She looked at him then. Her eyes softened.

I've got to tell you something, Charles. That terrible night in March. Outside the party. You told me you weren't good enough for me. The thing is, Charles, I was standing there thinking the same thing. That I wasn't good enough for you. I've felt so low, these years. Keeping such an ugly secret for my father.

Ah, don't talk about that, he said. March was a real long time ago. Don't you worry about that, Cat.

You're right, she said. That was a long time ago. A lifetime ago. The war had sped everything up. Sometimes I feel like I can't even catch my breath.

We ought to get going, he said, wondering, with a shiver of doubt, if the trenches they were digging over in Europe would be there forever too. Deeper even than scars, but like wounds that would never heal. I got to get you home.

Let's stay a minute, Catherine said, turning back to the fence. It's so peaceful here. Look at these mules. They're going to win the war.

PANIC

He took her back up to Everbright in the Ford. When he said good-night to her on the porch she looked so tired and delicate that he did not dare kiss her, as if it might do her some physical damage. His mind was spinning too fast to go back to the shack and try to sleep, so he returned to the depot to make sure the mules were set-tled for the night. Someone had fed them and they were all ripping great mouthfuls of hay out of the mangers. After he checked their water troughs he lingered a moment to watch them. He kept look-ing back at the roader's mules. Something was odd but he could not put his finger on it. Then he realized. They weren't eating.

He followed the fence line around to them. They were right along the rail. He leaned across to the nearest one.

What? he said. Ain't that hay to your liking?

He cupped his hand over the animal's nose and gave it a friendly push. The mule bobbed his head.

Well? What is it?

The mule nudged him. Charles caught his nose with one hand gripped like a claw. He looked the mule in the eye. Then the other eye. Then the mouth. Then he noticed, dripping from his left nos-tril, a fine stream of snot.

He swiped it with his thumb. Slowly, a new stream rolled down to take its place.

He let go of the mule and looked down at his hand. Rubbed his thumb and forefinger together. Clammy. Bird-limy. He stepped back and took another look at the animal, rubbing the back of his neck.

Probably nothing. A summer cold.

He bent at the waist, swung himself through the fence slats. He took hold of the mule's neck and grabbed his nose again and yanked it towards him to get a look into the nostrils. Not the healthy pink you wanted to see, but a dull iron gray.

The mule got impatient, began to fight him a little. Panic rising in his gut, Charles let him go, practically shoving him away, and went to the animal next to him, another of the roader's. He took the mule's face in his hands and turned it so that he could see into the nostrils. The left one was marked with the same trail of snot.

With a cold dread in his veins he went to the next mule. The same. And when he got to the fourth he was too disgusted to even touch him. He could see it, anyway. The trail of snot in the left nostril. The listlessness in the eyes.

They all had it, there was no doubt now. All four of them. That terrible word. That wanton word.

Glanders.

A FIX

Charles shook Billy awake.

Jesus, Joseph, and Mary, why'd you do that. I was having the most wonderful dream.

Do you know a cover for glanders?

Snow again, kid, I didn't catch your drift.

Glanders, Billy, shit. How do you cover it up?

Billy sat up and rubbed his face. His three-day beard was sparse and white. The scar on his forehead shone.

Never done it myself. It's a damn dirty trick.

Well come on. What do you need?

Billy kept rubbing his face. Let me think, he said. You need a wad of cotton batting. A vial of alum powder. A sheet of newspaper. And a pint of whiskey.

What do you do?

Billy dropped his hands and looked at Charles. Why you asking?

Come on. What do you do?

You roll the newspaper into a straw. You take a knife's edge of alum, blow it up into the nostrils. Then you plug it up good and high with a piece of cotton. Covers it up for a few days. Maybe a week. Long enough to put as many tracks as you can between you and that animal.

Charles looked to the door, then back at Billy.

What do you do with the whiskey?

Shit. You drink it. You don't want to mess around with glanders.

Charles went outside. He smoked a cigarette, fast, pulling it deep into his lungs. The gray moon was hoving into the sky. He went back in. Billy was up and dressed.

How many of em got it, Charlie boy? he said.

All the ones I got off that roader.

Billy turned his face to the wall. Ah, hell, he said. Gin.

Charles chewed his knuckle and leaned against the doorjamb. His heart raced.

All this time we're in here talking. They're up there spreading it. Breathing the same air. What am I doing? I ought to go get them—we can pull them out of there—

Billy shook his head. It's too late for that. Here's what you can do. You can go up there and take em all down to Nickerson's right now. Every single one of those mules in that pen. Call Bonnyman and tell him the deal's off. He scratched his face, studied the floor. It might not all be lost. Maybe this Huntington fellow will hire you anyway.

Charles braced his arms against the door frame and hung his head.

Shit. What kind of a fool am I gonna look like? I called him this afternoon and told him it was the greatest bunch of mules I ever seen.

Well, Billy said. Fine. You could cover it up. Take em down there. Cross your fingers and say a prayer. By the time it's discovered, they'll be in France.

After giving it to God knows how many more.

Caveat emptor, Billy said. Buyer beware. He shrugged. If Uncle Sam don't know that then he's a damn fool.

I could kill that old roader. I could kill him with my two hands.

Charles paced to the cold stove and crossed his arms and stared at it.

Billy. What should I do?

I don't know, Charlie boy.

Charles spun around to glare at him.

You'd cover it up and ship em down, wouldn't you? And it wouldn't bother you. You know why? Because you ain't an American. Well I am. Shit.

Billy didn't say anything to this. He was standing next to the girl in the Pears' soap ad. After a while he reached up and tapped her on the nose. You also got to think of that girl up there, he said. You do have to think of her.

What do you know about it, Billy? You've never been beholden to anything in your whole damn life. Charles grabbed his forelock and pulled. I got to think of the fellows over in the trenches counting on those mules, Billy! I got to think of my country. Shit. Those poor mules. They're all gonna die.

You know what, Charlie boy? Where we're sending them, it ain't no walk in the park either.

In the distance a train whistle blew. Charles looked up and listened to it and wished like hell he was on that train. Going anywhere but here. No one could help him. Not even Billy.

I could just go, he said. Jesus. I could just run. It's all we've ever done before.

Sure we could. Easy as pie. Billy lifted his palms. And that girl. I'm sure she'll be just fine taking care of herself. The way your ma did. Scrape by.

At this Charles walked out, right past him.

He ran up the road, to the lonesome empty Pike. Ran all the way back to town. The streets were deserted. The courthouse clock struck ten as he rounded the corner of East Main.

He walked and walked, smoking one cigarette after another. He took a turn somewhere and ended up in a strange neighborhood. It had once been respectable, but now it was crooked, overgrown yards with listing houses. The trees looked stricken. Trash in the street.

Someone was coming. Charles froze, frightened. But it was Twitch. Twitch, stumbling, drunk.

Twitch. Jesus. Am I glad to see you. Jesus. I need a friend.

I hear you're getting hitched, Twitch said. He slapped him on the back. Wise man! Catherine Hatcher. You'll be set up for life, won't you. Of all the slacker brides, you sure found the prize! Tell me. His breath was rank. You've been keeping a good secret. How the hell did you wheel and deal that one?

I ain't no slacker, Charles said, and pushed him away.

Twitch grinned. His small eyes were crazy. There was a fleck of dried blood coming off a scab on his nose. I got a secret too, he said.

That you're drunker than a skunk?

Twitch crooked his finger. We did it.

Charles looked at him. He didn't understand. Did what?

Finally got that old Kraut out of here. Flushed him out like a damn rat.

Kuntz?

Twitch nodded.

You did it? You burned down Kuntz's barn?

Well. Not me by myself. Them other fellows had the plan. Same as with the paint and setting fire to that old cross. I just helped. They had me stand watch and I showed em where the kerosene's kept. Kuntz always kept plenty of kerosene around.

You sonofabitch.

You're the sonofabitch! Twitch said. People like you who don't care don't pay attention don't think don't act. People like you is dangerous.

Charles's blow took Twitch by surprise. He fell back, stumbling against the curb. Twitch hit back, but Charles ducked, got him again. It felt good to beat Twitch up. Just to pummel a face. Twitch got a hold of himself, threw a punch that got Charles in the eye socket. Charles grabbed him and took him to the ground. They wrestled, arm wrapped around leg, teeth on flesh, fingernails in eyes. With a slash of his arm Charles freed himself, jumped up, ran a few steps.

Coward! Twitch called after him. You call yourself an American? This is war, McLaughlin! War!

Charles ran until he found Court Square. Pasted on the side of the courthouse he saw the poster of the girl saying, Gee I wish I was a man. I'd join the Navy. He reeled away from it. Sat down hard on the courthouse steps. Touched his fingers to his nose. Blood.

He could call Bonnyman and tell him. He would surely not get the job. He would probably not keep the job he had. He did not know what he would tell Catherine, or Leland Hatcher, or— Christ—the newspaperman who was meeting him in the morning.

Or he could cover it up. Send them on. Take Catherine down to Columbia. Away from this place and her father and the weight on her shoulders. Be a good man for her, as he had tried to do from the start. The mules would die, but not before infecting who knew how many others. But as Billy said, it was no walk in the park where they were headed.

He coughed and spit. Wiped more blood from his face with the back of his hand.

Those beautiful Pendergrass mules. Rattler. All of them. All ruined. All doomed.

Closing his eyes and dropping his head into his hands, he saw Catherine in the pale yellow dress at the fence rail, smiling her new smile and saying she ought to get used to it, the sight of mules.

And he thought about Billy tapping the nose of the girl in the Pears' soap ad. *You got to think of that girl up there. Or is she gonna scrape by the way your ma did?* It was all lined up. Their life. Their beginning. He could not leave her the way his mother had been left. No matter what the cost. He could not deal her such a hand.

There was a drugstore on Front Street still open, keeping odd hours in order to supply the Red Cross canteen. He bought the things he needed and went straight to the depot. In the pen the dozing animals hardly stirred when he entered the gate. Even in the dark, he knew each one. He found the four he sought and took hold of the nearest by the nose. He took out the roll of newspaper and measured out the alum and blew it in and crammed in the batting and then did it to the next mule, then the next, then the next.

The mules did not put up a fight. It did not take long at all.

NASHVILLE

He woke at dawn in the shack, with Billy standing over him.

What are we doing, Charlie boy?

He lay there, looking at the magazine pages on the ceiling. Goodyear. Firestone. Wrigley's Spearmint Gum.

Hey, Charlie. We loading em up?

Charles sat up, put his boots on the floor.

What the hell happened to your face?

Charles reached up and touched the swollen flesh under his eye. Twitch. He's the one did it to Kuntz's barn.

He examined his eye in the mirror. Billy went to look in the kit to see if there was something to cover the shiner. It was a bad one.

You got to come with me down there, Billy.

Billy closed the kit, giving up, and slowly shook his head.

You got to come with me. Please. Please, Billy. Please.

Charlie boy.

Please.

They caught the interurban up to town. The morning was crisp and cool, the sky eggshell blue.

The newspaperman was waiting by the pen. A small man with a small mouth that moved in quick contortions.

I'm thinking we can do a feature, he said. One mule's journey, from farm to glory.

Billy did the talking. The man took fast notes in a little notebook. Dozens of sparrows hopped around in the pen, braving the mules' feet to pick up bits of hay. Charles watched them. He thought about the lion fed the glandered horse's meat, dead in a day. God. Could an innocent little bird get it too?

Shorty showed up to help load the boxcar. The mules loaded beautifully. Not a kick. Ears disappearing into the dark. Shorty and Billy did it while the newspaperman shot questions at Charles. At one point he lowered his pad to watch Shorty take two mules past.

Would you look at that, he said, his little mouth twisting into a grin. Two by two. There they go. And the Lord said, 'Noah, I kinda believe it's gonna rain.'

When they were loaded Charles gave Shorty a dollar. He was not much older than he himself had been when Billy showed up at Harkleroad's. He would always remember what Billy had said to him that day: Come with me, kid, and you'll see the world.

He looked around. Billy was standing with one hand against the boxcar door, breathing hard, holding his side. He saw why last night Billy had said what he'd said about his mother having to go it on her own. He said it because he knew it would make him mad and knew it would drive him to make a choice, one way or the other. Charles shook his head. Billy Monday, Jesus, he did know how to work a fellow.

They walked with the newspaperman up to the interurban turnaround. The conductor recognized them and refused to take their fare.

You're on official war business, fellas, aren't you? Then we ain't gonna charge you. Keep up the good work.

The newspaperman's pencil got busy, taking all this down.

They sat up front, in the smoking section. The car rang its bell and rattled south out to the Pike. They passed the gates of Everbright, the turn to Dillehay's. The green tobacco fields stretched out, broken up by the war crops, the wheat and corn and hemp. Someone was plowing a field for a winter crop behind two mules and a walking plow. The earth rose up behind them, soft, dark, rich-looking as cake batter.

At Arbuthnot some boys in uniform got on. They were home on leave, rowdy. Joking around. A row back an old woman knitted furiously, her needles clacking. Charles heard her scold the young girl next to her for not doing the same.

When all the soldiers freeze to death this winter and you die an old maid, it will serve you right.

They passed a Ford stuck in a ditch beside the road.

Git a hoss! one of the enlisted men shouted out the window, and they all laughed.

Hey, Billy said, hooking his finger at the newspaperman. You hear the one about the farmer and the banker and the car in the ditch?

A cloud that looked like a skull broke apart. The woman's needles clacked. They stopped at Amqui, where a pretty girl got on, dressed for a day in the city, carrying an alligator purse, looking like she didn't have a care in the world. They passed the vast military cemetery south of Madison. Charles watched the tessellating rows of identical stones change and flash as if it was they that were moving, all over the gentle hills.

The man on the opposite bench crossed himself with the thumb of the hand that held his cigarette.

Makes you think, doesn't it, the newspaperman said, craning his neck. I've got an uncle out there. Died in the Battle of Nashville. A bugler, a kid in short pants. Fifteen years old.

He shook his head and flipped forward a few pages in his notebook and licked his pencil.

Now where are you from, Mister McLaughlin? Tell me a little bit about your family. A little human interest.

I'm gonna close my eyes a minute here, Charles said.

Nearly there. They passed slowly into the Edgefield neighborhood on the east bank of the river, which had been ravaged by fire the previous spring. It was still a wasteland. Stacked brick, roving dogs that were nothing but rib cage and legs, lonesome chimneys like sentinels. Men with defeated-looking shoulders pushed wheelbarrows of rubble. There was a rustle in the car as people turned to gape.

I covered it, the newspaperman said, knocking the window with his pencil. Want to know how it started? Colored boy playing set a ball of yarn on fire by accident. Got scared his mama would switch him so he tossed it out the window. Wind was whipping through that day. Fifty miles an hour. Picked up the flames and spread them like a river. Five hundred houses burned. Four churches. The entire goddamn neighborhood went. He snorted. Imagine the beating the kid's mama gave him then.

Charles watched it go by. The devastation was complete. Even the trees were charred skeletons. The standing chimneys looked forsaken. Not only forsaken, but damned. Atop one, a buzzard ruminated, flew off. As if there would never again grow even a scrap of grass on this place. It looked like the pictures in the paper of the ravaged villages in France. A hellish malevolence to it, and this had been only an innocent accident. A spark, a scared child, a tossed ball of yarn.

A dog wove through the charred remains of a house, sharp-nosed as a wolf.

Into Charles's mind floated Bonnyman's voice.

The greatest tragedy of war is the realization that what lies at its center is the human heart.

The bridge was before them, the great wide brown Cumberland below.

River's awful high for this time of year, the newspaperman said, to nobody.

*   *   *

In America, you write your own story. You pick one and it's yours.

Lola Montez was born Marie Dolores Gilbert, in County Limerick, Ireland. She invented herself when she came to America. Just like that. New name, new story, new life. They named a gold mine after her. And a mountain. All she had to do was show the miners a little leg, and it rained in.

It's easy, in America. You make up a name, you pluck a story out of the air, out of nothing you create the image of what you want your life to be. Then you fight for it, tooth and claw.

*   *   *

They got off at the end of the line and walked down Second Avenue to the transfer station. The newspaperman headed to his office, arranging to meet them later at the Roan and Huntington yards. The coolness of the morning had been a trick. Heat came up off the paved streets in waves. Second Avenue stank of rendering fat, the smell coming from a soap-making business down the block. An undertaker, a harness maker. Traffic headed to the city market. Next to an Army recruiting poster of the Statue of Liberty was a sign for the state fair, advertising an airplane flown by a lady aviator, promising a display of fireworks to mimic the shell fire of the Western Front.

They went into the barbershop across the street. Charles needed a shave. There was a notice on the wall.

BUY A LIBERTY BOND

SOLDIERS WIN BATTLES—WEALTH WINS WARS

It was the old-fashioned kind of place where every customer kept his own shaving mug. Each was labeled with the man's name. Trabue. Wooster. Kirkpatrick. Martin. Galliano. Szyjek. Balajian. Morris. Saint Cyr.

Yes, the barber said, seeing Charles looking. We got men here from every rat hole and woodpile in the world. Where'd you get that shiner?

The poster above all those men's names made Charles remember one of Hatcher's Money Matters columns, something about the value of a man's life. Billy had told him that Ernestine refused to take money for her mule. He had not believed him at first, but when Billy recounted the conversation he had come to understand what was behind the gesture and he saw it for what it was, bighearted and true. He leaned back in the chair and let the man wrap the hot towel around his face, hoping it would get rid of the thought of poor doomed Rattler quick.

Back out on the street Charles looked down and saw a pamphlet in the gutter. He bent down and picked it up.

A SOLDIER WITH THE CLAP IS A TRAITOR

Looking at it, he remembered what Catherine had said last night about John Rich. How she could not look him in the eye. What will he say to his grandchildren, she said, when they ask what he did for the Great War?

Up the street their car was coming towards them, the Number Three car, out to Jo Johnston. Billy was looking at him. Standing in the crooked way he sometimes stood now, since the mare attacked him, shorter on one side than the other. Like half of him had collapsed. They stepped back from the track.

Here she comes, Billy said.

*   *   *

Maura. My dear Maura. I thought you knew a trick.

Well no trick's 100 percent foolproof, Bill Monday. You ought to know that as well as anyone.

*   *   *

The streetcar headed northwest on Fourth. They passed below the Capitol, and the fine houses in its shadow. Billy and Charles had to stand, hanging by straps in the front. Someone in the back was coughing, coughing, coughing.

Goddamn, said Charles finally, would he quit!

They turned onto Jo Johnston. Under the tracks and into a shantytown. Tin roofs, houses that looked as if they would collapse in a stiff wind. The smells shifted, grew stronger, ranker. The air grew even heavier.

Then, there they were. The Roan and Huntington mule yards. A line of great mule sheds nearly one block long that backed up to a wide swath of track. Bonnyman had once told them that here two stablehands could load seven hundred mules onto a line of waiting boxcars in thirty minutes. The figure had not impressed Charles because he could not imagine it. But when he stepped down off the streetcar and looked up the street and saw the size of the sheds, he could. There were more mules in there than he could even get fixed in his imagination.

And you could hear them. Christ you could hear those mules. Braying, hee-hawing, snorting. Smell them too.

A colored woman who had got off the streetcar with them hurried into a church on the corner. For a minute the big door swung open, revealing the darkness inside. Charles wanted to follow her. Just dart in there and hide himself away.

He turned. Directly in front of them was a park, where a few boys were playing stickball. Next to it the Union Stockyards, cows crowded into a pen so tight that chins rested on rumps. A lady's fancy hat dropped in the middle of the street turned out to be a dead rooster. A car passed, and its feathers lifted. A cow lowed.

*   *   *

Daisy, Daisy, give me your answer, do
I'm half crazy all for the love of you

*   *   *

I can't do it, Charles said to Billy. I can't send those mules over there.

He turned in the direction they had come. The Capitol, flag flying above the cupola, was a ship on the crest of a wave.

You saw that place back there, he said. One spark in one goddamn ball of yarn. One spark, and the whole thing gone.

He looked back at the mule barns.

There's got to be a thousand mules in there. When they unload that boxcar, who knows how quick it will spread. And after that—there's a nursery rhyme—my mother, she used to sing it to me. I can't—I've been trying to remember it all morning. 'For want of a nail,' it goes. 'For want of a nail, a shoe was lost. For want of a shoe—for want of a shoe—'

Billy sucked his tooth. Ain't the time for nursery rhymes, don't you think, Charlie boy?

Charles dropped his head and raked at the back of his neck. Again a cow in the stockyards lowed. Shit. I need a smoke. I need a drink. I need something.

Let's sit a while, Billy said.

They crossed into the park. There was a hot black shade under a stand of magnolias, big as a cave. They sat down on a bench at the edge of it. Charles took a nickel out of his pocket. He flipped it, smacked it down on his knee. He did this half a dozen times and then he sighed and put it back in his pocket. His hands were trembling. He grabbed his forelock and shook it and blew out a breath. His mother's voice was there, distant, singing out from the darkest corner of his mind.

'For want of a shoe,' he said again. 'For want of a shoe, a horse was lost. For want of a horse. For want of a horse. For want of a horse, a king was lost—'

He gave up.

Ah, shit. You know what it is, Billy? You want to know what happened? I gave my old rabbit's foot to Gus Kuntz. Lost all my last damn luck and then some. Serves me goddamn right.

Don't be foolish. That old rabbit's foot was a mail-order fake, Billy said quietly.

Charles swung his head to look at him. How do you know?

Billy waved his hand and coughed. Could tell just by looking at it.

Well my father was probably nothing but a mail-order fake himself, Charles said. She probably made the whole damn story up. She was so good at it, telling stories.

In a rush the whole rhyme came back to him then, and it came out of him with a force of its own in the singsong rhythm she always recited it in. He spoke it not to Billy but up into the leaves of the trees.

'For want of a nail, a shoe was lost. For want of a shoe, a horse was lost. For want of a horse, a king was lost. For want of a king, a battle was lost. For want of a battle, a kingdom was lost. And all for the want of a nail.'

He rubbed his face.

Ah, dammit, Billy. I can hear her voice plain as if she's right here singing it to me. It's terrible. It makes me want to lie down right here and cry into the damn dirt. Makes me want to cry like a damn baby. And I'm going to be a damn father myself.

Billy had taken off his hat. He was turning it slowly in his lap, staring hard at it.

I got to tell you, Charlie boy. I was in your shoes once. With a girl.

Charles's head swung towards the tracks. A switch engine and two boxcars screeched along the siding. Not theirs.

Yeah?

A real high-class girl, Billy said. A hell of a girl.

Charles looked down at his knuckle. He had chewed it up so bad it was bleeding.

She probably did. She probably did make that whole story up. I'm probably nothing but a low-down mongrel after all.

Well if you are, Billy said, his voice far away. If you are, there ain't nothing the hell wrong with that. He was looking towards the mule sheds. He rubbed at his cheek and Charles could hear the rough skin of his palm against the stubble of beard.

What do they say about an old mule, Charlie boy? 'No hope of progeny, no pride of posterity.' A mule's got nothing but his own life to prove himself by. A man's not much better off than a mule, in the end. A man's got his lifetime. No more and no less.

Charles picked at his bleeding knuckle. A woodpecker hammered three times in the branches above them.

You think that's true?

Billy shrugged. I reckon that's the beauty and the shame of it, all at once.

Charles wiped his hand on his pants, leaving a tiny smear of blood.

Kuntz once said to me that in America it don't matter where a man comes from. But look what happened to poor Kuntz. Run out of town for no reason but for the fact of where he came from.

Don't change the fact that he made of himself the man he wanted to be, does it? Billy raised his finger, tracing letters in the air. Painted it right there on the side of his barn. Kuntz and Son.

He told me that he believed that after this war would come a time of peace and prosperity and brotherhood the likes of which the world ain't never seen. Peace. All over the whole damn place, peace. That's worth anything, ain't it, Billy? That's worth everything a man's got.

Charles shook his head.

I don't know what to do. I don't think I can go through with it.

Billy was looking hard at him. What do you want, Charles?

It don't matter anymore what I want.

Maybe. But a man wants something even if it don't matter.

I want to be a good man. And Catherine. I want to deserve her. I want to be worthy of her.

The switch engine behind them squealed and jangled and screeched and hissed, slowing at the Marathon car works. On the other side of the tracks a massive foundry belched smoke. Under another magnolia close by two little girls held and rocked handkerchief dolls.

Then it's simple, Billy said. You're taking care of her. You're worthy of her.

I don't know. Not if I do this. I don't know.

*   *   *

William, William, I'll give you my answer true
I'd be crazy to marry the likes of you

*   *   *

Charles watched the little girls with their dolls. At the Crimson Shawl, in those last dark days, she would put him in the closet when the men came in. Tell him to put his hands over his ears. After it was over she would pick him up and he would press his face into her neck. Clinging to her would be the smell of the man who had fucked her. He would hold his breath against it. He had once said to another boy, in a moment of hating what had become of her, She ain't nothing, my ma. Sometimes still at night he would think about saying that. All his life he had regretted it, saying this that one time, in a hot moment of shame.

*   *   *

Billy could hear her now. He could hear her now plain as if she was right there singing to him. It was terrible and it made him want to lie down and cry into the damn dirt.

*   *   *

Charles turned back to Billy. He saw that his eyes were half closed, his face contorted, creased by dozens of lines. It must be the pain.

Well what did you do, Billy? Tell me what you did when you were in my shoes.

Billy let out a long breath. I'll tell you sometime. Let's just sit here a minute, Charlie boy.

They sat. The woodpecker hammered again and then he pumped off across the air to another tree. The girls were laughing. The streetcar went by.

Charles stood up. Billy rose beside him.

I can't do it, Billy. I'm going in there to tell him the truth. He can't send those mules. If those mules went I'd have to go too.

Billy put his hand on Charles's shoulder. You can tell him it was me, he said. That I'm the one who covered it up.

No. I'm gonna tell him the truth. It's gonna be alright. Charles knocked the dust off his hat and set it back on his head. Bonnyman and I will work something out. We'll work it out together. He's a sensible man. And the damn newspaper fellow, he can print whatever story he wants. I don't care what he prints because I'm doing the right thing and I'll tell Leland Hatcher that to his face. What you said, Billy, it's true. A man's got his lifetime to prove himself. No more. No less.

Charlie boy, Billy said, and Charles felt his hand tighten on his shoulder, then fall away.

Yeah.

You are a good man, Charlie boy. You're a better man than me.

*   *   *

Charles went. The streetcar came along and the newspaperman got off of it. Billy went over to him, meeting him at the stone wall of the park.

I talked to my boss, he said. We're gonna do a nice feature. We were going to do a piece on the suffragists but we'll hold that till next week. Now where'd he go? I don't want to miss nothing.

Hang on, Billy said. He didn't want him in there. That was something he could do for Charles. Keep it out of the paper. Hang on. I got another joke for you.

I don't want to miss anything.

Oh, it's going to be a while before anything happens in there. Stay out here. Sit down. I got a good one.

*   *   *

The office had a bare concrete floor, a potbelly stove, a lone sparrow hopping around, pecking at wisps of hay. A secretary put down her knitting and told Charles to wait. Bonnyman was on the telephone, she told him. Mister Huntington's train had been delayed.

She smiled at him, flirting.

So you're the Richfield man I've been hearing so much about. Mister Bonnyman sure does think highly of you. Just yesterday he was in here saying you're on the up-and-up.

He took off his hat and she caught her breath.

What happened to your face?

He reached up to touch his eye. It was throbbing, he realized.

Ah, that's nothing.

You got a steady girl?

Getting married.

She scowled and turned off her smile. Well don't everybody get a prize but me.

When Bonnyman came out and brought him into his office he told him as soon as the door was shut behind them.

Mister Bonnyman, sir. Four of them mules have glanders. I covered it up last night. You can't let em off that boxcar.

Bonnyman looked at him.

Huntington's going to be here in half an hour.

You can't unload those mules, sir. I covered it up. I blew alum up their noses and stuffed em with cotton batting.

Bonnyman's face contorted, finally falling to rest in a bitter disappointment. As if he had been waiting for this betrayal all along.

Do you know how bad I'm going to look?

I've had em three days, Charles said in a rush. That whole load's probably got it. We can't unload them.

Like hell we can't, Bonnyman said.

Sir?

You ever heard of something called the Old Army Game, McLaughlin? Pass the buck. Pass the buck. My neck's on the line here. They're gonna go through and tomorrow they're gonna ship off to Newport News. After that, hell, I don't care. They're gonna be someone else's problem.

Charles's heart fell. He saw in Bonnyman's hard face that it was hopeless to argue. It was too late. He could not stop what was set in motion, coming down the siding, sliding and screeching towards him now.

Bonnyman ran his thumb and forefinger down the lines on either side of his nose. Brought them together under his lip. Charles looked into his undertaker face, the eyes that saw the half-empty glass, worst in all things, and he understood for a moment the magnitude of war, the force so much greater than both of them that it rendered them utterly powerless, less than men.

Do you have any idea what my wife's doctors' bills are, kid?

*   *   *

Billy couldn't keep the newspaperman any longer. He was desperately trying to come up with another joke when he heard another switch engine on the siding. He turned to the tracks and saw the boxcar. Their mules.

The man jumped up and jogged across the park. Billy was slow in following him, his side aching, a growing dread in his heart. When he got into the office there was Bonnyman and the newspaperman, but no Charles.

Where's McLaughlin?

He's gone, Bonnyman said.

Gone.

I ain't got time to stand around and talk about it. I got Virgil Huntington coming in ten minutes. Virgil Huntington. The big boss.

We're gonna make it a feature, the newspaperman was saying to the girl. On the other side of the office window there was a great commotion of stablehands going out to meet the boxcar.

Bonnyman turned his back on Billy and put his arm around the newspaperman and hustled him out towards the barns.

Billy went to the girl at the desk.

You see which way that kid went?

He was in a real hurry. Rushed right past me. Got on the streetcar.

Heading which way?

Streetcar goes by fifty times a day. I don't pay attention. North. South. East. West. I'm stuck here in this office stinks to high heaven of mules. Probably will be till I'm an old maid too. Streetcar comes and goes all day long. What's it matter to me?

Billy stayed in Nashville three days, looking for him. Three days he walked the streets, checking the hotel registers and the blind tigers, the camps down by the river. At night he slept under his coat on the southern edge of town, out beyond the mansions south of Broadway, in a lot across from the City Cemetery.

On the evening of the third day he found his name in the newspaper, in a list of those newly enlisted. Buried among those of thirty other men.

McLaughlin, Charles. Hometown: Richfield, Sumner County.

He went back up to Richfield. He didn't know where else to go. Mice had ruined all the food in the shack. Waiting at the post office was the check from Bonnyman for the last load. He went to the bank and cashed it. The young clerk counted out the bills and then wouldn't hand them over, trying to talk Billy into buying a Liberty Bond. He grew more and more persistent until finally Billy told him where he could shove his Liberty Bond. Two old women were waiting in line behind him, whispering.

Irish, he heard one of them hiss when he passed, and when he opened the door he turned around and said, Boo!

He took the money from Bonnyman's check up to Freedman's Hill and laid it by Ernestine's door. He didn't knock, because he didn't need to see her. And he did not need to know what she would do with it. He did it because he did not want the weight of that money bearing down on his soul, nor did he want it fanning the flames of war, and he thought she might understand that and couldn't think of anyone else in Richfield who would.

He slept down by the creek. The creek didn't give a shit about him and he liked that. It didn't give a shit about the war. It had been there since before France and Germany and before the U. S. of America and it didn't give a good goddamn.

He stayed away from town, because people recognized him and wanted to ask about their mules. But then his beard grew out and no one recognized him anymore and everyone was too busy anyway doing his bit for the war to pay much attention to an old vagrant. And one day when the leaves were just changing to red and yellow he was picking through a rubbish barrel and saw a notice in the paper announcing that Catherine Hatcher would be married to Wad Taylor.

AFTER A LONG HONEYMOON IN THE ROCKY MOUNTAINS, THE COUPLE WILL RETURN TO LIVE IN RICHFIELD.

The kind of long honeymoon—eleven months, a year—from which a girl came back with a baby unusually big for its age.

Tell a story enough times, and it doesn't matter that it's a bald-faced lie. You can start to believe it yourself. The gun tangled in the dress. The missed turn onto the bridge over Defeated Creek. Your father was a big man. You are forgiven. A pair of painted-up mules with air blown into the sunken hollows over their eyes.

He could have told Charles. The straight story. He had started to tell him sitting there in the park and he had stopped himself because he saw that it was not what Charles needed. But he could have told it to him then or at any moment of the nearly ten years they were together. Maybe he should have. He didn't know. He didn't know what he should have done or if he could have changed anything. He had not told him, and now he was gone. He missed him like a limb, like a piece of his own heart. If he was here, they would leave this place, go together to a place where no one had heard of the war. To the moon.

Some mornings he would walk along the creek to the graveyard to set rabbit snares, passing under the twin magnolias at the gates and hunting out the paths the rabbits followed along the tree line. Hatcher's plot was here at the edge, in the new section, where he had spent a lot of money trying to emulate the old Richfield families. His plot, like theirs, was girded by a wrought-iron fence with an elaborate gate, and marked at the center by a tall obelisk, but his fence was bright black and new, not peeling with rust, the gate's hinges were still strong, and the obelisk shone with harsh brightness, and wasn't muted and mottled with green and black lichen as the old ones were.

Every time he passed, Billy was sad for him, the Hatchet. He had tried hard to make this place look like the others but in the end couldn't have what he wanted. Couldn't buy the lichen. Couldn't buy the rust. Couldn't buy a fence rail swallowed by a tree. All those other families had something on him and that was time, and no amount of money in the world could buy that.

Hatcher's wife's headstone, alone inside his iron fence, was oddly modern. Not a headstone at all but a concrete sculpture of a tree stump, realistic down to the leaves of the concrete ivy on its sides and the growth rings cut into the top. The inscription was chiseled in a peeled-back section of the delicately textured bark.

MORNING ROBERSON HATCHER
1873-1915
LOVING WIFE AND MOTHER
SHE IS JUST AWAY

When Edmund Hatcher came home from the war, Hatcher had thrown a parade. But Edmund had not shown up for it. Hatcher, up on the podium on Court Square, had kept the crowd waiting for over an hour, giving a speech that broke down into mumbled, feverish nonsense. The people stayed and listened, trying to make sense of his words, because he was Leland Hatcher, and because Edmund Hatcher was a hero, their first hero, to return from the Great War. A few did venture to whisper, He's been under quite a strain. Finally the mayor came up and put his arm around him and walked him off and they all went home.

And then, Monday morning, it was back to business as usual. The troop trains kept coming and going, and Hatcher was back at work making hobnail shoes for the Army. Leland Hatcher, Billy suspected, would endure. He might crack, and crack again, but he would never break.

One November morning Billy saw Edmund Hatcher at the Hatcher plot. The Pierce-Arrow was parked on the other side of the path and there was Edmund Hatcher, standing outside the gate of his father's fence, looking in at the obelisk. He wore a pair of glasses but otherwise he seemed unchanged. He did not even carry a cane.

When Billy went by he looked over.

Who the hell are you?

I'm just passing through.

Edmund Hatcher stuffed his hands into his coat. Smart man, he said. Get out of here quick as you can.

Billy hesitated, then went to him.

Your sister, Catherine, he said. I saw in the paper she got married.

Edmund Hatcher grunted.

I knew her, Billy said. Know her. Blessings on the union.

Edmund grunted again. Wad's a lucky man.

Was there . . . another fellow? Another she was meant to marry?

You mean the one who ditched her?

Sure.

Well can you keep a secret, buddy? Edmund took his hands out of his pockets and opened them and stared into them. My father managed to put the right spin on it. Told everyone he was called away on government business. There you are. You've got it now. Another secret for the Hatchers. I'm starting to lose sight of what I'm allowed to say. King Midas has ass's ears. He waved his hand towards Billy. I'm thinking I might just start telling it all to strangers. Sometimes a man's got to scurry off and whisper it all to the rushes if he doesn't want to explode.

Did he ever write to her, the other fellow?

Edmund Hatcher ignored this. He looked up to the railroad trestle beyond the trees.

Wad saves the day. Old Kissam Quick. It's funny. Ever since his accident he was the one who was never going to get married. Now it's me. Good old Wad. Straight-up, square, and on the level. He's 110 percent, Wad.

He looked at Billy and took off his glasses. The lower half of his face came off with them.

Jesus.

Billy had seen some awful things in his time but nothing like this. He looked where Hatcher's nose and mouth should have been and instead felt he could see all the way down his throat. Without the mask he wasn't even a man. He was a body and a neck carrying around a few scraps of flesh. A stump, like his mother's headstone.

He put the glasses back on, and his face became whole again. Billy let out his breath. Edmund Hatcher tapped the cheek of the mask.

Pretty convincing, wouldn't you say? Copper. You would never know, would you, unless you got close to me. Well I don't got to worry about that. Anyone getting close to me, that is. He reached out and touched the gate, dropped his hand. Well now you know another Hatcher secret. My face ain't a face. Those Frenchmen are artists, you know. Just look at that damn statue up there in New York.

What did that to you?

I just hope it doesn't turn green. Then I'd really be a monster. He laughed a strained terrible laugh.

What happened to you? Billy said again.

You want to know what happened? No one wants to know. No one asks. They want to pump my hand and tell me I'm a hero but they don't ever ask. Just want to tell me what I am. 'Edmund, you're a hero.' Well Jesus. I'm not.

Edmund Hatcher looked again to the trestle. A train crossed. They were both silent, watching it.

I'll tell you what I am, he went on. I'll tell you gladly. Because in this case it's no damn secret, except nobody wants to hear it. We had been sitting in that trench for days. Just waiting. Waiting. Waiting. Wet and dark and the stink. Going crazy. Like we were all sitting in our grave. Bernard and I played about a thousand hands of poker, which I taught him, with these dirty playing cards, which were his. I can still see those girls. They're stamped on my brain. Those Frenchmen, I'm telling you, they're artists.

They know how to sculpt a sculpture and they know how to take a dirty picture. It's because they're free, you know, or freer than us, anyhow. I mean, these pictures, Bernard's wife sent them to him. His *wife*. They've got something figured out.

But you want to know how this happened. Well this is how it happened. This is my war story. I got bored. I couldn't stand the waiting any longer. 'I got to get out of here,' I says. 'I'm just gonna take a little stroll and have a little smoke and then I'll come right back. Just pass me a lucifer.' That's what they call matches, you see. 'Give me a lucifer, Bernard, I'm gonna have a smoke and then go back and try to get some sleep.' I climb out of there. Start walking towards no-man's-land. Walking like I'm down here on East Main Street and I can walk wherever I please.

And Bernard, he leaps out after me and he says, ''Atcher, *non!*'

'What are you worried about, Bernard, for Christ's sake' I say. He takes my arm. ''Atcher, please,' he's saying. '*Allons.*' Tugging my arm. 'If they see a light they will shell you. *S'il vous plaît.*' So damn polite, those goddamn Frenchmen. And I say, 'Bernard, we've been sitting here in silence for five damn days. There isn't even anybody out there. Relax. This war has made you all too damn jumpy.' I strike the match. The lucifer. Next thing I know I hear a sound like a dozen champagne glasses dropped in a bathtub. Turns out that's my face. And Bernard. Well. Bernard. Bernard just suddenly wasn't there anymore. Bernard was just scraps and rags. Bernard. Blown to bits because I got bored. Shit.

Edmund Hatcher turned back to the gate.

If one more person calls me a goddamn hero, I am going to goddamn bust his goddamn face.

It was time to get moving again. Before the snow began to fall. Billy got the Raymond sold, and the lot it sat on too, to a man who was exempt because of rheumatoid arthritis. Pennies on the dollar for what it was worth. He traded the wagon for a riding horse, dumb as rocks but reliable. He traded a string of hares for a saddle-bag and packed it with his few possessions. He left Richfield on a cold bright morning, headed north, with a hell of a lot less than he had come in with.

AMERICAN WAKE

Ireland
JULY 1886

The night before William O'Maonlai leaves for America, he nearly drowns in a sea cave with a stolen calf. He is too drunk to remember what got him into the cave, which is filling with the rising tide. It had been a dare at the party, his American wake, the first of what will be many such parties in the coming years as more and more young people leave for America, which might as well be Tír na nÓg. The land of eternal youth from which no man ever returns.

The cold water is rising fast in the tiny cave. Billy has climbed onto a ledge, then onto the calf's back. Her sides heave like a bellows. They both have their necks stretched towards the ceiling to breathe the last pocket of salty air, their faces together, close as lovers or twins in a womb.

I am going to die, Billy thinks. Right here in this tomb of a cave with this calf, her and me together, before I ever even get to America. And he lays his head against her warm wet neck and closes his eyes.

Then, in a flash, he sees a secret. The answer to the riddle of the goggle-eyed witch, high above him in the cave atop East Hill. The answer to the question of whether she is tearing herself open to receive a man or to give birth to one.

She is not one or another, he sees. She is both. And yet, more than both. She is All. She is the constant loop of decay and regeneration, of blood and milk, the entire world slipping now and forever from the gash between her legs. With her claws she stretches that cave of herself so wide that it encompasses everything and the edges come around to meet on the other side of the universe, screaming an endless spiral of joy and pain and pain and joy until it is beyond pain, beyond joy, beyond suffering, beyond lover or mother or even man or woman or human or cow. She is the unknowable. She is what does not die.

Seconds or minutes or hours later, the calf reaches out her black tongue and licks Billy's face. He laughs. She licks and licks and he keeps laughing and then he feels a shift at his neck, a tickle. The water has begun to recede. Slowly the tide pulls away and then it is low enough that they can splash out. He races up the strand towards home. Returns the calf to her pen. Changes into his traveling clothes, grabs his suitcase, pins his money inside his shirt. Thinking only one thought: America!

That day the entire island gathers at the harbor to see him off. His mother is smiling at him through her tears, holding her shawl at her chin against the breeze.

He runs to his friend Paddy.

I figured it out! he whispers. The riddle of the witch! I'm gonna live forever!

Well, Paddy says. What is it?

Can't remember! Ask the calf! She was there!

Billy is already running down the strand to where his father waits at the water's edge with the curragh to take him across to Skibbereen. When they push off into the choppy water, the islanders cheer. Each man and woman on the shore has a vision of where Billy is headed, this paradise, America. It fills them with hope, to see one of their own on his way. Their hearts lift as if they themselves are setting off for Tír na nÓg, the land of eternal youth, heaven on earth. What a wonderful world, to contain such a place.

What a wonderful ocean that would carry you there. What a wonderful sky, to stretch over it all!

Look out for Italians! they call. Watch your money! Eat a watermelon! Send letters home!

There will be gold and silver in the ditches, boy! And nothing to do but gather it.

MAURA CARRIES HER BABY UP THE STAIRS OF THE CRIMSON SHAWL

Bristol
SPRING 1898

In her arms, the newborn baby makes a sound in his sleep. A grunt. He moves his tiny lips.

Maura's legs are still shaking from her long labor, smeared with blood that has seeped from the rags stuffed between her thighs. Her knees keep buckling. With each step the hot, thick air grows hotter and thicker, almost choking. From the landing above come the moans and murmurs of a whorehouse.

She hates to be here in this hateful place. But a baby boy will only rise in the world if he is carried up a staircase before the sun sets on his first day of life. Back home in Galway, the nearest house with two stories and a staircase was miles away on bad roads. Most women in her family were too weak from labor to make the journey. Misery plagued them for generations. This was no coincidence, she knows.

Her baby too was born in a house without stairs, but Maura has a friend here, at the Crimson Shawl, and she arranged this with her, weeks ago. And as soon as Maura had the strength to stand, she swaddled the tiny baby and came and her friend opened the door and let her in. In spite of the pain, not coming never even crossed her mind. Because this is America, not Ireland. There are no limits here. Up in America means all the way to the stars.

On the landing she stops. She looks down at the baby. His red face is peaceful, serene.

When she first knew that she was pregnant, she had prayed that he would die. More than that. She had let herself fall down the embankment of the river. She had spent a week's paycheck to rent a bicycle. Riding a bicycle, some girls said, would do it for sure. When nothing worked she still did not give up hope. She still believed that there was some way out of it, that a plan of escape would come to her suddenly, as all her best ideas came, as her idea for that trick with the monkey had come, but then Billy came back down off of Holston Mountain. With Billy back, the hope disappeared. The two of them caged in the terrible house on Second High. She had run before the walls fell in on them. Run blind, with her cigar box full of money, and had only made it as far as Nashville, where she was robbed while she slept, exhausted, in Union Station. Had to beg for the money to get back to Bristol, grabbing well-dressed women's arms as they brushed past her to the tracks. Even then she knew that it was all over, that if she could have sprouted wings and flown, it would not be fast enough to catch him, that he was gone. But she went back. She had no place else to go.

Missus King fired her. When Maura explained her condition, she had not taken pity, but instead said she would make sure she had trouble finding work anywhere in Bristol again.

And it will get harder and harder to find work. Finally she will end up here, at the Crimson Shawl, where she once vowed to Billy she would rather die than be found. But by that time, she *is* dying, without the strength to do anything but lie back and let men do to her what they want, what they will. Because the boy needs to eat. And the boy needs books for school. And when she knows she has only weeks left to live, in a bedroom just below where she now stands, she will tell the boy the story. Because she is going to die, and has nothing else to give.

Blood will tell, she will say to him.

But on the stairs that is all years ahead. At the moment Charles is only a few hours old. Named not for anyone but because it was the finest name she could think of. From the moment she saw his face she knew her life would now be dedicated to one purpose only. If she could not have what was promised, then he would.

And so she came here as soon as she could stand. Single-minded. With hackles raised and teeth set. A fox, Billy used to call her. Foxy little Maura McLaughlin. He had loved her. She does know that.

When she reaches the top stair she leans against the wall and closes her eyes against the small explosions of pain inside her. She has done it. She can carry him no higher. Her knees buckle again. Dizzy. When the wave passes she opens her eyes to look down at her boy, so new, still sleeping. All the world at his feet.

SOMEWHERE IN FRANCE

Get up, you damn mule. Please.

The mule groans, struggles again, digs himself deeper into the mire.

Charles is on his knees. Another shell, much closer, sends up a rain of mud.

He rolls himself tight against the mule's body. Catherine. Sometimes he tries to call her up, to remember the taste of her, her bare flesh under his hand in the Everbright springhouse, but he cannot.

Other things, he can remember. Clear as the night sky.

Can you do the Bunny Hug? The Turkey Trot? The Grizzly Bear?

Jones, before he died, had talked on and on about his girl back home. Charles had only said Catherine's name once.

You don't know nothing, Jones, till you've known a girl with a gap-toothed smile.

How many times had he wished Jones was Billy. Wished he would turn around and see Billy standing there, grinning. But he doesn't even have Jones anymore.

Another thought of Catherine that comes back, clear: watching her eat an ice cream sundae in the window of the soda fountain that summer day when he knew little more about her than her name. Dragging her tongue along the spoon and studying it carefully, like it was the most important job in the world. Sometimes he thinks he ought to have just stayed put, there on the other side of the window, unseen. Just watching her. He could have saved her from all of it. He tried to say that, in the letter he sent her from Nashville.

But he had wanted her so badly. And it was no use, saying it to her then, and it is no use thinking about it now. Edmund Hatcher was right. The war made you want to forgive everybody. Even yourself.

The boom of the big artillery has started now. He feels it in his belly. The mule flinches. They've got to get up. The sky is lightning.

He struggles to his feet and leans back on the mule's lead. His shoes slide in the mud, go out from under him.

Get up, Champ. Get up. Please get up.

Champ, with a groan and a great sucking sound, gets up out of the mud.

Charles jumps out of the way of the floundering feet. The mule shakes himself like a dog, sending the gun and ammunition clattering.

He kisses Champ on his nose.

Oh, you mule. You good mule. Come on, good buddy. Come on. You and me, let's go.

They go on. Towards the sound of the guns.

MORNING

Tennessee
1924

When Billy heard about the memorial they were building in Nashville, that they had put out a call to collect all the names of the soldiers who had died, he wrote a letter.

> *To whom it may concern,*
>   *A boy named Charles McLaughlin was in the fight. I lost track of him. He enlisted in September 1917 and that's as far as I know. I don't know if he's dead or alive or running around in France but if he is dead, I know he'd want his name up there on that wall more than anything. That is why I am righting to you. If this ain't the write address please right me back and let me know where I ought to send this letter. Like I say he would want his name up there real bad I know and I hear you want to be sure to get them all and I wouldn't want him to be missed.*
>
>   *Sincerely,*
>   *William Monday*

He put it in an envelope and put a return address care of the post office in the town he was in. The reply came quickly, in an official-looking envelope.

We regret to inform you that Private Charles McLaughlin was killed in action—

He didn't finish it. He threw it away. Now he wished he had never written that damn letter in the first place. Sure enough he was never going down to Nashville to take a look at that wall.

There had been a bird whose story had been everywhere for a while. A carrier pigeon named Cher Ami. She carried a message ten miles through the flying shrapnel and bullets of no-man's-land, not quitting when her leg was shot off, her eye shot out. She had saved five hundred men with that message, not knowing what she carried. Only to go. To fly. Fly.

There was a British cavalry mare who learned the difference between enemy aircraft and friendly aircraft by the way it sounded. She would give warning at the approach of the former but not the latter. After a while, her men figured out it was a good idea to pay attention to her.

And the dogs that carried guns, food, messages. And the canaries kept in cages to warn of mustard gas. What were their names? Where was their memorial? The mules. All those mules they had loaded onto the boxcars. Tennessee mules, the finest in the world.

All gone. All mud.

The next summer he went through Sumner County with a string of horses. He stopped at a service station on the outskirts of Richfield to water them. The young man who came out to work the pump for him wore a wristwatch. That was something new, after the war. The wristwatch was a lot easier on the battlefield. Pull out your shiny pocket watch, get shot. Dangerous as striking a lucifer.

Other things had changed. There were times it felt the world had been knocked off its axis. Just a little, but enough to throw off the spin. The bottom had fallen out of the horse-and-mule market after the war. Just fell out completely. But prices were back up. In fact, they were the highest they had ever been. Booming. A man would always be able to make a living dealing in horses. And Billy had little use for money these days. Living on wind, weeds, and water, just like an old horse put to pasture. But it was a fine feeling. As if he might just lift up on the breeze and float away.

He did have an ache, when it rained. His keepsake of Leland Hatcher's mare.

You didn't see horses like her anymore. They were gone from the world. When the prices fell after the war, the breeding stock had suffered. Generations of bloodlines had been lost. There would never be another like her.

The horses sucked at the water in greedy pulls. They were hot and breathing hard, lathers of sweat on their bellies. He spoke to them and moved the bucket a little closer. Then he squatted, his bad knees popping, and dipped his hands in it and wet the back of his neck. He thought about all the boys in Richfield. Twitch. Jack Dillehay. Ernestine's son, and Doc Walker's, John Rich IV, all of them, and he knew they had either gone to war or hadn't. They were either dead or alive or, like Edmund Hatcher, had been destroyed by it. But he did not want to know their fates. Just as he never wanted to see that wall in Nashville. There were times when not knowing was better than knowing. A man didn't have to know everything.

A line of cars was waiting at the gas pump. One by one the fellow filled them up and they drove off. Then a big Chevrolet pulled in, and a man got out. He walked up to the door of the filling station on a cane.

Wad Taylor. Running behind him was a little girl. Hair the color of ash bark, and a blue dress. He called her name, and she streaked past him through the door. It closed with a bang behind them.

Billy got out of there fast. He did not want to be there when they came out. He did not need to see her face.

That night he camped in a field by the road. There was a three-quarter moon, no clouds. Fast crickets. The air was hot and heavy.

He staked the horses and laid out his bedroll and stretched himself out on it. He did not bother to make a fire. He lay there uncovered to the stars and waited for some relief from the heat. Sometimes it felt as if he waited all day for it, the short hours in the middle of the night when a coolness opened up like wings.

That little girl.

How strange, that he had seen her. Yet maybe not so strange at all. This was something that happened, to a traveling man. If you did not push yourself in any one direction, something seemed to pull you. Put you in the right place at the right time.

Morning Hatcher Taylor. With a name that meant beginning. A child who would never have to hustle. She had been there all along, Billy thought, even before she was born. All those years that Maura survived, fighting to stay alive and to keep her boy alive. She was there, this little girl, the way an entire tree was held in a tiny seed, folded, waiting.

She will never know your story, Maura, he thought. Not a hint of it. But that's alright. By now the story doesn't matter. If only we could bring back the dead, just for one moment or two, to show them. But the mystery was too great for such a simple solution, in spite of what Ernestine promised those who sought one. Maybe the other animals understood the mystery, as Harkleroad had said. But man had to go on faith, and faith alone.

He looked up at the stars. For the first time in decades he thought of his baby sister, the one dead from hunger, buried on top of East Hill, next to the cave where the goggle-eyed witch still howled. She had died and he had not. He survived the Winter of Darkness. He survived the caverns of the Bowery. He survived his drunken night in the cave with the calf and he survived the Neversink mine. All those times he ought to have died but for some reason, luck or wits or strength or otherwise, he had survived.

But Charles. Charles had been born at the wrong time for young men. He had gone into the flames of the crucible and never came out again.

Well there would never be another one. That was what they all said, that was the good that could come out of the madness. That was what they all died for. The men, the pigeons, the horses, the dogs, the canaries, the mules, all those lost, gone in places with names Billy could not even pronounce.

Morning Hatcher Taylor. He said the name aloud. Morning McLaughlin. Morning Monday. The mongrel Morning, in her starched blue dress. She would never know her story but she would be alright. He was certain of that, if nothing else.

He was tired in all his bones but he did not sleep deeply. He woke up many times in the night. Once it was a whip-poor-will. Later it was the almost weightless patter of a field mouse running across his legs. Once he sat bolt upright, heart pounding. He got up and hurried over to check on the horses. Whatever woke him must have woken them too. Their ears were pricked and their heads were raised. Their eyes were shining in the dark.

ABOUT THE AUTHOR

Lydia Peelle holds an MFA from the University of Virginia and is the author of the acclaimed story collection *Reasons for and Advantages of Breathing*. Her short stories have appeared in numerous publications, have won two Pushcart Prizes and an O. Henry Prize, and have been featured in Best New American Voices. She lives in Nashville, Tennessee. *The Midnight Cool* is her first novel.